MURDER!

'You killed them,' Eugene said. 'You killed them both.'

'I know I did. So?'

'Nothing,' Eugene said, and shrugged. 'Nothing.'

Rodiz got behind the wheel of the police car with his heart pounding and the stupid blood-stained state police hat down over his ears, aware that there were two dead troopers in the trunk behind him and wondering whether or not their blood was seeping through the trunk and onto the highway. He drove at forty miles an hour, and the low speed seemed intolerable; he was sure that everyone in the world knew there were two dead men in the trunk . . .

Also by Ed McBain in Sphere Books:

JACK AND THE BEANSTALK
SNOW WHITE AND ROSE RED
CINDERELLA
PUSS IN BOOTS
THE HOUSE THAT JACK BUILT

The Sentries

ED McBAIN

At a time when a single clash could escalate overnight into a holocaust of mushroom clouds a great power does not prove its firmness by leaving the task of exploring the other's intentions to sentries . . .

JOHN FITZGERALD KENNEDY

SPHERE BOOKS LIMITED

A Sphere Book

First published in Great Britain in 1965 by
Hamish Hamilton Ltd
Published by Sphere Books 1986
Reprinted 1986, 1988, 1991

ISBN 0 7221 5762 2

Printed and bound in Great Britain by
Cox & Wyman Ltd, Reading

Sphere Books Ltd
A Division of
Macdonald & Co (Publishers) Ltd
Orbit House
1 New Fetter Lane
London EC4A 1AR
A member of Maxwell Macmillan Pergamon Publishing Corporation

This is for Rees and Jerry Mason

ACKNOWLEDGEMENTS

While simultaneously absolving them of any blame for inadvertent errors I may have made, I would like to thank the following gracious and helpful people for the valuable information they supplied to me during the writing of this novel:

Mr. Gordon E. Dunn, Chief Tropical Meteorologist of the United States Weather Bureau in Miami; Miss Geraldine B. Kamp of the Miami-Dade County Chamber of Commerce; Mr. L. R. Verchereau of the Lower Keys Chamber of Commerce; Mrs. Tom Cadenhead of the Upper Keys Chamber of Commerce; Mrs. Gloria Strassner of the Key West Chamber of Commerce; Mrs. Frank Malone of the Key West Garden Club; Mr. Michael E. Hart of the Chris-Craft Corporation; Mr. Robert Wacker, Jr., of the American Cyanamid Company; Mr. Daniel Mountain of the National Rifle Association; Mr. J. Fuller of the Southern Bell Telephone and Telegraph Company; Capt. W. K. Thompson, Jr., of the United States Coast Guard Headquarters in Washington; Lt. George Mitchell and Lt. Bobby Wilks of the Coast Guard Air Station at Floyd Bennett Field; Lt. J. C. Goldthorpe of the Third Coast Guard District . . . and especially, for their untiring patience and willingness to answer the hundreds of questions I put to them:

Lt. (jg) C. L. Larance of the Seventh Coast Guard District in Miami, and . . .

Lt. Commander Rudy Roberts of the Third Coast Guard District in New York.

EMcB

PART ONE

1

It was still raining.

There were no stars, no moon. A high keening wind sent dark clouds scuttling across the Miami sky, lashed the waters of the bay against the public dock where the man and woman stood in embrace. A twenty-seven-foot cabin cruiser was tied up at the dock behind them. At the far end of the dock a truck was waiting, its motor idling.

The woman was pregnant. She wore a loose black raincoat and white sneakers. A black kerchief was tied around her head, which she kept ducked into the man's shoulder, away from the wind. The weather did not seem to bother the man. The rain was light, but the strong wind drove it across the dock in a piercing needlelike spray that was cold and penetrating; the man was wearing only khaki trousers and shirt.

From the truck someone called, 'Jason, it's a quarter to three.'

He did not answer. He simply nodded and then said to the woman, 'Will you be all right?'

'Yes.'

'Are you worried?'

'No.'

'Good.'

'Only about you is all,' she said.

'My part is easy,' he said.

'No. It isn't. You know it isn't.'

He smiled. There was assurance in his smile and something more, something she could not easily define, but which had been there since that night several years ago when he had first told her of the plan. She had not liked the

3

plan then, and she was not sure she liked it much even now –
but he was her husband.

'If something goes wrong, you'll call if off,' she said. It
was not a question.

'Nothing will go wrong.'

'But if it does. If it does, you'll call it off.'

'Yes.'

'Fatboy and the others in Key West . . .'

'They know they're not to move out until I call them.'

'And you'll radio us on the boat if we're to go ahead.
Otherwise we'll come back to Miami.'

'Yes.'

'Jason,' she said, 'there's still time.'

'For what?'

'To change your mind.'

'Why should I?'

'Because even if this succeeds, we can all be dead
tomorrow morning.'

The dock went silent. She could hear the wind rattling in
the distant palm fronds, could hear the creak of the boat
against the dock, and the steady pounding of the waves, and
beneath that a tiny sharp rush of air as Jason pulled in his
breath.

'It'll succeed,' he said.

'Yes, but even if it does . . .'

'Annabelle, we've been over this.'

'Yes, but . . .'

'Annabelle, listen to me. You just listen to me. This
doesn't get called off unless something goes very wrong
with my part of it, do you understand? It doesn't get called
off unless something terrible happens when I get down
there to Ocho Puertos. That's the only thing can call this
off. This isn't something where I can say *now*, standing here
on this dock, with everything ready to go – this isn't
something where I can say, Okay, let's not do it. This is too
important.'

'I know, Jason, but . . .'

'To the world,' he said.

'Jason . . .'

'Important to the world.'

At the far end of the dock she could hear the idling motor of the truck, the wind flapping in the tarpaulin that covered the rack. She had the feeling that if only she could think of the right thing to say, Jason wouldn't have to climb into the back of that waiting truck. She would not have to board the cruiser, the plan would not be set in motion, if only she could think of the right thing to say. Give me another moment, she thought, another thirty seconds, and I will be able to explain why we can't go through with this scheme of yours; give me another twenty seconds.

From the deck of the cabin cruiser, Randy Gambol cleared his throat. 'Jason,' he said, 'I'd like a word with you.'

'Just a second.' He lifted Annabelle's chin and looked down into her face. 'Go on,' he said, 'get aboard. Get some sleep. I'll be looking for you later.'

'If anything goes wrong –' she began, and he immediately said, 'Everything will go just the way we planned it.'

'I hope so.'

'Come on now, give me a kiss and go get some sleep.'

She nodded. 'All right,' she said, and she nodded again. 'Jason . . . please be careful. If anything goes wrong, if there's even a *sign* that anything is going wrong, promise me you'll call it off. Even if it means putting the boat in danger. Promise.'

'Go on, get aboard. It's almost time.'

'Jason, I want to talk to you,' Randy said.

'Go on, Annabelle,' he said, and kissed her. She threw her arms around his neck and returned the kiss lingeringly. Then she turned away from him swiftly and went to the boat, taking Randy's hand as he helped her aboard, mumbling 'Thanks,' and going immediately below. Randy came down onto the dock.

'This is the advisory I called you about at the warehouse,' he said.

'What about it?' Jason said, not taking the sheet of paper from Randy's extended hand.

'The Weather Bureau's 8 P.M. advisory,' Randy said.

'I know what it is.'

'This hurricane . . .'

'She isn't a hurricane.'

'They've named her already, Jason. They don't usually name them until they're real hurricanes.'

'She's a tropical storm, that's all.'

'Then why'd they name her?'

'Randy, there's a truck waiting for me at the end of the dock there. Now, will you please say what the hell's on your mind?'

'This is what's on my mind,' Randy said. He lifted the sheet of paper so that it was close to his face, but there was no light on the dock, and it was clear to Jason that he had memorized its contents, even though he pretended now to be reading. 'What's on my mind is a storm they've named Flora, the centre of which is fixed near latitude 20.5 north, longitude 77.2 west. Her highest winds –'

'You told me all this on the –'

'Her highest winds have been estimated near hurricane force, extending out a hundred and seventy-five –'

'So?'

'They've got gale warnings up,' Randy said, lowering the sheet of paper. '*The Golden Fleece* is a small craft.'

'I know what it is. Don't worry about Flora. She plays right into our hands.'

'I just don't like the idea of putting out to sea when –'

'I spoke to Arthur down in Key West just a little while ago,' Jason said. 'He told me the sun was shining there all day long, and the breezes are like an angel's kiss.'

'Well, the sun wasn't shining here in Miami,' Randy said, 'and the breezes are expected to hit gale force. Now, what do you want me to do?'

'Put out to sea, same as you're supposed to.'

'With a hurricane coming?'

'Can you think of a better time?'

'Jason . . .'

'I asked you a question.'

'Yes, Jason, I can think of a better time to be in a small boat than when a hurricane is coming, okay? Yes. If we capsize out there . . .'

'You won't capsize.'

'I hope not.' Randy paused. 'I just thought that with the seas the way they're going to be, and considering Annabelle's condition –'

'Annabelle's fine,' Jason said quickly.

'Jase, I'm afraid of this, I really am. We really might sink out there if those winds –'

'You won't sink. Stop worrying.' He glanced towards the waiting truck.

'And even if *this* part of it works . . . well, Jase, with a hurricane blowing –'

'Don't worry about it,' Jason said.

There was a note of finality in his voice. He lifted his arm and again looked at his wristwatch. 'They're waiting for me,' he said. 'It's almost three.' He paused. 'Do you know what time Alex is coming aboard?'

'Yes. Five-thirty.'

'You know what time you're supposed to shove off, right?'

'Dawn,' Randy said.

'If everything goes as planned, we'll radio the boat by eight-thirty, nine o'clock. If you don't hear from us by ten at the very latest, you turn around and head back. Is that clear?'

'I know the plan,' Randy said wearily. 'But I wish . . .'

Jason extended his hand. 'Good luck,' he said.

Randy took it. For a moment the men stood facing each other with their hands in each other's grip. They could not see clearly in the dark, but something unspoken passed between them. They knew what they were about to attempt, they knew the chances they were about to take, they knew the possible consequences.

'Good luck,' Randy whispered.

Jason smiled briefly, and then nodded and dropped Randy's hand and walked quickly towards the waiting truck. From inside the truck a pair of hands threw back the tarpaulin flap. Another pair of hands reached down to help Jason up. A voice said something that was unintelligible to Randy. The truck ground into gear and then moved forward. Randy watched its disappearing tail lights. He looked at his watch. It was 3 A.M.

He sighed, wiped his face, and went back aboard the boat.

The Golden Fleece was a custom-built cruiser with her name lettered in a semicircle across her transom, together with the name of her home port: NEW ORLEANS, LA. She was a good-looking boat, newly painted maroon and white and black, the maroon covering the solid longleaf yellow pine of her bottom, the white marking her waterline, the black painted over her African mahogany topside. She had been designed for a British naval officer in the Bahamas during 1953, costing him £3,500 to build and had been sold only three months ago to Jason Trench for $4,300. She was a good, steady offshore boat, propelled by twin, eight-cylinder, 185-horsepower engines, and capable of a top speed of thirty knots. Randy walked across the open cockpit, listening to the howling wind with misgivings, and then went into the wheelhouse and past the sink and icebox to where the charts were stowed overhead, near the primus stove. He found the chart he wanted, and then went to the starboard side, unrolling the chart on the flat surface to the right of the binnacle. He flicked on the overhead light in the wheelhouse and then glanced below to see if Annabelle had gone to bed yet. She was already asleep in the lower berth on the port side, one of four that hung two abreast on either bulkhead. He watched her for a moment. She was covered with a blanket, and the blanket rose and fell steadily with her even breathing. He wondered how she could sleep at a time like this, and then turned away and looked down at the chart, studying it nervously for perhaps the hundredth time.

On the chart, Ocho Puertos Key resembled nothing so much as a loin lamb chop, its eye tilted to the northeast, its tail straggling down towards Key West. For Randy, the image was instantly transformed into a more easily remembered one of sand and coral, of ocean rolling in against an essentially isolated shore. The drive down from Key Largo was sixty-two miles over a road that spanned the water skewer-straight, piercing island after island – sky, ocean, and bay blending into an incredibly open vista on either side of the highway. Marathon was forty-nine miles from Key Largo, and Knight Key was just beyond it. The Seven Mile Bridge began there, a two-lane span built across the open water and running, as its name made clear, for seven miles to Little Duck Key at the western end of the bridge. There were markers on all the keys leading to Ocho Puertos, each designating the name of the island, each passed in a wink, a network of short bridges connecting uninhabited Little Duck to uninhabited Missouri, uninhabited Ohio, Bahia Honda with its single house on the eastern end – and then the thousand-foot bridge and Ocho Puertos with a fixed bridge on its western end.

Offshore, the chart showed Hawk Channel and beyond that the Florida Reef.

Later today Alex Witten would be navigating through that reef and into that channel. If everything went the way Jason anticipated, they –

If.

If, of course, Hurricane Flora did not roar into Miami and the keys sometime today or tomorrow. And *if* Annabelle Trench, who was eight months pregnant and carrying her baby like a mountain waiting to erupt, if Annabelle did not get sicker than hell in high seas and gale-force winds, and vomit or deliver or some damn thing long before their rendezvous with Jason on Ocho Puertos.

If.

Randy stowed the chart and snapped out the light. He went below and crawled into his bunk. Two feet away from him, he could hear Annabelle's gentle breathing, and above that and beyond it, the high keening of the wind.

Gale force, he thought.

Alex would be coming aboard at five-thirty. They would

put out to sea at dawn. He sighed, rolled over, and tried to get a little sleep before then.

She heard Randy as he came below, and she longed for a moment to talk to him, to voice her doubts about what they were doing and about to do, but then she felt this would be unfair to her husband; she should not express any fears that might later undermine his authority. She turned her head towards the bulkhead. The berth was tight and cramped, her baby kicked inside her, and she grunted and listened to the wind, and wondered where the truck was now. She should have stopped Jason. She should have thought of the right thing to say there on the dock ten minutes ago.

She should have thought of the right thing to say in New York City in the summer of 1961, when he first told her of the plan that had been taking shape in his mind for the better part of three months. He had been turning it over and over, he said, searching for a way to succeed where others had only failed before, and then recognizing that the only hope for success lay in complete failure. They were living on Second Avenue at the time, in a two-room apartment near Houstin Street, and all the windows were open because it was one of the hottest days of the year; his voice had automatically lowered as he outlined the plan to her.

'There are two things a person can do, it seems to me,' he had said. 'He can sit back and let others shape his destiny, he can let everybody walk all over him and not worry about a thing until the day that bomb falls – that's one of the things he can do. Right, Annabelle?'

'I suppose so, Jason. But we *do* have a government, you know. We *do* have –'

'Why yes, *cer*tainly we have a government! That's my whole point, honey! It's the *government* I'm trying to preserve. That's the whole point.'

'I don't think I understand you, Jason.'

'Honey, it's a matter of knowing what this country wants, and knowing how to help this country *get* what it wants.'

'How do you know what this country wants?'

'If you read the papers, if you read between the lines, you

10

know *exactly* what it is we want. But more to the point, you know exactly what it is we do *not* want.'

'Jason, I'm going to make some lemonade,' Annabelle said, and she started to rise from where she was sitting by the window, and it was then that he put his hand on her shoulder and said, 'Wait, you just wait,' with his eyes looking directly into hers, his voice so low she could hardly hear him, the heat a stifling, penetrating force that seemed to capture each of his whispered words and hold them suspended in the air like bloated poisonous balloons.

'You love this country?' he asked.

'Yes.'

'I love this country, Annabelle, I really do. Why are we here in this lousy city of New York, if not for love of this country, would you tell me that? You think I like this city, with its dirt and its noise and . . . Annabelle, I *hate* this city, that's the truth you know that.'

'I know that, Jason,' she said quietly.

'But this is where the influence is, right? This is where you have to be if you hope to convince anyone that what you believe in is right.' He paused. His fingers still gripped her shoulder. 'Now, we can go along doing what we've been doing – I'm not saying that's bad, Annabelle. I think we've had an effect, I think it's all to the good. But I have the feeling it's the same thing as watching the world go by and allowing *other* people to make the decisions for us, *other* people to shape our destinies. We can go right on doing that, mind you. I'm not saying it's bad to do that.'

'What *are* you saying, Jason?'

'I'm saying I would rather shape my own destiny.'

'How?'

'By taking action.'

'What kind of action?'

'More than the leaflets, Annabelle. More than the meetings.'

'Then what?'

'I want to contact the others.'

'What others?'

'Alex and Goody and Arthur and the rest.'

11

'Why?'

'They'll help me,' Jason said.

'Help you?'

'With this plan I've been working on. Annabelle, I think I know how to get the results this country wants, and I know how to do it with only a handful of men, fifty, sixty men at the most. What do you think of that?'

'I don't know what the hell you're talking about,' Annabelle said, and she pushed his hand off her shoulder and rose and walked to the refrigerator. He sat silently by the window while she searched for lemons in the vegetable tray, watched as she cut them and began squeezing them. He sat silently while she mixed the lemonade in a pitcher beaded with moisture. The ice clinked against the inside of the pitcher. Her hand kept moving the spoon in a circular motion as she stirred.

'I'll contact Arthur first,' he said, almost to himself.

Annabelle said nothing. She poured two glasses of lemonade and brought one to him.

'I was always closest to him,' Jason said, taking the glass. 'Of all of them. And he was the only one who realized what was going on, who realized they'd set a trap –'

'Are we going to talk about *that* again?'

'No, we are not going to talk about *that* again,' he said.

'Good.'

'Because I know, of course, it bothers you.'

'Yes, it bothers me,' she said.

'Yes, I know that. But it's too damn bad about what bothers you because I'm going to have to contact Arthur whether it bothers you or not. And all the others too. I need help. I can't do this alone.'

'I don't know what it is you need help with,' she said. 'You haven't told me yet.'

'This isn't handing out leaflets on street corners,' he said, and he grinned.

'Then what is it?'

He rose and walked to the window. He looked at her with a curiously boyish expression on his face, almost mischievous, and then he closed the window.

12

She should have thought of the right thing to say then in the summer of 1961, the first time she heard the plan. But she had listened to him and then had said only the wrong thing. She had listened to him and said, 'You sound like a fanatic.'

'No,' he had answered, his eyes serious, his mouth set, 'I am not a fanatic.' And then, his voice very low, he had said, 'I'm an American citizen who is extremely concerned about the future of this nation.'

He rose and walked to the window, opening it again, making it absolutely clear he would say nothing more about his plan that day.

Now, in the cabin of a boat that would be putting out to sea in a matter of hours to execute a part of that plan, Annabelle rolled over onto her back and looked up at the overhead and listened to the wind and wondered what time it was and wondered where the truck was now and wondered what would happen in the daylight hours to come and wondered if she could do all that was expected of her and wondered why she had not said something back in 1961, when there was still time.

Dawn on Ocho Puertos that Sunday of October sixth was expected at 6:17 A.M.

The truck was a 1964 Chevrolet, her rack fitted with inch-and-a-quarter tubular supports over which hung the tarpaulin cloth that covered the top, front, sides and rear of the rack. The cab, wheel rims, and stakes of the truck – showing only occasionally when a sharp wind lifted the tarpaulin – were painted red. The truck had been rented from the Paley Systems Corporation on South Bayshore Drive ten days ago. Last night the lettering had been stencilled onto the side of the cab. The name and address of the firm had been invented by Jason and together became something of an inside joke: PETER TARE, 832 MISSION.

Goodson Moore was the one driving the truck.

Clay Prentiss was the man sitting beside him in the cab.

They were both wearing khaki trousers and shirts.

Neither of them spoke very much. They had made this identical run with a loaded truck exactly seven times during the past week, and they knew precisely how long the trip should take because they had loaded up at the warehouse at 2:30 A.M. each of those times and left Miami at 3 A.M. The warehouse, like the truck, had been rented. Unlike the truck, they had had to take the warehouse for a month, which was not too bad because they had managed to find uses for it during that time. The first time they made the trip down, they had tried changing speeds whenever the speed limit changed, but that had not worked too well because the speed limit jumped to sixty-five miles per hour just outside Cutler Ridge, and Jason had said sixty-five miles an hour was too fast to be driving on those narrow black roads with water on both sides of them, especially once they got past Key Largo. Jason was in charge, of course, so Goody and Clay listened when he talked. The next time down, Goody tried maintaining an average speed of fifty miles an hour, dropping down to thirty-five when the limit called for it, and goosing the truck up to sixty once they had passed Cutler Ridge. Jason said this was still too fast. Jason said they would drive the truck clear into the Caribbean, that's what they'd do, and that would be the end of the whole damn shooting match. Goody and Clay had listened while he yelled at them – well, that wasn't quite true; Jason rarely yelled. Jason just stared at you with his cold blue eyes, nothing on his face moving except those eyes, and they seemed to jump right out of his skull to nail you to the wall. They had listened and said, Well, Okay, Jason, how fast you *want* us to go?

No faster than forty-five at any time, he said, right? Try to average it out so you'll be making forty miles an hour. That'll put us in Key Largo an hour and a half after we leave Miami, and then figure fifteen minutes each to Tavernier and Islamorada, and forty-five more to Marathon. That'll bring us right to the Seven Mile Bridge about three hours after we start, right?

Okay, they had said, if that's what you want, Jason.

That's what I want, Jason had replied.

14

The truck passed the town of Naranja now, darkly shrouded at the side of the road, and moved steadily southward on U.S. 1, the speedometer needle nudging forty-five, the wind lashing at the tarpaulin cover, a wind that worried Goody. The men's faces were intent in the light of the dashboard, Goody's lean and drawn, with grey eyes and blond hair that almost faded completely in the feeble illumination; Clay's a rougher face, with a harsh cleaving nose and massive cheekbones, dark bushy brows over brown eyes.

'You reckon they asleep back there?' Clay asked.

'Not with Jason watching them,' Good answered.

In the back of the truck, beneath the tarpaulin cover lashed by strong winds, twenty-one silent men sat opposite each other on two long benches. Jason Trench was the only man wearing khaki. The rest wore dark blue dungaree trousers and pale blue chambray shirts.

He lifted his wrist and peered at his watch in the darkness.

There were hours to go yet.

There were hours to go.

The feeling of isolation was intensified by darkness.

The headlights of the truck picked out the narrow ribbon of road ahead, two lanes that spanned coral and water and sand. On one side of the truck were Florida Bay and the Gulf of Mexico. On the other side was the Atlantic Ocean. There was the persistent feeling that an over-elaborate engineering feat had been performed only to link civilization with a scarcely inhabited wilderness. There were forty-two bridges between Key Largo and Key West, but the bridges seemed to connect islands that sometimes supported only a single small house hidden in the mangroves, or a cluster of a half-dozen dwellings along the beachfront, or at best a real community of shops and restaurants and houses complete with a post office and a Chamber of Commerce but built flanking the highway like a two-bit honkytonk town erected overnight. In the darkness the uninhabited keys seemed the same as those that were

15

populated. The truck pushed south and west over the black highway, the water black on either side of it, the towns, the small clusters of dwellings, the uninhabited strips of sand and coral and twisted mangroves all presenting an identical impression of flat silent blackness somewhere at the farthest reaches of the earth.

The water was the first thing to come alive with light.

Long before the sun was up, the water began to take on colour, brightening from its total black to a deep and velvety blue, and then changing blue tones steadily as dawn approached, moving upwards through the spectrum so that by the time they reached the Seven Mile Bridge there was visible on either side of the truck a vastness of ocean and bay that was overwhelming.

Jason Trench threw back the flap of the tarpaulin cover and looked out at the miles of bridges they had already crossed. The sun had not yet cleared the horizon, but the water on either side of the bridge was now touched with pre-dawn silver, each separate ripple looking like the filigree on a fine medieval tool or weapon. The bridge spanned the sea relentlessly, the highway falling behind the truck as it maintained its steady speed, driving away from the approaching dawn.

Jason looked at his watch. It was five minutes after six, and they had come halfway across the bridge, and dawn would light the sky in twelve minutes. He felt a sudden lurch of excitement as he thought of what lay ahead, and then he lowered the tarpaulin as though reluctant to watch the sky turn pink. Dawn would be the beginning, and he hated beginnings. The departure from the Miami warehouse, the long drive down to the bridge – these were preliminaries to the real beginning that would take place when they crossed those three small uninhabited keys to the west, and then Bahia Honda, and then Ocho Puertos and the sign for S-811, the sharp turn to the left; that would be the beginning. That would be dawn, a dawn in every sense of the word, and he anticipated this beginning with a high excitement that was somehow coupled with a cold gnawing dread. If anything went wrong.

16

Nothing would go wrong.

And yet, as he allowed the tarpaulin to drop from his hand, as he turned to look at the other twenty men in the rear of the truck, he wondered if this should not have been a night time manœuvre. Why had he decided on dawn? Suppose the people of that creepy damn town all got up at five in the morning, and were standing there in the road, waiting with pitchforks?

The people of that town don't get up at 5 A.M., he reminded himself. We know the getting-up and sleeping habits of every person in Ocho Puertos, and we know that on Sunday morning nobody's stirring before 7:30 A.M. Dr. Tannenbaum and his wife Rachel get up at seven-thirty on Sunday morning and drive all the way to Marathon to have breakfast and to buy the New York *Herald Tribune*. Only this morning they are going to be awakened by twenty after six at the latest and they are not going to drive to Marathon or anyplace else. The next person to wake up in that town on a Sunday morning is Lester Parch, and he lives in the first house on the beach, and he sets the alarm for eight o'clock. The waitress and the short-order cook both drive in from Big Pine by eight o'clock, in separate cars, but Lester doesn't open his diner to customers until nine, too late to catch Dr. and Mrs. Tannenbaum who are usually in Marathon having their breakfast by then. Lester Parch's wife, Adrienne, sleeps until ten on Sundays. By that time all of Ocho Puertos is usually wide-awake, except for Rick Stern, the bachelor in the third house on the beach, who generally has some poontang with him, picked up in Marathon the night before. He wouldn't roll out of the hay until eleven, and then he'd roll right back in again ten minutes later to polish off a morning matinée. This morning he was in for a slight surprise.

Jason smiled.

He looked at his watch again, and briefly wondered how many times he had stared unseeingly at its face since they had left the warehouse three hours ago. Then he looked across the width of the truck to where a red-headed youth with a crew cut was sitting staring at the floor, and he said

17

very softly, 'Benny, I think it's time we armed up. We're almost there.'

Without a word Benny rose and glanced at a huge Negro sitting three places away from him on the bench, towards the rear of the truck. With practised balance, they both moved spread-legged towards the front of the truck where a painter's stained dropcloth covered an angular pile beneath it. Benny pulled off the cover and began handing out rifles to the big Negro.

Some of the rifles were new and some of them were used, but they had all been purchased over the counter in gunshops in different states, because there was not a single state in the union that required a licence for the purchase or possession of a weapon other than a handgun. The rifles varied in model and calibre from a Mossberg .22 with a seven-shot clip magazine to a .30-06 Savage with a staggered box-type magazine, and ranged in price from a low of $17.25 for a single-shot Springfield .22 to $155.00 for a .243 gas-operated Winchester. The rifles were tagged, and Benny and the Negro – whose name was Harry – handed each rifle to the man whose name tag was on it. As they walked between the benches facing each other, Jason got to his feet.

He could hear the rattle of bolts being tested, of clips being slammed home, of cartridge belts being clasped into place around waists. He cleared his throat.

'We're approaching Ocho Puertos,' he said.

The men fell silent. A single clip rattled, the rifle was shifted, the clatter of metal, silence.

'In a few minutes this truck is going to swing off the main highway and on to S-811 into the town,' Jason said. 'We'll make all the stops we've been rehearsing this past week, but this time is for real. This time we are setting our plan in motion.'

Benny and Harry had handed out all the pieces by the time Jason had finished this part of his speech, and were giving Colt .45s to the two group leaders in the truck, Johnny and Coop. Only nine states in the union required a permit or a licence to purchase a handgun, and so it had been comparatively simple to buy the two .45s and the various other revolvers and pistols that were needed. A total of twenty-five handguns of varying calibres had been bought, seventeen for the men who would hopefully be coming up from Key West later, two for the group leaders in the truck, three for the crew of *The Golden Fleece*, and one each for Jason, Goody, and Clay. Jason's personal preference had been for a .45, only because he felt the gun looked lethal and would be psychologically effective against small-town hicks.

'You all know what we're about to do,' he said. 'We've gone over that enough times. I have no doubt we will accomplish our part of the operation, and be able to carry out the subsequent parts as well. I have no doubt. I have no doubt, men, because I know that what we're about to do today will change the history of the United States and the world. That is how important I feel our mission is.'

Jason cleared his throat again, and then paused.

'We are the sentries of freedom,' he said, his voice low. A man near the back of the truck coughed. 'We are the sentries of freedom, and we are standing on the bulwarks of a great nation and defying the world to challenge our greatness, defying the world to abandon its opinion of the Unites States as a weak and compromising nation instead of the great and powerful nation it is. That is what we are doing here today in Ocho Puertos. That is exactly what we are doing here today.'

He strapped on the gun, letting the holster hang low on his right thigh. There was an air of excitement in the truck now, and the men began to murmur when Clay turned on his seat in the cab and knocked on the small rear window. Clay pointed dead ahead to indicate they were coming off the bridge. Jason nodded.

'I want that town,' Jason said. 'There are seven houses in that town, all on the beach, really eight if we want to count the Westerfield house across the main highway – but that's empty until December, so we don't have to worry about it. Seven houses and a diner and a tackle shop and a marina, and that's it, and that's our objective. I want that town, and I want it by 8 A.M.'

They heard the smoother rumble of the truck wheels as they came off the bridge and on to Little Duck. The inside of the truck went still at once. They waited, and suddenly the wheels made a brief thudding sound and they knew they were crossing another short bridge, the smooth rumble once more, they were on Missouri Key, they waited, another bridge, there, they were on Ohio now, they held their breaths, it took forever to cross Bahia Honda, the truck tyres whined, any moment now, they were crossing another bridge, and then the sound changed again, there was the feel of solid land beneath them.

'Ocho Puertos,' Jason whispered.

2

From where Luke Costigan stood on the deck of the catamaran, he could see the red truck turning off U.S. 1 and rolling past the sign advertising the diner and its good food and drink. The truck came out of the rising sun, almost as though a small red section of the sun had slipped free of the horizon and somehow spilled onto the highway and bounced off onto the dusty cutoff leading to the town. The truck took the turn faster than it should have, but then began slowing almost at once, not quite stopping outside the diner, but dropping speed considerably, and then immediately picking up speed again until it was just abreast of the white shanty that was Bobby's Bait and Tackle Shop. There was a great deal of dust behind the truck, and for a moment Luke was not quite sure he had really seen two men in the road behind it, both wearing blue. Then the truck was in motion again, and there was a great deal more dust obscuring his vision as the truck gained speed and headed for the marina. Luke watched the truck coming down the road, his eyes squinted, one hand resting on the deck rail. The truck slowed again, just outside the marina, and, as Luke watched, two men carrying rifles dropped from the rear of the truck, bent at the knees as they hit the dusty road, and then sprang erect almost immediately and began running towards the marina with their rifles at the first of the beachfront development houses. Luke glanced only briefly at the moving truck, and then quickly turned back towards the two men, both of whom were wearing dungaree trousers and blue chambray shirts, watching them as they came across the lawn towards the pier, where he was clearly visible on the boat's deck. He was not at all frightened, not even

21

apprehensive about the appearance of two men with rifles on his lawn. He was curious and somewhat puzzled, but a part of his mind told him this was only some sort of Navy drill, probably some sailors from the base in Key West.

The first man stopped some four feet away from the boat and slowly lowered his rifle so that the barrel was level with Luke's midsection. In that same moment Luke caught movement on his right and turned his head only briefly, really turned only his eyes, and saw that two other men in dungarees and chambray shirts were breaking in the door to Bobby's shop not two hundred yards away. The truck was moving off up the road, raising dust behind it; two men in blue were rushing across the lawn of the Parch house, heading for the front door. Luke Costigan suddenly smelled danger and immediately reached for the socket wrench lying near the ladder.

'Hold it,' one of the men said. He was redheaded and had a crew haircut, and he could not have been older than twenty. He held the rifle steady, his finger inside the trigger guard.

'What is this?' Luke said.

'Just you keep your hands away from that wrench, mister,' the redhead said. 'Raise 'em up over your head, go on.'

'What is this?' Luke said again.

'Mister,' the other man said, 'this is pretty damn serious, whatever it is. So just pick up your hands, like Benny told you, and put them up over your head.'

'Come on,' Benny said.

Luke hesitated another instant. Curiously, and seemingly without reason, he thought abruptly of Hurricane Donna in 1960, and how she had destroyed the marina he had owned in Islamorada. And then he remembered Omaha Beach and the bullet that had caught him in the right calf, and suddenly the two memories merged, France in June of 1944 and Islamorada in September of 1960. He looked at these two men with rifles in their hands and all he could think of was that he had been hurt twice before.

'Mister, you want me to shoot?' Benny asked.

'No,' Luke said. 'No, don't shoot.' Slowly he raised his hands over his head.

'Anybody here yet?' the man with Benny asked.

'No. I was moving some boats into the cove,' he explained. 'There's a hurricane supposed to be coming.'

'Bobby and Sam ain't arrived yet, huh?' Benny said, and he grinned at Luke, and for the first time since they had entered his yard, Luke felt a shiver of dread. 'We better get inside, huh?' Benny said. 'We're gonna have company soon.' He gestured at Luke with the rifle. Luke began limping towards the side door to the marina office. Beyond his buildings he could see the two other men in blue entering the bait shop, and he suddenly wished that Bobby would not be drunk this Sunday morning.

The battering on the door of the shanty had not awakened him, and neither had the splintering of the wood on the jamb, or the rasp of the lock screws ripping loose. He had blinked only partially awake when he heard the sound of heavy work boots on the loose floor planking, but now a man stood over him, shaking him, and Bobby Colmore squinted up at him and then he thought he was having a bad dream, and tried to roll over against the wall. The man's hand was firm on his shoulder and he could not turn. He opened his eyes wider.

The man was a Negro.

He was wearing a blue shirt and blue pants, and he was holding a rifle in one huge hand, the hand wrapped around the middle of the piece, just about where stock joined barrel. There was a scar across the Negro's nose, and his eyes looked bloodshot. For an instant Bobby had the notion the man was an escaped convict. For an instant only, he was sure the man would demand food and drink and civilian clothing.

'You awake?' the Negro asked.

Bobby blinked and said nothing. The Negro shook him. 'Don't do that!' Bobby said.

'You awake?' the Negro asked again.

'I'm awake, goddamit! Stop shaking me.'

He freed his shoulder from the Negro's grip and sat up in bed. He looked around the room, as though trying to ascertain that this was really the back of his small shop, where he slept every night of the week, those were *his* nets hanging there, and that was *his* picture of Ava Gardner which he had cut out of a magazine and pasted on the white wooden wall, that was *his* empty bottle of bourbon lying on the floor next to the bed, those were *his* flowered curtains leading to the front of the shop, Bobby's Bait and Tackle Shop, the only goddamn thing he owned in the world.

'Is this a stickup?' he asked.

The Negro grinned and said, 'He wants to know if this's a stickup, Clyde.'

'Tell him, Harry,' the other man said, grinning back. He was white and tall, wearing the same blue clothes, his rifle hanging loosely at his side as though he recognized Bobby Colmore would be no threat to anyone in this room.

'No, sir,' Harry said, 'this ain't a stickup. Now, Mr. Colmore, we would like you to get out of that bed there and put on some clothes, because we has to take you over to the marina.'

'How do you know my name?' Bobby asked.

'We know it,' Harry answered. 'Would you put on your clothes, please?'

'Why?'

'Why, because we *asking* you to.'

'Suppose I don't want to?'

'Mr. Colmore, we gonna take you over to that marina whether you want to go there or not. Now, it's entirely up to you whether you leave here dressed up Sunday-go-to-meetin', or whether we carry you over in your skivvies. I think I ought to tell you, though, there might be a lady or two present. Now, which'll it be?'

'Suppose I won't let you take me?'

Grinning, Harry said, 'I'd have to shoot you dead, Mr. Colmore.'

Bobby wiped his hand across his mouth and then looked up at Harry. Very slowly he said, 'I don't believe you.'

'Mr. Colmore, the reason we're taking you over to the marina is because we don't want you acting like a old drunk, you dig? A old drunk is what you're acting like right now, which is just what we expected from you. But we can't take no chances, is why we're getting you out of this shop. You dig, Mr. Colmore? Put on your clothes.'

'I'm not an old drunk,' Bobby said with dignity.

'I guess our information is wrong, then,' Harry said. 'Any case, put on your clothes. We ain't got time to fool around here with you.'

Bobby Colmore did not answer. He got out of bed and walked to the chair where his trousers and shirt were draped. Silently, sullenly, he began dressing.

The Ocho Puertos Diner was a classic diner in the shape of a railroad dining car, with silvered sides, and a sign running the length of the building. In the entrance box – a small four-sided glass square appended to the main body of the diner – there was a second, smaller sign upon which was lettered the information that Lester Parch was the proprietor of the place. Lester had been proprietor since 1961 when he had floated a building loan and put in his eating place shortly after Fred Carney built the waterfront houses. The marina was not built until later. It had been good for Lester's business, but he had not counted on it when he built the diner. All he had counted on was the state-maintained road running off U.S. 1. He figured he was bound to catch at least some of the truck traffic heading for Key West, and he was right. Even before Luke built the marina, Lester Parch was taking home a fat pay cheque each month.

The entrance doorway to the diner divided it exactly in half. There were four leatherette booths to the left of the entrance, and six to the right. The counter ran the length of the place with twenty stools in front of it. The rest rooms and telephone booth were on the left-hand side of the diner, adjacent to the kitchen which occupied the entire rear half

25

of the building. The men who dropped from the back of the truck and ran to the rear of the diner that morning knew that Lester Parch and his wife lived in the first house on the beach and would not be rising until at least eight o'clock. All they were supposed to do was knock out the alarm wires in the box at the rear of the diner, and then force the lock on the kitchen door and enter. For the remainder of the day, and throughout phases two and three of the operation, they were to stay inside the diner and use it as a makeshift guard post, stopping anyone who tried to enter the town on S-811.

They did not know what kind of wiring the alarm box alongside the rear door contained. They had cased the area near the garbage cans out back on two separate occasions the week before, and knew definitely that the diner was wired, but they could not tell whether they would come up against an open-circuit alarm system, a closed-circuit system, or a combination system. They knew that in an open-circuit system, the cheapest kind, the alarm would sound the moment the current was closed. In order to knock out this type of alarm, they would only have to cut the wires. The closed-circuit system, on the other hand, always had a weak current running through the wiring, which meant that even if the wires were cut, the alarm would sound when that current was broken. The combination system was the most modern and the most expensive, and it combined both the open and closed circuits. The men did not expect to find such an elaborate system in a chintzy little diner on a crumby little Island in the middle of nowhere. The first of the two men pulled over a garbage can, climbed on to it to reach the wiring box and then unscrewed the cover, studied the system and discovered that it was closed-circuit. He nodded to his companion and then smiled.

In ten minutes' time they had made their cross contacts, cut the wires, and forced open the rear door.

They closed and locked the door behind them, and then walked to the front of the diner. One man carried a Winchester. The other, because he was a group leader, carried a .45. They drew all the Venetian blinds except the ones in the corner booth on the right. Through the wide corner window they could see the full sweeping curve of S-811 as it ran up to U.S. 1. One of the men lighted a cigarette, and the second adjusted the corner blinds to keep the rising sun out of his eyes.

The truck had dropped off twenty of the men, leaving the last two at the Tannenbaum house at the end of the beach, and then gunning the engine and making the steep climb up S-811 to where it rejoined the main highway. Goody Moore, still at the wheel, made the sharp right turn and then stepped on his brake pedal and pulled to the side of the road. He opened the cab door, climbed down onto the road, and then walked swiftly to the back of the truck where Jason was just lifting the tarpaulin flap.

'Here you go,' Jason said, dragging a wooden road barricade to the back of the truck and then handing one end of it down to Goody. In the cab of the truck Clay Prentiss watched the road ahead through the windshield, turning his eyes to the rearview mirror every few seconds to check the road behind. He could see Bahia Honda ahead, and beyond that the Seven Mile Bridge racing off into the sky in the distance, pink and gold, the water stretching on either side of it like cotton candy.

'You got it?' Jason asked.

'I've got it,' Goody replied, and the men eased the barricade down and out of the truck. The barricade had white legs and a black-and-white diagonally striped cross support. The words FLORIDA STATE ROAD DEPARTMENT were painted across the side of the cross support, and as Goody set the barricade across the mouth of S-811 where it rejoined the highway, Jason went into the truck again and came back with one of the wooden signs Clay had painted for them. The sign was a white rectangle upon which were the simple black letters:

ROAD CLOSED
FOR REPAIRS

Goody took the sign from Jason, and then carried it to the barrier where a spike had been driven into the centre of the cross support. He hung the sign on the spike and stepped back to admire it.

'Let's move,' Jason said.

Goody ran forward to the cab of the truck, climbed in, threw it into gear, and drove east on U.S. 1, heading back in the direction from which they had come, towards Bahia Honda and the Seven Mile Bridge. In the rear of the truck Jason leaned on the second barricade and watched the road through the open tarpaulin flap.

The cop had hit him with his club; that was the final indignity. The barricades had been set up on the pavement in front of the theatre, as though the New York City police were circumscribing a definite area in which citizens of the United States could peaceably state their views. The barricades had annoyed Jason. He had told Annabelle he would not picket within a narrow defined area; you could not limit freedom of speech to an area designated by fascists in the uniforms of policemen. There were a half-dozen pickets in all, including Jason and Annabelle, and they carried signs on long sticks, crudely lettered to simulate a vaguely Oriental calligraphy, huge black letters on a white field. The police insisted that Jason and the others stay within the corridors defined by the barricades and Jason, who was younger then, and more hotheaded – this was in the spring of 1950, three months after they had come up to New York from New Orleans – told the cop he was a fascist who was trying to limit the rights of free citizens.

'I'm trying to keep this from becoming a riot, you Communist fink!' the cop shouted.

'Me?' Jason asked incredulously. 'Me a Communist? Do you know why we're here? Do you even know why we're here?'

'Let's stay inside the barricades,' Annabelle whispered.

'Why? So he can prove his point? Are we supposed to excuse him the way this play excuses the lousy Japs?'

'Jason, we won't prove *anything* if they won't let us picket.'

The others in the group – a fat and ugly girl who was a Political Science major at C.C.N.Y., a pimply-faced boy who was on Fordham's basketball team, a Long Island matron who was in her second month of pregnancy, and a tall and sombre-faced boy from Kentucky – agreed with Annabelle that it was best to stay within the barricades. Jason reluctantly went along with them.

They marched along the pavement in front of the theatre entreating passers-by to stay away from the play. Their signs read LET'S REMEMBER PEARL HARBOUR and WHY WHITEWASH THE JAPS? and DID OUR BOYS DIE IN VAIN? and the people walking past the small and solemn group marching in a steady oval within the barricades looked up at the signs with smiles of wry amusement, and then glanced beyond the pickets to the posters outside the theatre and then up to the marquee where the name of the play was announced together with the names of the actors. One of the actors was a well-known Hollywood star who was Japanese and who had been playing heavies in war movies as short a time ago as 1948, but who was now starring in a vehicle set in a Japanese command post in the South Pacific. Jason had not seen the play, but the reviews had made it abundantly clear what the play was about. The play attempted to show the Japanese position, attempted to explore 'the Japanese as human beings caught, even as we were, in the terrible throes of a horrible conflict,' as one of New York's major critics had put it. In other words, the play was a whitewash of a people, a *race*, who had been our enemies only five years ago, which fact the producers of the play and apparently the public too – the play was an enormous hit – had already chosen to forget. Jason Trench did not choose to forget anything that threatened the United States of America. The play was a threat to the nation because it lulled people into a sense of security that was dangerous. It was ridiculous to believe that the Japanese had suddenly been transformed overnight into a sweet and loving people who wanted only to tend their gardens and paint their lovely little pictures. It was foolish to believe that, it was dangerous, it was suicidal. If you forgot who your past enemies were, then you were halfway down the road to forgetting who your *present* enemies were. If you let them get by with a play that took a sympathetic view of a philosophy that was totalitarian and imperialistic, you were opening the door for an acceptance of *any* ideology, so long as you presented it in terms of 'human beings'.

It began to rain as they marched.

The rain, the idea of the play, the idea that such a play could be pulling in throngs of people who were willing to pay to see what amounted to a propaganda vehicle probably sponsored by the goddamn Japanese government, the idea of the barricade that limited Jason's right to free speech while the author of an atrocity was grandly allowed a pulpit from which he could reach thousands of people every week – all this rankled in Jason. When the cop said, 'Why don't you all go over to Moscow, you love it so much?' Jason raised his sign and swung it at the cop's head.

The cop was startled for a moment, and then he reacted the way he was supposed to. He lifted his billy and struck Jason on the arm with it. Jason yelled, 'You fat Irish fascist bastard!' and the cop hit him again, and Annabelle reached for his arms and tried to restrain him from attacking the cop, and it was then that the others in the picket line began running. Smelling a riot, wanting no part of it, they ran. The police arrested Jason for disorderly conduct, and the court magnanimously allowed him to go free, albeit with a suspended sentence, since disorderly conduct was only a misdemeanour, and since this was his first offence. The funny part of it, he realized later, was that the cop who had hit him with the club and also the judge who had heard the case both thought he was a Communist – that was the funny part of it. They were allowing a play with a fascist point of view to be presented eight times a week, and they were using the methods of a police state to squelch anyone who opposed the play's thesis, but they were calling *him* a Communist; that was what got him.

The truck was coming to a stop at the eastern entrance to S-811, the entrance they had used not more than ten minutes ago. Goody made the turn again, from the opposite direction this time, coming off the macadam highway and hitting the oiled road, and then stopping some ten feet in from the highway. By the time he got out of the cab and walked to the back of the truck, Jason had the second barricade in position and ready to hand down. They set it up much as they had the first one, effectively closing the side road to traffic on both ends. Goody got into the truck again, and they drove to the diner. Jason came out of the rear carrying a small cardboard sign. He hung it on the front door and then waved to the drawn Venetian blinds, behind which he knew were Johnny and Mac, covering the road.

Nothing stirred.

With its CLOSED sign hanging on the front door, with its blinds drawn, the diner seemed sealed tighter than a crypt.

The baby began crying the moment the two men entered the house, working much more effectively than the alarm on the diner had, setting up a fearful fuss that would not be controlled by cutting wires or crossing them. The house was the second one on the beach, just beyond Lester Parch's house. Lester heard the baby go off next door and woke up to find a rifle pointed at his head. He did not say a word. He simply jabbed his elbow hard into Adrienne's ribs, and she jumped up cursing and was ready to take a good swat at him when she realized they were not alone in their bedroom.

The two armed men standing at the foot of the bed both seemed to be about thirty years old, though the one with the beard looked older. Adrienne studied them unbelievingly, as though somehow Lester had dreamed them and they had escaped from his goddamn head and materialized at the foot of the bed. She looked at her husband furiously, her eyes demanding an explanation. Lester simply shrugged and said, 'Well . . . what's the guns for, fellers?'

The one with the beard very softly said, 'You're going to spend the rest of the day in this house, Mr. Parch. Would you and your wife kindly get dressed, please?'

'The rest –' Lester began and then closed his mouth. He

thought for a few seconds and then asked, 'Who'll open the diner?'

The man with the beard smiled and said, 'It's already *been* opened, Mr. Parch.'

Next door the baby was wailing up a storm.

Pete Champlin, who was the baby's father, rolled over, pulling half the sheet off his wife, and then mumbled, 'Rosie, you want to get him?'

'No,' Rosie said, 'you get him.'

'Forget it,' a strange voice said, '*I've* got him.'

Pete was used to all kinds of kooky things because he happened to be a real estate salesman in Marathon, and he got crazy nuts in the office every day of the week. The craziest nut of them all had been Frederick Carney, for whom Pete had handled this whole waterfront development after buying one for himself at thirty thousand, ten grand less than the next five sold for. He was used to all kinds of strange, mysterious real estate happenings, but not to a man's voice just outside his bedroom door at – what was it, six o'clock? – on a Sunday morning.

'Did you hear something?' he asked his wife.

'No,' Rosie said.

He probably would have let it go at that if the voice had not said, very loud and very clear this time, 'Your son's pants are wet, Mr. Champlin, and he's soaking through my shirt. You want to get up and take care of this?'

He popped up in bed immediately and saw a man standing in the doorway of the room with Pete, Jr., slung over his shoulder and with a rifle in his left hand. Right alongside him was another man, and he was holding a rifle too, and looking very serious.

'All right,' the second man said, 'nobody gets hurt if we all relax.'

'Who is it, honey?' Rosie mumbled beside him.

The men broke in through the french doors leading from the lanai at the back of the house, both of them wearing dungarees and blue shirts, both carrying rifles, both at least three inches shorter and twenty pounds lighter than Rick

32

Stern. They had been warned that the occupant of this fourth house on the beach was six feet four inches tall and weighed two hundred and twenty pounds bone-dry. They had been further warned not to take any chances with him because he had been an Iwo Jima Marine during World War II. At that time he had stormed a Japanese pillbox carrying nothing but a bayonet and two hand grenades. He had flushed out six enemy soldiers while demolishing two machine guns and, just for good measure, a mortar emplacement alongside the pill box. Jason's men had been told to shoot immediately if Rick Stern so much as lifted his pinky. So they broke the glass panel on one of the french doors, and then reached in to twist the knob, and then turned one rifle on him as he sat bolt upright in bed, and the second on the girl who was spilling out of the front of her nightgown and getting ready to scream.

'I've got the girl, Willy,' the man on the left said, pointing his rifle at her.

'I've got the guy, Flack,' Willy answered, and they both stood motionless across the room while the girl decided whether or not she should scream.

'Go ahead, lady, scream,' Flack said. 'There ain't nobody to hear you.' Whereupon the girl immediately closed her mouth and concentrated instead on pulling the sheet up over her exposed breasts.

It was at this point that Rick Stern burst into laughter.

He could not have explained why he began laughing at that precise moment. There was certainly nothing very comical about two snotnose kids busting your french doors and coming into your bedroom where you were entertaining a lady. Nothing was less funny than a Springfield rifle, either, unless it happened to be two of them, one of which was pointed at your lady friend's exposed left breast – well, exposed until just a moment ago – with the other pointed at a spot about three inches above your own bellybutton. There was nothing terribly funny about Lucy's dilemma, either, the dilemma being that she was the daughter of Walter Nelson, who was deacon of the church on Big Pine Key, and who happened to be up in Miami on church business, but who certainly wouldn't have appreciated his holy little flower being in bed with the rake of the Lower Keys, even if the rake happened to be a World War II hero. Oh, no, there was nothing comical about Lucy's dilemma. Perhaps, then, perhaps what made Rick burst into laughter at this particular tense juncture of his life was the look worn by the intruder on the right, the one called Willy.

Willy was nineteen years old, and he had a little blond moustache and fierce brown eyes. He kept his mouth curled in a sort of sneer that was supposed to be menacing but only managed to look petulant. That was funny enough in itself, but the look that had flashed over his face when he broke through those french doors was worth the price of admission alone. Lucy had popped up in bed, spilling out of the front of her gown, and Willy had frozen to a spot just inside the french doors, his eyes opening wide, his jaw dropping.

It had taken Lucy approximately thirty seconds to get her mouth ready for the scream, during which time she kept sitting up in bed with her open gown pointed right at Willy's gaping jaw. It had taken another thirty seconds for Flack to deliver his clever little speech about screaming and there being nobody to hear and all that, during which time Willy kept leaning over farther and farther towards Lucy, though still rooted to that spot just inside the french doors. Then at least ten more seconds went by before Lucy decided not to scream and pulled the sheet up over her breasts instead.

It was then that Rick burst out laughing, because Willy just kept right on staring at Lucy as if fiercely willing her to drop that sheet, and his partner, Flack, kept trying to be tough by waving the rifle at Rick and saying, 'Don't try nothing funny, Stern. Our orders are to shoot to kill.'

'Well, well,' Rick said, and wondered immediately how Flack had known his name, but said nothing further. He was already trying to figure a way out of this, because everything in Rick Stern's mind usually broke down eventually into a matter of logistics, and the logistics of this situation was simply how to disarm and break into little pieces two nineteen-year-old punks who had invaded his bedroom, how to do this without causing harm to our holy flower of Big Pine Key, God bless her.

'All right, what is this?' he asked. 'A gag?'

'This ain't a gag, Stern,' Flack said. Willy, on his right, kept staring at the sheet that Lucy held clutched to her bosom.

'Then what are you doing here, would you mind telling me?'

'You better get up out of that bed,' Flack said. 'We have to tie you up.'

'Why?'

'Because we've got to keep you here until –' Flack began, and suddenly Willy nudged him with the barrel of his rifle and said, 'Shut up, Flack.'

'What's the matter, Willy?' Flack asked.

'Don't tell the bastard nothing,' Willy said, and Rick looked at Willy's mouth again, curled into a sneer below the silly blond moustache, and wondered all at once whether the menace there wasn't true enough after all.

'Keep me here until what?' Rick asked.

'Until we decide to let you go,' Willy answered. 'Get out of that bed.' He paused and then said, 'The girl, too.'

'Uh-uh, Willy.'

'You better listen to me, Stern,' Willy said. 'When I tell you to do something, you do it, and fast. You got me?'

'I got you fine,' Rick said. 'The girl stays in that bed until we get her a robe. And then she dresses in the bathroom.'

'She dresses where I say she dresses.'

'Over my dead body,' Rick said.

Willy smiled and said, 'Any way you want it, Stern,' and then pulled back the bolt on the rifle.

'Don't make me laugh,' Rick said.

'I'm counting to three,' Willy answered, his finger moving into position inside the trigger guard. 'I want you both out of that bed and starting to dress by the time I hit three, you got me?'

'And if we're not?'

'If you're not, you're dead,' Willy said. 'One.'

'Save your breath. I'll get the girl a robe, and she can –'

'Stay where you are,' Willy shouted. 'Two.'

'I thought you wanted us –'

'I'm giving the orders around here, not you. You think I'm gonna let her out of this room?'

'The bathroom's right in the hallway. Your friend can follow her down and stay right outside the door while she dresses.'

'Suppose she busts a window and gets out,'

'There's no window in the bathroom,' Rick said. 'There's only an overhead vent.'

'The girl dresses right here,' Willy said. He paused and then said, 'Three.'

The room went silent.

'You getting out of that bed? Both of you?'

'No,' Rick said.

The bullet took him completely by surprise, smashing into his abdomen, and lifting his behind from the bed, and slamming him back against the headboard. He felt only instant impact and agonizing pain, and then his vision blurred and he felt himself falling forward on the bed, his body bending from the waist, pulling the sheet out of Lucy's hands as he fell, Lucy clutching for the sheet wildly, trying to cover her breasts, the sheet suddenly turning a bright pulsing red, as Lucy's scream bursting from her mouth as red and as strident as the shrieking spreading blood. 'You killed him!' she shouted. 'You killed him, you killed him!' And then unmindful of her naked breasts, she threw herself headlong onto his body and tried to hold him close while his blood and his life drained out of him and soaked into the mattress.

Across the room Willy watched her wordlessly for several moments, his heart pounding in his chest. Then he turned to Flack and said, 'Get Jason.'

3

Dr. Herber Tannenbaum and his wife Rachel were not in their bed; two other people were. The two other people were a lot younger than the Tannenbaums were supposed to be. The girl seemed to be twenty-five or -six, and the man sleeping beside her seemed to be maybe a few years older than that, but where the hell was old Tannenbaum and his wife?

Virgil Cooper took the surprise well. After his first Mongolian cavalry attack in Korea, he was incapable of being surprised any more; he simply gestured to Leonard Crawley to keep the slumbering pair covered while he went out to check the rest of the house. He was coming through the hallway and heading for the other bedroom when he received the second surprise, and the second surprise was Dr. Tannenbaum himself coming from the bathroom at the opposite end of the corridor, tying the strings on his pyjama bottoms. Tannenbaum was sixty-eight years old, a tall spare man with a good tan on his arms and his face and spreading up on to his forehead and the beginnings of his bald pate fringed with white hair that clung to the back of his head and formed a narrow shelf above his ears. He had been the orthopaedic specialist at Montefiore Hospital in the Bronx before he had retired and come to Ocho Puertos with his wife the year before. He came down the corridor now tying his pyjama strings, completely unaware of Coop who stood frozen at the opposite end, holding the .45 loosely in his right hand, waiting for Tannenbaum to discover him.

Tannenbaum sensed Coop's presence before he actually saw him. His step faltered and he raised his eyes first and then his head, and the first thing he saw was the gun in

37

Coop's hand. He stopped dead in the hallway, his eyes continuing upwards to Coop's face, settling on Coop's mouth, which was thin and smiling faintly, moving upwards to Coop's eyes, which were pale and vaguely amused. Tannenbaum wet his lips. As though afraid he would wake the sleepers in the house, he said in a whisper, 'Who are you? What do you want?'

'Who's that in the big bedroom?' Coop whispered back.

'My son and his wife. What do you want? What do you want here?'

'Get dressed, Dr. Tannenbaum,' Coop whispered, and then shouted over his shoulder, 'Wake 'em up, Leonard!'

In the master bedroom of the two-bedroom house, Leonard Crawley kept his Springfield trained on the bed and watched the young man and woman in the bed come immediately and unbelievingly awake.

Marvin Tannenbaum sat up and stared at what seemed to be a man holding a rifle. He heard Selma gasp beside him as he fumbled for his glasses on the night table. He put them on, blinked at the man, cleared his throat, and said, 'What the hell is it?'

'Mister, get dressed,' Leonard said.

'Who are you?' Marvin said.

'Get dressed,' Leonard answered. His eyes searched the room. He picked a blue robe from the armchair near the bed, threw it to Selma and said, 'Here, lady. You can put this on.'

'Thank you,' Selma said.

'Pop!' Marvin shouted suddenly. 'Pop, are you all right?'

'He's all right,' Coop called from the hallway. 'Shut up and do what you're told, and nobody'll get hurt.'

Marvin got out of bed in his pyjamas and walked past Leonard to the doorway of the room. He was five feet ten inches tall, but somehow managed to convey an impression of squatness, despite his height, perhaps because his legs were short in proportion to his torso and arms. He had black hair and brown eyes and a peculiarly

38

sensitive and sensuous mouth in a dark and brooding face. His black-rimmed eyeglasses gave him a scholarly appearance that was contradicted by the squat power of his body, as though an ape had accidentally picked up his trainer's glasses and perched them on his broad flat nose. He looked into the hallway without fear, somewhat sleepily, a man who had been awakened without any reasonable cause and was now trying to get at the root of the problem. Coop turned partially to face him as he peered out into the corridor.

'What's this all about?' Marvin asked conversationally.

'We're taking you over to the marina,' Coop answered, just as conversationally.

'What for?'

'We need this house,' Coop said.

'Why?'

'To watch this end of the road.'

'To watch it for what?'

'For anybody who might come down it,' Coop said, and smiled, 'You want to get dressed?'

'I don't get it,' Marvin said.

'You're not supposed to. Get back in there and hold up a blanket for your wife while she dresses.' Coop looked at his watch. 'I want to be out of here in five minutes.'

Marvin nodded, sighed, and went back into the bedroom. 'What's this all about?' he asked Leonard.

'Didn't you hear what he told you, mister? We want to be out of here in five minutes. So let's hustle, huh?'

'Yeah, but what's it all about?' Marvin asked.

'Get dressed,' Leonard said, and Marvin shrugged. He walked to the bed where Selma was sitting upright, fully covered by the cotton nightgown she wore – why the hell didn't she ever wear nylon like other women did, like Marvin supposed other women did?

'We'd better do what they say,' Marvin suggested. He took the blanket from where it was folded at the foot of the bed and held it up in front of his wife, his arms spread. Selma got out of bed and nodded a small thank-you, and then slipped the nightgown up over her shoulders and head

39

and took her undergarments from the chair beside the bed and quickly began dressing.

From across the room, Leonard Crawley, who was thirty-five years old and whose education had not gone further than the twelfth grade in high school, watched Marvin Tannenbaum's rigid back and outstretched arms, saw Selma's pale and expressionless face appear above the top edge of the blanket again as she pulled her dress over her head, and immediately sensed something that had managed to elude the older and wiser Dr. Tannenbaum from the moment his children had arrived yesterday afternoon.

Leonard Crawley, with a gun in his hands and more important matters on his mind, knew immediately and intuitively that something was wrong between these two kids.

'There's two houses on the beach where we won't have any trouble at all,' Coop had said. He had said this to Jason immediately after he had first scouted Ocho Puertos Key and was making a preliminary report. 'One of them is the second house on the beach, the Champlin house, right here' – pointing to an enlarged map of the key – 'and the other is the sixth house down, just before the Tannenbaums.' Coop had paused for effect, the way he had often paused for effect in Korea when he was surrounded by boys his own age whose toes were freezing and who kept slapping their hands against their sides and looking to their sergeant for answers he did not have. He had looked up at Jason and grinned and said, 'The reason we won't have any trouble is that there's kids in both those houses.'

The kids in the Hannigan house were both little girls, six and eight years old respectively, and they were in the living room in their pyjamas playing Chinese checkers when the two men came through the lanai. They looked at the men curiously, without fear, and then got just a little frightened when the men picked them up and carried them into the bedroom where their parents were still asleep. The men put the little girls down at the foot of the bed, and one of them went to the bed and shook Jack Hannigan by the shoulder, and when he woke up, the man said, 'Those are your kids, there, Mr. Hannigan. We don't expect any trouble from you.'

There was no trouble.

Jason looked first at Willy, who stood opposite the bed with the rifle hanging loosely from the end of his arm. Then he turned to the bed where the man Stern was lying pitched forward halfway on his side, bent awkwardly at the waist, the sheet sticky with blood and clinging to his stomach and thighs and crotch. The half-naked girl was sobbing against Stern's shoulder and back, covered with blood herself, unaware of Jason's entrance, seemingly unaware of anything but the man who lay bleeding beside her.

'What happened here?' Jason said. He did not raise his voice, nor was there any indication in his manner that he was angry. He faced Willy calmly, studying him with a careful, interested look on his face.

Willy smoothed his sparse blond moustache with his free left hand and then looked at the floor first and the ceiling next, and then said, 'He wouldn't do what I told him, Jase.'

'Well, now, let me hear it all, okay?' Jason said, and he smiled a pleasant, encouraging smile. Beside him, Flack nodded in sympathetic appreciation of the way Jason was handling this, without getting excited or anything, just peaceful and calm. Across the room the girl was still sobbing.

'You said we shouldn't take no chances with this one, Jase,' Willy said. 'So I warned him to do what I said, and when he didn't, I shot him.' Willy shrugged. 'That's all.'

'What was it you asked him to do?' Jason asked quietly.

'Just to get dressed,' Willy said, and shrugged again.

'Mmm-huh. And where does the girl fit in?'

'The girl?'

'Right.'

'Gee, she's got nothing to do with it,' Willy said, and smoothed his moustache again.

'Get her something to put on,' Jason said, and then quickly, 'Not you, Willy.'

41

Willy checked his forward movement and shrugged. Flack picked up Stern's white shirt from where it was lying in crumpled heap on the floor. He brought it to the bed and held it out to the girl. 'Miss?' he said. She did not answer him. She kept her face pressed to Stern's muscular back, her cheek smeared with blood, sobbing. 'Miss, you want this?' Flack asked.

'Take it,' Jason said suddenly and harshly, and the girl looked up for an instant and met Jason's eyes and then slowly sat up and took the shirt from Flack. There was nothing to hide anymore, there was nothing they had not seen. She pulled the shirt on slowly, and then held it closed over her breasts, not buttoning it, her arms folded across its front. She looked at Jason again, and then sniffed once, and then wiped her nose on the long sleeve of the shirt.

'What's your name?' Jason asked.

'Lucy.'

'Lucy what?'

The girl did not answer. Jason walked to the bed and lifted Stern's wrist. He felt for a pulse and then turned to Willy and said, 'You goddamn butcher, he's still alive.'

'I thought he was dead,' Willy said.

'He's not.'

'I thought sure he was dead,' Willy said again, as though that would make it so.

'No,' Jason said. He kept staring at Stern, still holding his wrist.

'There's a doctor here in town, ain't there, Jase?' Flack said.

'Yeah.'

'What do you need a doctor for?' Willy asked.

'The guy's dying,' Flack said.

'Yeah, but the plan –'

'Shut up,' Jason said.

The girl looked up at him. 'Are you . . . will you get a doctor for him?' she asked.

'Yes,' he said. He looked again at Stern, and then suddenly frowned. He kept holding Stern's wrist silently for what seemed like a very long time. At last he let it drop.

42

'We don't need a doctor any more,' he said, and the girl began screaming.

Samantha Watts had awakened at five-twenty to the sound of an engine starting. She had supposed Luke was moving his boats into Pasajero Channel, and she further supposed she would go down to the pier to help him, but she lay in bed wide-awake, searching the ceiling, reluctant to rise, and yet unable to sleep. One of the Siamese leaped onto the bed. Although the room was still dark, she knew at once it was Fong, not Fang. She could tell by the gentler sound of his purr and the scratchy feel of his tongue, so unlike Fang's across her wrist. She took a playful swat at him, and then said aloud, 'Oh hell, I might as well get up,' but remained in bed anyway for the next ten minutes. Her eyes were growing accustomed to the predawn gloom. She wondered where the other cats were. She owned ten cats in all.

At five-thirty she got out of bed and took off her pyjamas and looked briefly at her tanned and slender body in the full-length mirror on the back of the closet door. She quickly pulled on panties and bra, denim trousers, a pair of tattered sneakers, and an old grey sweatshirt. From the dresser top she took a comb which she put into her back pocket, and a lipstick and her house keys, which she put into the right-hand side pocket. At the back of her mind someplace was the half notion that she would meander down to the marina and give Luke a hand with the boats. Her house was the fourth in line on the beach, between Rick Stern's – she noticed that all the shades were drawn; that meant he'd picked up a girl in Marathon the night before – and Mr. Ambrosini's, who was a retired tractor salesman from Des Moines. Mr. Ambrosini's shades were never drawn, but she saw no sign of him this morning. Mr. Ambrosini was a nice little man who was seventy years old if he was a day.

By the time she had had a cup of coffee and come out through the lanai and into the backyard, all thought of helping Luke with his boats had vanished. It was perhaps ten minutes before dawn, and she scanned the horizon over the Atlantic and then turned in a slow circle, her eyes taking in the Ambrosini house to the west, and then the Tannenbaum house, and then moving in the same slow circle across the highway to the north where the big grey Westerfield house squatted behind its stand of hardwood trees. As she watched, she saw the upstairs bedroom light go out. She was surprised because she had not known the Westerfields were here; they did not usually come down until after Christmas. Well, perhaps the house was being rented; she would ask Luke when she saw him. If he was out moving boats, he had undoubtedly seen the light too. She turned eastward towards Bahia Honda and watched the sky beginning to brighten and wondered why on earth Luke was moving the boats into the cove. She had, of course, heard the Weather Bureau's advisories the night before, but that certainly did not look like a hurricane sky.

She wondered what it was like out on the water, and then – because she was thirty-one years old and had been directly translating thought into action since the time she was six – she walked rapidly to the dock and jumped down into the boat. She threw off the bowline, and then started the outboard and freed the stern line. She nosed the boat out and away from the dock. The offshore waters deepened quickly, dropping from three feet to eight feet to thirteen feet in the space of half a nautical mile. Beyond the inshore shelf the waters dropped away swiftly to form Hawk Channel, where the depths ran to forty feet and more, enough draft to accommodate an ocean liner. She did not go out as far as the channel. She headed due south for several miles, and then cut the motor and allowed the boat to drift. She figured the water beneath her was some twenty-five to thirty feet deep.

She looked at her watch now and saw that it was five minutes to seven. She stood up in the small boat, stretched her arms over her head, and ran one hand through her close-cropped blond hair. Then, smiling for no reason other than that it looked as though it would be a beautiful day, she started the outboard, and cheerfully headed back towards the island.

The chart was affixed to a clipboard, and the clipboard was resting on Luke's desk where he could see it plainly, just alongside the telephone. Luke was sitting in the chair behind his desk, and Benny sat on the edge of the desk, his eyes on the telephone. Across the small marina office, the second man in dungarees and chambray shirt idly trained his rifle at Luke's chest.

The chart had been typed on an inked grid [see overleaf].

Looking at the chart, Luke knew instantly that the numbers under each name were the last five digits of telephone numbers on Ocho Puertos. His own telephone number was 872-8108, and the second listing for the marina was the number of the outside booth. Bobby Colmore's number was 872-8217, and Sam's which he also knew by heart – was 872-8826. He glanced up at the clock hanging on the marina wall opposite his desk. The time was five minutes to seven.

'Figured it out, Costigan?' Benny asked.

'No, I haven't,' Luke said.

'Well, stick around. Maybe it'll come to you.'

'You know,' Luke said, 'if you think there's any money in the safe, there isn't. I made my bank deposit Friday afternoon.'

'Is that right?' Benny said.

'Yes,' Luke answered.

'My, my,' Benny said, and Luke had the positive feeling he had known all along the goddamn safe was empty. He heard voices outside and then the screen door opening. A moment later the inner door opened wide, and a tall man wearing khakis came into the room carrying an open bottle of Coke which he'd undoubtedly bought from the machine just outside. He stepped into the office and glanced immediately at Luke, and then gave him a wide smile, and then tilted the Coke bottle to his mouth and took a long pull at it, and then walked to the desk and put the bottle down on

	700	705	710	715	720	725	730	735	740	745	750	755
MARINA 2-8103 2-8985												
THE DINER 2-8369												
COLMORE 2-8217												
PARCH 2-8670												
CHAMPLIN 2-8989												
STERN 2-8406												
WATTS 2-8826												
AMBROSINI 2-8348												
HANNIGAN 2-8105												
TANNENBAUM 2-8572												

its top, directly in front of Luke, banging the bottle down hard, and keeping his hand wrapped around it, smiling all the while, and then saying very softly, still smiling, 'Morning, Mr. Costigan.'

Luke looked up at the man and said nothing. The man's eyes were blue and steady, and they studied Luke's face, unwaveringly, the smile still on the man's mouth, his fist still wrapped around the narrow neck of the Coke bottle. There was unmistakable challenge in the stiff extended arm of the man and the hand curled tightly around the bottle neck. Luke did not know why the challenge was being issued, but there it was, as certain as a dropped gauntlet at his feet.

'I said, "Good morning," Mr. Costigan,' the man said.

'Who are you?' Luke answered.

'Well, now, that's impertinent, isn't it?' the man said, and turned to the blond man who had followed him into the room. 'Isn't that impertinent, Willy?'

'It sure is impertinent,' Willy said, and then moved his hand up to stroke his moustache.

'I say "Good morning" to a man, and next thing you know he's asking me who I am. That's not very good manners, Mr. Costigan.' He smiled at Luke again and abruptly released his grip on the bottle. 'My name is Jason Trench,' he said.

'What do you want here, Mr. Trench?'

Jason smiled, and at that moment the telephone rang. He walked to the phone and said, 'If it's for you, Mr. Costigan, I'll just say you're out on the water – you won't mind, right?' He lifted the phone from its cradle. 'Costigan's Marina,' he said. 'Hello there, Johnny, how are you? Yep, we're all set here. Did you see us when we hung the "Closed" sign on the door?' Jason chuckled and then said, 'Figured you did. All right, keep in touch,' he said, and hung up. He turned to Benny and said briefly, 'That was Johnny at the diner. It's secured, you can check it off.'

Benny took a pencil from the pocket of his chambray shirt, and in the space alongside the diner's listing and phone number, under the column headed 700, he put a

47

small check mark. Luke glanced up at the clock. It was exactly 7 A.M. He looked again at the chart. The next call will come from Bobby Colmore's place, he thought, and it will come at 7:05.

'Is Goody in the phone booth outside?' Benny asked.

'Right,' Jason said, and the office went silent.

At 7:05 by the wall clock, just as Luke had expected, the telephone rang again.

'Hello there, Harry,' Jason said. 'How's every little thing? Well, that's just fine. You lock up there and bring him on over. Right,' he said, and replaced the receiver in its cradle. 'The tackle shop,' he said to Benny. 'It's secured. They'll be bringing the wino on over.'

The wino, of course, would be Bobby, and for some reason they were going to bring him here to the marina. Luke watched as Benny put a check mark next to Bobby's name, in the column headed 705. The calls, then, would come into the marina at five-minute intervals and would obviously be reports from Jason's men scattered throughout the community. The chart went only as far as 755, which Luke now knew was five minutes to eight o'clock. Did this mean the reports would cease at that time? He then noticed that this particular chart was only the top page of a sheaf of papers attached to the clipboard. Was it possible that the sheet under this one began with the numerals 800 and proceeded to 855, and then on through the day, on the next sheet and the one after that, for as long as these men intended to stay in Ocho Puertos?

He listened to the next several calls intently, trying to establish some sort of pattern. Jason took each call in high good humour, chatting briefly with each of his men, giving instructions, and then turning to Benny each time and telling him where to put another check mark. The progression of check marks seemed to be absolutely clear, running down the chart vertically, and across the chart horizontally, the calls coming in order from the diner, the tackle shop, the Parch house, and then the Champlin house. When Jason hung up after the call from the Champlin house, he told Benny to check off the Stern house as well,

48

since he positively knew that was secured. Luke assumed he must have come directly from the Stern house to the marina.

The next listing on the chart was for Samantha's house.

The palms of Luke's hands were suddenly covered with sweat.

His hands had begun sweating that day long ago as the landing barges approached Omaha Beach. He had repeated the words over and again to himself, don't be frightened, don't be frightened, but his hands had begun to sweat, and then he was enormously frightened when the ramp went down and he found himself running across the wet sand with the machine-gun bullets spraying the beach. He had wanted to turn and run back into the water, but they were dead and dying behind him, so he threw himself flat on the sand and began to crawl, listening to the shattered screams around him and the roar of the shells and the angry clatter of the machine guns. Nobody ever talked about the sounds of war; nobody ever told you that dying in pain had a terrifying sound all its own. That was when the enemy bullet struck him.

He had been lying flat, so nothing really happened when the slug pierced his calf except that he felt a sharp stinging pain, and then he looked back and saw that his leg was bleeding just a bit above the top of his combat boot. Well, he had thought, it's over; I get a Purple Heart and a trip home. Then the man crouching in fear not a foot from him in the sand took a slug right in the mouth, the bullet shattering his teeth and blowing away the back of his helmet and his head. Luke felt neither guilt nor relief. He had not asked for the bullet that caught him in the calf, and he experienced no joy when the man lying next to him got killed. Years later he would hear the combat clichés repeated so many times in so many different ways that he came to believe perhaps he *had* been overjoyed when the bullet smashed into the soldier beside him. But at the time he only winced when the blood spattered up on to his own hands from the man's broken face.

He came very close to breaking on that strange beach

with a stranger's blood spurting onto his hands; he began weeping like a baby. In 1960 he again came very close to breaking on the edge of his hurricane-demolished pier in Islamorada. He was thirty-six years old, too old to cry; this was no longer the kid who had trembled in fear on a beach in France. He looked out over the water. Donna had smashed his pier to splinters, taking away each of the slips and even knocking down most of the pilings. She had torn through the big sign he had erected facing the Atlantic – WELCOME TO COSTIGAN'S MARINA, and then had extended her welcome into the marina office itself, destroying it completely. Undiminished, unwearied, she had ripped the sides off three of Luke's sleeping units and shattered the windows and torn the shingles off all the others. Luckily he had moved his customers' boats northeast to Windley Key and into Snake Creek the moment he had heard the first advisory. They, at least, had been saved.

His insurance, he knew, would cover only part of his investment.

For the first time since 1944, he was filled with an overboiling sense of unfairness, a choking self-pity that bordered on rage. For the first time since he had been wounded, he came very close to accepting himself as a cripple who just could not make a go of it, the hell with it, the bloody goddamn rotten *hell* with it.

He kept staring at the debris floating offshore.

I could sell the derrick hoist, he thought. I could get maybe thirty-five thousand for it, less than I paid, but at least I'd be able to settle with the bank.

When Luke Costigan discovered Ocho Puertos in 1961, it was a community of seven beachfront houses on the southern side of the island and one large house on the northern side. In addition, the community could boast of a diner owned and operated by one of the charter residents, a man named Lester Parch. Luke decided at once that it would be a good spot for a marina. The waters just off Spanish Harbour were full of amberjack and wahoo, king mackerel and yellowtail. Up north towards Bahia Honda Channel, and among the myriad small keys dotting Florida

Bay, were tarpon and red snapper, muttonfish and trout. In the Gulf Stream you could expect to pull sailfish or bonita, Allison tuna or dolphin. Luke knew the fish were plentiful; the thing he did not know was whether he could persuade anyone to leave a boat at a small marina on an essentially isolated key. He hoped that he could. He asked the bank for another loan, and they gave it to him.

The new marina was nothing pretentious, but at least it was a beginning. His pier had only thirty-five slips, back-in slips at that, no sleeping facilities, and only a small travel lift. There were three Esso pumps at the end of the pier (two for petrol, one for Diesel fuel) and also a sign identical to the one that had dominated the marina entrance in Islamorada: WELCOME TO COSTIGAN'S MARINA. The welcome included fuel and docking facilities, as well as the limited amount of marine supplies (lights, flags, bolts, pumps, horns) he carried in the small store behind his office. In addition, there was a locker where he hoped to store boat covers and batteries for his customers, a men's room and a ladies' room, a Coke machine alongside the marina office, a machine selling block ice and ice cubes, a telephone booth, and the long repair shop with its big overhead doors where he would work on his customers' boats. That was it. He watched it rise on the edge of the ocean with a feeling of pride and determination; he would not let this bastard life kick him around and make him the cripple he never was and never wanted to be.

Samantha came into the office the week after the new marina opened for business. It had been in construction for close to six months, but he had never seen her before, and he was surprised when she told him she lived there, fourth house on the beach, right between Stern and Ambrosini.

'I inherited it,' she said. 'From my mother, when she died.' She paused. 'Do you like it here?'

'Yes,' he said. 'Very much.'

'So do I.' She paused. 'I've got ten cats,' she said. 'I have to feed them every day of the week, twice a day. I'm running out of money.' She paused again. 'I need a job.'

'I can't hire anybody right now,' Luke said.

'I wouldn't expect you to pay me much in the beginning.'

'I couldn't pay you anything.'

'Okay,' she said. 'It's a deal.'

'Look, Miss . . .'

'Watts,' she supplied. 'Sam. Well, really Samantha.'

'I just don't need any help.'

'If you start getting customers, you will.'

'I haven't got a single boat yet.'

'You'll get them. It'll be too late then to set up an office system.'

'What do you know about office systems?'

'I used to work for a savings and loan company in St. Pete before my mother died.' She paused. 'I know how to run an office. Also, I know most of the boat captains in the area. Once you get going, you'll need charter boats for fishing parties.'

'Maybe, but –'

'Try me,' Samantha said.

She began work the following Monday, answering mail and telephone, getting out circulars, soliciting customers, contacting boat captains, talking to salesmen. She knew boats. She could discuss them intelligently and affectionately. She harassed and badgered and cajoled all the captains in the area, until she finally succeeded in lining up a dozen of them who agreed to carry charter parties for Luke, giving him first call over the marinas on the bigger islands. She talked to fishermen, learning where the fish were running best and then passing on the information to marina customers. She was tightfisted with money; she constantly argued with salesmen about the price of canvas, or varnish, or block ice. Attractive but not beautiful, she did not scare away the customers' wives. Instead they enjoyed stopping by the office to ask her about the shops in Key West or Miami, or sometimes to have a glass of iced tea with her, away from boats and the stink of fish. She worked hard in those early days of the business – but more than that, she set a tone of relaxed efficiency that coloured the entire operation and was in no small way responsible for its success.

Accepting Samantha on her own terms, of course, was certainly simpler than any attempt to know her as a complex woman would have been. She ran the marina for Luke, and she did it easily and efficiently. He never questioned her about herself. Their relationship was pleasant and businesslike. In February of 1962, some five months after she began working for him, he found himself involved in a way he had neither anticipated nor desired.

The last fishing party had come in at about nine o'clock that night and had paid Luke for the charter boat. He had squared it away with the captain – a one-eyed man who lived on Ramrod and had miraculously escaped being called Popeye – and then, because it was late and because both he and Samantha were exhausted after a long day, he asked her if she would like a drink before she left. He felt a slight pang the moment the words left his lips, as though this puncturing of their businesslike understanding would inescapably lead to complications.

'I'd love one,' Samantha said, and she looked at him steadily and lingeringly, with much the same expression that had been on her face the day she applied for the job and told him she had ten cats to feed.

They drank a great deal that night, and they talked a great deal. They talked in the small, marine office, Luke with his feet up on the desk, Samantha curled up opposite him in the battered leather chair that was a survivor of the marina in Islamorada. She spoke softly and easily, the way she seemed to do everything, and he listened to her with growing interest, filling their glasses, watching her intently. She had been married when she was eighteen, she told him, to a man who ran a seaquarium just outside St. Pete. That was where she was born, that was where she had lived most of her life until her mother bought the house down here in Ocho Puertos. He was a very nice man, her husband, older than she; she always seemed to go for older men. She supposed that was because her father died when she was seventeen – Electra and all that jazz, you know. She looked up at Luke and smiled wanly, and then sipped her drink and leaned her head against the side of the chair, burnished blonde against

53

black leather. She did not know whether the marriage had been a good one or not, she said. It had seemed very good to her, but that was because she had loved him so much – he had a moustache, one of those very black handlebar things; he took great pride in his moustache.

He had left her when she was twenty-two years old. There was a water ballet company – you know, aquacade swimmers – and he told Sam he had fallen in love with one of the girls in the company. Sam looked her up one day; she was a very pretty little thing with good legs, a swimmer's legs. Her husband sold the seaquarium to a man from Texas, and left with the swimmer a week after the divorce was final. She had never seen him since. She heard once that he was running a sideshow at the Seattle Fair, but she was not sure it was true.

He had left her five years ago, and she had lived with her mother until two summers ago, when her mother died of cancer. So here she was, a divorced lady of property – she looked up and smiled wanly again – living on the edge of the world 'with ten cats, ten, count them'.

She sipped her drink. The ice rattled in her glass.

Without looking at him she said, 'I'm very lonely, Luke. I'm so very goddamn lonely,' she began crying.

They made love in his room behind the marina office. He could remember everything they did together, could remember the taste of her mouth, and the softness of her hair, and the gentle sound of her weeping.

He could also remember telling her he loved her.

The telephone rang.

It was seven twenty-five.

Jason lifted the receiver.

'Costigan's Marina,' he said, and waited. 'This is Jason.'

Luke, sitting behind the desk, caught his breath. She's all right, he told himself; don't worry about her, she's all right. He found himself staring at Jason's shoes, tracing the crisscrossed ladder pattern of his brown shoelaces, and then the knot at the top of each shoe, and then the pale tan socks Jason was wearing. She's all right, he thought.

'What? What do you mean?' Jason said.

There was, in the next ten seconds, an eternity of time during which Luke felt as though he were sliding towards a black uncertain abyss.

'What do you mean, you don't know?' Jason said. 'Sy, don't give me stupid answers.' He paused. 'Let's start from the beginning, right? Did you go into the bedroom? Fine. Was the bed slept in? Fine. Then she was there last night, is that right? Right. Did you and Chuck go through the whole house? You did. And she's not there. Was her boat at the dock?'

Jason was waiting. Luke, watching him, felt suddenly relieved. It was entirely possible that Samantha –

'Sy, was her boat at the dock?' Jason repeated. 'What? You *what?*'

It seemed to Luke in that moment that Jason would tear the phone from its wire and hurl it against the wall. His face went white and his grip tightened on the receiver, and he began trembling with the sheer physical exertion of controlling himself. Very quietly, as though forcing himself to be gentle, as though he would explode into a hundred flying fragments if he did not speak softly, he said, 'Well, Sy, suppose you just go out and take a look at the dock now, huh? Would you do that for me? Go ahead, I'll wait.'

He stood beside the desk with the phone pressed to his ear, waiting. Benny and Willy watched him silently. The fifth man in the room, who was thus far nameless to Luke, continued leaning against the filing cabinets with his eyes closed, as though he were asleep. Patiently Jason waited. At last he said, 'Hello, yes, what did you find?' He listened carefully, and looked up at the clock. 'Any sign of her out on the water?' he asked. 'Mmm,' he said. He looked at the clock again. 'Mmmm. Well, you just sit there on that dock and call me the minute you've got her. Right.' He put the phone back onto its cradle.

'What is it?' Benny asked.

'The Watts girl. She must be out on the water. We'll have to wait till she gets back.'

Benny looked at the clock. 'It's almost seven-thirty, Jase.'

'I know what time it is.'

'Three more calls and the check-ins are done.'

'I know that.'

'When will you call Fatboy?'

'As soon as we get the girl.'

'When'll that be? She might stay out there all day. Maybe she took the boat out for a long trip. How do we know? She can be heading for Miami for all we know.'

'All she has is a fibre glass outboard,' Jason said. 'I don't think she'd head for Miami in it, not with the possibility of a hurricane coming.'

Benny still seemed concerned. He was obviously a worrier, and Jason was obviously used to his fretting. 'Maybe we ought to call Fatboy anyway,' he said. 'As soon as all the others report.'

'No,' Jason said. 'Not if there's the possibility of trouble here.'

'Do you think there *is* the possibility of trouble, Jase?'

'Well, the girl's out on the water there someplace,' Jason said gently, 'and until she's in our pocket, we haven't got the town. Until we have the town, Benny, why yes, I think there's the possibility of trouble, yes.'

The telephone rang.

The clock read seven-thirty.

'Costigan's Marina,' Jason said. 'Yes, this is Jason. Right,' he said, 'right. You just keep him happy there.' He hung up. 'Ambrosini,' he said to Benny, 'secured.' And Benny marked the chart.

Luke watched him. Something was beginning to bother him about that chart. He did not know quite what, but something was wrong with it. The something that was wrong had to do with the fact that Samantha was not in her house, where these men had obviously expected to find her, but was instead out on the water. He began to worry about how they would treat her when she pulled up to the dock. These men were armed; they might react badly to an unexpected situation.

'Got it all doped out, Costigan?' Jason said, and smiled.

'Not yet,' Luke answered.

'Give it time,' Jason said, but offered no explanation.

At seven thirty-five a call came telling Jason that the Hannigan house was secured. As Benny put his check mark in the 735 column, Luke looked at the chart again, and again wondered what was wrong with it. He was beginning to suspect that he had really discovered nothing peculiar about the chart, but was instead playing an intellectual guessing game designed to take his mind off Samantha. The possibility of Jason's men harming her seemed extremely remote, and yet he felt anxiety gnawing inside him, felt a premonition of dread that terrified him.

At seven-forty the last of what Benny had labelled 'the check-ins' came through. Jason picked up the phone and said, 'Costigan's Marina,' and waited, and then said, 'Hello, Coop, how'd it go? Yes, everything here is under control.' He listened. 'All right, tell Leonard to bring them over. What?' He paused, listening again. 'Well, that's a surprise, isn't it? We're getting all kinds of surprises this morning. Well, you bring *them* over, too. Right.' He put the receiver down and turned to Benny. 'That was Coop over at the Tannenbaum house. It's secured. You can check it off.'

'What was all that other stuff?' Benny asked.

'Oh, unexpected company,' Jason said. 'The doctor's son and daughter-in-law are visiting him.'

'How come we didn't know that?'

'They only got here yesterday,' Jason said, and it was then that Luke realized what was wrong with the chart. He was glad the telephone rang in that moment because he was sure his sudden knowledge showed immediately on his face. And then he realized this call could be about Samantha, and he gripped the edge of the desk as Jason lifted the receiver.

'Costigan's Marina.' He paused. 'Yes, Sy. Yes. All right, Sy. Bring her here. We'd better keep a close watch on her.' He hung up. 'The Watts girl,' he said to Benny.

'Is she all right?' Luke asked suddenly.

'She's fine,' Jason said briefly. He turned to Benny. 'The house is secured. You can check it off.'

Benny sighed deeply, relieved. 'Then that's everybody,' he said.

'That's everybody,' Jason answered.

Luke, sitting behind the desk, said nothing.

There was no listing on Jason Trench's chart for the Westerfield house across the main road. At four-thirty this morning, when he had begun moving his boats, a light was burning in the upstairs bedroom of that house.

4

The telephone rang in the Key West motel room at exactly seven forty-five. Fatboy, who was dressed and waiting by the phone, lifted it from the receiver at once and said, 'Hello?'

'Arthur?'

'Yeah.'

'This is Jason.'

'Yeah?'

'We've got it. You can move out.'

'Okay,' Fatboy said, and hung up. He looked across the room to where Andy was studying him with a quizzical expression. 'Jason,' he said, nodding assurance. 'They've got it. We're to move out.'

'Good,' Andy said, and rubbed his hands together briskly.

'Put the bags in the car,' Fatboy said. 'I'll contact the others.'

'This is good,' Andy said again. 'It's good, ain't it, Fatboy?'

'I knew they'd do it,' Fatboy said.

'So did I. But . . . well . . . things can go wrong, you know that.'

'Not when Jason is doing the planning. Come on, we've got to move.'

'Yeah,' Andy said, and he grinned and went into the bathroom.

Fatboy stood by the telephone with his hand on the receiver, motionless, knowing he should make the call to Fortunato, and yet delaying the call, savouring this moment of satisfaction.

His small black eyes were sparkling. He was pleased by

59

the knowledge he now possessed, the fact that Ocho Puertos was in Jason's hands, and that he and the others could now proceed there from Key West where they had been since last Monday. But he had expected Jason to take the town all along, and he knew this did not account for the major portion of his pleasure. The pleasure was something that went much deeper than the surface accomplishment of Jason's capturing the town, deeper perhaps than the magnitude of the entire scheme. The pleasure went back as far as 1945, when Fatboy was the only one who had had the sense to lie, the only one who had known instinctively that a careful trap was being set, and that to tell the truth would be dangerous to Jason's well-being. He had known at once that the questions were being framed to elicit a denial – 'You *were* gambling, weren't you? There *was* a big game, wasn't there?' Every instinct for self-preservation had urged him to shout, 'No, sir, we were *not* gambling,' and then he recognized the trap. That was what they wanted from him, a denial. He was too smart for that. He told them there had been a game, when of course there had not, told them further that it was a high-stakes game, corroborated every lie Jason had previously told – not that it made any difference in the end. But there had been pleasure in knowing he had come to Jason's assistance, even if he had not been able to save him.

Arthur Stuart Hazlitt had been called Fatboy since the time he was nine years old. In the summer of 1961, when Jason called him from New York City, he said, 'Hello, Arthur, how are you?' using Fatboy's real name, the way he had done from the day they met.

Fatboy smiled. 'I'm fine,' he said. 'How're you, Jase?'

They exchanged courtesies, how's your mother, fine, how's Annabelle, fine, what kind of work are you doing, all that, and then they reminisced a little, and then there was a long pause.

Jason cleared his throat.

'Arthur, can you come to New York?' he asked.

'What for?'

'I need your help.'

'Are you in trouble?'

'No. But I need your help.'

'With what?'

'A plan. I'd appreciate it if you could come, Arthur. I hope to call Alex and the others, but I wanted to talk to you about it first. You're the first one I've called.'

'Well, I certainly –'

'Arthur? Can you come?'

'Well . . . well, what's it for, Jase?'

'It's for America,' Jason said.

There was a silence on the phone.

'I'm not sure I know what that means,' Fatboy said.

'I can't say more than that on the phone.'

'Well, this . . . uh . . . this sounds pretty important,' Fatboy said.

'It is.'

'When . . . when did you want me to come, Jase?'

'Now. Today.'

'I've got a job, Jase, I can't just –'

'Then come Friday night and stay for the weekend. We can talk about it over the weekend.'

'I'll see if my mother –'

'I'd rather you didn't tell her anything about this,' Jason said, and the line went silent again.

'All right,' Fatboy said at last. 'I'll come.'

In the Second Avenue apartment that Friday night, Jason outlined the plan to him. It was not a polished plan at the time; it was instead nothing more than the most rudimentary of schemes, with none of the details worked out. They would need a town, yes, that was apparent, someplace to effect the transfer, but Jason knew only that it should be somewhere in Florida; more than that he had not planned. Fatboy suggested that the Florida Keys might serve their purposes, making his suggestion even before he was completely convinced he wanted to throw in with Jason. Jason said yes, the Keys *might* be a good place for them, and Fatboy said they could even use one of the uninhabited Keys, hell, there were probably a dozen uninhabited Keys down there. No, Jason said, we need someplace to keep the men, you see; we can't just have them roaming around loose in broad daylight after the transfer is made. That's right, Fatboy said, we need a place with buildings, don't we, someplace we can keep them, that's right. That's right, Jason said, but I'm sure we can find the place down there, the Keys might just be the right place for us, I'm not sure yet, it would have to be investigated. Oh, sure, it would have to be investigated, Fatboy said, still not knowing if he wanted to go along with Jason or not, liking Jason a hell of a lot, and respecting him, but not knowing if he wanted to risk, well, his life on a scheme like this one.

He decided to throw in with Jason the next night.

That Saturday night they began by talking about the old days, and the things they had done together, and then Jason started telling him what he had been doing since they had last seen each other in 1946. He had gone back to New Orleans, of course, because that was his home town and that was where Annabelle was waiting for him. He had a college degree, a bachelor of science from the University of Louisiana, well, Arthur knew that (Yes, I knew that, Fatboy said), and he was a trained mechanical engineer, but after what had happened (Well, *that*, Fatboy said) he didn't much feel like taking a job working for anybody. He felt there were more important things to be done in the world – here, have some more of this bourbon. (Thanks, Fatboy said.) What he had done was join a volunteer group that called itself The Sons of American Freedom, which he later found out was a racist group, not that he much gave a damn one way or the other. The war had been over for more than a year when Jason joined the group, which was at the time agitating for death sentences for the Nazi war criminals. This was in July or thereabouts, not too long after Lieutenant General Homma, the Jap who had ordered the Bataan death march, was executed, so the group felt it had a precedent and they were running around handing out leaflets and making speeches, while also rousing out a few niggers every now and then, but that was more or less kidding around and the war criminals thing was the important issue. After the verdict came in October, the group got down to its major business, which was keeping the nigger in his place in Louisiana, and a couple of months later fighting broke out in Indochina between the French and the Reds, and it was then that Jason realized just how vast and unrelenting the Communist conspiracy was. He broke with The Sons of American Freedom and joined a group that called itself The Indochinese Assistance Committee, ICAC, which was mostly a fund-raising group, though they did put out some pamphlets that tried to explain what was behind all the fighting in Indochina. Luckily, he had managed to save a little money, plus what he could steal, huh? (and Fatboy laughed here) so he was able to devote almost all of his time to these various committees and organizations, moving from one group to another as the dangers presented themselves: the Communist seizure of power in Czechoslovakia, for example, and the Russians stopping traffic between Berlin and the Western occupation zones in June of 1948, and the Russian veto of an atomic control plan in that same month, and the sentencing of Cardinal Mindszenty to life imprisonment in Hungary, and the revelation by President Truman in September of 1949 that Russia had set off an atomic explosion. That was it, that was when the danger *really* became clear and present, that was when the Commies were ready to clear the decks for the Korean invasion in 1950, nothing could stop them now, they had the goddamn bomb and nothing could stop them.

Fortunately for this country, there were men around who recognized the danger immediately and who tried to do something about it. In October of 1949, a month after the Russians set off their bomb, Jason organized a group called the McCarthy Men, which independently tried to assist the Wisconsin senator in his early battle against subversive forces within the United States. He went to New York with Annabelle not three months later, in early January of 1950, where he formed a new group called Americans for America, figuring he could distribute his energies more liberally without an organization name that linked him to any single person. Actually, he was ready to assume a leadership of his own at that time, and did not want to seem a follower of *anyone*, even someone he respected as much as McCarthy. In April of 1950, he had a run-in with the police in New York when he and his new group – there were half a dozen members at the time, including himself and Annabelle – picketed a pro-fascist play with a Japanese leading man, and he was forced to reorganize again in September of that year, with new people – well, Arthur got the picture, didn't he? It was a constant battle, a constant effort to be heard against the complacent idiots in this country who were unwilling to recognize the fact that Russia was nibbling away at the world, piece by tiny piece, nibbling up the world while it talked of coexistence with a full mouth, swallowing countries or pieces of countries one by one, Albania, Bulgaria, Czechoslovakia, Germany, Hungary, Poland, Romania, North Korea, North Vietnam, Cuba, half the goddamn new African nations.

'Where does it end, Arthur? Where does it end?'

'I don't know?' Fatboy said. 'Where does it end, Jason?'

'Arthur,' Jason said, 'I love this country. I want this country to survive.'

'I do, too.'

'What's there in the world for men like us, Arthur?'

'What do you mean?'

'What is there for us, unless we make it ourselves?'

'Ourselves,' Fatboy repeated softly.

'Yes.' Jason paused. 'Ourselves.' He paused again. 'I want *action*, Arthur. I'm tired of leading groups of mealymouthed malcontents who think we're agitating for free love or folk singing. We are agitating for a stronger America, the America we *fought* for, Arthur, the America we risked our *lives* for. Is all that going to go down the drain? Was all that for nothing? Arthur, I need your help. Say you'll help me. Say you'll join me in what can only be a glorious day for America, for our country.'

Fatboy nodded.

'I'll join you,' he had said. 'I'll help you.'

He picked up the telephone now. He had been the first one Jason called in September of 1961, and he was the first

64

one to be called today, and the knowledge that he was so respected, so trusted, so necessary to the plan, filled him with a pleasure that was almost a religious glow. Quickly he dialled the number of the Magnolia Motel on Simonton Street and asked to talk to Mr. Fortunato. They rang the room and Fatboy said, 'Sal?'

'This is Sal,' Fortunato answered.

'Fatboy. We roll.'

'Check,' Fortunato said, and hung up.

Andy came out of the bathroom with two small overnight bags. He waited until Fatboy hung up, and then said, 'You leave a tooth brush or anything in the medicine chest?'

'No.'

'Nothing?'

'No.'

'Okay,' Andy said, and went out.

Fatboy dialled the number of the Waterview Motel on Pearl Street. When Rodiz came onto the line, he said, 'Rafe?'

'Yes?' Rodiz answered.

'Fatboy.'

'Yes?'

'We roll.'

'*Comprendo*,' Rodiz said, and hung up. He sat looking at the telephone for just a moment, and then he grinned and rose and walked swiftly to the dresser on the other side of the room, tapped his zippered overnight bag with the palm of his hand, and then called to the bathroom, 'Eugene, hurry up. That was Fatboy. We roll.'

There were mornings when everything just went wrong, and it was on those mornings that Amos Carter figured it was a pretty goddamn sorry mess when a Negro found himself living in Monroe County, Florida, just a stone's throw from Dade County, with a name like Amos to boot, so that every comedian who walked into the diner could say, 'Hey there, Amos, where's Andy?' Very funny, and usually he would reply, 'Out back with the Kingfish,' but that was only on days when he was feeling some sort of self-respect as

65

a human being, and could take jokes from white men. On the mornings when everything went wrong, he did not choose to take either jokes or crap from any white man walking the face of the earth, and this Sunday morning was one of those mornings.

It had started with Abby bugging him again about how come he didn't go to church any more. He had tried to explain to Abby that he had to be at the diner at eight o'clock on Sunday mornings to get the stoves going before Mr. Parch came in at eight-thirty. Abby told him there was a seven o'clock Mass over to the church on Big Pine, and Amos told her that was a white man's church, and he didn't want to start his Sunday by having trouble with white men. You afraid of white men? Abby had asked, which had started him off just fine because he wasn't afraid of *no* damn white man walking the face of the earth, and yet he was scared to death of *every* damn white man he'd ever met. But he didn't like no skinny little girl with her hair all wrapped up in rags to go reminding him about it. She had told him to fetch his own breakfast after he'd given her a clout on the ear, and then he'd burned his damn hand lighting the wood stove, and had left the house without having no breakfast at all, figuring he'd get to the diner just a little early and mix himself a batch of eggs.

Now here he was on Ocho Puertos Key at five minutes to eight o'clock, and there was a goddamn roadblock telling him the road to the diner was closed for repairs. Now, when the hell had they put *that* damn thing up? He sat looking at the barricade for several moments in silent disbelief, knowing it had not been there last night when he left the diner at six o'clock, and knowing today was Sunday when road gangs didn't ordinarily work, so how had the barricade got there and what purpose did it serve? Amos scratched his head and got out of the car and walked over to the barricade and studied the sign solemnly, as though suspecting Allen Funt was lurking in the mangroves with his crew and his cameras, ready to pop out and tell Amos this was all a joke. But Allen Funt didn't pop out so Amos figured the roadblock was real enough.

66

He looked down the road past the barricade and saw no work gang in sight, but that didn't necessarily mean they couldn't be working just out of sight around the bend. Then, because this was only another nuisance on a morning when everything seemed to be going wrong, Amos did a very brave thing for a Negro living in the state of Florida. He moved the barricade to the side of the road, got back into his 1952 Plymouth, drove onto S-811, stopped the car, got out again, and then moved the barricade back where he had found it. You go to hell, he thought, you *and* your goddamn roadblock; and he got back into the car and drove directly to the diner.

He parked the car behind the diner, facing the beach, and then he walked to the back door, and the first thing he noticed was that one of the garbage cans was not where it was supposed to be. Somebody had moved it closer to the door. He picked up the can and moved it back with the others and was reaching into his pocket for his key when he noticed the scraps of wire lying on the ground near the door. Some of the wires were red and some were yellow, and he could not figure what the hell they were from, unless the telephone company had been here to make some repairs. Seemed like everybody in the world was out making repairs, though he sure as hell hadn't *seen* nobody making any, that was for sure.

He was inserting his key in the lock when the door opened.

'Come on in,' the white man said, and Amos took one look at the .45 in his hand and decided three things in as many seconds. He decided to punch the white man right in the mouth because nobody walking the face of the earth was going to push him around this morning when everything else was going wrong; he decided to turn and run like hell before this sonofabitch white man put a bullet in his head; he decided to be sensible and go into the diner, just like the white man with the .45 had suggested.

'Come on, nigger,' the white man said. 'I got a itchy finger here.'

Amos, his heart pounding furiously inside his chest,

squeezed his eyes shut for just an instant, and then went into the diner.

Ginny woke up at eight-fifteen and, as seemed to be the case more and more often these days, did not know at first where she was. Boston, Norfolk, Baltimore, where? And then she remembered that this was Big Pine, and she rubbed her eyes and wondered why she hadn't heard the alarm, and then looked at the clock and saw what time it was. Oh my God, she thought, eight-fifteen! Why hadn't the alarm gone off, or had she even bothered to set it last night? Oh brother, Mr. Parch would take a fit when she walked in. She was supposed to be there at eight o'clock. What was wrong with that darned clock, anyway? She picked it up in both hands and held it close to her face, like a jeweller giving it a checkup, and saw that she had indeed set the alarm for ten minutes after seven, and that she had pulled out the little button on the back of the clock just the way you were supposed to. Oh, brother. She wanted a cigarette.

She got out of bed and walked to the dresser where she had put her bag and her ear-rings and the nice pin with the turtle on it last night when she'd come in with the fellow from Sugarloaf who started to get fresh the minute he was in the room. Some men were that way; they saw a woman thirty, thirty-five years old and on her own, right away they figured, well, what the hell. Where were the cigarettes?

She found the package – only one left in it, she'd have to get some more at the diner – and she lighted the cigarette and then crumpled the package in her hand and threw it at the waste-basket near the easy chair, missing, and then walked barefoot to the bathroom and looked at her face in the mirror and went 'Blaaaah' to herself, and then sat down to smoke the cigarette. She was wearing a shorty nightgown, and she still had good legs at forty-two years old which was what she was, and her breasts were still full, though somewhat pendulous or, to be downright honest with herself, sagging, okay? She took a last drag on the cigarette, rose, and threw it into the toilet bowl. Sagging breasts, she repeated to herself, as if repetition would remove the curse. But good legs, so drop dead, mister.

I'd better call the diner, she thought, tell Amos I'm gonna be a little late.

She went out of the bathroom and to her easy chair over which she had draped her clothes last night after the octopus had decided to leave. The phone rested on a battered end table alongside the easy chair, which was pretty battered itself, but which was as comfortable as an old shoe, if you enjoyed sitting in old shoes. She sat and felt one of the springs poking her in the behind (I wonder if I should have let him, she thought) and she adjusted her bottom and then pulled the phone to her and thought for a moment about the number of the diner, not having really forgotten it, but not remembering it off hand either. She puffed her cheeks out as she thought, letting her breath escape in a slow steady *phwwwwh*, and then nodded as the number came to mind. She dialled slowly, not wanting to make any mistakes; if there was one thing she hated it was dialling a number twice because she'd made a mistake the first time. She could have let him, she supposed, but what the hell was the percentage? He was a salesman on his way down to Key West. What was in it for her? What was she supposed to be, a free soup kitchen for every bum who staggered through? Yeah, well, never mind *that* jazz; she'd been had by enough salesmen all up and down the Eastern Seaboard, and there was no percentage in it, no percentage at all, half of them left you hanging anyway. The only decent one had been the guy in Richmond, and he turned out to be married, so what was the –

'Hello?' the voice said.

For a moment she thought she had dialled the wrong number. She looked at the dial and grimaced and then jerked the receiver away from her ear and studied it as though it had played a horrible trick on her.

'Hello,' the voice said again.

She put the phone back to her ear. 'Who's this?' she asked, frowning.

'Johnny,' the voice said again.

'I must have the wrong number,' she said.

'What number did you want?'

'Listen, is this the diner?'

'That's right.'

'The Ocho Puertos Diner?'

'That's right.'

'Well, who are you?'

'You don't know me.'

'Where's Amos?'

'Out back.'

'Is Mr. Parch there?'

'No, he hasn't come in yet.'

'Well, this is Ginny McNeil,' she said, and paused. 'I work there.'

'Okay, Ginny.'

'My alarm didn't go off this morning, so I'm gonna be a little late. Would you tell Amos to tell Mr. Parch?'

'What time did you plan on getting here, Ginny?'

'Well . . .' She looked across the room to where the clock was resting. 'It's almost eight-thirty. I guess I'll be in around nine, okay? Would you tell Amos?'

'Sure, Ginny.'

'Or maybe a little later. Maybe nine-thirty. Yeah, I still have to get dressed and all. Nine-thirty, okay? Tell Amos.'

'I'll tell him as soon as he gets back.'

'Thanks,' Ginny said, and hung up.

She was taking off her nightgown when she suddenly wondered how this Johnny guy, whoever he was, had managed to get into the diner when the diner didn't open until nine o'clock on Sundays, and here it was only eight-thirty, not even.

Well, what the hell, she thought. One of life's little mysteries. She shrugged, and then picked up her underclothing from the chair.

5

Luke Costigan's pier came out of the Atlantic Ocean like the shaft of a primitive arrow, its triangular head formed by the three buildings of the marina – the storage locker, the shop, and the office. Of these three buildings, the office was the smallest and farthest inland, the tip of the arrow. On the left of the office, facing the ocean, was the windowless storage locker. On the right, also facing the ocean, was the repair shop.

The repair shop was built of plywood with a corrugated metal roof and two huge overhead doors on its seaward side. The building was some seventy-five feet long and forty feet wide, with a door at one end, just beyond the spar rack holding small masts and riggings. The door was marked NO ADMITTANCE, and it opened on the joiner's shop where Luke and Bobby (and any extra help Luke hired from time to time) did their carpentry work. There was a keyboard just inside the door, containing tagged keys for all the boats in the marina and, to the right of that, shelves containing shafts, and rudders, and gaskets, and other boat parts. Scattered throughout the room were an electric saw, a planer, a sander, and a drill press. The room behind the joiner's shop was called the engine room, and it was here that Luke and whatever local mechanics he could get worked on inboard engines needing repair. The room was lined with benches containing tools and parts. More often than not, an engine would be hanging from the chain hoist in the centre of the room. Along one wall was a spark plug tester, an air compressor that belonged to a mechanic on Saddlebunch, and a part-washing tank.

A half wall, plywood, with wire mesh spreading from the top of it to a beam in the ceiling, divided this section of the shop from the larger section beyond. Luke called that area the paint shop, although more than painting was done there. The overhead doors opening into the paint shop admitted boats up to thirty feet in length, for repairs on their bottoms, for new shafts or propellers, for any job that could not be handled in the water. In addition, the shop doubled as a repair shop for outboard motors and contained a tank for testing. The area was usually cluttered with motors on racks or lying on the concrete floor with sawhorses and cartons of empty oilcans, with paint cans and bottles of thinner on open shelves, with greasy overalls hanging on pegs, with empty Coke bottles rolled under worktables, with idle cradles. The carpentry shop was certainly the cleaner of the two, with its smell of sawdust and its feeling of electrical efficiency.

There were eight people in the paint shop section of the building when Willy took Luke over there at rifle point.

Jason had made a call to Key West, first turning to Luke and saying, 'You won't mind if we make a long distance call, right?' and then immediately asking the operator for the number. When he reached his party, all he had said was 'Arthur?' (Pause) 'This is Jason.' (Pause) 'We've got it. You can move out.' And hung up. Whoever Arthur was, Luke surmised he was (a) not overly talkative, and (b) capable of understanding the tersest sort of directions from his leader. Obviously, he was in Key West. Apparently, he was now about to move *out* of Key West. Seemingly, if Luke's speculations were correct, he would be heading towards Ocho Puertos; otherwise, why had Benny and Jason been so concerned about not having control of the entire town before placing their call to him?

Jason, observing the furrow on Luke's forehead, perhaps reasoning that Luke was doing a little too much reasoning of his own, had said to Willy, the one with the scraggly blond moustache, 'Take Mr. Costigan over with the others, huh, Willy?'

Willy had grunted and shifted his rifle to a sort of overly smart military ready position and then said, 'Lezgo, Costigan.'

72

Luke got to his feet and limped towards the door, and then stopped just before opening it and turned towards Jason and smiled and said, 'Sure you can manage here without me?'

He could not have explained why he had felt the need for some rapport with this man, why he had felt the need for an exchange of wisecracks at this point. But he knew he was totally unprepared for what followed next.

Jason turned from the phone lazily, and looked at Luke steadily, no trace of a smile on his mouth. 'I don't think we need a cripple hanging around, Mr. Costigan,' he said, and continued to stare at him without smiling. Luke returned the stare, the smile frozen on his lips, his face gone suddenly pale. He opened the inside door and then the screen door and then limped out of the office with Willy following him. They walked in silence to the repair shop. Luke seemed to be favouring his good leg more than he ever had before.

Willy jabbed the Springfield into his back.

'Inside,' he said, and opened the door marked NO ADMITTANCE at the western end of the building. They walked past the power tools and through the opening in the plywood-wire-mesh wall into the paint shop. The first person Luke saw was Samantha sitting across the shop on the edge of an empty cradle. He almost went directly to her, but something warned him that secrets were valuable here, and that a hoarded treasure could conceivably be something to spend later in the day. Sam seemed to recognize his masquerade and made no gesture or movement towards him. She continued sitting on the cradle's edge as Willy came into the room and again poked the rifle barrel into Luke's back. Luke turned and said, 'Sonny, don't do that.'

'What?' Willy said.

'I said don't do that.'

'*You're* telling *me* what to do, Costigan?' Willy asked incredulously.

'Lay off, Willy,' a Negro standing near the cradled speedboat on the far end of the shop said. He was a big man with immense hands and a bullet-shaped head. There was a scar across his nose, and his eyes were bloodshot, and he

73

seemed capable of lifting the speedboat over his head and hurling it clear across the shop and into the Atlantic.

'You hear what he said to me, Harry?' Willy asked.

'Maybe he don't like you poking that gun in his back when there ain't no reason for it,' Harry answered.

The two men stood staring at each other for a moment, Willy seemingly searching for a rejoinder, and Harry waiting for him to reply so he could cut him down again. There was no love lost between them, Luke realized, and wondered immediately how he could use their animosity.

The door at the far end of the shop was opening again.

A small skinny Negro, perhaps forty years of age, came into the paint shop, followed by a white man holding a rifle.

'Hey, what you got there, Mac?' Willy said.

'Oh, he just wandered into the diner,' Mac said, grinning. 'Ain't that right, Amos?'

'Hey, Amos,' Willy said, 'where you got Andy hiding?'

Luke glanced first at Amos, saw the deep look of hatred that flared in his eyes, and then glanced quickly to where Harry stood.

Harry smiled. 'Aren't you gonna say hello to him, Mr. Costigan?' he asked.

'Say hello to who?'

'Mr. Costigan,' Harry said chidingly, 'we been casing this town for a long time now. We know exactly who's who, and who *knows* who, and even who's *sleeping* with who, so don't give us no snow job, huh? Say hello to Amos and then go on over there and sit with your girl.'

Luke hesitated, and then sighed. 'Hello, Amos,' he said.

'Hello, Luke,' Amos replied and then wiped the back of his hand across his mouth and looked around the room nervously.

Harry turned to Willy. 'You supposed to stay here?' he asked.

'What?' Willy said.

'Did Jason tell you to stay here or what?'

'He told me to bring Costigan over.'

'And stay?'

'He didn't say nothing about staying or anything.'

74

'Then why don't you shove off? Clyde and me can take care of this detail.'

'Where you want me to go?' Willy asked.

'Didn't you have a house assigned to you?'

'Sure,' Willy said, and made a short awkward gesture with his head. 'The Stern house, up the beach.'

'Then why don't you go there?' Harry suggested.

Willy wet his lips. 'You think I ought to?' he asked. 'Flack's up there, you know.'

'Supposed to be two in each house, ain't there?' Harry said.

'Well yeah, but –'

'Then go on up there. I mean, Jason didn't tell you to stay *here*, did he?'

'No, he just told me to bring Costigan over, like I done.'

'Then go on. We got this wrapped up here.'

'Okay, whatever you say,' Willy said, and shrugged and walked to the door. At the door he stopped, turned towards Harry, and asked, 'You sure now?'

'What's the matter with you?' Harry asked suddenly.

'Nothing,' Willy said. 'Nothing.' He went out.

'I'm gonna head back to the diner myself,' Mac said. 'Johnny's there all alone.'

'Okay,' Harry said. 'Thanks.' He watched as Mac went out, and then he turned to the others and said, 'Let's get some kind of order in here, I guess you've all made a count by now and decided there's only me and Clyde here to watch over you, which makes it odds of four to one against us.' Harry grinned. 'These rifles sort of tilt the odds our way, though, and I want to tell you we're both pretty good shots and have orders to kill anybody who tries to get out of here.' Harry paused to let this sink in. His eyes met with Amos's across the room, and he suddenly said, 'Something troubling you, mister?'

For a second only, Amos seemed not to realize he was being addressed. It was almost as though he was certain the colour of his skin would provide immunity from someone who – like himself – was black. But Harry had indeed addressed him, and he looked up at him blankly now, his eyes wide, a dumbfounded expression on his face.

'You hear me?' Harry said.

'You talking to me?'

'I'm looking straight at you, ain't I?'

'Nothing's troubling me,' Amos said briefly.

'You looked like something fierce was biting on your behind,' Harry said, and laughed. Clyde burst into laughter at the same moment. Amos, watching them, saw a Negro like himself laughing at him. Worse, he was laughing with a white man.

'Yessir, orders to kill,' Harry said when his laughter had subsided. 'Everybody got that?'

Nobody said anything.

'Mr. Costigan? You got that?'

Luke nodded.

'Reason I'm asking you, Mr. Costigan, is because just a minute ago you made believe you didn't know our coloured friend there' – and he indicated Amos with a sideward flick of his eyes – 'which makes me think you might be hatching some plans inside that head of yours.' Harry smiled pleasantly. 'Forget them, Mr. Costigan. Take the advice of somebody who knows. You got any notion of busting out of here, forget it now. Right, Clyde?'

Clyde nodded and laughed again, plainly tickled by just about everything Harry had to say. Harry, mindful of such an appreciative audience, seemed to deliver each word with one eye on Clyde and the other on Amos, as though challenging Amos to elicit the same respectful laughter from a white man. Amos, instead, eyed him dourly from the opposite side of the shop.

'Anyway, eight people is a little unwieldy,' Harry said, 'so I'm gonna separate you in groups of twos. How's that? Nice and cosy, right? Clyde and me here, we'll be able to keep a better eye on you that way, and avoid any trouble in case some of you get ideas. Right, Mr. Costigan?'

'Whatever you say,' Luke answered.

'Ahh, now, there's a smart man,' Harry said. 'Whatever I say, that's right, Mr. Costigan. Whatever I say. Okay.' He put down his rifle and looked across the room thoughtfully.

'Dr. Tannenbaum,' he said, 'I'm gonna pair you up with Mr. Colmore here. Is that all right with you? You know Mr. Colmore, don't you?'

'Yes, I know him,' Tannenbaum answered. He spoke with a faint Yiddish accent, holding his head high in a manner that was intended to be dignified but succeeded only in looking comically offended.

'Then you know he's a alcoholic, is that right, Dr. Tannenbaum?'

Tannenbaum did not answer.

Harry's face became extremely serious. He cocked his head to one side and looked at the doctor balefully and said, 'He's not gonna be drinking none today, Dr. Tannenbaum, so maybe you'd better keep an eye on him, huh? I want you both to pull up one of those empty parts crates and sit right there near the bow of the boat, side by side, and facing me right over here. Go on.'

Bobby Colmore, picking up one of the crates from against the wall, abruptly said, 'I'm not an alcoholic.'

'Yes, I know, Mr. Colmore,' Harry said. 'You already told us that.'

'I drink a little,' Bobby said.

'Uh-huh.'

'But I support myself, I have my own shop right across the . . . right across the yard there . . . and I'm not an alcoholic. I'd like you to remember that.'

'Uh-huh,' Harry said.

'And I'll thank you not to say it again.' He glanced at Marvin and his wife and said, 'There are some people here I don't know, and I wouldn't like them to get any wrong impressions.'

'Oh, I'm terribly sorry,' Harry said with a mock bow, and Clyde laughed.

'And I don't need any of your sarcasm, either,' Bobby said.

'Bobby,' Luke said gently, 'do what he says.'

'I just don't like him calling me a drunk, Luke.'

'I know.'

'He doesn't even know me, Luke.'

'I know that.'

'Nothing gives him the right to call me a drunk.'

'You're right, Bobby.'

'You gonna sit down now, Mr. Colmore?' Harry asked.

'Yes, you just take your goddamn time,' Bobby said. 'Don't play this so big.'

'Sure, they're big shots,' Tannenbaum said suddenly and angrily. 'He's right, you're making a big thing out of *what?* A cheap stickup? What do you want, my watch? My wife's pearls? What? So take them and go back where you came from, go back in your sewer someplace.'

'Why, I do believe the doctor is getting angry,' Harry said, and Clyde laughed. 'Doc, you just sit down there and don't get yourself all fussed up, huh?'

'Sure, hoodlums,' Tannenbaum said, and sat on the crate alongside Bobby. 'With guns, sure,' he said. 'Breaking into a man's house so his family can't even sleep in peace.'

'Take it easy, Pop,' Marvin said.

'Don't give me take it easy,' Tannenbaum answered.

'Pop, these men aren't kidding around.'

'So? Am *I* kidding around? If they want to shoot me, then let them shoot already. I know snotnoses like them from when I was interning in one of the worst hospitals in New York. I had them come in *there* with guns, too.' He nodded angrily and then stood up and pointed his finger accusingly at Harry. 'You don't scare *me* with your guns, mister!'

'Sit down, Pop,' Marvin said.

'Sure, sit down,' Tannenbaum said, and did sit down. He glared at Harry angrily, and then looked to where his wife was watching him reproachfully. 'Never mind,' he said to her, and then turned to scowl at Harry again.

'Your father's got quite a little temper there ain't he, Mr. Tannenbaum?' Harry asked.

'Listen to me,' Marvin said slowly. 'My father has a bad heart. That's why he retired and came down here to Florida. I don't want him to get excited. Can you understand that?'

'Why, sure, Mr. Tannenbaum,' Harry said, opening his

eyes wide, 'I can understand that. Just what is it you'd like me to do about it?'

'Just don't provoke him, that's all.'

'I'll try not to,' Harry answered, and then smiled briefly, and quickly said, 'You take that bench and sit over there against the doors with your mother.'

'What does he want?' Rachel Tannenbaum asked.

'Come on, Mom,' Marvin said. 'Over here. Near the doors.'

'There's a draught near the doors,' Rachel said.

'Mom, this is Florida.'

'Sure, we'll all catch pneumonia here besides,' Rachel said, but she went to sit alongside Marvin on the bench in front of the overhead doors.

'Mr. Costigan, if you'll carry another one of those parts crates over near the fantail of the boat, I think you and Miss Watts can sit there. Facing me, please. Good. Now, that leaves only our coloured friend and the younger Mrs. Tannenbaum. Amos, you want to move over to where those outboards are standing? You see those five-gallon oil drums?'

'I see them,' Amos said.

'Good. You want to roll them over here, just about across the room from where Mr. Tannenbaum and his mother are sitting? That'll set us up in sort of a square, huh? Harry said. 'That'll make a real pretty pattern, huh, Clyde?'

'Mighty pretty,' Clyde said, and burst out laughing.

'I'm glad it's so funny,' Tannenbaum said. 'Everything is so funny, you ought to be in vaudeville, both of you.' He looked at his wife across the room and again said, 'Never mind.'

'Pop,' Marvin said, 'try to control yourself, will you?'

'You want to sit down now, Amos?' Harry said, turning towards Amos who had rolled the two oil drums over and was looking down at both of them.

'They're dirty,' he said. 'They got oil on them.'

'Oh! Oh, my!' Harry said. 'Oh, my, we don't want to get you all dirty, do we? Oh my, no!'

'We'd better do what he says,' Selma whispered.

'You'd damn well better, lady,' Harry said.

'Tough guy,' Tannenbaum said, and Harry suddenly shoved himself away from the workbench and crossed the room to where Tannenbaum and Bobby were sitting near the cradled bow of the speedboat.

'I think I've had about enough from you,' he said. 'Just keep your mouth shut.'

'You're not talking to a woman now,' Tannenbaum said, and he raised his hand and shook his finger at Harry.

'Put your hand down,' Harry said.

'You're a hoodlum,' Tannenbaum answered vehemently.

'I'm a hell of a lot more than a hoodlum!' Harry said, and he slapped Tannenbaum's hand aside. He wheeled away and strode across the room, back towards the workbench where Clyde was sitting, the rifle on his lap. He turned again to look at Tannenbaum, and again said, 'A hell of a lot more than a hoodlum.' He nodded in agreement with his own words, pleased with their sound, and then – instead of walking back to the bench – began pacing the rectangular area in front of it. As he paced, he glanced in turn at each of his prisoners: Marvin and Rachel Tannenbaum who sat on a backless bench against the overhead doors on the long side of the paint shop; Luke and Samantha, who sat on an upturned crate in front of the cradled speedboat towering above them; Dr. Tannenbaum trembling in anger, sitting beside Bobby Colmore on another upturned crate near the bow of the speedboat; and Amos Carter and Selma Tannenbaum who sat on the third side of the rectangle on the oil drums Amos had dragged over. Clyde, with his gun in his lap, closed the rectangle on the fourth side.

'Okay, we had a lot of fun up to now,' Harry said, pacing. 'It's been a real laugh riot in here, but that's all finished. I don't want no more of that. I want everybody quiet, you hear me? We'll be getting something for you to eat and drink from the diner in a little while, so don't go telling me you're hungry, and don't go telling me what to do about

80

heart attacks or nothing. I don't want to hear it. You just sit there and shut up, and that's *it!*'

He walked back to the workbench.

'Clyde,' he said, 'shoot the first one moves.'

'Now or later?' Clyde said, grinning, and Luke had the sudden feeling he was making a grim, prophetic joke.

The seventeen men in their three cars left Key West at five-minute intervals starting at 8 A.M. There were only five men in Fatboy's car, including himself, the extra room having been decided upon by Jason as an accommodation to Fatboy's extreme girth. His car was the first to pull out; he called Fortunato just before he left and said, 'We're off, good luck.'

Fortunato waited five minutes and then called Rodiz. 'I'm leaving now,' he said.

'Good,' Rodiz answered. 'Take it easy, yes?'

Five minutes later, at eight-ten, Rodiz and his partner, a tall Bostonian named Eugene Miller, left the Waterview Motel. They were carrying two small overnight bags, each of which contained their toilet articles and a .38 revolver. They put the bags into the trunk of the rented car and then drove through Key West picking up their men, who had been alerted and were waiting outside their hotels and motels with similar overnight bags. They did not drive out of town – past the sign advising motorists that this was the beginning of U.S. 1 at the southernmost point of the United States of America and that the other end was up in Maine someplace – until close to eight-thirty. The men in the car, two on the front seat with Rodiz who was driving, and three more on the back seat, looked like a group of faintly bored businessmen, dressed in tropical suits of various weights and hues, wearing short-sleeved dress shirts and ties. Rodiz was the best-dressed in the lot because he had been born in a tropical climate and wore lightweight clothing with authority. He was sporting a brown Italian silk which might have been a little too heavy had the thermometer registered a bit higher that morning but which, a tribute to his weather sense, was perfect for the day. His shirt was tan, and his tie was a gold-and-brown stripe held to his shirtfront with a simple circular gold pin fashioned from an old Austrian coin. His hair was coal-black, his eyes only a shade less dark, his cheekbones high and massive like those of a San Blas Indian, the taut skin covering them the pale white of a pure Castilian. His fingers were long and thin, and he guided the rented car effortlessly, assiduously observing the speed limit as they came up Truman Avenue onto Roosevelt Boulevard to U.S. 1. The men did not seem overly tense, but they were nonetheless relieved when they moved safely out of the town, which contained too many naval installations for comfort.

It was thirty-five miles from Key West to Ocho Puertos, give or take a few hundred feet, and Jason's instructions had been to drive slowly and safely. Slow and easy, that was the way it had been outlined. Slow and easy, that was the way Rodiz was handling it.

They got the flat as they were crossing the bridge connecting Sugarloaf with Cudjoe. They had been driving no faster than forty miles an hour, and so there was no question of losing control of the car. Rodiz cursed softly, and Eugene – sitting in the middle on the front seat – said, 'What is it? A flat?'

'Mmm,' Rodiz said. He slowed the car. 'Should I drive off the bridge or what?'

'I think you'd better,' Eugene said. 'It's pretty narrow here to be changing a flat.'

Rodiz nodded and said nothing. He glanced at his watch. This was going to spoil their time. He started the car and drove slowly off the bridge. The car was rented, but Rodiz held a high respect for property, and it would have pained him to ruin the punctured tyre by driving too fast. He pulled to the side of the road some hundred feet onto Cudjoe and then went to the trunk and unlocked it.

'I'm gonna get my clothes all dirty,' he said to no one, raising the trunk lid. 'How we gonna reach that spare?' he asked Eugene when he came back.

'Have to take the bags out,' Eugene said.

They took out the men's overnight bags, and put them in

the road behind the car. They lifted the spare out then, and pulled out the jack. Rodiz looked at the flat tyre distastefully and then put the jack in place under the bumper. Eugene began loosening the lug nuts while Rodiz jacked up the car. The other four men stood at the side of the road watching the work, wanting to help but knowing this was a two-man job at the most, and knowing there wasn't much they could do but wait until Rodiz and Eugene were finished.

The car was up on the jack, and the flat tyre was off, when they heard the sound of another car coming down the road from the opposite direction.

'Rafe,' one of the men at the side of the road whispered, and Rodiz looked up and nodded, and then went back to wheeling the spare tyre into place.

The approaching car belonged to the Florida Highway Patrol.

There were two troopers in it.

It seemed at first that the car would continue right on past and onto the bridge leading west to Sugarloaf. But instead, it stopped on the other side of the road, about a hundred yards past Rodiz where he was hoisting the spare onto the wheel rim. The door on the highway side opened and a tall muscular man wearing a light tan uniform, with a holstered pistol at his side, a mean suntanned look on his face, began walking towards the car. Eugene and Rodiz had wrestled the wheel into place by then and were screwing on the lug nuts. The other four men stood at the rear of the car and slightly away from it, watching the approaching trooper.

'Hi,' the trooper said.

Rodiz looked up, seemingly surprised, and said, 'Hello.'

'Need some help?'

'No, thanks a lot,' Eugene said. 'We must've picked up a nail back there. We drove off the bridge so we wouldn't block traffic.'

'Mmm,' the trooper said.

The two men continued working on the wheel. All the lug nuts were in place now. Eugene picked up the wrench and began tightening them. Rodiz went back to the jack, ready to lower the car. The trooper went with him, glancing at the canvas overnight bags in the road behind the car, and then nodding and smiling at the four men who stood silent just behind the right wheel, watching.

'You fellows coming up from Key West?' the trooper asked.

'That's right,' Eugene said.

'Mmm,' the trooper said.

'You can lower it, Rafe,' Eugene said, and Rodiz released the jack. Up the road, the second trooper had come out of the patrol car and was approaching the sedan.

'What was it?' the trooper asked. 'Convention or something?'

'What was what?' Eugene asked.

'I mean, all six of you travelling together,' the trooper said, and smiled.

'I don't get it,' Eugene said, deadpan.

'The six of you travelling together,' the trooper repeated, as if that made it much clearer.

'Well, what's wrong with the six of us travelling together?' Eugene asked.

'He didn't say nothing was wrong with it,' the second trooper said, padding up swiftly and silently to stand just alongside his partner, his thumbs looped in his belt.

'We work for the same company,' Eugene said. 'We were down in Key West on business.'

'What kind of business?' the second trooper asked.

'Boats.'

'What kind of boats?'

'Inboards, outboards, you name them.'

'What's the name of the company?' the first trooper said.

'Framingham Boats,' Eugene said.

'Where at?'

'What do you mean?'

'Where's your home office?'

'Framingham, Massachusetts.'

'You happen to have a business card with you?' the second trooper said, and the highway went silent.

84

Eugene smiled pleasantly and said, 'I don't understand, officer. What's wrong?'

'Nothing. We were just wondering how come six respectable businessmen are travelling together with only this luggage, that's all.'

Again the highway was silent. Off in the mangroves Rodiz could hear a bird calling stridently.

'There are six bags,' Rodiz said.

'Six *overnight* bags,' the trooper said.

'So?'

'So nothing. Six overnight bags, all the way from Framingham, Massachusetts.'

'We're travelling light,' Rodiz said.

'What's your name, mister?'

'Rafael Rodiz.'

'You Spanish?'

'Panamanian.'

'You're from Panama?'

'That's right.'

'Where in Panama?'

'Colón.'

'Mind if I see your passport?'

'I'm an American citizen,' Rodiz said. 'I've been in this country seven years.'

'In Framingham?' the trooper asked.

'That's right.'

'Got any proof of citizenship? Naturalization certificate? Draft card?'

'No, but –'

'All right, mister, you want to open those bags,' the first trooper said, and he drew his pistol. 'You fellows get over here on the side of the car, let's go,' he said, waving the pistol. The second trooper, following his lead, came over to Rodiz with his pistol in his hand and pointed to the bags with it. 'Go on, open them,' he said.

Rodiz nodded and kneeled behind the closest bag.

'I don't understand this, officer,' Eugene said. 'Why are you –'

'Let's just hold the violins a minute, huh?' the first

trooper said. 'Maybe you don't see anything fishy about six guys driving along a highway at nine o'clock in the morning, but we do, okay? So if everything's all right, you'll be on your way in just a few minutes, provided your friend here can come up with some kind of satisfactory identification. You don't expect us to –'

The first shot took the trooper between the eyes, and the second one was placed just a trifle lower to the left so that it passed through his left cheekbone and blew away half of his skull as it exited. The other trooper stood stock-still as his partner collapsed to the highway dripping blood, and then, his reaction time just a few seconds too late, he raised his pistol and was about to pull off a shot at Rodiz when the next three bullets came in rapid succession, each thudding into his chest and sending him reeling back against the trunk of the car. He said something unintelligible – it could have been 'Martha', it could have been 'Mother' – and then rolled onto the highway and lay still and bleeding beside his partner. Rodiz looked at them both silently. In the mangroves there was the flutter of wings, and then stillness. The men on the highway stood motionless. Rodiz said, 'Get the patrol car, one of you.'

'What do we do?' Eugene asked.

'You, Vinny!' Rodiz snapped. 'Get the car, hurry! The rest of you, pull them off the road, behind the car there. Go ahead.'

He threw the .38 into the bag again, zipped it shut, and hoisted it into the trunk.

'The flat,' Eugene said.

'In the back.'

'The other bags.'

'Hurry.'

'Here comes Vinny.'

'Get them.'

'What'll we do with them?'

'The back. The trunk of their car.'

'Vinny, open the trunk.'

'Which key?'

'Find it.'

'This?'

'I need a hat from one of them.'

'There, it's open.'

'This doesn't fit. Give me the other one.'

'There's blood on it.'

'Hurry.'

'You want them both in the trunk?'

'Yes, hurry. Is this better?'

'It's all right. You going to drive them?'

'Yes.'

'Where?'

'Into the water?'

'The ocean?'

'No, a swamp. We'll find a swamp someplace.'

'Where?'

'I don't know. This is the Florida Keys. There's got to be a goddamn swamp or a marsh someplace, doesn't there?'

'Rafe, they're in.'

'Close the trunk.'

'There's blood on the fender.'

'Wipe it off.'

'What about the road?'

'They'll think an animal got hit. How does this hat look?'

'Fine.'

'I'm gonna sit behind the wheel. Can you tell I'm not a trooper?'

'Rafe, let's get moving.'

'In a minute, Vinny. What do you say, Eugene?'

'You look okay. Shall we follow you, or what?'

'You'll have to.'

'Suppose we don't find a marsh?'

'I'll drive them right into the goddamn Atlantic.'

'Rafe?'

'What?'

'You killed them,' Eugene said. 'You killed them both.'

'I know I did. So?'

'Nothing,' Eugene said, and shrugged. 'Nothing.'

Rodiz got behind the wheel of the police car with his heart pounding and the stupid blood-stained state police hat hanging down over his ears, aware that there were two dead troopers in the trunk behind him and wondering whether or not their blood was seeping through the trunk and onto the highway. He drove at forty miles an hour, and the low speed seemed intolerable; he was sure that everyone in the world knew there were two dead men in the trunk. What the hell had that last marker said? What key was this, Summerland? Was this Summerland already? God, they were getting too close to Ocho Puertos! He began searching for a cutoff and found it at the eastern end of the island, a road marked S-492. Abruptly he made a screeching right turn and headed for the ocean. He recognized at once that he was driving into a community of houses built on long stretches of packed coral and that he could no more dump the police car here than he could in the middle of Key West's Duval Street. He made a dusty U-turn, passing Eugene and the others in the car behind him, and then glancing into the rearview mirror to see if they had executed the same turn and were still with him. He was beginning to sweat profusely in the Italian silk suit now. He wondered whether he could conceivably pull the car off into the mangroves someplace and hope that it would be hidden from the road. He doubted it. And then suddenly he was on Ramrod Key with the road heading straight for Big Pine and still no place to dump the car, and then he was on Big Pine itself. He wet his lips and became really frightened then because he seemed to remember from the map that Big Pine was just that, a *big* island with plenty of people and houses and stores, and here he was sitting in a police car with a silly hat on his head and two dead men in the trunk. But wasn't there a long spit of land here, jutting out into the Atlantic, pointing west? Hadn't he seen that on one of the charts Randy and Jason had gone over repeatedly in the Miami warehouse? Wasn't there a beach on that chart? He followed U.S. 1 until it curved right at Bogie Channel to parallel Spanish Harbour, and then continued on down, ignoring the bridge that led to the Spanish Harbour Keys. He drove south and then turned west onto Long Beach. He'd been right; there *was* a beach. Desperately he began searching for a spot to sink the car. He passed the single house on the beach and then there was only sand and mud and grass. He wished he had one of those charts *now*, wished he knew how deep the inshore waters were, and then suddenly realized he would have to do something soon, sink or swim, before he reached the end of the beach. He slowed the car, searching for an incline, dropping speed to the point where he almost stalled, and then throwing the car into second and hearing the police radio on the dashboard erupting with a call – was it for this car? He spotted a small shelf of land sloping into what looked like deep grass and mud, and wrenched the wheel sharply until the car was poised on the edge of the drop, ready to plummet below. The radio in the car was still calling when he carefully opened the door and stepped into the road. Eugene had parked the rented sedan some twenty feet behind him. Rodiz looked down the slope again and then threw the borrowed hat onto the front seat and placed his arm stiffly against the door plate and shoved. The car began rolling at once. He watched it silently as it gathered speed going down the slope and then began sinking into the mud.

It sank quickly to the hub caps, sucked up mud noisily into the wings of its fenders and then hesitated a moment as if undecided whether to submerge completely or not. Grass slapped the fenders, and then the car gave a sudden lurch sidewards, like a prehistoric beast rolling over, and seemed ready by sheer weight and bulk to overwhelm the resisting mud and tangled grass.

It did not sink farther.

It sat where it was in the shallow mud, twisted partially on to its side, the left fender lower than the right and covered with mud, the right fender and indeed the entire upper portion of the car jutting out of the slime, the domed red light on the roof clearly announcing that this was a police car.

Son of a bitch, Rodiz thought, and then began running up the road to where Eugene and the others were waiting for him in the rented car.

6

The United States Coast Guard cutter *Mercury* was a 165-foot vessel with five officers and fifty enlisted men in her crew. Her single armament was a three-inch, 50-calibre gun on her bow, but she was also equipped with mortar flares, and her gun locker on the after bulkhead of officer's country carried ten carbines, ten M1s, and eight Colt .45 automatics. She was a small ship and not a particularly fast one, her top speed being thirteen knots. Sometimes when she steamed along with her canvas awning flapping over the fantail, she resembled an old-fashioned gunboat on a Chinese river during the Boxer rebellion.

From the bridge deck of the *Mercury*, in Key West, Lieutenant Commander Nathaniel Cates could see the *Androscoggin*, WOG-68, where she lay alongside her dock. For a moment he wished the larger cutter were going out on patrol these next six days instead of his own vessel. His longing had nothing whatever to do with the hurricane warnings that were still pouring from Miami's Weather Bureau into the Coast Guard's Rescue Co-ordination Centre on Southwest First, and thence into the radio room of every Coast Guard vessel in the area, all travelling with the speed of light and the frequency of gossip. The advisories bothered Cates not at all, because he had seen hurricanes galore and this did not look to him like any hurricane. They could yell all they wanted to, but the fact remained that the *real* storm was not moving a hair from its position over the centre of Cuba, and the winds and rain up there in Miami this morning were probably nothing more than a good solid nor'easter.

The reason Cates wished it were the *Andy*'s turn to go out and not his own ship's was that he had a toothache and there was no dentist aboard the *Merc*. His own dentist was a man named Feldman who had come down to Miami on vacation in 1949 and had stayed on to open an office on Collins Avenue at the Beach. Cates enjoyed listening to Feldman talk about New York. Not that Cates was a New Yorker. His home town, in fact – before he had joined the Coast Guard in 1936 – was a place called Tantamount, Iowa.

He had joined the Coast Guard because the United States of America in that August of 1936 had just barely stopped selling apples in the street, and the salary of an apprentice seaman was twenty-one dollars a month, plus three squares a day and a bed to sleep in every night. He wouldn't have cared where they sent him, so long as it was away from Tantamount, Iowa; actually, the choice was between the boot camp at Cape May, New Jersey, or the one in Alameda, California. The Coast Guard, reversing the old military principle that it was best to send a man as far from his home as possible, decided on Cape May. He trained there for ten weeks, and then was sent as a seaman second class to a 327-footer operating out of Boston, Massachusetts.

He loved Boston. He loved the city itself, and the surrounding countryside, this was autumn and wild colours claimed the landscape, there was a sudden cruel bite to the air – and he loved the flat nasal speech of the people, and the feeling that at last he was in America, that at last he had shaken the dust of Crackerbarrel Falls, Iowa, and come to grips with what America was really about.

He had yet to discover New York City.

He made his first liberty into the largest city in the world when he was seventeen years old, falling immediately in love with a girl who worked at a club on 63rd Street, falling in love at first with her long dancer's legs in black net stockings, and then falling overwhelmingly in love with the rest of her the night they tumbled eagerly into bed in her apartment on West 48th Street.

Her name was Celeste Ryan, and she was twenty years old. She told Cates that she had been born in the Bronx, but that she had been living alone in Manhatten for the past two years. She also told him she was still a virgin, and he believed her. Actually it didn't matter whether she was or not, because Cates very definitely was, and that was virgin enough for both of them.

She loved him.

He was seventeen years old when he met her, and from November of 1936 to June of 1938 he was possibly loved more than he would ever be loved again in his life. He would jump onto that train whenever he had liberty, and then count the minutes into New York, ticking off the station stops – Providence, New London, New Haven, Stamford – and there she was, waiting at Grand Central Station with those magnificent legs signalling wildly to him. She would rush into his arms and shower his face with kisses, and then pull back from him and look into his eyes with her own green eyes wide and questioning to ask each time, 'Do you still love me, Nat?' And each time he would say the same thing, 'I love you, Celeste,' and then they would go to her apartment and drink some gin and get into the king-sized bed she owned. He spent almost two years aboard the cutter, learning what it was like to live afloat, being promoted to seaman first class and deciding to become a quartermaster striker, and then studying to take his petty officer test in June of 1938. But in all that time, working as hard as he did, he still managed to spend a good many hours each week in bed with a girl who taught him things they didn't sing about at prayer meetings in Backwater Gulch, Iowa.

Cates had witnessed the death of prohibition, he had seen the NRA eagles in every shopwindow in Iowa, and then Massachusetts, and then New York, and now he felt the country shaking itself alive again, throwing off the desperate grey coils of its long illness, felt its renewed strength coursing into his own expanding muscle. In June of 1938, two weeks before he was to take the test for quartermaster third, Celeste Ryan discovered she was pregnant and asked him what she should do. Cates told her he would marry her on the spot as soon as she gave the word and as soon as he could obtain permission from his commanding officer. Celeste said that she appreciated the gesture, which she thought was very sweet of him and all that, but she really enjoyed being a dancer and she would –

A showgirl, you mean, he said.

Yes, a showgirl, if that was how he wanted to put it; she really enjoyed dancing though, and it didn't seem she'd be able to do much dancing in the future if she had a baby and was married to a sailor who might be assigned God knew where.

Cates admitted she had a point. To tell the truth, he was a little relieved. He was barely nineteen and just starting his Coast Guard career. He didn't particularly feel like embarking upon a marital career at the same time, not to mention a paternal one. So he told Celeste the best thing they could do would be to seek an abortion, and she told him she had already checked with a couple of the girls in the line and one of them said she knew a very good woman who did a lot of theatrical work and who could take care of this for three hundred dollars. By this time Celeste was three months pregnant, which made it all seem very fair, a hundred dollars for each month. The only trouble was that Cates and Celeste had been living somewhat extravagantly on his fifty-four dollars a month seaman-first-class salary and her forty dollars a week earned as a dancer-cum-drink hustler. They barely had thirty dollars between them, let alone three hundred. Cates got off a wire to his folks back in Overall Patches, Iowa, saying SEND ME THREE HUNDRED DOLLARS AT ONCE I AM IN DIFFICULTY WILL EXPLAIN LATER. The return wire said THREE HUNDRED DOLLARS ARE YOU KIDDING EXPLAIN NOW. Cates did not explain then – or *ever*, for that matter. Instead, he went to Celeste and assured her he would rustle up the three hundred dollars somehow, somewhere, just give him a little time, after all he was just about to take the quartermaster test, and he was studying and –

Celeste looked into her lover's eyes and wisely saw neither solvency, solution, nor salvation in them. 'Okay,' she said, 'do your best, Nat,' and then she went to the owner of the club where she worked and asked him for a

94

three-hundred-dollar advance on her salary, which he gave her at ten per cent interest. The next week-end she got rid of the baby. She called Cates in Boston to tell him it had all been taken care of, and he said something like 'Oh gee, that's great, baby. I passed the test, I'm a quartermaster third. Wait'll you see my rating patch.'

Celeste never got around to seeing Cates's rating patch, nor did Cates ever get an opportunity to show it to her, because the next time he went to her apartment her landlady told him she had moved. When he went over to the club, he discovered she was not in the line any more. One of the girls said she had gone to San Francisco with a drummer from the Cotton Club band, who had paid off her debt to the owner. All Cates could think of to ask was 'A *coloured* drummer?'

In July of 1938 he was taken off the cutter with his quartermaster rating and sent to the buoy depot in Portsmouth, Virginia. The thing that troubled him all during his two years there, the thing that continued to trouble him after he was transferred onto a buoy tender and promoted to quartermaster second, the thing that bothered him constantly all during the war when he served aboard a Navy AKA, making chief quartermaster in 1945, and finally marrying a girl from Norfolk, Virginia, where he was stationed on weather patrol, the thing that annoyed him constantly was the certain knowledge that he had done something wrong back there – but he didn't know just what the hell it was.

She had *said* she didn't want to get married, hadn't she?

He had offered, he had told her he would marry her as soon as he got permission, but she had said she wanted to be a dancer. He could remember those were her exact words, because he had corrected her like a goddamn jackass; he had said, 'You mean a showgirl, don't you?' and she had said, 'Well, yes, if that's what you want to call it.' Was *that* the mistake he'd made? He'd tried to get the money, he'd honestly tried. He'd wired his folks – fat chance of getting anything there in Hayseed, Iowa – and then he'd begun borrowing from every friend of his on the ship and had managed to raise a hundred and thirty-two dollars, but by that time Celeste had called to say it was all taken care of.

'What do you mean?' he'd said on the phone.

'The baby. You know.'

'Well, when –'

'Last week. It's all taken care of.'

'Well, that's great, honey,' he'd said. 'Hey, I'll be coming in week after next. Wait'll you see my patch.'

Late in 1947, Nathaniel Cates entered OCS and emerged from it four months later as an ensign in the United States Coast Guard. Now, at forty-four, he was a lieutenant-commander, his hair still brown, his figure somewhat paunchier than it had been back in 1938, his face showing the puffiness of a man who had been drinking gin since 1936 when he was only seventeen. His wife, Helen, was forty-two, a slight blonde woman with fine bones and beautiful brown eyes. (Celeste's hair was black, her eyes were green, there was an Irish sauciness in the switch of her backside, there was a wild promise in her legs, she was the only real woman he had ever known in his life.) His son was sixteen years old and hoped one day to enter the Coast Guard Academy in New London, Connecticut. His daughter was fourteen; she had won a French medal during her sophormore year in high school. (*Tell me about Tantamount, Celeste said, There's nothing to tell. There's a petrol station and a store and railroad tracks running through, that's all. Oh, you poor dear baby coming from such a dead town. Kiss me, you hear? Kiss me, baby, I'll take you out of that horrid little town. Kiss me, baby, I'll take you where you've never never been before.*) He had served aboard a 125-footer until June of 1949 when he'd made j.g. Then the Korean War broke out, and he had worked picking up Navy DEs in Green Cove Springs, Florida, ferrying them to the Coast Guard Yard at Curtis Bay, Maryland, near Baltimore, and then across the Pacific to Hawaii where he was stationed until 1953. (*When I'm dancing, I feel like I could fly, do you know what I mean, Nat? I feel as if I can kick my legs higher than anybody in the world, that I can kick them right up to the ceiling, the sky! Look at me, baby, I'm flying!*) In 1955,

Nathaniel Cates made full lieutenant and was assigned to a buoy tender as executive officer of the base on MacArthur Causeway. He did not earn his lieutenant-commander's stripes until April of 1960, and shortly after that he was given command of the *Mercury*.

He still did not know what the hell he had done wrong back in 1938.

'Excuse me, sir.'

Cates turned. For a moment he looked at the man standing before him without recognizing him, and then realized it was one of his electronics technicians. Quickly he said, 'Yes?'

'Captain, shore tie's broken for water and electricity, and the telephones are all aboard,' the technician said.

'Very well,' Cates said. He turned to his talker, who was wearing sound-powered phones and gazing blankly off to starboard. 'Take in three and four,' he said.

'Fantail, bridge,' the talker said. 'Take in three and four.'

Cates waited. In a moment the talker said, 'Number three aboard, sir.'

'Very well.'

'Number four aboard, sir.'

'Very well, take in number one.'

'Forecastle, bridge,' the talker said, 'take in number one.'

Cates glanced at the clock on the after bulkhead. It read 0904.

'Number one aboard sir,' the talker said.

'Very well,' Cates answered. 'Left standard rudder.'

'Left standard rudder,' the helmsman replied.

'Starboard engine ahead one-third.'

'Starboard engine ahead one-third, sir,' the engine order telegraph operator said, and in a moment added, 'Engine room answers starboard engine ahead one-third, sir.'

'Very well,' Cates said.

The 165-footer cutter was a ship that responded quickly. He heard the *chug-chug* of the engines almost immediately and then felt the familiar surge of the ship as she moved forward against the single spring line holding her to the dock. 'Port engine back one-third,' he said immediately.

'Port engine back one-third, sir. Engine room answers port engine back one-third, sir.'

'Check two,' Cates said.

'Check two,' the talker said into his mouthpiece. 'Forecastle checking two, sir.'

'Rudder amidships. Starboard engine stop. Take in number two. Shift colours.'

Behind Cates the quartermaster of the watch blew a mouth whistle, signalling a shift of the ensign to the after stick. The cutter began backing out of the dock. 'Sound three short blasts,' Cates said. He heard them sounding behind him. 'All engines stop.'

'All engines stop, sir. Engine room answers all engines stop, sir.'

'Right full rudder. Port engine ahead one-third.'

'Right full rudder, sir. Rudder is right full, sir.'

They were moving out and away from the dock now, past the Naval Station light, the buoys dead ahead marking the Key West main ship channel.

'Rudder amidships,' Cates said to the helmsman. 'Steady on course two-zero-four, sir. All engines ahead one-third, sir.'

'Steady as you go.'

'Small boat bearing three-five-zero, range five thousand,' the lookout called down.

'Very well,' Cates answered. 'Come right to two-zero-nine.'

'Right to two-zero-nine, sir.'

Cates turned to Michael Pierce, the full lieutenant who was his executive officer, and who was standing just a few feet to his left, staring through the wheelhouse windshield at the three-inch 50-calibre cannon on the bow, and past that to the channel beyond. 'Someday we'll cut one of those damn boats right in half,' Cates said, and then turned his head over his shoulder and said to the quartermaster, 'Sound one blast.' The whistle sounded in warning, high and sharp and strident on the clear Key West air, telling the small boat that the cutter was coming right. The boat went past on the cutter's port bow, and the pilot waved up at the bridge. Cates did not return the wave.

'Left to one-eight-three,' he said.

'Left to one-eight-three, sir.'

As the ship began its swing, Cates said, 'Move those men off the forecastle and onto the lee side,' and then to Pierce, 'No sense getting them soaked out there, Mike.'

The cutter moved slowly down the main channel, changing course and speed as she went, the helmsman watching his compass, Cates peering ahead through the windsheild, Pierce silent at his side, the other men in the wheelhouse waiting for sight of the sea buoy. At the buoy Cates said, 'Come left to zero-eight-five.'

'Coming left to zero-eight-five, sir.'

'Meet her.'

'Steering zero-eight-five, sir.'

'Steady as you go.'

'Steady as you go, sir. Course zero-eight-five.'

'Secure the special sea detail,' Cates said. 'Set the sea watch.'

Into the p.a. system the quartermaster said, 'Secure the special sea detail. Set the sea watch.' He turned to Cates. 'That's watch section three, sir.'

'Very well. All engines ahead two-thirds,' Cates said.

'All engines ahead two-thirds, sir. Engine room answers all engines ahead two-thirds, sir.'

'Very well. As soon as we're relieved up here, Mike, let's go down to the wardroom for some coffee.'

'I can use some, sir,' Pierce said. 'This weather gets in your bones.'

'Quartermaster, ask the engine room when they'll be able to give us standard speed,' Cates said.

Sitting in the pilot's seat on the port side of the Grumman Albatross, Frank Randazzo looked off to starboard past his co-pilot, Murray Diel, and down to where the keys were clearly visible. He had checked the weather map and the weather reports at the Miami Air Station before take-off, and so he was not surprised by the visibility here, and yet there always seemed to be something mysterious and magical about the way weather could change in the space of a few miles. He pressed the ICS button under his left thumb on the yoke. He was wearing soft earphones with a boom mike an inch from his lips. Through the static coming from the HF and VHF circuits he said, 'We'd better check in with Bluerock, before *he* calls us.'

'Right,' Diel said.

'Bluerock, this is Coast Guard seven-two, seven-two,' Randazzo said into his mouthpiece.

There was a pause and then the radar station answered, 'Coast Guard seven-two, seven-two, Bluerock. Go ahead with your position.'

'Bluerock, seven-two,' Randazzo said. 'Long Key at three-seven, one thousand feet. Heading, two-two-six. Speed, one-fifty. Estimating ADIZ at five-seven in position twenty-four forty-five north, eight-oh-four-oh west. Over.'

'Bluerock, roger.'

Randazzo pressed the ICS button and said to Diel, 'That ought to hold them for a while.'

'Fuel transfer's coming off about now, Frank,' Diel said. 'We're reading seventeen fifty in each.'

'Right,' Randazzo said, and watched his gauges as the petrol was automatically transferred from the 300-gallon drop tanks into the mains. Penner, one of the two mechanics, came into the cockpit with two paper cartons of coffee, handing one to Randazzo and the other to Diel.

'I take three sugars,' Diel said, tasting it. 'You always forget.'

''Cause I can't understand how anybody can drink it so sweet, sir,' Penner said, and went aft again with the carton of coffee. Like every other man aboard the plane, he was wearing a flight suit over his work uniform, and a life vest over that. The flight suit was orange, and the life vest was a bright yellow; the colours were supposed to enable searchers to spot the crew more easily in the water if ever they had to ditch. In addition, and also in the interests of survival, the life vest was equipped with a battery-operated

100

light that could be switched on at night, a shark repellent, a survival knife, a dye marker to spread on the water, and a day and night signal marker. Murray Diel, who had a reputation for thin-bloodedness in a warm climate, was wearing a non-regulation, blue poplin flight jacket over his orange flight suit and under his yellow life vest, and therefore was the most colourful man aboard. The jacket was adorned with two patches. He had brought one of them with him from Floyd Bennett Field where he had been stationed before his transfer to Dinner Key. The Brooklyn Air patch showed a red, white and blue American shield against which soared a brown eagle clutching a yellow rubber life raft in its claws. The Miami Air patch, which Diel wore on the opposite side of his jacket front, showed the Florida coastline in the background in green and, against that, the yellow numeral 7 with an ever-watchful eye painted up near its top, Miami being in the Seventh Coast Guard District, and Miami Air calling itself 'The Eyes of the Seventh'.

'Coffee, sir,' Penner said. 'Three sugars, sir,' and he grimaced.

The soft rubber earphones against Randazzo's head erupted with sound.

'Coast Guard seven-two, seven-two, this is Miami Air, over.'

'Miami Air, seven-two, seven-two.'

'You see anything of that cruiser out of Bimini?'

'Nothing yet,' Randazzo said.

'She's a fifty-footer, twin Cadillacs, overdue three days.'

'Got that before I took off,' Randazzo said dryly.

'Thought you might have spotted her. I'm reading you kind of scratchy. Want to give me a short count?'

'Short count,' Knowles, the radioman, answered 'One, two, three, four, five.'

'Still reading you scratchy,' Miami Air said. 'Let's try eight-nine.'

'Shifting to eight-nine,' Knowles said. 'Is that correct?'

'Affirmative,' Miami Air said.

By the time Knowles and the air station had decided on a

frequency, it was time to call Bluerock again. Randazzo made contact and told them he was checking ADIZ.

'Go ahead, seven-two,' Bluerock said.

'Inbound heading two-three-three,' Randazzo said. 'One thousand feet, speed, one-fifty. Squawking mode three, zero-six.'

'Roger, out,' Bluerock said.

It was going to be a quiet morning. The ocean below, despite the hurricane advisories, seemed calm and unruffled, glinting with touches of golden sunshine. There were very few small boats out on the water; those damn advisories had probably scared hell out of everybody. Off to port, and far out on the horizon, Randazzo could see what looked like a Russian trawler, but no, the lines were different. Still for a moment it had looked like one. Dead ahead, a tanker plodded down towards Key West, its white masts gleaming in the sunlight. It was going to be a quiet morning.

At 0930, Randazzo contacted the radar plane on VHF.

'Checkmate,' he said, 'this is Coast Guard seven-two, seven-two with a position.'

'Go, seven-two,' Checkmate answered.

'Saddlebunch at three-oh. One thousand feet. Estimating Key West at three-four. Relay to Bluerock.'

'Seven-two, Checkmate. Roger your position.'

At 0934, Randazzo swung over Key West, and switched course to Key pat four-alpha, a flight path that would take him farther south of the reef line, and then north-east.

It was going to be a quiet morning.

From the moment he had come aboard at five-thirty that morning, Alex Witten had been making snide remarks. He had hailed Randy from the dock, climbed aboard *The Golden Fleece*, walked into the wheelhouse where Annabelle was standing in a flannel robe preparing coffee at the two-burner Primus stove, and had immediately said, 'Gee, you two are barely out of bed,' and then grinned pointedly at Randy to make his meaning absolutely clear. Randy chose to ignore the innuendo. Annabelle seemed not to catch the tone of Alex's voice. She turned the flame a little higher and then said, 'Excuse me, I want to get dressed,' and went below, closing the slatted swinging doors behind her.

'Did Jason get off all right?' Alex said.

'Yes.'

'What have you heard on the hurricane?'

'Nothing yet this morning. We'll be under way long before the next advisory is due.'

'Hmmm,' Alex said, 'well,' and shrugged.

Annabelle came up the ladder wearing the black raincoat. The rain had abated considerably, but there was still a wet sprinkle in the air driven by the wind, more a sharp cold penetrating mist than a real rainfall. Her long brown hair was tucked up under the rubber folds of a yellow rainhat, and the spray in the wet air put an immediate glossy sheen on her cheeks. She was five feet nine inches tall, a big woman, and she carried her unborn baby with all the monumental grace of an Egyptian pyramid. There was about her face with its high cheekbones and narrow slitted eyes, its generous mouth and strong jaw, the suggestion of a hill peasant in Wales or Ireland. This hint of peasant stock was echoed in her body as well, big-boned, full-breasted, wide-hipped, and magnified by her current state of pregnancy. She seemed capable of planting crops and harvesting them, of grinding grain and milking cows and chopping wood. It was perhaps this very impression of something primitive, the country girl in bursting pregnant bloom, that provoked the steady barrage of remarks from Alex.

As she came up the ladder, he said, 'Ahh, the lovely bride,' and again glanced at Randy.

'I was just going to pour the coffee,' Randy said. 'How do you take it, Annabelle?'

For an instant the slitted eyes in the angular face flared with an intelligence that denied any primitive heritage, that threw aside any false illusions her face and body had permitted. 'Black,' she said, and paused for the briefest instant while her eyes flicked Alex's face like a whiplash.

She smiled wickedly. 'Like my heart,' she added.

Her voice had dropped a decibel, had become almost a knife-like whisper that slid past the evil smile and across the cockpit to lodge in Alex's heart. Alex ignored the thrust. He was having too much fun pulling Randy's leg, and he did not intend to stop now, Jason's wife or no. He had to admit that her eyes and the sound of her voice back there just a second ago had carried something reminiscent of Jason Trench himself, oh, going away back to when he'd been skipper of the 832, and Alex had been his exec. Even then, though Jason had been only twenty-two, there had been an icy resonance to his voice whenever he snapped a command, and Alex had heard that same distant chill in Annabelle's voice just now. 'Like my heart.' You choose your mate, he thought, and then said aloud, 'This is like a little honeymoon cottage, ain't it?' and enjoyed the look of pain on Randy's face, and the angry intelligence that flashed again in Annabelle's eyes, and suddenly wondered if they had.

The Golden Fleece got under way at dawn.

Even coming down the Intercoastal Waterway, shielded as it was from the Gulf Stream by the Florida Keys landmass through which it cut south and then west, Alex felt again the thrill of piloting a vessel on water. It was a miserable grey wet dawn, and he piloted the boat from inside the wheelhouse and wished there were a flying bridge so he could feel the spray on his face and smell all the mysteries of the ocean deeps, smell fish and coral and sunken treasure and dead men floating, smell all that secret teeming life. He piloted a lousy twenty-seven-foot boat down a protected coastal waterway, and felt the same thrill he had known whenever Lieutenant (j.g.) Jason Trench gave him the conn of PT 832, in the middle of the Pacific Ocean. There was a big difference between this twenty-seven-foot pleasure craft and an eighty-foot United States Navy motor torpedo boat, and the difference wasn't so much in the handling as in the knowledge that the two torpedo racks on either side of the Navy boat were capable of wreaking immediate destruction on anything that happened to float into their way. The biggest thing that had ever floated into the way of the 832 was a Japanese minesweeper. Goody Moore had been gunner's mate second class aboard the boat, and had been standing bow lookout watch when he spotted the Jap vessel far out on the horizon and called it up to Alex, who had the conn. Clay Prentiss, who was the boat's radioman second, had come up onto the bow and taken the glasses from Goody, verifying the ship as a Jap, and then they had gone below to wake Jason.

There would normally have been no question about attacking. The PT boat carried four torpedoes and was equipped with a pair of twin .50-calibre machine guns, and a 20-millimetre cannon. Her most effective weapons, of course, were her speed and her manoeuvrability, and normally Jason would have plotted an attack course with Alex and with Fatboy, who was the boat's chief torpedoman. They'd have made their run then, and dropped their fish, and got the hell out of there before anybody aboard the Jap ship knew what hit them. That was normally. But the boat had been heading back under orders for drydock in Pearl when Goody spotted the minesweep, and the reason she was going into drydock was that a blade was damaged on her screw, which severely limited both her speed *and* her manoeuvrability. The question was should they continue on their course which was away from the minesweep's and heading towards Pearl, or should they alter course and attack?

Jason decided to take the chance.

They had come in on the minesweeper's fantail, on the hunch that the jerrybuilt superstructure there had created a blind spot, and then swung out past the ship and come in abeam for their one and only run, firing two fish almost simultaneously, connecting with both and apparently hitting a storage locker of live mines somewhere below. The Jap ship came out of the water in two pieces, splitting in the centre and rising like the steeple of a church, and then cracking and falling back into the ocean while the 832 raced away.

They had taken the chance and won.

That was in 1942, and that was a long time ago.

Almost twenty years later, in January of 1962, they met again in a Second Avenue Apartment. There was snow in the streets of New York, and the windows were rimmed with frost, and Goody Moore came into the room blowing on his huge brown farmer's hands and joking about how it never got this bad down in Georgia, even when the snow froze out all the crops. He had not changed a bit; he was still tall and lean, with ridges radiating out from his grey eyes, his hair almost as blond as when the South Pacific sun had bleached it day after day. They shook hands all around, Jason and Fatboy and Goody and Clay and Alex himself. Then Jason introduced them to Randy Gambol, whom he said he had worked with in a group called America in Distress, and then he'd broken out the whisky and they sat around reminiscing about the days aboard the 832 while Annabelle went into the bedroom to watch television.

He didn't get around to telling them about his plan until almost eleven o'clock, and they were still arguing it and discussing it when dawn broke against the frost-rimmed windows at six o'clock the next morning. Annabelle had fallen alseep in the next room with the television set on, and Jason went in to turn it off, and then he came back and put a pot of coffee on the stove and went to where the men were seated and said, 'What do you think?'

'It would have to be Florida some place,' Clay said.

'Well, Arthur has suggested the Keys, as you know,' Jason said.

'It's pretty isolated down there, isn't it?' Goody asked.

'Well, that's the point,' Fatboy said.

'I don't think that's the difficult part,' Alex said. 'Taking the town, I mean.'

'No, that would be simple.'

'It's the rest that seems risky.'

'The rest seems just as simple to me,' Randy said.

'Well, you and Fatboy are already convinced of all this,' Alex ventured, 'so naturally you'd think *all* of it was pretty simple.'

'I feel the plan has value,' Randy said, 'if that's what you mean.'

'I didn't say it had no value.'

'Then what, Alex?' Jason asked.

'Look, if you simply want me to agree with everything you propose . . .'

'You know that's not what I want. You're here because I think your ideas are valuable.'

'All right, then, I've got to say I don't think there's a chance in hell of the *second* part succeeding. Not with fifty men, not with a hundred men. I don't think it would work, that's all.'

'Why not?'

'Because you wouldn't get anywhere near her, not with the situation as tense as it is today. Any small boat making an approach would be immediately suspect.'

'He's got a point,' Clay said.

'And especially a small boat carrying armed men. I'm sorry, Jason, it wouldn't work.'

'He's right,' Goody said.

'So there goes your plan,' Alex said. 'Without the second part, it's worthless. Without the second part, there's no need to take the town. You'd never get to make your transfer at all.'

'Besides, Jason,' Goody said, 'even if it was to work, we're not sure what the reaction would be. We're not sure we'd get what we were after.'

'I think we would.'

'Yeah, but there's no guarantee.'

'That's true. That's the biggest chance we'd be taking.'

'But don't you see, Jase? If we can't be sure, why then all the rest of it is for nothing.'

'I think the reaction will be what we expect,' Jason said.

'Maybe,' Goody said.

'Maybe isn't enough,' Clay said.

'Then you don't like the idea, right?'

'I'm a married man,' Goody said.

'All right, then we'll count you out,' Jason said. 'Who else wants –'

'I didn't say to count me out, Jase,' Goody paused. 'You know how I feel about things. Goddamnit, we spent enough time together for you to know how I feel about things.'

'I thought I did, Goody.'

'But you can see how weak the second part is, Jase.'

'That can be worked out.'

'I'm not so sure it can,' Alex said, shaking his head. 'That business with the boat –'

'The business with the boat,' Randy said angrily, 'is simply a matter of finding an approach that will not be suspect.'

'Like what?' Alex said.

'I don't know yet. How should I know?' This only came up a few minutes ago.'

'It should have come up long ago. It's the weakest part of the plan. You're going to risk men's lives taking a Godforsaken town down in Florida, and you don't even know how the hell to –'

'I'm sure we can think of a hundred approaches,' Randy said.

'Yeah, you can think of a hundred,' Alex said, 'but so far I haven't heard a single one.'

'We're not moving on this thing tomorrow, you know,' Jason said. 'We've got all the time we need. The situation isn't going to change overnight, you can count on that.'

'What do I tell my wife?' Goody asked.

'Nothing. You tell her absolutely nothing.'

'I just take off one morning, huh? Knowing I might never come back.'

'That's a possibility,' Jason said.

'And she won't wonder how come I'm not going out on the tractor. She won't ask me, Hey, Goody, where you off to? You should've heard her when I told her I was coming up to New York for a renunion, Jase.' He shook his head. 'I don't know. I just don't know.'

'Then drop out,' Jason said flatly.

'I let you down once,' Goody said.

The men in the room were silent.

'You don't owe me any favours,' Jason said. 'If you're thinking I called you because you owe me something, you're mistaken.'

'He called you because he thought he knew what kind of men you were,' Randy said.

None of the others said anything.

'Well,' Jason said, 'the only thing I can do is ask you not to talk about this to anyone.'

'A woman might be able to pull it off,' Alex said suddenly.

'What?'

'The boat. Why don't we use a woman?'

'It looks as though it's clearing up,' Annabelle said.

Alex turned his eyes from the water ahead. She had come from below to stand beside him, her belly protruding, the same live intelligence sparkling somewhere behind the slitted eyes, like a fire burning in the depths of a cave.

'I was worried,' Annabelle said. 'When Jason radioed to say we should go ahead, I was worried about the weather.'

'I don't imagine Jason would have set us in motion if the weather was going to be a hang-up,' Alex said.

'Wouldn't he?' Annabelle asked, and smiled.

'I don't think so,' Alex said.

'You don't know Jason.'

'I know he wouldn't risk the whole thing collapsing.'

'Jason never even *imagines* anything collapsing,' Annabelle said flatly. 'In Jason's world everything comes off like clockwork, just the way he planned it.'

'That's sunshine up ahead,' Alex said, and shrugged. 'Jason knows what he's doing.'

The winds around Key Largo had worried Alex, but now as they approached the bay side of Long Key, now as sunshine broke through the overhanging clouds in radiating spikes like a miracle in a religious film, now as sunshine touched the water ahead and set it aglow, now as a milder breeze sifted into the wheelhouse for the first time since they had left Miami, Alex suddenly felt that everything would be all right. The day, the plan, the wheel in his hands, the twin engines humming smoothly belowdecks, the boat's prow knifing the water and sending a spuming spray back against the sides – everything felt fine, everything was good, everything *was* going to come off like clockwork, just the way Jason had planned it.

'These cracks you've been making,' Annabelle said abruptly.

Alex did not take his eyes from the windshield. He steered into the sunshine, and fantastically thought for a moment that the rays would snap off as the boat passed through them. The wheelhouse was bathed in sudden warmth and light. He squinted and said, 'What cracks?'

'You know what I mean, Alex.'

'No, Annabelle, I don't think I do.'

'Your hints that Randy made love to me last night,' she said flatly.

'Did I hint that?'

'Alex,' Annabelle said slowly and clearly with an almost painful precision, 'if you say something like that one more time, I'm going to kill you.' She kept watching him. His eyes flicked from the windshield and then back to the water ahead. 'You hear me, Alex?'

'I hear you,' he answered, 'but I don't know what you're talking about.'

'Look at me, Alex,' she said. He did not turn. 'Alex, look at me.'

She was holding a .22 in her hand. The butt of the small gun rested on her immense belly, and the muzzle was tilted up so that it pointed at Alex's mouth as he turned to look at her. Her face was unsmiling; the gun was steady.

'Say it one more time, Alex,' she said.

'Say what?'

'That Randy made love to me last night aboard this boat.'

'I never said that, Annabelle.'

'We're coming to the bridge, Alex.'

'I see it,' Alex said.

'Say it before we pass under the bridge, Alex,' Annabelle said. 'That way I can kill you and dump you overboard as soon as we come into the Gulf Stream. Go ahead, Alex.'

'I never meant anything like that, Annabelle.'

'You sounded like that was what you meant.'

They were passing under the Bascule Bridge now, through Channel Five, the bridge some fifty feet above them, momentarily shading the bow and then the wheelhouse and then the cockpit. The boat came out into sunshine again. Annabelle stood alongside him with the gun resting on her belly and pointed at his head.

'What do you say, Alex?' she asked.

'I'm not afraid of you, Annabelle,' he answered.

'No?'

'No.'

'Then you go right ahead and make another crack. Either now or later, or anytime you feel like it. If you're not afraid of me, you just make another one of those smart cracks of yours.' The wheelhouse was silent. Into the silence, with deadly calculation, Annabelle pulled back the hammer of the .22 cocking the gun even though it did not require cocking before it could be fired. The hammer going back made a tiny ear-shattering click.

'Okay?' she said.

'You're gonna hurt somebody with that thing,' Alex answered. He was sweating and his throat was dry. He did not believe for a minute that she would shoot him, and yet he was sweating and his throat was dry.

'I'm waiting, Alex.'

Alex nodded briefly. 'I won't say anything else that might upset you, Annabelle.'

Annabelle smiled, and then eased the hammer back down. She lowered the gun.

'Thank you, Alex,' she said sweetly.

7

Even moving as fast as she could, Ginny couldn't get out of
the apartment until amost nine-thirty, and then with a run
in one of her stockings which she didn't have time to go
back and change. She pushed the old Chevy as hard as she
could, and was about to make the turn onto the Spanish
Harbour Bridge when a car came barrelling up the
secondary state road to make a turn just ahead of her. She
jammed on the brakes and yelled 'You stupid idiot!'
through the open window on her left, but the driver of the
other car – a 1964 Ford – had not heard her and was indeed
already on the bridge and driving east towards the Spanish
Harbour Keys and Ocho Puertos. She continued to nurse
her anger as she drove onto the bridge, mixing her full
repertoire of swear words with an equal amount of
Sunday-driver criticism and also with several devout wishes
for accidents that might befall the car ahead, already out of
sight. She was completely exhausted by the time she crossed
the bridge to Ocho Puertos. Her normal routine was to
enter S-811 from its western end, driving past the
Tannenbaum house and the other houses on the shore-front
road leading to the diner. But this morning, as she
approached the cutoff, she saw a car parked just at its
mouth, right on U.S. 1. She recognized the car immediately
as the one that had cut in ahead of her on Big Pine, the 1964
Ford, and her anger suddenly renewed itself and flared into
life again. She slowed her own car and would have come to a
stop behind the Ford had not its doors suddenly opened. As
she came up behind the other car, three men stepped into
the road and walked to the barricade that was across the
mouth of S-811. Ginny immediately swung her old Chevy
out into the other lane, passed the Ford, and then glanced

back to see the three men moving the barricade aside. She had noticed that three other men were in the car, and now, as her own car moved out of viewing range, she wondered what six men in business suits were doing coming off the Long Beach road on Big Pine and racing here to Ocho Puertos where they were moving aside a highway department barricade to enter 811. She suddenly remembered, as though it had been there in a corner of her mind all along, waiting to fall into place, that a strange voice had answered the phone at the diner early this morning, long before the diner was supposed to be open for business.

Ginny pulled the Chevy to the side of the road.

She wanted a cigarette desperately, but she had smoked her last one back in the apartment and was waiting to buy a new package from the machine in the diner. A cigarette would have helped her to think this out more clearly, but she couldn't get a cigarette until she got to the diner – and the thing she was trying to figure out was whether or not she should go to the diner. Or even onto 811, for that matter. She sat impatiently behind the wheel of her old car with the engine running and probably overheating itself, tapping her painted fingernails on the steering wheel and wondering what she should do. There probably was nothing at all sinister about a stranger answering the diner phone before eighty-thirty. It was probably some truck driver, or somebody, who had driven up and knocked on the door, and Amos the nigger had probably opened up for him, even though Mr. Parch wasn't in yet. After all, the guy had given her his name on the phone, hadn't he? He had said This is Whatever-His-Name-Was, so there probably was nothing wrong with his being there. A guy doesn't give you his name if he's up to something. Of course, nobody said it had to be his *right* name. Mmm.

Ginny wet her lips and then put her thumb into her mouth and began chewing off the nail polish.

And if she hadn't seen that Ford coming so fast off the Long Beach road, she probably wouldn't have thought anything about the three men moving aside the barricade to get into Ocho Puertos. She'd probably have moved the barricade herself – how else could she get to the diner? But where had that barricade come from, anyway? It certainly hadn't been there when she'd left last night.

Something was funny.

She didn't know what it was, but she knew that something was funny, the same way she could tell when some guy was going to make a pass at her the minute the door to the apartment was locked. Something was funny, and her first instinct was to call the police, but that would mean driving all the way back to Big Pine, which was where she'd find the nearest phone. Besides, suppose she was wrong? Suppose nothing at *all* was funny, except maybe a silly middle-aged waitress who was imagining all kinds of crazy things? They ought to make nail polish in different flavours, she thought.

So come on, she thought. How about it?

Well, I could drive back to Big Pine, she thought. And call the police from there. And meanwhile, Mr. Parch'll be in already and What's-His-Name who answered the phone would have told him I'd be there at nine-thirty. By the time I get to Big Pine and back, it'll be ten, maybe ten-fifteen, and I'll be arriving with cops, no less. That'll sit just fine with Mr. Parch, the state troopers coming into his place. That's just what he needs. Though maybe we'll all have a good laugh at how silly and suspicious women can be, yeah, fat chance. Amos'll be yelling his bloody nigger head off about the diner being full and nobody to wait on customers – assuming those six guys in the Ford had even *gone* to the diner. But where else could they have gone? To Luke's marina maybe, to hire a boat, how about that?

Hey, brainless, what do you say to that?

They're businessmen who want to rent a boat for the day, get out on the water, fish a little, drink it up.

Ginny shrugged.

Yeah, it's possible, she thought.

With everybody saying a hurricane is coming?

Mmm.

Maybe I *ought* to drive back to Big Pine and get to a

phone, she thought. But suppose I call the cops and this is nothing? Maybe I'd better check first.

How?

I can't move the barricade aside and drive the car into town because if something *is* funny, well, that'd just be asking for it. But I can't leave it parked here on U.S. 1, either. If everything's all right in there, all I'll get is a ticket for my troubles, besides being late and in dutch with Mr. Parch. So where can I –

Hey, she thought.

The Westerfield house.

There's nobody there this time of year. Myron Westerfield and his wife don't come down till after Christmas. I'll just park the car in the driveway, and then cut across the highway into the thicket – probably get eaten alive, but I can't just go marching down 811, can I? Not if something's wrong in there. Well, maybe I can work my way along the beach instead. I'll have to see.

Ginny pursed her lips, thinking furiously. Then she nodded, shrugged, put both hands on the wheel again, glanced into the rearview mirror, and immediately made her U-turn.

Roger Cummings was fifty-four years old, a tall man with hair greying at the temples – he rather enjoyed the cliché of distinction – a well-preserved athletic body, and a manner of speaking that left a person feeling he had been severely reprimanded for a grievous wrong he had committed.

When the car pulled into the driveway of the Westerfield house, Cummings was in the upstairs bedroom, shaving. He frowned and put down the razor and then, because the bathroom window was made of frosted glass, went into the bedroom to take a look from there. He could not see beyond the bend in the driveway, but he was sure an automobile was on the road because he heard the sound of its engine being cut, and then silence.

'What is it?' Sondra said from the bed.

'Shhh!' he said sharply.

The bedroom was silent as they listened. The car did not start again. They heard the sound of birds in the mangroves outside, the sound of water gently lapping against the Westerfield dock, the sound of an aeroplane somewhere high overhead, the sound of plumbing in the house, and of palm fronds rattling in the backyard – but not the sound of an automobile engine.

'Is it a car?' Sondra asked.

'I think so,' Cummings answered.

'Can you see it?'

'No.'

'Did you order anything, Rog?'

'No.'

'Then who can it be?'

'I don't know.'

Sondra Lasky sat up in bed, a troubled look on her face. She was a slender girl with features that seemed even more youthful than her twenty years, a palely turned delicate beauty in her face, a narrow mouth, large inquiring eyes. Her neck was long and graceful, her hair blonde and clipped very close to her head, exaggerating the impression of extreme youthfulness. Her breasts were small and immature, the nipples suggested rather than defined. There was about her an appearance of vulnerability which was not too terribly far from the truth and which, in part, accounted for her attractiveness to men. Sitting up in bed naked, with the sheets twisted around her long legs and narrow waist, her lower lip caught between her teeth, she seemed the total picture of perplexed innocence.

'You don't think your wife –' she began, and Cummings immediately said, 'No.'

'Then –'

'I don't know Sondra. I'll go down and check it now.'

'All right,' she said, and nodded.

He went back into the bathroom to finish shaving, and then washed his face vigorously, and dried it. Quickly he threw the towel into the hamper and went back into the bedroom to put on a shirt. As he went out of the room, he said, 'Get dressed, Sondra.'

116

'Be careful,' she said.

He would not admit to himself that he was in any way concerned about the unexpected arrival of this automobile. He had not even seen the car yet, and so his mind had an opportunity to create several varied images of its appearance, but none of the images pleased him. The first car he visualized was one driven by an imaginary private detective who had been hired by Faye and who had followed him and Sondra all the way down here to the tail end of the country. The car was a rented automobile and had been waiting for the private detective at the airport in Miami. He had immediately hopped into it, and come after them to Ocho Puertos. He was now making his way up the driveway with a camera and a witness, but Cummings was going to surprise him by meeting him halfway, instead of in bed and on top of Sondra.

The second car he visualized was one driven by the Florida Highway Patrol who had noticed that the Westerfield house was occupied and were wondering why, since Westerfield and his wife never came down until the end of December. They had parked their patrol car at the top of the drive because they didn't feel like crossing that narrow ditch just before the bend. They were now striding to the front door in suntanned splendour, where they hoped to knock and – in the approved polite manner of cops everywhere – ask just what was going on here. Cummings would then have to explain to the best of his ability what he thought was going on here.

He would have to say that he was a very good friend of Myron Westerfield, who was the tax collector in the small Connecticut town where Cummings owned a large rambling stone house and forty acres of land that his great-great-great-grandfather had fought for in the American Revolution. He would then go on to explain that usually he lived in that house with his wife and his nineteen-year-old daughter when she was home from Vassar on holidays, but that he also maintained an apartment in Arlington, Virginia, because – well, he'd have to be careful about that, he supposed, about mentioning

117

Arlington at all. That's right, he would leave Arlington out entirely; there was no need to mention it. He would simply say that Westerfield was a good friend of his and that he had given him the house for a nine-day vacation starting yesterday, October fifth, and running through Sunday, October thirteenth, by which time he expected to be out of Ocho Puertos and back North. Maybe he ought to be careful about mentioning his friendship with Westerfield, too. But if they were policemen, he had to tell them something; he had to explain what he was doing in Westerfield's house.

He had told Faye he would call her at the Connecticut farm whenever he had the opportunity, but not to be upset if she couldn't reach him during the next week, since he expected to be occupied almost continuously with meetings. His plan was to telephone her from Ocho Puertos on Tuesday and again on Thursday, telling her he was calling from Arlington each time. He wasn't sure whether or not that part of it mattered too damned much, whether Faye discovering he was an unfaithful husband would change their lives one way or another. Maybe they were already too far gone for that.

The screen door closed noisily behind him. He glanced up at the bedroom window and saw Sondra standing behind the drapes, a blue robe thrown over her shoulders, her blonde hair touched with early morning sunshine. For a foolish moment he entertained the hope that the car would turn out to be an Ocho Puertos version of the Welcome Wagon. And then, because he knew the situation had to be faced realistically, he pulled back his shoulders and lifted his head and started up the driveway.

The birds in the mangroves set up an unholy chatter as he continued up the driveway. Up ahead, a huge egret fluttered into the air in an awkward flapping of fuzzy feathers, its long neck bobbing. Cummings, startled, brought both hands up in front of his face, as though expecting an attack. The birds swooped up and then gracefully circled away into the mangroves on the other side of the driveway, vanishing. A new cacophony of bird calls shattered the air as Cummings approached the bend and rounded it.

The car was a green Chevrolet, circa 1958.

It was empty.

Cummings stood staring at the car for perhaps three minutes, unmoving.

He had met no one in the driveway.

Now he wondered if whoever had parked the car wasn't somewhere in the thicket silently watching the house.

He turned and began walking back.

The incoming security calls from the diner and each of the houses on the beach had been switched to the phone booth outside by nine o'clock, thereby freeing the office phone for any possible calls from Costigan's clients. Jason had insisted that each of the men on the beach call in at five-minute intervals, right down the line starting with the diner and working west to the Tannenbaum house, and then back to the diner again. In that way, any trouble in any of the houses could immediately be spotted by the simple fact that the security call had not been made. At the same time, he had realized that such an operational plan would effectively monopolize the single telephone in the marina office, and had supplied the alternate number to his men for use after 9 A.M. It was now 10:05, and Willy still had not found the courage he needed to take him back to the Stern house where the girl Lucy was being guarded by Flack. Instead, he stood some ten yards from the glass phone booth outside the office and heard the phone ringing, and saw Goody Moore lift the phone from the hook and say something into it. Willy wiped the sweat from his moustache and walked over to the booth. Goody was just hanging up the phone.

'Everything okay?' Willy asked.

'Fine,' Goody answered.

Willy gestured to the three new cars parked in front of the marina office. 'I see they made it from Key West all right, huh?'

'Yeah, last of them pulled in about ten minutes ago.'

'Who was that?' Willy asked.

'Rafe.'

'What took him so long?'

'Didn't take him too long,' Goody said. He watched Willy for a moment and then said, 'Where're you supposed to be, Willy?'

'I took Costigan over to the repair shop,' Willy answered. 'Like Jase said.'

'That must've been an hour ago,' Goody said. 'Where've you been since?'

'Harry said I should go back to the Stern house.'

'So why don't you?'

'I've *been* there,' Willy said. 'I was looking around outside.'

'What for?'

'I was checking the water.' Willy licked his tongue over his moustache. 'I figured maybe some of Costigan's customers might be coming this way, you know. Over the water.'

'Yeah,' Goody said. 'But that's why Clay's on the end of the dock with binoculars, Willy. To let us *know* if any boats are heading in. See?'

'Yeah.'

The telephone rang. Goody pulled it immediately from the hook. 'Goody here,' he said. 'Yep, Walt. Right, thanks,' he said, and hung up. 'Walt over at the Ambrosini house,' he said to Willy, and then grinned. 'When he busted in this morning, the old guy was on the pot.'

'Who?' Willy said grinning.

'Ambrosini. He looks up at Walt and says "What're you doing in my toilet?" '

Both men burst into high almost female giggles. The laughter helped to ease some of Willy's nervousness. He fished into his pocket for a cigarette and started to light it. Goody's laughter trailed. 'You better get back,' he said. 'Jase won't like it if he sees you hanging around this way.'

'Back where?' Willy said, puffing on the cigarette as he lighted it.

'To the Stern house. That's where you're supposed to be, isn't it?'

'Flack's there, you know.'

'I know. Two men in each house, though, that's the plan.'

'That's right,' Willy said, and shook out his match. 'You want me to go back, Goody?'

'Yeah, you'd better get over there.'

'Right,' Willy said. 'See you.'

He started up the road. His heart was fluttering wildly in his chest. He could hear the sound of the surf rolling in against the shore and up on the main road the sound of a truck racing past, but these were almost lost in the pounding of his own heart and the rush of blood to his ears. He could remember the way the girl looked when they had broken in through the french doors, could remember her trying to cover herself with the sheet, could remember the feel of the rifle in his hands and the trigger against his finger and then the gun bucking and the man on the bed jerking back in bloody spasm. He forced himself to walk at a normal pace because Goody was watching him from the booth, but there was a furious propelling force within him – his mind was already in that bedroom with the girl again, his eyes were coveting her breasts, he was watching the steady ooze of bright red blood against the white sheet. He wondered if Flack would object to his taking the girl and then he thought, He damn well better *not*, I'm the one got him into this; if it wasn't for me, he wouldn't even be here.

It was exciting the way Willy and Flack had got involved in this operation; oh, not exciting the way his thoughts of the girl were as he moved steadily towards the Stern house up the road, his heart beating in his chest, not that kind of wild, fluttering excitement, but a different kind of excitement, right from the beginning, right from the first time Clay Prentiss talked to him in Goldman's drugstore. Even then he'd known something big was about to happen to him. Otherwise, why would Clay – who was an older man and a war veteran and all – even bother talking to him? 'Willy,' he had said, 'I'd like to discuss something with you. Whyn't you stop by the agency one day?' The agency he meant was the Buick agency he owned downtown on

Columbia Street. Since Willy was about to graduate from high school that June, he figured maybe it was about a job, but there had been something very mysterious about Clay's manner, something that was exciting even then about the slight pressure of his hand on Willy's arm, as though they were already sharing a secret; this wasn't about no job.

He didn't get around to visiting Clay until Friday of that week. Clay showed him into his private office, and then they sat opposite each other at Clay's desk, neither of them speaking, Clay smiling, and Willy's sense of mysterious excitement mounting as the clock on the wall ticked off minutes.

'Willy,' Clay said at last, 'I was wandering around uptown, oh, last month sometime, around where the old Porter Theatre used to be, you know where I mean?'

'Yes, sir,' Willy said.

'There's a bookstore on the corner there, do you know the one?'

'I'm not sure,' Willy said.

'Well, the reason I mention it is that you went into that bookstore.'

'I did?'

'Uh-huh. You stood outside looking in the window for a while, and then you went in.'

'Oh yes,' Willy said. 'Uh-huh, I remember.'

'I wonder what caught your eye in that window, Willy.'

'A book, I guess,' Willy said, and shrugged.

'What book?'

'I don't know,' Willy said cautiously.

'It was a book called *The Communist Peril in America*, wasn't it?'

'Is that right?'

'That's right.'

'What's this all about, Mr. Prentiss?' Willy asked.

'Well, when you went inside there, it seems you asked about that book. And you also asked a few questions about the organization sponsoring the bookstore. Do you remember that, Willy?'

122

'I was just curious,' Willy said. 'I don't have anything to do with that organization.'

'I know you don't. But you *are* interested in Communism, aren't you?'

'No more and no less than anybody else.'

'Well, certainly interested enough to go in and ask about that book.'

'I only wanted to know how much it cost.'

'Four-fifty,' Clay said.

'That's right,' Willy said.

'You told the man in the shop that four-fifty was more than you cared to spend.'

'That's . . . listen, how do you know all this?'

'Leonard is a friend of mine.'

'Leonard? Who's Leonard?'

'Leonard Crawley. Working in the bookshop.'

'Oh.'

'Do you remember now?'

'I remember asking the price of a book, yes.'

'A book about the Communist peril?'

'Well, yes, but that don't mean . . .'

'What doesn't it mean, Willy?'

'Nothing.'

'Willy,' Clay said gently, 'there's nothing wrong about hating Communism.'

Willy said nothing.

'Were you thinking of joining that organization?'

'No,' Willy said immediately.

'Then why did you ask questions about it?'

'I was just curious about how come they had only books about Commies in the window, that's all. I thought maybe it was a Commie organization, that's all.'

'But it isn't as you found out.'

'That's right, but I still wouldn't want to belong to it. I've read a couple of things about it in the papers and in magazines since then, and I don't think it's the kind of group I want to get involved with.'

'Why not?'

'It just doesn't appeal to me, that's all.'

'You're not in *favour* of Communism, are you?'

'Hell, no! Who said that? Listen, would you mind –'

'I mean, you *might* be interested in a group that was against Communism, though not that par*ti*cular group, isn't that right?'

'No. I'm not interested in any group,' Willy said. 'Not *that* one, and not any other one, either.'

'Oh,' Clay said. 'I see.'

'Why? You got a group?'

He put the question flatly and abruptly, leaning across the desk at the same time. Clay's dark brows lowered for an instant. Then he grinned and said, 'Yes. We've got a group.'

'Who?'

'Some interested Americans.'

'Some interested Americans interested in what?'

'In the same thing that interests you.'

'Which is what?'

'The Communist peril.'

'Yeah?' Willy said.

'Yes.' Clay answered.

'So?'

'*Are* you interested?'

'No.'

'You seemed interested.'

'Seems and is are two different things.'

'Okay, Willy, then let's forget it.'

Willy was silent for a moment, thinking. 'What's the name of this group of yours?' he asked.

'It hasn't got a name.'

'Who's in it?'

'A few people here in town,' Clay said, and paused. 'And some people elsewhere.'

'Where elsewhere?'

'New York, Chicago, Richmond, Boston, few other places.'

'How many people are in it?'

'Why do you want to know?'

'Because I do. Look, Mr. Prentiss, *you* sent for *me*, not vice versa.'

Clay seemed to hesitate. Then he said, 'All right, six of us started it. There are now twenty of us. We need forty-two.'

'Why forty-two?'

'Why not?'

'It just seems like a funny number to hit on.'

'It wasn't *hit* on. It's what we need.'

'For what?'

Clay smiled.

'For *what*, Mr. Prentiss?' Willy asked.

Clay continued smiling.

'Mr. Prentiss,' Willy said, 'did you want to tell me what this is all about, or did you want to just waste time bullshitting?'

The smile dropped from Clay's face. Willy listened to the clock ticking in the silence of the room. Very slowly Clay said, 'We need forty-two men to prepare for an action that will protect our nation and preserve our American way of life.'

'What kind of an action?'

Clay shook his head and said nothing.

'You've got a group thinks it can do all that, huh?'

'Yes.'

'How?'

Again, Clay shook his head.

'What is it, a vigilante group?' He had learned about vigilante groups in Social Studies II. They were supposed to be bad.

'No,' Clay said patiently. 'Not a vigilante group.'

'Then what would you call it, Mr. Prentiss?'

'I would call it a group of patriots like yourself who would not like to live under Red domination. That's what I would call it, Willy.'

'Patriots, huh?' Willy said. 'Lots of speeches and slogans, huh?'

'We have no slogans, Willy.'

'What *do* you have?' Willy asked.

'Guns,' Clay replied.

125

The office went silent.

'That is,' Clay said, smiling, 'we'd planned to do a little target shooting over at the range near the old Granger place, in case you're interested in joining us.'

'With rifles?' Willy asked.

'Uh-huh. Rifle practice.'

'I wouldn't mind a little rifle practice,' Willy said. 'I'll probably be going in the Army next few years, anyway, you know.'

'That's right,' Clay said.

'I wouldn't mind a little rifle practice at all.' Willy paused. 'When did you plan on going up there? To the range?'

'Sunday morning.'

'Could I bring a friend?'

'Who'd you have in mind?'

'Flack. Frank McAllister. We call him Flack.'

'I'll let you know.'

'What's you gonna do?' Willy said, smiling. 'Check with Leonard to see if *Flack* was in there asking about some books, too?'

Clay returned the smile.

'I'd have known already if he was,' he said.

Willy saw a sudden burst of white among the pines up ahead.

For a moment he thought it was a large white bird swiftly moving through the tangled vegetation. There was a sudden flutter, like that of wings, and then an unexpected silence – whatever was in the thicket had been observed, but had observed as well. The silence lengthened. He heard an insect buzzing somewhere off to the side of the road, and then there was movement again, lower, more cautious this time, a stealthy measured crawl – that was a human being in there. Willy pulled back the bolt on his rifle and eased a cartridge into the firing chamber.

'Who's there?' he said.

There was no answer.

He moved down the road quickly, taking up a position

near where he had spotted the intruder. He held the butt of the rifle in tight against his hip, the muzzle pointing into the scrub palmettos, his finger curled inside the trigger guard. His thoughts of the girl in the Stern house and his first talk with Clay, and now this unexpected encounter with someone, the prospect that he might within the next few moments be squeezing the trigger again, be killing again, filled him with an almost unbearable excitement.

'Who is it?' he said again, and again received no answer but the whispering friction of someone crawling swiftly through the tangle. He wet his moustache with his tongue, and left the road.

The mosquitoes were upon him instantly. They swarmed up from a thousand hidden pores and filled the air in a dense humming cloud. He swatted at them and swore loudly, tripping on exposed pine roots, pushing his way deeper into the thicket, the muzzle of his rifle brushing aside the fans of palmetto leaves. There was cactus too in the tangled confusion of the thicket, and always the high omnivorous hum of the mosquitoes and beneath that in the distance the sound of a human being pushing steadily towards the main highway. There was a sudden loud crashing sound, a startled moan, the flutter of wings, the strident note of a bird in flight – and then silence.

He's fallen, Willy thought.

Something quickened inside him. He thought again of the man in the bed, waiting to be killed, daring Willy to kill him, and somehow he equated him with the fallen man ahead. The tangled vegetation became a wilful adversary now as he chopped his way through with the muzzle of his rifle, the mosquitoes a formidable enemy determined to overwhelm him as he swatted and slapped and swore and stumbled. There was a patch of white in the clearing ahead. Willy's heart began pounding fiercely. He swallowed and came closer; his hand on the muzzle of the Springfield was cold with sweat.

He pushed into the clearing.

It was a woman.

She was lying unconscious on the ground, a cut on her

forehead, the blood trickling down slowly past her eyebrows and along the side of her nose. She wore white, rubber-soled flat shoes. Her nylons had been ripped by the cactus, torn to their gartered tops which showed where the white skirt of her uniform had pulled back over her thighs.

8

Marvin's gaze roamed the walls of the paint shop in secret, brown eyes behind black-rimmed glasses, searching. He had never before realized how much junk there could be in a room, and his eyes recorded the trivia as dutifully as a ribbon clerk taking stock.

He was looking for something he could use.

He did not know what this was all about, nor did he particularly care. He knew only that he was a prisoner. Being a prisoner, he automatically planned escape. He did not know how he would escape or when he would escape, but he knew that he would. That was the only thing on his mind. Escape.

He knew he would have to do it alone.

He could not count on Costigan because he was a cripple. He could not count on his mother or father, or on Selma, either, though a man was certainly supposed to be able to count on his wife. Nor could he count on the old guy they'd dragged in, who looked like a prime example of a Bowery bum if ever Marvin had seen one. As usual, it got down to a simple fact, and the fact was that Marvin Tannenbaum, B.A., M.A., and working for his Ph.D. at Columbia University in the city of New York, Marvin Tannenbaum, as had always been the case throughout his entire life, from when his father was a general practitioner on Bathgate Avenue in the Bronx, and then after that to when his father began specializing and they moved to the Grand Concourse just off 183rd Street, all those years Marvin Tannenbaum – B.A. from City College, M.A. from Columbia – had been looking out for number one, and there was no one he could count on now but number one.

He had married Selma Rosen because she was a helpless

fluttering sort of girl who wouldn't know which subway to take to school if he didn't direct her, had loved her for the very scatterbrained cute puzzled way she had of turning life's simplest matters into vast and complex mysteries. The teen-age girl who was Selma Rosen was very pleasant to have around. There was a nice wholesome quality about her clean-scrubbed face and brushed brown hair, her lithe body, legs long and coltlike, breasts comfortably pleasant but not too enticing to other fellows, almost a shiksa look about her, almost. She was a cute teen-age kid when they got married, nineteen years old and both of them still in college, and he loved the open-eyed innocence of her in bed, the giggling sweetness she brought to the act of love, the kooky college-girl things she said, the odd shocked way she had of laughing at even a mildly dirty joke. She was a frolicsome teen-ager when they were graduated from City College together, twenty-two years old and cute as a button, moving impulsively and with an awkward grace, brimming with plans that were nutty and unrealistic. She was still a frisky little teen-ager – but she happened to be twenty-six years old.

Marvin did not know when he had become a father to the world at large, but he knew he did not enjoy the role. He was twenty-eight years old, and he had been playing father to Selma from the moment he'd met her, and father to the elder Tannenbaum ever since he had had his coronary. Marvin wanted a father of his own who would pick him up in his arms and carry him up the three flights of stairs to their third-floor apartment on Bathgate Avenue; he wanted a father with strong arms; he wanted somebody he could go to and say, 'Pop, I'm having trouble with Selma. Pop, I don't love her. What shall I do?'

'What is the trouble, son?' his father would say.

Pop, he would say, she's still a teen-ager. Pop, I don't want a teen-ager in my bed any more. I don't want to come home at the end of the day and listen to all these cockamamie problems she's made up out of nothing. I'm tired when I get home, I want to rest. She's always crying, Pop. She cries about everything. If she can't get the car in the garage she starts bawling. Pop, I can't stand it any more. That's why I came down here; I had to talk this over with you. I want to divorce her, Pop. I can't deal with everything all alone any more. I need some help, she's too goddamn helpless, I'm sick of it. That big wide-eyed crap in bed. Pop, we've been married close to six years. When the hell is she going to become something more than a person I do things to, a person who lies back on the pillow with a shocked awed almost religious look on her face? I'm sorry, Pop, but isn't marriage supposed to be something *special?* Isn't it? Pop, I don't love her, I want out!

He didn't have a wife, and he didn't have a father either.

Oh, God, he wanted to be on a tropical island someplace.

He wanted sixteen girls to wait on him hand and foot and bathe him in oil and feed him coconut and pineapple and make love to him with the ocean murmuring against the shore and the breeze wafting through the palm fronds, balmy. God, oh God, he did not want to carry the whole damn world, he wanted to rest, he wanted to relax, he wanted to escape.

He wanted to escape.

There were a great many tools in the shop. He silently weighed each one against the rifles carried by Clyde and Harry. He had no idea what kind of rifles they were, but they looked uncommonly deadly. He imagined they were capable of putting rather large holes in a person, especially if a person were foolish enough to come charging across the room with something like, well, a monkey wrench in his hand. No, the tools were out, even if he could get to them, which he couldn't possibly since some of them were hanging on the pegboard clear across the room behind the racked outboards. No.

'Marvin?' his mother said.

'What is it, Mom?'

'What are they doing here?'

'Who?' Marvin asked. His gaze had moved to a wall calendar to the left of the workbench, advertising a hardware store in Key West and showing a photograph of a semi-nude girl on a surfboard.

'These men.'

'I don't know.'

'If it's a holdup, why don't they hold us up already?'

'Maybe they've got something bigger in mind,' Marvin said.

'Like what?'

Marvin shrugged. His scrutiny had shifted from the calendar to the open door in the half wall, and then to the shelves on the wall beyond. 'Maybe a bank,' he said. There were parts manuals on the shelves, and several soiled rags.

'A bank where? There's no bank here,' his mother said.

'Maybe the next town.' He shrugged again. 'Mom, I don't know *what* they want.'

'Could it be the post office?' Rachel asked. 'There's a post office next door on Big Pine. They keep money in post offices, don't they?'

'Uh-huh,' Marvin said. He was examining the outboard motors on their racks now, the socket wrenches spread before them on an open cloth carrying bag. Several packing crates containing parts were against the pegboard wall on the far end of the shop, and a boat's propeller was resting on its side near some stacked petrol cans. What looked like a short mast was standing in the corner. Three opened packing crates were near the bow of the boat, excelsior overflowing their wooden edges. The boat on its cradle hid almost the entire wall on the left side of the shop.

'But not so much,' his mother said.

'Not so much what?'

'Money.'

'Where?'

'In post offices.'

'Oh. No, I guess not.'

'Keep quiet there,' Harry warned. 'Both of you.'

A closed door with a hand-lettered sign, TOILET, was in the corner of the room behind the boat's stern, and hanging to the left of the door was a fire extinguisher. The wall where Marvin sat began just there, with the overhead doors behind him and running almost the entire width of the room, stopping some three feet short of the joining perpendicular wall. A short row of shelves occupied those three feet. The shelves were laden with cans of paint and varnish, bottles of what seemed to be either turpentine or paint thinner. On one of the shelves several brushes with drilled handles were hanging in a pan of water.

The workbench was against the adjacent wall. Harry was leaning against one end, near the vice. Clyde was sitting on the bench, his feet off the floor, his rifle across his lap. There were some tools and paintbrushes and wood chips on the bench itself. On the wall behind the bench there were more shelves with cans and bottles. Under the bench there were two Coca-Cola cases, one of them containing only empty bottles. That was it. Several feet past the bench was the hardware store calendar, which was just about where Marvin had come in.

He could see nothing that he could use, and the lack of a weapon, the lack of an idea, the lack of a workable attack frustrated him enormously. Exactly opposite him, across the room on one of the oil drums Amos had carried over, his wife Selma sat against the white pegboard wall, white blouse, white skirt, white against white. She caught his gaze. She looked at him questioningly. For a moment he felt something close to what he must have felt a long time ago, when Selma Rosen was sixteen years old and a junior at Evander Childs High School. He returned the questioning look, but a larger question was in his eyes, the question that had been troubling him for the better part of a year now, the question he had carried inside him day and night. Where do we go from here, Selma? What do we do with this marriage of ours that has gone stale and rotten? What do we do, Selma? How do we get out of it without destroying each other?

He turned his head aside.

His gaze came to rest on the fire extinguisher hanging alongside the door to the toilet.

He supposed he could reach for the extinguisher and, well, wait, he would need some excuse to take him over to that side of the shop – why not the bathroom? He could tell Harry he wanted to go to the bathroom and then he could grab the extinguisher from the wall and turn it full on Harry's face and, sure, they'd shoot him full of holes before he even got the damn thing off the wall. And even if he did manage to get it before anyone saw him, he'd still have to come clear across the room with it before he could hope; the hell with it.

He became angry with the stupidity of the idea, and then irrationally angry with the fire extinguisher itself. Because it could not serve his purpose – escape – he immediately berated its ability to serve any purpose whatever. It seemed too small for a room this size, and it probably hadn't been checked or refilled in years. How could it possibly function effectively if a fire broke out? He moved his eyes towards the shelves of paint and varnish and thinner and turpentine, towards the petrol cans stacked near the rear wall, towards the oil drums, towards the excelsior sticking out of the packing crates, and his anger at the extinguisher turned to something bordering on anxiety. He suddenly hoped no one was smoking, and he felt instantly relieved when he glanced around the room again and saw no lighted cigars or cigarettes. If a fire broke –

Fire, he thought.

It became something more than a word almost at once, flaming into his mind in a self-igniting flash of inspiration.

Fire.

Cautiously, because the idea had been conceived in searing intensity and accepted immediately as workable; cautiously, because he did not wish to arouse the slightest suspicion now that he had come upon something he could use; cautiously, he took his handkerchief from his pocket and blew his nose, and allowed his gaze to drift towards the three-foot section of shelves on his right. He discounted the cans of paint at once. Paint was inflammable, yes, but not particularly volatile. He needed something that would give him immediate and sudden flame, something that could be ignited in an instant. For a terrifying moment he wondered whether or not the clear colourless liquid in the half-gallon bottles on the middle shelf was water. No, he thought, please. It's not water, it can't be water.

He closed his mind like a trap.

The clear colourless liquid in those two bottles was either turpentine or paint thinner.

'Don't be so angry,' Bobby Colmore said to Dr. Tannenbaum.

'They make me angry,' Tannenbaum answered at the top of his voice, glaring at Harry.

'It doesn't pay to get angry with these kind of men,' Bobby said. He was very angry himself. He was so angry that his hands were trembling, and to hide their trembling he had put them behind his back. He had been offering advice to himself more than to Tannenbaum, knowing that every time he got angry he began drinking, and every time he began drinking it only made him angrier. There were two quart bottles of bourbon back in his room on the shelf over his bed near the picture of Ava Gardner, but they wouldn't do any good if he got angry here in the paint shop. He tried to control his anger by talking to Tannenbaum, but Tannenbaum was so angry himself, with veins standing out on his jaw and with his hands clenched, that it did no good at all to talk to him. In fact, Bobby was afraid that Tannenbaum's anger would jump right over into his own, like electricity leaping from one terminal to another.

'These kind of men,' Bobby said, 'are the kind who push into your lives without any reason. That's the kind they are. If you get angry at them, you only hurt yourself. Anger is a terrible vice.'

'I know it,' Tannenbaum said. 'But I don't like being pushed around for no reason.' He looked across the room and said, louder so that Harry would be certain to hear him, 'I don't like being pushed around for no reason.'

'Lower your voice, doc,' Harry said. 'Clyde here is trying to get some sleep.'

Clyde laughed. His eyes were closed, but he wasn't sleeping. He laughed and then wet his lips. He laughed at everything Harry said. Bobby wondered if he really thought everything Harry said was so funny.

'What they said, you know . . .'

'What?' Tannenbaum asked, glaring at Harry, and then turning again to Bobby.

'What they said, it isn't true,' Bobby said.

'What's that?'

'About my being a drunk.'

'Oh,' Tannenbaum said.

Bobby's hands were clenched in tight anger behind the crate upon which he sat.

'I drink a little,' he said to Tannenbaum, 'but that doesn't make me a drunk.'

'Argh, they're crazy,' Tannenbaum said. 'What do you listen to them for?'

'I'm not,' Bobby said. 'I'm not listening to them, Dr. Tannenbaum. It's just we've got a little community here, and I don't want my neighbours to get the idea I'm a drunk just on their say-so, do you know what I mean, doctor?'

'Sure, sure, don't worry. You think we'd pay attention to what a bunch of hoodlums have to say? Don't worry.'

'Look, I said I want it quiet in here,' Harry said, 'and I mean *quiet*.'

Bobby glanced at him quickly. Behind him, his hands were still clenched.

The men who had invaded Ocho Puertos, the men who had broken into his shack this morning and pulled him out of bed, had deprived Bobby of an early-morning half tumbler of bourbon and the reassuring knowledge that more was in the back room whenever he wanted it. He was not in the back room now, and his isolation from the bottles made him angry, as did the intrusion of these men who were seriously threatening Bobby's concept of what a drunk was or wasn't. You weren't a drunk if you got drunk in private, if you clung to whatever dignity a human being possessed. These men had invaded his privacy and cut him off from the source of his supply, and this made him angry, and his anger intensified his need for a drink. He could only remember one other Sunday like this, last year, around September it was, when he'd run short and had driven over to Big Pine forgetting it was a Sunday and had found the liquor stores closed. He had come back to town wondering

136

what to do and had gone over to the paint shop where Luke was working on the hull of a small outboard, and had flatly asked Luke for something to drink. Luke had only a pint bottle of Scotch, half full, which was light and smooth and delicious and gone in four seconds flat.

A man is not a drunk, Bobby told himself, if he gets drunk in private and clings to his dignity.

He had waited until Luke left the shop, and then had gone to the shelves near the overhead doors. He had taken a bottle of paint thinner from one of the shelves, and carried it back to his room. In his room he strained the liquid through his handkerchief into an empty can. He had no vanilla extract with which to disguise the taste, so he drank the filtered alcohol neat and hard, and was drunk within the quarter hour. It was not a good drink; paint thinner had never been a particular favourite of his.

A narrow smile touched Bobby's mouth now.

He scratched his jaw and looked across the room to the shelves just left of where Marvin Tannenbaum was sitting.

The man was squatting opposite her when she regained consciousness.

Ginny saw first the branches of the pine tree overhead and the sun blinking through in a radiating dazzle. She propped herself on one elbow and saw the bloodstains on the breast of her uniform, and then raised her eyes and saw the man across from her.

She drew her breath in sharply, surprised by his immediacy and surprised too by the rifle in his lap. She remembered then, and all surprise fled, leaving only a cautious fear. He had looked older when she had watched him through the palmettos. She had seen him just as she was about to step into the road, and had immediately turned back into the thicket, but not before the rifle had registered on her mind. She had stopped to study him, crouching behind a thick pine, and had dropped to her knees to hide. When he had yelled 'Who's there?' she had begun crawling through the thicket towards the main highway, anxious to get to the nearest telephone, sure now that something was terribly wrong; a man didn't carry a rifle in broad daylight unless –

'You must've hit your head on that big branch up there,' he said.

'What do you want here?' she asked immediately.

'Where, lady?'

'In Ocho Puertos.'

'Oh. I thought you meant here in the woods with you.' The man grinned. 'That's what I thought you meant.'

She followed his gaze, a knowledgeable lowering of his eyes to her exposed legs, and suddenly became aware of her skirt, and lifted herself quickly and pulled the skirt down over her knees. She noticed her torn nylons at the same moment, and thought, Oh, goddamnit, as if the torn stockings were somehow more serious than this young man who sat opposite her with a rifle, more important than whatever was happening in the town of Ocho Puertos.

'What's your name?' the young man asked.

'What's yours?' she answered.

'Willy.'

'My name is Ginny McNeil. I work in the diner.' She paused. 'What's going on?' she said.

'You always come to work through the woods, Ginny?'

'No.'

'Then how come you did this morning?'

'Because there's a barricade up on the road.' She paused again. 'I couldn't bring the car in. So I parked it and decided to walk down, that's all.'

'Oh?' he said.

She felt immediately that she had told him the wrong thing, that if only she had said the right thing to him he would have let her go. She could see him frowning as he thought it over. He nodded, and then suddenly smiled.

'You brought a car to work, huh?'

'Yes. It's a 1959 –'

'Where'd you leave it?'

'Up there,' she said, and made a vague gesture with her head. She had decided to be very careful about what she told him. She had not liked the way he had studied her legs;

well, she had good legs but that didn't mean some young kid could look at them that way. And she didn't like the way he was smiling now, which was somehow more frightening than when he had been frowning and thinking.

'*Where* up there?' he asked, and made the same vague gesture in imitation.

'Off the road.'

'Where?'

'I parked it in the Westerfield driveway.'

'Where's that?'

'Across U.S. 1.'

'Anyone apt to see it there?'

'Well . . .'

'Yes or no?'

'It's about ten feet off the road, I guess.'

'Mmm,' he said.

'I'll go move it if you like,' she said.

He gave a short mirthless chuckle and then got to his feet, holding the rifle in one hand and dusting off the seat of his dungaree trousers with the other. 'We'll *both* go move it,' he said. 'Get up.'

He watched her legs as she rose awkwardly, grasping one of the branches for support. 'My head still hurts,' she said.

'You gave yourself a good whack,' he answered. He had apparently been considering what she had told him earlier because he then said, 'Did Mr. Westerfield see you park the car?'

'There's never anyone there this time of year. The house is empty.'

'Oh?' he said again, and again he nodded and the smile came back onto his face. 'Let's go get the car, huh?'

'I feel a little dizzy.'

'You'll live.'

As they moved out of the small clearing and into the thicker growth, the mosquitoes attacked again in force, swarming over Ginny's arms and legs and the back of her neck. She swatted at them and swore under her breath, and then turned to look over her shoulder.

'Aren't they biting you, too?' she asked.

139

'They're biting me,' he said flatly. 'Let's just move a little faster, okay? Then we won't get bit so much.'

It was twenty minutes after ten when they reached the main highway. Ginny looked at her watch in much the same way she had earlier looked at her torn nylons, registering the time, and thinking how late she was going to be, and then wondering if the diner were open at all.

'It's across the road there,' she said.

'Go on,' Willy told her. 'Hurry up before we get traffic.'

They ran across the highway and into the Westerfield driveway. Willy glanced over his shoulder and then said, 'Get in the car. Quick.'

'Are we going back to town?'

'Yes. Get in.'

They got into the car, Ginny behind the wheel, Willy beside her with the rifle. She started the engine, and then said, 'I'll have to back out into the road.'

'No, I don't want you doing that,' he said. 'Drive on up ahead. If there's a house up there, there ought to be a turnaround.'

She nodded and set the car in motion.

At first she was only aware of his eyes on her legs. She tried to pull her skirt down, but her extended leg on the accelerator made this impossible. She pulled back her hand quickly, grasping for control of the wheel. The driveway was badly rutted, and the car bounced and lurched as they came closer to the distant grey house. She could not have said exactly when his interest turned to genuine excitement, but she felt it in the automobile suddenly, like an overpowering animal stench, primitive and wild, felt his excitement beside her as surely as if they had just entered her bedroom and locked the door. She drove with her legs widespread, the skirt pulled back over her knees, the car lurching and bouncing. From the corner of her eye she could see his hands moving along the stock of the rifle. She dared not glance at him because she did not want to encourage him in any way, and yet she was tempted to look at him, to *see* the excitement on his face and on his body; did he have a hard on?

She was suddenly frightened.

'How old are you, Ginny?' he asked.

She decided to lie, and then changed her mind and said, 'Forty-two.' She had begun trembling. Her legs trembled, and her hands on the wheel trembled. She was sure he could see her trembling, and sure too that her fear, if it *was* fear, was exciting him.

'You're preserved pretty good for forty-two,' he said.

'Thank you.'

'What?'

'I said thank you.'

'Yeah, you got pretty good legs there,' he said.

'There's the house up ahead,' she answered. 'We can make the turn.'

She pulled the wheel to the left as they approached the house, swinging into the circle before the front door, making the turn in a wide lazy arc.

'Just a second,' he said.

'What is it?'

'Pull over there a minute, will you?'

Ginny braked the car to a slow, gliding stop. She put her hands in her lap and sat quietly beside him. She could hear the gulls shrieking over the bay.

'Let's take a look inside,' he said.

'What for?'

'Just to check. I didn't even know there *was* a house here.'

'It's probably locked,' Ginny said.

'Well, let's try it, huh?'

'I'll wait here,' she said.

'Well, now, that'd be pretty silly, wouldn't it?'

'I won't go anywhere.' She pulled the key from the ignition. 'Here,' she said, and turned partially on the seat to hand it to him.

'Why, thank you,' he said, accepting the key.

'I'll wait here.'

'Mm,' he said.

'I won't go anywhere.'

'Mm.'

141

'I'll just sit right here.'

'Mm.' He smiled and nodded and said 'Mm' again and then said, 'I think you better come along with me, Ginny.'

'I told you I –'

'Get out of the car,' he said.

'I . . . I want to stay here.'

'Why?'

'I want to.'

'You afraid of me?'

'Yes.'

'Don't be afraid, honey.'

She looked up into his face to find the same fixed smile there. He was young and strong and frightening and she could smell sex on him, and sweat, and viciousness. Her eyes lowered inadvertently. She turned away quickly but too late to stop her own sudden unbidden response, hot and rushing. Her hands were trembling violently now.

'Get out of the car,' he said slowly.

He had said only that he wanted to check the house, but as she opened the car door and prepared to slide off the seat, she turned her head over her shoulder and whispered, 'What are you going to do to me?'

He did not answer. He only smiled and nodded.

She got out of the car silently and walked ahead of him to the front door of the house, silently, and then waited for him to try the knob.

'It's locked,' he said.

'I figured it'd be.'

He thought for a moment, and then said, 'Get back in the car.'

'All right,' she said.

'Hey.'

She turned to look at him.

'I know where we can go.'

Fatboy was pacing the small marina office. 'Where did you leave it?'

'On Big Pine.'

Fatboy glanced to where Jason was standing alongside the filing cabinets. The television set in the corner was on, the sound lowered. An old cowboy movie was showing.

'Where on Big Pine?'

'The road leading to the beach.'

'Long Beach?'

'Yes.'

'I don't like it,' Fatboy said. He was now wearing a khaki shirt and trousers similar to Jason's. A .45 was hanging in a holster on his right thigh. 'What do you think, Jason?'

'He had no choice,' Jason said, and shrugged.

'I'm only arguing with the way he disposed of the car,' Fatboy said.

Jason nodded. 'You should have brought it here, Rafe,' he said.

'With two dead men in it?' Rodiz asked.

'There are two dead men in it where you left it, right?'

'Yes, but that's over on Big Pine, not here. Suppose they start looking for that car? If I'd brought it here –'

'We could have hidden it here,' Fatboy said.

'How?'

'In the paint shop. There're two big overhead doors on the south wall. We could have driven it right in there.'

'I didn't think of that,' Rodiz said.

Fatboy would not let it go. 'This way, as soon as they find that car in the mud, they'll come looking.'

'So what?' Rodiz answered. 'They won't find anything, will they?'

'They'll find a town full of armed men.'

'They'd have found that even if the car was in the paint shop.'

'You don't seem to under –' Fatboy began.

'Take it easy,' Jason said.

'He doesn't seem to understand there are two dead cops in that car,' Fatboy said angrily.

'I understand that fine. What did you want me to do? Let them take us in? Our whole operation would have –'

'I'm saying you should have brought the car here. You

panicked, that's what happened. You weren't thinking straight.'

'I'm saying it doesn't make any difference.'

'It makes a *hell* of a lot of difference,' Fatboy said. 'When they find that patrol car, they'll also find two dead men. That makes it murder, you understand? That means if cops come here, they come here investigating a homicide.'

'If I'd brought the car to the paint shop –'

'Yeah?'

'It'd have been the same.'

'No. Because then the car would only be *missing*, you understand? *Missing*. And headquarters would think maybe they'd had a flat, or their radio was out, something like that. The other cars'd just be cruising the roads looking for it, that's all. They wouldn't stop to ask questions, they'd never get anywhere *near* that paint shop.'

'And if they did?'

'They wouldn't,' Fatboy said. 'This way, somebody's gonna stumble on that car sooner or later, sticking out of the mud like that. The whole damn police force'll come looking for a murderer.' He shook his head. 'I don't like it, Jase.'

'Neither do I,' Jason said.

'What do we do?'

'We wait.'

'For the cops to get here?'

'*If* they're coming,' Jason said.

'They'll come, don't worry about that.'

'I did what I had to do,' Rodiz said. He looked at Jason. 'I followed your orders, Jason.'

'I know you did.'

'You should have brought the car *here*,' Fatboy insisted.

'Lay off,' Jason said.

'I'd just hate to see this thing get screwed up,' Fatboy said. 'Especially now, when this part of it's gone so –'

'. . . for the latest news on Hurricane Flora.'

'Hold it,' Jason said, and moved quickly to the television set, turning up the volume.

144

'This is the eleven o'clock advisory from the Miami Weather Bureau,' an announcer said. 'Hurricane Flora is still centred near latitude 20.4 north, longitude 78.4 west. This position is about seventy statute miles south-south-west of Camagüey, Cuba, and three hundred and eighty miles south-south-east of Miami. Flora is moving westward about four miles per hour.'

'Jason, do you think ?'

'Shh!'

'Highest winds are estimated at a hundred and ten miles per hour near the centre. Gales now extend outward in occasional squalls some four hundred statute miles in the northern semi-circle, two hundred miles in the south-east quadrant, and a hundred and thirty miles in the south-west quadrant.'

'What the hell does he mean?' Fatboy asked.

'. . . will move very little during the next twelve hours. Since a large portion of the circulation will remain over Cuba, little intensification is expected. The threat to South Florida has not increased significantly, but gale warnings are up along the Florida coast from Stuart to Everglades City. Seas are very rough throughout the Western Antilles, in the south-east Gulf of Mexico, and in the Atlantic off the Florida east coast. Small craft in these areas should remain in safe harbour. All interests should keep in touch with further advisories. While little movement is expected during the next twelve to eighteen hours, some radical changes in the direction of movement are probable thereafter. The next regular advisory will be issued at five P.M. Eastern Standard Time, with an intermediate bulletin at two P.M.'

Jason turned off the set.

'What do you think?' Fatboy said.

'I think we'll be all right.'

'You think the water's okay?'

'I think so.'

'I mean, I was wondering about *The Golden Fleece*.'

'I know.'

'It won't be too rough, will it?'

'Alex knows how to handle a boat in rough water.'

'Yes, but . . .'

'Don't worry,' Jason said. 'They'll get here.'

9

The boat seemed to be adrift.

Murray Diel was the first of the six crew members to spot her, and he immediately passed the information to Randazzo over the plane's intercommunication system. 'One o'clock,' he said. 'About two miles. On the water.'

Randazzo glanced off to his right and grunted. They were still maintaining an altitude of one thousand feet on this leg of the patrol back from Key West, and the boat below was clearly visible.

'She looks to be adrift,' he said to Diel.

'That's what I thought.'

'Let's go down for a closer look.' He paused, pressed the ICS button again, and said, 'Photographer, pilot.'

'Aye?'

'Samuels, there's a boat at one o'clock, about two miles, seems to be adrift. We're going down for a look. Want to get some pictures?'

'Wilco.'

'She'll be on our starboard side. You can shoot when I bank. After station, stand by.'

'Standing by, sir.'

'Look sharp. We'll compare stories after the pass. Let's go, Murray.'

He shoved forward on the yoke, and the plane began its descent, sunlight flashing on its wings. The boat below loomed closer as the plane dropped. Randazzo could see the numbers on her bow, could see a man standing in the cockpit, waving his arms. The plane banked to the right and began climbing again.

'We'll make another pass,' Randazzo said. 'Across the stern this time. Knowles?'

'Yes, sir?'

'Want to try to raise them?'

'Aye, aye,' Knowles said. 'Sir, this isn't that boat out of Bimini, is it?'

'I don't think so,' Randazzo said into his mouthpiece. 'Murray, what was that boat out of Bimini?'

'Blue fifty-footer, twin Cadillacs,' Diel answered.

'Sir?' Penner said.

'Go ahead, Penner.'

'This one isn't no fifty-footer.'

'I figured thirty, thirty-five,' Randazzo said.

'Twenty-seven, sir,' Penner said.

'Maroon hull and black trim, sir,' Acadia, the other mechanic said.

'Roger. Anybody get the numbers?'

'6024, I thought,' Diel said.

'That's what I saw, too. Samuels, did you get your picture?'

'I think so, sir. You going to be banking to the right again?'

'Affirmative.'

'Standing by, sir.'

'Here we go,' Randazzo said, and brought the plane around for its second pass. He came in over the stern, some fifty feet above the water and the boat, and then banked to the right and began climbing.

'Name's *The Golden Fleece*, sir,' Penner said.

'That's what I saw, too,' Acadia said.

'Out of N'awlins,' Diel said with a phony accent, and then laughed.

'What do you think, Murray?'

'I think she's in trouble. The guy was waving his arms on this pass, too.'

'Sir, he was wearing a lifejacket, did you notice that?'

'Yeah. Knowles, any luck raising her?'

'Negative, sir.'

'Let's drop a message block. Penner?'

'Yes, sir?'

'Want to bring some paper up here?'

148

'Aye, aye, sir.'

'You've got it, Murray,' Randazzo said, and released the yoke and pulled a pencil from the long slit pocket on the sleeve of his flight suit. Penner came forward immediately with a sheaf of papers attached to a clipboard. Diel had the controls now, and Randazzo put the clipboard on his lap and wrote:

If you are out of gas or otherwise disabled, raise one hand over your head.

If you need medical assistance, raise both hands over your head.

'Message block, sir,' Penner said.

Randazzo took the six-inch-long, hollow, balsa block and pulled the cork from its end. He folded his message, stuffed it into the block, and then sealed it again. 'Better get a red streamer on that,' he said.

'Aye,' Penner answered.

'We'll come in over the stern again,' Randazzo said, 'give you a nice long target. I expect you to drop it right in his lap, Penner.'

'I'll try, sir,' Penner said, smiling, and started aft with the message block.

'You want to take her down, Murray?'

'Rog, I have it.'

'Standing by the after station, sir,' Penner reported.

'Got your streamer on?'

'Affirmative.'

'Take her down, Murray.'

The plane began its descent again. It came in directly over the stern, some forty feet above the boat.

'Bombs away!' Penner called over the ICS.

'Did you get him?'

149

Penner, who was looking back at the boat from the open hatch in the side of the plane, did not answer for a moment. The block with its trailing red streamer fell like a bleeding gull. 'Right in his lap, sir!' Penner shouted.

'Okay, we'll give him a few minutes to read our love note, and then we'll make another pass. Hold it here, Murray. Just circle above her, about three hundred feet or so.'

'Wilco,' Diel said.

'He's still reading our note, sir,' Knowles said as the plane gained altitude.

'He must be a lip-reader,' Acadia put in.

'Doesn't want to make any mistakes,' Randazzo said. 'Wants to make sure he raises the right number of hands.'

'Lucky thing he's only got two, sir,' Penner said, and everyone laughed.

'You want me to get this back to base, sir?' Knowles asked.

'Well, let's see what he tells us first, okay?'

'Roger,' Knowles said.

The plane circled over the boat like a giant patient bird.

'One thing I always hated doing,' Randazzo said.

'What's that?'

'Circling.'

'How come?'

'I don't know. Makes me feel stupid. As if I'm not going anywhere.'

The plane continued its lazy circling.

'Shall we take her down?' Diel asked.

'Guy's had time to read *War and Peace*,' Randazzo said. 'Let's go.'

The plane began dropping.

'He's standing in the middle of the cockpit, sir,' Penner said.

'I see him.'

The plane was coming in low now, a hundred feet above the water, seventy-five, fifty, forty. 'Pull her up,' Randazzo said.

'He had both hands over his head, sir,' Penner said.

★ ★ ★

150

The radioman first class who took the message in room 1021 of the Coast Guard's Rescue and Co-ordination Centre in downtown Miami immediately went into the room next door and handed it to the chief quartermaster who was on duty. The chief, whose name was Osama and who happened to be a full-blooded Cherokee, read the message slowly and almost tiredly and then waited for his superior officer to get off the phone. His superior officer was Lieutenant Abner Caxton, and he was talking at the moment to an admiral who wanted to know just what the hell that damn hurricane was doing. Caxton was trying to explain that Flora seemed to be sitting still at the moment, but the admiral kept asking Caxton *why* it was sitting still, and what the Coast Guard was doing about its immobility. Caxton finally succeeded in mollifying the admiral only to hang up and find Big Chief Osama looking at him dourly.

'What now?' Caxton asked.

'Boat adrift, sir, needs medical help,' Osama said.

'Where?'

'Twenty-five miles, zero-nine-zero radial of Key West OMNI.'

'Get me latitude and longitude,' Caxton said. 'Do we need a chopper?'

'I don't know, sir. The message doesn't say how bad the situation is.'

'Who'd it come from?'

'The Seven-two, sir.'

'Who's flying?'

'Randazzo.'

'He's a good man,' Caxton said generously. 'If his message doesn't give details, then there aren't any to give. Where's the *Merc* right now?'

'Don't know, sir. She won't be reporting until 1500.'

'Tell Di Filippo to raise her. Go ahead, I'll finish that.'

He went to the charting table. A sign on the door of the message centre warned that the area was restricted to authorized personnel only. Caxton watched the chief disappear through the doorway and then leaned over the chart. The chief, he saw, had already positioned the plotting arm on its proper bearing. Caxton counted off the twenty-five miles from Key West and put a dot on the chart. Latitutde 24.33.8 north, longitude 81.19.2 west. He looked at the big clock hanging on the wall above the status board. It was 1107. The *Merc* had left the base in Key West at 0900, and she was probably travelling at eleven knots or so, just outside the reef line, which would put her at about, oh, somewhere south of Summerland Key. That was, mmm – Caxton consulted the chart again, moving the plotting arm and marking off the area beyond the reef – well, somewhere around latitutde 24.30 or .32, and longitude, oh, 81.27, he would guess. He put another small dot on the chart, and then lighted a cigarette and waited for Big Chief Osama to come back with the *Merc*'s actual position. If the *Merc* was indeed where Caxton thought she should be, there'd be no need to send out a helicopter. She could be alongside the disabled boat within a half hour, probably sooner if she really poured it on.

Unconcerned, Caxton smoked his cigarette and waited for the chief to return.

The message was received in the radio room of the cutter by Curt Danby, a radioman second. He immediately hit his buzzer, and the quartermaster on the bridge heard the three buzzes, knew there was a radio message, and dispatched the coxswain to pick it up. The coxswain brought the message to Ensign Charles Carpenter, who was O.D. on the forenoon watch. Carpenter walked over closer to the porthole to read it by the light streaming through the glass.

P 061620Z
FM CCGDSEVEN
To CGC MERCURY
INFO CGAS MIAMI
GR 31
BT

UNCLAS
FROM 0

1. 27-FOOT C/C GOLDEN FLEECE MAROON HULL WITH BLACK TRIM DISABLED AND REQUESTING MEDICAL ASSISTANCE. NO RADIO. POSIT 24.33.8N 81.19.2W.

2. CG 7272 ORBITING.

3. PROCEED AND ASSIST.

BT

'Very well,' he said, and initialled the original. The coxswain went into the chart room and attached a copy to the clipboard there. He was on his way down to the captain's cabin when Carpenter picked up the sound-powered telephone.

'Captain here,' Cates said, answering.

'Captain, we've got a proceed-and-assist from Miami. Coxswain's on his way down with it now.'

'I'll be right up,' Cates said.

'Yes, sir,' Carpenter answered, and the captain hung up. He had been lying on his bunk on the starboard side of the small cabin (he had shared larger quarters as chief quartermaster aboard the Navy AKA) and sat up now to put on his shoes. The knock sounded on his door just as he was rising. 'Come in,' he said, knowing it would be the coxswain. He read the message quickly and then initialled it and went out of the cabin into the passageway, and then up the ladder to the bridge.

'Where are we now?' he asked Carpenter.

'I've plotted the position of the boat, sir, as well as our own. Would you like to see the chart?'

'Yes, I would,' Cates said, pleased by his first lieutenant's efficiency and foresight, but nonetheless suspecting him of being a first-rate ass-kisser. He studied the chart, and then went back into the wheelhouse.

'How does she head?' he asked the helmsman.

'Zero-seven-zero, sir.'

'Our speed?'

'All ahead standard, sir.'

'Come right to zero-nine-zero,' Cates said. He paused only an instant, and then said, 'All engines ahead full.'

It was almost 1145 by the time they reached the boat. They spotted the circling plane first and Cates ordered his radioman to try to raise it, and then they saw the boat out on the horizon, bobbing on the waves soundlessly, moving in an eccentric drifting pattern. Cates's hospital corpsman was a second-class petty officer named Emil Bunder, whom everyone aboard – including Cates – called Doc. Bunder had prepared his emergency kit, not knowing what to expect once he got to the boat, and now he stood by, waiting to leave the ship, holding the kit in one hand and – in the other – a portable FM radio in its canvas carrying bag. The ship was equipped with two boats, a twenty-foot pulling dinghy on its port quarter, and a twenty-foot motor launch on its starboard quarter. For the trip to the disabled cruiser, the motor launch would be used. The seas were not rough, and the three men who would accompany Bunder in the launch were all skilled boat handlers. Bunder himself detested boats and was prone to seasickness, a failing which had led him to choose medicine (offering proximity to all sorts of pills) as his line of work in the Coast Guard.

The ship slowed to a stop some five hundred yards from the drifting cabin cruiser, and the crew lowered the launch into the water, hand over hand. A Stokes litter was passed down into the launch. The seaman serving as line handler cast off from the mother ship. The chief bosun turned the bow out, and the launch began moving across the water. Bunder, sitting alongside the engineman in the stern sheets, hoped he would not get sick. He also hoped the person needing medical assistance hadn't been cut or shot or anything like that because he hated the sight of blood, which was one reason he'd almost decided *against* a life of medical adventure, in spite of his tendency towards seasickness. He also hoped the passengers wouldn't turn out to be bare-assed, dirt-poor Cuban refugees half dead of malnutrition. Bunder had been aboard the *Merc* long enough to have answered a hundred and twenty-nine calls for assistance. More often than not, these small refugee boats were authentic distress cases even before they left Cuba. Equipped with makeshift sails or propelled by oars, they put out into the Gulf Stream overcrowded and under-supplied, hoping somehow to reach the United States. The last distress call the *Merc* had answered was only two weeks ago. They had overtaken and come aboard a fifteen-foot sailboat thronged with twenty-two sick and starving refugees. The stench of vomit had almost caused Bunder to jump overboard. The search party had gone through the boat looking for weapons, and then the *Merc* had taken all twenty-two passengers aboard, abandoning the rotting sailboat to the sea.

'Nice-looking boat,' the bosun's mate said. 'Custom job.'

'*The Golden Fleece*,' the engineman said, reading from the transom.

'Yeah,' Bunder said. 'Chief, are you coming aboard to make a search?'

'You know it,' the bosun's mate said.

They could see a man standing in the cockpit now, wearing an orange life jacket, and waving his arms at them as they approached.

'He doesn't look sick to me,' Bunder said.

'Must be somebody else aboard,' the engineman said.

They were approaching the drifting boat rapidly now. They could make out the face of the man in the boat. He was a good-looking man; they were close enough to see the colour of his skin now; he was not a Cuban, his eyes were blue. The bosun cut the engine and allowed the launch to drift alongside. The line handler hauled himself into the cockpit of the other boat, tied them together and then dropped a rope ladder over the side. Roxy, the bosun's mate, came aboard and Bunder followed him up the rope ladder.

'Thank God,' the man in the cockpit said.

'What's the trouble, sir?' Roxy asked.

'We've got a pregnant woman down below,' the man said. 'Did you bring a doctor with you?'

'We don't carry a doctor,' Roxy said. 'Bunder, you want to go down there?'

Bunder nodded and went below. Roxy looked at the man standing before him, obviously recognizing him as an American, and wondering whether he should go through a routine search anyway.

'Are you an American, sir?' he asked.

'What?' The man seemed surprised. 'I'm sorry, what did you –?'

'I asked if you were an American, sir?'

'Yes. Yes, of course,' the man said.

'What's your destination, sir?'

'Ocho Puertos. But you see –'

'How many people are aboard, sir?'

'Just the three of us.'

'Who's that, sir? The three of you.' Roxy had taken a small green book out of his jacket pocket, and he opened it now and poised his pencil over a clean page.

'I'm Alex Witten.'

'Yes, sir. Is that W-i-t-t-e-n?'

'That's right. And Randolph Gambol, G-a-m-b-o-l.'

'Yes, sir,' Roxy said, writing. 'And you said there was a pregnant woman aboard. Is she your wife?'

'No. No, she's not.'

'Is she Mrs. Gambol then?'

'No. Her name is Annabelle Trench. Mrs. Jason Trench.' Roxy looked up, puzzled. 'Mr. Trench is an associate of ours,' Witten explained. 'He's in Ocho Puertos at the moment. In fact, that's why we were going down there from Miami. To join him. We figured –'

'I see,' Roxy said, and paused. 'Sir, I wonder if I could see some identification.'

'What for?' Witten asked. Again, he seemed surprised.

'Regulations, sir.'

'What do you mean?'

'Sir, we get a lot of Cubans up this way.'

'Do I look like a Cuban?'

'Sir, we get lots of Cubans who look just like you and me, and who were educated at Harvard.'

Witten sighed and reached into his back pocket for his wallet. He rummaged through it for a moment and then handed Roxy his driver's licence. 'Is this all right?' he said.

Roxy studied it for a moment, and then looked up. 'Where do you live, sir?' he asked.

'In New York City.'

'Where?'

'1130 East Sixty-fifth Street.'

Roxy looked at the licence again. He looked up at Witten's hair. He looked at the licence again. He looked up at Witten's eyes. He handed the licence back. 'This your boat, sir?'

'No.'

'Mr. Gambol's?'

'No.'

'Whose?'

'It belongs to Mr. Trench.'

'What's its registry?'

'New Orleans.'

'Whose name?'

'Jason Trench. Or maybe Annabelle's, I'm not sure. We can ask her later. Look, maybe you don't understand. That woman below is –'

'Sir, the doc's with her and doing his best, I'm sure. Can you tell me –'

Roxy heard footsteps on the ladder behind him, and turned. The man coming up the ladder was wearing white duck trousers and a life jacket over a pale blue windbreaker. He was suntanned and good-looking, but there was a harried, frantic look about his eyes and his mouth.

'Are you in command here?' he asked immediately.

'Yes, sir,' Roxy said.

'We've got a woman below who needs help desperately,' he said, and then turned to Witten and said, 'I knew we shouldn't have put out, Alex. I knew it.' He swung again to the bosun's mate and rested his hand on Roxy's arm, as though confiding something terribly personal to a good and trusted friend. 'She's expecting the baby any minute. When the engine went out –'

157

'Are you Mr. Gambol, sir?' Roxy asked.

'Yes, that's right. Randolph Gambol. How –'

'Didn't either of you gentlemen know there were gale warnings up when you left Miami?'

'Yes, but we'd talked to Jason . . . to Mr. Trench . . . and he said the weather was clear down this way. We thought –'

'What time did you leave Miami?' Roxy asked.

'At dawn,' Witten answered.

'We thought we'd be in Ocho Puertos by now,' Gambol said.

'But she conked out, and we haven't been able to get her started again.'

'We've got plenty of gas.'

'It read full when we left this morning.'

'It still reads half. Take a look at it yourself.'

'Yeah,' Roxy said, and grunted.

In the sleeping compartment below, Emil Bunder looked at the huge belly of the woman in the upper starboard berth and immediately swallowed and then wet his lips. The woman was breathing through her mouth. Her eyes were closed. Her face was sweaty, and each breath she took seemed to send a ragged shudder through her enormous body.

'Ma'am?' he said.

The woman grunted, and then suddenly gripped her stomach and opened her eyes wide, and squinched them shut again almost immediately, her fingers twisted into the covering sheet. 'Oh my God!' she said, and Bunder wet his lips again, and again said, 'Ma'am, can you . . . is it . . . are you in labour?'

'Yes,' the woman said. 'Oh my God, please help me.'

Bunder tried to remember if the Coast Guard had ever taught him anything about the delivery of babies, and the only thing that came to mind was the need for timing the frequency of the labour pains. He turned to the engineman who had come below after him, and nervously said, 'Time her pains, Jack.' Then he opened the canvas carrying bag of the PRC/59, lifted the telephone-like receiver and radioed the ship.

'You'd better get me the captain personally,' he told the radioman who answered aboard the *Mercury*.

'Stand by,' the radioman said, and Bunder waited with the receiver to his ear, and the woman lying at his elbow, groaning and writhing. She suddenly gave a convulsive shudder, her hands gripping the edges of the bunk.

'There's another one,' he said to the engineman. 'How many minutes was that?'

'Four.' The engineman looked up into Bunder's face. 'Is that good or bad?'

'Well, it gives us a little time, anyway.' Bunder said.

'I've already broken water,' the woman advised him.

'Yes, ma'am,' Bunder answered, embarrassed.

'I'm soaking wet,' she said.

'Yes, ma'am.'

'What does that mean?' the engineman whispered into his ear.

'What does *what* mean?'

'Breaking water.'

'I don't know,' Bunder whispered back.

'Quicksilver One, this is Quicksilver. Over.'

'Go ahead, Quicksilver,' Bunder said into the phone.

'Doc, hold on, here's the captain.'

'Mm,' Bunder said.

The captain's voice came onto the line immediately. 'Doc? This is the captain.'

'Yes, sir.'

'What's the situation there?'

'Sir, I've got a pregnant woman here who's already in labour. Her pains are about four minutes apart.'

'There's another one,' the engineman said.

'There's another one, sir,' Bunder said into the phone.

'Tell him about the water,' the engineman whispered.

'Sir, she's been breaking some water,' Bunder said, embarrassed.

'What do you advise, Doc?'

'Sir, I've never delivered a baby before, and I'd rather

159

not try it here. I'm below with the woman now, and this sleeping compartment is about maybe six by eight, sir, with two bunks on each side and a passageway of about a foot between her and the overhead, sir. So I don't think this is the place to go delivering a baby, sir, especially since I've never done this kind of thing before.'

'What do you want to do?'

'I'd like permission to take her back to the ship, sir. And I'd suggest, sir, that you get the wardroom set up for an emergency delivery, and ask around aboard the ship, sir, for any of the men who'd had experience with this sort of thing and who can lend me a hand.'

'Very well, bring her back.'

'Yes, sir. And, sir, we're going to need someplace to get her ready for the delivery. I was thinking someplace in officer's country, sir, maybe Mr. Pierce's cabin or –'

'She can have my cabin, Bunder,' Cates said. 'Get back here as fast as you can.'

'Yes, sir.'

'Bunder?'

'Sir?'

'Is she an American?'

'Yes, sir,' Bunder said.

'Very well. At the double.'

'Yes, sir,' Bunder said, and put the receiver down. 'We're taking her back to the ship,' he said to the engineman.

'What did he say about that water she busted?'

'Nothing,' Bunder said, and shrugged and went topside. 'Who's this lady's husband?' he asked.

'Why? What is it?'

'Are you her husband?'

'No, my name's Gambol. I'm a close friend. What is it?'

'Well, we want to take her aboard ship. She's in labour, and –'

'All right, let's do it,' Gambol said.

'Well, that's just it, sir. I wanted to get permission from her husband.'

160

'Her husband isn't aboard, Doc,' Roxy said. 'He's in Ocho Puertos.'

'Oh. Then I guess I'll have to get permission from her.'

'Look, would you mind –' Gambol began.

'We'll probably need a release, too. Don't you think so, Roxy?'

'Yeah, most likely.'

'What kind of release?'

'She's coming aboard government property, Mr. Witten,' Roxy said.

'What's that got to do with –'

'We wouldn't want to be held responsible if anything –'

'I never delivered a baby before,' Bunder said.

'Can't you take care of a release after she's aboard?' Witten said impatiently.

'Yeah, we'll have to check it with the captain,' Roxy said. 'You want to use the stretcher, Doc?'

'I don't know. Let me ask her if she can walk.' As he went down the ladder, he paused, and then said, 'She may not be able to with all that broken water, you know.'

The engineman looked up as Bunder came down the steps into the sleeping compartment.

'How's it going?' Bunder asked.

'Every three minutes,' the engineman said.

Bunder squeezed past him, nodded and bent so that his mouth was close to the woman's ear. 'Ma'am?' he whispered.

'Mmm?'

'Can you walk?'

'I think so.'

'We're going to take you aboard ship, ma'am. We'll be able to help you better there.'

'All right.'

'We've got a stretcher and we can use that if you like. But it's kind of tight down here, and if you can walk, I think we'll save a lot of time. What do you think, ma'am?'

'I think I can walk.'

'Okay. Ma'am, I think we'd better hurry, if you know

what I mean, because three minutes apart is getting kind of close. We don't want to deliver the baby here under these conditions.'

'No,' the woman said. She wiped her hand across her mouth and opened her eyes, and sat up as far as the low overhead would permit, leaning on one elbow. 'Would you help me down, please?' she said.

Bunder and the engineman helped her out of the bunk, one on each side of her, and then guided her to the ladder. She came up into the wheelhouse and the cockpit, the back of her skirt wet, moving like a ponderous mountain, her size magnified even more by the life jacket she wore over her black smock.

'How do you feel?' Witten asked anxiously, the moment she was on deck.

'Weak,' she answered, and then suddenly clasped her hands over her belly, her face twisting in pain.

'Get her in the launch,' Roxy said. 'Hurry it up!'

They lifted her over the side of the boat, three men above her, three men below her, guiding her gently and slowly into the waiting motor launch below. Witten and Gambol kept murmuring assurance to her, kept snapping instructions to the sailors who, for the most part, ignored the two civilians and concentrated on getting the woman into the launch safely and with as little discomfort as possible.

'Can one of us come with you?' Gambol asked.

'Go ahead,' Witten said. 'I'll stay here with the boat.'

'I don't know,' Roxy said. 'What do you think, Doc?'

'Look, let's just get started, huh?' Bunder said testily. 'I mean, let's not cut this goddamn thing too close, okay, Roxy? If he wants to come, let him come, for Pete's sake!'

'Hop aboard,' Roxy said, and started the engine. Gambol leaped into the launch. As it pulled away from the cruiser, Witten shouted, 'If you can send a machinist over to take a look at the engine, I'd appreciate it.'

'I'll ask the captain,' Roxy said, and the launch swung out in a wide foaming arc towards the cutter.

'How is she?' Gambol asked.

'I'm all right, Randy,' the woman answered. 'Don't

talk about me in the third person. It makes me sound as if I'm dead already.'

'That's nothing to say, ma'am,' Bounder said, and wiped sweat from his upper lip.

'Oh my God,' the woman said, and clutched her abdomen.

'Annabelle?'

'Shhh, shh, shhh,' she said, rocking with the pain. 'Shhh, shhhh, shhh.'

The men fell silent.

The woman's eyes were closed.

There was only the sound of the launch's engine, the gentle slapping of waves against the boat's sides.

'Ma'am?' Bunder said.

'Annabelle?'

'Yes, I'm all right.'

'Sir, what . . . what is her last name, sir?' Bunder asked.

'Trench,' Gambol said. 'Mrs. Trench.'

'Thank you, sir.' Bunder was beginning to feel a little sick. He did not know whether the sickness was caused by the motion of the launch or the certain knowledge that this delivery would necessarily be accompanied by blood and afterbirth. 'Mrs. Trench,' he said, 'have you . . . uh . . . have you ever had a baby before?'

'No,' she answered.

'Oh, then . . .' he began, and fell silent and tried to control his rising queasiness.

'We're almost there,' Roxy said.

Aboard the cutter, the p.a. system announced, 'All hands not actively on watch lay to the starboard side to pick up the number one boat,' and then repeated the announcement as the launch came closer.

'Stand by,' Roxy said to the line handler.

'Standing by,' the handler answered, and Roxy guided the launch alongside. A line came down almost immediately from the ship to the boat. The handler secured it to a thwart, and the boat rode the sea painter into the ship, coming up gently against the hanging fenders. As the men in the launch and on the ship prepared to hoist the boat aboard, Bunder sat beside Mrs. Trench and timed her labour pains. 'Hooked on forward!' someone shouted. He hoped he'd have time to get her ready before they brought her into the . . . God would he have to shave her? 'Hooked on aft! Heave away together!' and a sudden bowel-trembling fear caught hold of Bunder, chasing away whatever sickness he had been feeling only a moment before.

The boat was leaving the water. The men on the deck responded to each command quickly and efficiently; the boat was coming up higher and higher. 'Handsomely now, handsomely.' He would sure as hell have to shave her; should he try the delivery without anaesthesia? Weren't you *supposed* to leave the woman awake? Wasn't there something about her being unable to bear down if she was unconscious? 'Ohhh! Ohh, you son of a bitch!' the woman said, and clutched her stomach, three minutes on the dot, almost as if the baby were wearing a wristwatch. 'Two blocked!' came the order from the deck. 'Let's get her out of here,' Roxy said.

'How is she?' It was Captain Cates.

Bunder nodded. 'All right, sir,' he said, and swallowed.

'The wardroom's ready for you,' Cates said.

'Thank you, sir.'

Two stretcher bearers were waiting on the starboard side. They lifted the woman immediately and started forward with her. Bunder walked alongside the stretcher, his right hand inexplicably twitching at his side.

'One of our cooks has four children,' the captain was saying, 'and helped deliver two of them. He's washing up now.'

'Yes, sir. That's very good, sir.'

'And I've asked both our technicians to assist.'

'Sir?'

'Our electronics technicians,' the captain said.

'Thank you, sir,' Bunder said, and hurried to open the bulkhead door for the stretcher bearers. This is fine, he thought. I've got a cook and two electronics technicians to

164

assist me. What the hell does this son of a bitch think we're doing here? Baking a cake? Fixing a radar set?

'Go right in,' the captain said as they approached his cabin. Bunder threw open the door. 'Put her on my bunk there,' the captain said. 'I'll get some brandy.'

The stretcher bearers helped Mrs. Trench into the captain's bunk. 'Thank you,' she murmured.

'Sir, I'll need a razor,' Bunder said, embarrassed.

'You can use mine,' the captain said as the stretcher bearers went out. 'How much time do we have, Bunder?'

'Still . . . still three minutes apart, sir.'

'Oh?' the captain said, and turned from the chiffonier where he was opening his safe.

'Yes, sir.'

The captain took a two-ounce bottle of medicinal brandy out of his safe and began pouring the contents into a coffee cup.

'Sir?' Bunder said.

'Yes?'

'Sir . . .' Bunder said, and swallowed. 'Sir, could . . . could I have one of those, sir? I . . . I think I'm going to need it.'

'Very well,' the captain said, and looked up as a knock sounded on his door. 'Come in.'

The door opened. Bunder looked at the man in the doorway and then said, 'It's Mr. Gambol, sir. He's the lady's friend, sir.'

'Come in, Mr. Gambol,' the captain said. He handed Bunder a water tumbler partially filled with brandy. 'Here you are, Bunder. I haven't given you much. Do you feel all right?'

'Yes, sir.'

'How is she?' Gambol asked, closing the door behind him and leaning against it.

'She seems all right, Mr. Gambol,' the captain said. He picked up the cup of brandy and carried it to the bunk. Bending, he said, 'Madam?'

Bunder was not watching the captain. Bunder was turned

slightly away from the bunk, tilting the water tumbler to his lips. But in the silence that followed the captain's gently spoken 'Madam?' he suddenly knew that something was wrong. For a heart-stopping instant he thought, Oh my God, she's dropped dead, and he turned swiftly, expecting the woman to have gone pale and limp, expecting the captain to be standing beside her with a shocked and numb expression on his face.

The woman was holding a .22 in her hand.

10

Cates looked into the barrel of the gun the woman had pulled from inside her life jacket. It was a small gun, and he wondered if he should try to take it away from her. The woman swung her legs over the side of the bunk. Moving faster than he had ever seen a pregnant woman move in his life, she backed away to where he couldn't possibly reach the gun without being shot first.

'Don't move, either one of you,' she said. 'Randy, lock the door.'

There was a sharp sudden crack in the stillness of the cabin, the sound of the bolt being thrown.

'It's locked, Annabelle,' Randy said.

'What –'

'Shut up, Captain,' Annabelle said.

Cates looked at her and again wondered if he should try to charge her and try to wrest the gun out of her grip. There were only two of them, and if he could get the gun away from her, even if she shot him first, why then Bunder? . . .

He had the feeling all at once that he was about to make a mistake almost as serious as the one he'd made with Celeste back in June of 1938. He thought it was funny for him to be thinking about a young black-haired Irish girl when a gun was being pointed at his heart, but the notion that he was going to make another mistake loomed large and frightening in his mind, and the terrible thing about it was that he didn't know what the mistake would be or even how he could prevent it. Would it be a mistake to jump her? Would it be a bigger mistake to hear her out and delay any action until he knew what the full score was? He didn't know. It was 1938 again, and every fear he had ever nurtured sprang full-blown and weedy into his head, like Jack's beanstalk, leading to a giant who devoured confused sea captains. The giant was a pregnant woman holding a tiny little gun and staring at him with the deadliest eyes he had ever seen on any human face.

'Do you have a gun in this cabin?' she asked him.

He debated lying. It seemed to him that every decision he made in the next few minutes could be the one that plunged him into that spinning nightmare of error executed but not understood.

'Yes,' he answered.

'Where?'

'The safe.'

'Randy,' Annabelle said, and he moved quickly to the open safe door and reached into the safe and pulled out a holstered Colt .45. He took the gun out of its holster and waved it at Bunder.

'Get over there,' he said.

Cates watched Bunder as he moved to the chair Randy indicated. He could have sworn there was a look of immense relief in the corpsman's eyes, almost as if he were delighted he no longer faced the prospect of delivering a baby. He sat heavily in the chair near Cates's bookrack and blinked vapidly at the .45 in Randy's hand.

'What do you –' Cates began.

'Just shut up, Captain, and do as you're told,' Annabelle answered.

'What do you want? How –'

'And remember one thing, Captain,' Annabelle said. 'I won't shoot *you*, if you try anything funny, but I *will* shoot your pharmacist's mate there.'

'*Ho*spital corpsman,' Bunder corrected, and then blinked and looked apologetically at Cates.

'You wouldn't want to sacrifice a man, would you, Captain?' Annabelle asked.

'No.'

'Good. That's very smart, Captain. Especially since we don't intend to harm anyone aboard this ship . . . provided you do exactly what we tell you to do.'

'And what's that?' Cates asked.

'First, you will answer anyone who knocks on that door, or calls down on the voice tube or the sound-powered telephone. You will answer in your normal voice, and you will give no indication that anything at all is wrong. If you attempt a signal of any kind whatsoever, I will immediately kill the Corpsman. Do you understand that?'

'Go on,' he said.

Annabelle smiled. She was very pretty when she smiled. He noticed the difference the smile made on her face, and then remembered again that she was holding a gun in her hand and threatening murder.

'*Do* you understand it, Captain?'

'I do,' he said.

'Good,' she said. 'Randy, give him the first sheet.'

Randy reached under his life jacket and into the pocket of his windbreaker. He took out a folded sheaf of papers, unfolded them, consulted the top sheet, and then handed it to Cates.

'Read it,' he said.

Cates glanced at the typewritten sheet:

THE BOAT OUT THERE HAS ENGINE TROUBLE. YOU WILL MANOEUVRE TO PICK HER UP AND SECURE HER TO THE FANTAIL FOR TOWING. BRING HER PASSENGER ABOARD AND SHOW HIM TO MY CABIN.

'That's what you're going to call up to the bridge in just a moment, Captain. What's your O.D.'s name?'

Again he was tempted to lie. The O.D. was Lieutenant Forman, who had relieved Carpenter at 1145. But if he called the bridge and asked for Mr. Carpenter instead, would they –

No. Forman would only inform him quickly and politely that this was Mr. Forman, sir, was there anything he could do?

'His name is Forman,' Cates said.

'What do you usually call him?' Annabelle asked.

'Mr. Forman.'

'See that you call him that when you give him this message. Read it just the way it's typed, Captain, and don't say anything that isn't on that sheet of paper. Go ahead. Call him. Use the voice tube; we want to hear his answers.'

From the other side of the cabin Randy said, 'I've been briefed on shipboard voice procedure, Captain. No tricks please.'

Cates nodded and went to the voice tube. He lifted it from its clamp, blew into it and said, 'Bridge, this is the captain.'

'Bridge, aye,' Forman's voice answered.

'Mr. Forman, the boat out there has engine trouble. You will manoeuvre to pick her up –'

'Aye, aye, sir.'

'– and secure her to the fantail for towing.'

'Aye, aye, sir.'

'Bring her passenger aboard and show him to my cabin.'

'Aye, aye, sir.'

Cates replaced the voice tube on its clamp.

'That was very good, Captain,' Annabelle said. 'Don't you think it was very good, Randy?'

'Very good,' Randy said.

'We don't *really* have engine trouble, Captain,' Annabelle said, smiling. 'But that was our story, you see, and we wouldn't want any of your men to begin wondering. Give him the second sheet, Randy.'

'Would you mind telling me –'

'Shut, up, Captain. Give it to him, Randy.'

Cates glanced at Bunder, who was sitting wide-eyed on the edge of the bunk. He sighed then and took the extended sheet of paper.

Skip Forman had relieved the deck at 1145. It was now 1230, and he stood on the bridge and watched as the *Merc* manoeuvred closer to the disabled cruiser. He was grateful for the activity. He did not know what there was about the afternoon watch, but he considered it the longest watch anyone ever had to stand, even longer than the midwatch. All this business with the pregnant woman and the disabled boat, though, had made the past forty-five minutes speed

170

by. He wondered if they'd taken her to the wardroom yet. He could just imagine Bunder deliver.

'Bridge, this is the captain.'

Forman put his mouth to the voice tube. 'Bridge, aye.'

'Mr. Forman, we're going to have to change our plans here. This woman is not as close to giving birth as we seemed to think she was.'

'Very well, sir,' Forman said.

'I do not think we will have to attempt a delivery here at sea.'

'Very well, sir. What shall I do with the men standing by in the wardroom?'

There was a long pause.

'Sir?' Forman said, and then waited.

In a moment the captain's voice came over the tube again. 'You'd better secure them, Mr. Forman. We definitely will not be attempting the delivery.'

'Aye, aye, sir.'

'I would like to put the woman ashore,' the captain said, 'but it would take us several hours to get back to Key West, and I would not want to risk that.'

'Yes, sir,' Forman said, and frowned at the voice tube. The captain sounded funny as hell, as if he –

'Nor do I feel her condition is serious enough to warrant radioing for a helicopter,' the captain was saying, and Forman glanced at the helmsman to see if he had noticed anything strange in the captain's manner. The helmsman was gazing placidly through the windshield, probably dreaming of all the teen-age girls he knew in Kansas city. Forman wondered when anyone aboard this tub had ever called a helicopter a helicopter, and then realized the captain was still speaking.

'. . . closer perhaps.'

'I'm sorry, sir. Would you say that again, please?'

'We may have to put in closer perhaps.'

'Yes, sir,' Forman said. 'Where did you have in mind, sir?' Again there was a long silence. 'Sir?' Forman said. 'Captain?'

'I haven't decided,' the captain said.

'Very well, sir.'

'Have you picked up the disabled boat yet?'

'Yes, sir, and securing her to the fantail now.'

'Very well. Is the passenger aboard?'

'Should be on his way to your cabin, sir.'

'Very well,' the captain said, and Forman heard the click of the voice tube being replaced on its clamp. He turned to the helmsman. 'Farringer,' he said, 'what do you call a helicopter?'

'Sir?'

'What do you call a helicopter?'

Farringer shrugged. 'A helicopter, I guess, sir.'

'Farringer, don't be a jackass!' Forman said.

'A chopper you mean, sir?'

'Thank you, Farringer,' Forman said, and nodded and began nibbling his lower lip. He tried to remember whether he had ever heard the captain call a chopper a helicopter, tried to remember whether the captain always sounded like such a stuffy –

Oh, wait a minute, he thought.

Of course.

The old man had company aboard. A woman – and pregnant, at that. Which was probably why he hadn't come up to the bridge personally to manoeuvre for the pickup. He preferred staying below and showing the civilian types how cordial and charming the U.S. Coast Guard could be in any kind of emergency, even though it turned out not to be an emergency at all.

Forman nodded.

Of course.

The reason the captain hadn't taken the conn was just that. He was too busy impressing his guests with his precise clipped speech and his elocution course commands. Well, it didn't matter. Forman had manoeuvred up to the disabled boat and they'd thrown her a line and taken her passenger aboard. Forman had not been as charming or as courteous as the captain, he supposed; he had not left the bridge to greet the gentleman. But he *had* sent the quartermaster of the watch back to welcome him aboard and to lead him to the captain's cabin.

Roxy, the chief bosun, came into the wheelhouse. 'Boat's secured aft, sir,' he said.

'Aye. What do you call a helicopter, Roxy?'

'A chopper,' Roxy said. 'I understand she isn't going to have the baby, after all. Is that right?'

'Well, not right now, anyway,' Forman said.

'We taking them back to Key West?'

'I don't know,' Forman said.

'She sure seemed ready to pop when we were on the boat.'

'Well, you can't always tell with these things.'

'I knew a girl in Fort Worth used to pop out babies like water-melon seeds,' Roxy said. 'Why'd you want to know about a chopper? Are we going to need one?'

'Captain says no.'

Roxy looked up to where the amphibious plane was still circling. 'What do we do with the fly-boys?' he asked.

'Send them on their way, I guess. Soon as the captain decides what we're doing next.'

'Well, I'm gonna get down below,' Roxy said, and left the bridge.

At 1304 the captain's voice came over the tube.

'Bridge, this is the captain.'

'Bridge, aye.'

'Mr. Forman, we'll be getting under way for Ocho Puertos.'

'Ocho Puertos, yes, sir,' Forman said.

'We'll want to go past Looe Key and into Hawk Channel.'

'Into the channel, yes, sir. I'll –'

'These are your approximate headings, Mr. Forman.'

'Sir?'

'These are your approximate headings,' the captain said again, and Forman could have sworn he was reading from a sheet of paper. 'Two-zero-five will take us to Looe Key and the channel mouth. Come right to three-three-zero at Looe Key. Inside the channel, steer zero-six-five.'

'Zero-six-five, yes, sir.'

'A boat will meet us, Mr. Forman.'

'Sir?'

'A boat will come out to meet us.'

'To *meet* us?'

'To *meet* us, Mr. Forman.'

'What kind of boat should we be looking for, sir?'

There was a long silence.

'Captain?'

'It'll be coming out from the marina,' the captain said.

'Yes, sir,' Forman answered and the tube went dead. He looked again at the helmsman. He could not understand why they were taking the ship into Hawk Channel when they had never as long as he had been aboard gone anywhere inside the reef line on patrol. Well, all right, the captain wanted to put the woman ashore; that was reasonable. She *was* pregnant and they'd even thought for a while she was going to have the baby right here on the ship. Well, okay, grant the old man his gallant gesture. He was going to take her right into the channel, and maybe clear up to the island itself – no, he couldn't do that; the inshore waters were probably too shallow.

'Quartermaster, let me see a chart for Hawk Channel, Ocho Puertos, around there.'

'Yes, sir,' the quartermaster answered.

That's probably why the boat is coming out, Forman thought. Our draught is nine feet, six inches, which means we won't be able to come in too close; well, the chart'll tell me just *how* close, but I'll bet it won't be less than four or five miles. Which is why the boat is coming out. If the old man wants to put that woman ashore, a boat would have to –

'Here you are, sir,' the quartermaster said, spreading the chart on his table. Forman walked to the table and bent over it.

'Mmm,' he said. 'Better than I thought.'

'Sir?'

'We can come in as close as a mile offshore. Closer in some spots.'

174

'Offshore where, sir?'

'Ocho Puertos.'

'We're going inside the reef line, sir?'

'Looks that way,' Forman said.

'I thought only the forty-footers went in there.'

'Mmm,' Forman said, and frowned and looked at the chart again, wondering why the captain had thought it necessary to give him all those headings. Forman wasn't as experienced a ship handler as either the captain or the exec, but he could see nothing on the chart that looked even remotely difficult or dangerous. Well, yes, there *were* some rocky spots to the east of Looe Key, but even they were deep enough for safe passage. Besides, any experienced navigator would automatically enter the channel just west of Looe Key. Once inside the channel, there was nothing that could cause the slightest possible difficulty. So if the captain had decided not to take the conn himself (which was understandable since he had guests aboard and since manoeuvring into the channel was a very simple job), why had he read off all those headings? Either he trusted Forman to handle the ship, or he didn't. And if he didn't, then he should have taken the conn himself, or given it to the exec.

'Take a look at this chart, Bannerman,' he said to the quartermaster. 'Our position's about here. Show me how you'd take us to Ocho Puertos.'

Bannerman leaned over the table for several moments, and then placed his forefinger on the chart. 'I'd go back here, sir, to Looe Key, and then come right, into the channel. Then I'd steer right again, down the centre of the channel.'

'Uh-huh,' Forman said. 'Thank you.'

And another thing, Forman thought. How did the captain *know* a boat was going to come out of the marina when there hadn't been any radio messages or signals of any kind? How in hell did he *know?*

'Bridge, this is the captain.'

Forman went into the wheelhouse. 'Bridge, aye,' he said into the tube.

'Let's get under way, Mr. Forman. Is that plane still orbiting overhead?'

'Affirmative, sir.'

'Tell her the situation is under control, and she may carry on.'

'Aye, aye, sir.'

'Do that by radio, if you can.'

'I think we were able to raise her earlier, sir.'

'Very well. And send me a messenger.'

'Aye, aye, sir.'

The ship got under way at 1330, on a heading of two-zero-five, just as the captain had ordered. Standing on the bridge, Forman gave his commands to the helmsman and the engine order telegraph operator, and watched the amphibious plane dip its wings in farewell, and then begin climbing and moving in the opposite direction, back towards Miami.

As the ship steamed past Looe Key and turned right, into the channel, the coxswain walked into the radio room with a clip-board. He went directly to the transmitter, where Danby was reading Erskine Caldwell.

'Hey, man,' the coxswain said. 'Captain wants this to go out right away.'

'Check,' Danby said. He put down his book, and looked at the message:

To CCGD Seven

Info CGAS Miami

ZUG

1. C/C GOLDEN FLEECE IN TOW.

2. PASSENGERS ABOARD MERCURY. WOMAN PREGNANT AND IN NEED OF MEDICAL ASSISTANCE. HELICOPTER UNNECESSARY.

3. PROCEEDING BEST POSSIBLE SPEED
   NEAREST PORT.
4. CG 7272 RESUMING PATROL.

Danby was not in the mood for cut-and-dried reports to Miami, not after Erskine Caldwell. He looked at the message again, reading it over briefly in preparation for sending, and hesitated a moment when he saw the word ZUG preceding the text. He almost asked Reiser, who was a radioman first class and his superior, whether he should send the message just this way. But Reiser was over on the other side of the radio shack, talking to one of the ship's cooks, probably about getting some pies for the radio gang if he would only pipe into the galley some of that corny country and Western music the cooks liked so much. Danby looked at the message again. Well, he thought, it's in the captain's handwriting, I guess he knows what he's doing. His finger hesitated over the transmitter key only an instant longer.

Then, rapidly, he began sending.

A copy of the message was brought to Forman on the bridge a few minutes before the boat came alongside. Forman read the message and initialled it, and then asked the coxswain, 'When did this go out?'

'Few minutes ago, sir.'

The message did not bother Forman at all. There was something unassailable and trustworthy about the bold capital letters of a radioman's typewriter. If anything, the message seemed to clarify and simplify all the events of the past few hours. Moreover, the boat about to come alongside imbued all of the captain's earlier commands with an almost poetic inevitability.

'You'd better lay to the starboard side, coxswain,' Forman said. 'Roxy may need a hand there.'

'Aye, sir.'

The boat came alongside at a minute before 2 P.M.

She was a thirty-four-foot cabin cruiser with two men on the command bridge, and another four men in the cockpit. The bridge was perhaps twelve feet above the boat's waterline, so that Forman had to look down on the boat from where he stood just outside the wheelhouse of the *Mercury*. The two men on the bridge were wearing khaki. The men in the cockpit were wearing dungaree trousers and chambray shirts. For a moment Forman felt as if he were looking at some Coast Guard officers and enlisted men who had accidentally put to sea in a Chris-Craft.

'Ahoy,' the man sitting at the wheel said. 'My name's Clay Prentiss. We're supposed to pick up a woman here and take her back to shore.'

'That's right,' Forman called down. 'Stand by a minute, will you?'

He went back into the wheelhouse and picked up the sound-powered telephone. He waited until the captain answered it, and then said, 'Captain, the boat's alongside.'

'Very well, ask them to come aboard for the woman.'

'Will we need a stretcher, sir?'

'Negative,' the captain said, and hung up.

He thought he had handled it well up to now. He thought he had got by without making the mistake he'd been dreading ever since the pair had come aboard. He still did not know what they wanted, other than passage to Ocho Puertos. Well, he'd given them their goddamn passage, taken them through the channel and close to the beach, and now their boat was alongside and they'd be going ashore.

He thought he had handled it well.

The two men came up the rope ladder on the starboard side of the *Mercury*. Lieutenant Forman, having been relieved of the deck, had come down from the bridge and now stood just aft of the forward stack, waiting to greet the men. Roxy, the chief bosun, crouched to the right of the ladder and offered his first man as he reached the top rung. The man took Roxy's hand, sprang onto the deck and began reaching into his shirt just as the second man's head showed above the deck.

Forman saw the quick motion of the first man's hand, and knew instantly he was reaching for a weapon.

'Roxy!' he shouted. 'Watch it!'

Roxy turned at the sound of the lieutenant's voice and saw the gun coming out of the man's shirt. For a moment he was too stunned to move, and then the opportunity for movement, the opportunity for action, was gone. The second man had reached the top of the ladder. His elbows were clear of the ship's side and resting on the deck; there was a pistol in his hand. Don't, Roxy thought, you're too late, and then ignored his own advice to himself and kicked out at the gun. The man with his elbows on the deck wasn't fooling around. He fired twice, catching Roxy in the groin with the first shot and in the stomach with the second shot. Roxy, caught by the momentum of his own powerful kick knocked backward by the force of the high-calibre slugs, performed an awkward sliding fall, one leg high in the air, the other slipping back in the opposite direction as he skidded across the deck and then fell backward on to his own arm.

Forman grunted and closed his hands around the first man's throat and then gasped in surprise at what felt like the flat end of a railway tie being slammed into his stomach. The blow sent him spinning back some five feet to collide with the bulkhead of the radio room. He reached for the grab rail, suddenly unable to breathe, and then looked down and saw that the front of his khakis was covered with blood. More armed men were scrambling up the rope ladder. An armed man came out of the passageway leading from the captain's cabin. The door to the radio room opened. There was another shot. Forman saw Danby, the radioman who had come rushing out of the radio shack, suddenly clutch his hand to his face and pull it away and fall back with a giant red smear between his eyes. Oh my God, they've killed me, Forman thought; there's a hole in my belly.

He staggered towards the ladder leading to the bridge, wanting to blow the whistle or use the p.a. system or warn the captain that the ship was being overrun by armed men, but as he walked, he realized there was no strength in his legs, his legs were giving out under him. He dropped to his knees on the deck and shouted, 'Man your . . .' and nothing else because he fell face forward, dead, in the next instant.

'The ship is in our hands!' a voice said over the p.a. system. 'We're armed, and we'll shoot to kill! Resist and you are dead. Resist and you are dead. Resist and you are dead.'

PART TWO

11

'You're dead!' he shouted.

'I am not!'

'I got you!'

'You didn't get nothing!' she answered. 'And I don't want to play this stupid game.' She threw the toy rifle on to the ground, and he stood in the centre of the road staring at it, his lips pursed, a look of utter exasperation on his face.

'What do you have to throw the gun down for?' he asked.

'Because it's stupid.'

'Yeah.'

'And *you're* stupid,' she said.

'Yeah.'

'And the beach is stupid,' she said and giggled.

'What *do* you want to play, if you don't want to play this?'

'I want to play stupid,' she said.

'How do you play stupid?'

'You just be stupid,' she said and shrugged, and giggled.

She was five years old, and he was six, and he stared at her with the eternal patience of older brothers everywhere in the world, wondering why he always had to go out and play with her after he got home from school each day, and all day Sundays. Her nose was running and her underpants were falling down, and she stood in the middle of the road just a few feet behind the rifle she had thrown down, and he looked at the rifle and then at her and thought, Boy.

'Well, what *do* you want to do?' he said. He was always asking her what *she* wanted to do, it seemed. She was just a snotty-nosed little kid, but she was the one who always decided what they were going to do. Boy, he couldn't figure *that* one out.

'Let's play Sunday,' she said.

'What's Sunday?'

'Sunday is you put on your hat and go for a walk.'

'I don't have a hat.'

'You put on a make-believe hat.'

'What for?'

'So we can take a walk.'

'I don't want to take a walk.'

'Why not?'

'What was wrong with what we *were* playing?' he asked.

'You always shoot me,' she said.

'You can shoot me, too, you know.'

'I don't want to shoot my own brother.'

'I'm not supposed to be your brother.'

'You *are* my brother.'

'I mean, in the game.'

'Put on your hat,' she said. 'We'll take a walk. Come on.'

He picked up the rifle and looked at her patiently, waiting for her to relent. She stared at him unperturbed, and then tugged at the elastic waistband of her panties, and then wiped the back of her hand across her running nose. They stood in the centre of the road, staring at each other.

'Come on,' she coaxed.

'Well, I'll go for a walk, but I'm not gonna put on no stupid hat.'

'To play Sunday, you *have* to put on a hat.'

'I don't want to.'

'Papa always does. When him and Mama go for a walk, he always put on a hat.'

'Oh, all right,' he said, 'I'll put on a damn hat.' He went throu͝ an elaborate pretence of putting an imaginary hat on ͟ ͟.

͟ ͟ ͟ nice,' she said.

͟ ͟ ͟ your nose with your hand,' he told her.

͟ ͟ ͟ he centre of the road. He held one of ͟ ͟ hand. She walked beside him, trying to keep up with his longer stride.

'What we are,' he said, 'is Arabs in the middle of the Sumara Desert.'

'Where's that?'

'Someplace, I don't know. We don't have any water. The camels are all dead.'

'You're playing something else,' she said. 'You're not playing Sunday.'

'I am, too.'

'Then why are there dead camels?'

They walked for a while in silence. The water close inshore was clogged with mud and grass.

'What we are,' he said, 'is the first people to land on Mars.'

'We are the first people to land on Mars!' she shouted. A spoonbill preening in the tall grass squawked at the sound of her voice. She turned to the bird and giggled, and then shouted again, 'We are the first people to land on Mars!'

'You don't even know where Mars is,' he said.

'Sure I do.'

'Where is it?'

'Someplace,' she said.

'In the desert?'

'No.'

'Then where?'

'I know,' she said.

'In the water?'

'No.'

'In the sky?'

'Of course not.'

'Ha!' he said. 'It *is* too in the sky!'

'Ha-ha,' she said, 'the *moon* is in the sky.'

'So's Mars. Ask anybody.'

'There's nobody to ask,' she said. 'Show it to me. If it's in the sky, show it to me.'

'You can't see it. You need a telescope.'

'Make believe we have one.' She put her clenched fist to her ear and said, 'Hello, this is Cynthia Griffin, let me talk to Mars bars,' and then giggled.

'It's not Mars *bars*,' he said. She was still giggling. 'And it's not a telephone, it's a tele*scope*. It has a thing you look through.' He made his thumb and forefinger into a circle and peered through it.

'Let me see, too,' she said, and immediately pulled his hand to her eye. 'Ah-ha!' she said. 'Ah-ha! I see it!'

'What do you see?' he asked her, thinking there were times when she was okay, times when he almost liked her.

'I see Mars,' she said.

'How does it look?'

'It has grass and water and mud.'

'Do you see any people?'

'No. Only us.'

'We must be the only ones on the planet,' he said. 'Do you see any sign of our ship?'

'What ship?'

'The rocket ship.'

'Yes,' she said. 'I see a sign of the ship.'

'Where is it?'

'In the mud.'

'What does it look like?'

'It has a red light on top.'

'That's probably the escape hatch,' he said.

'No, it's a red light,' she answered.

'Are you sure it's our ship?'

She suddenly pulled her eye away from his hand and looked up at him. 'Jackie,' she said, 'will you get mad at me?'

'What is it?'

'I can't see our ship,' she said. 'All I can see is Mr. Hogan's car sticking out of the mud.'

Will͟ ͟d driven Ginny's car past the barricade and onto
S͟ ͟͟ping at the diner to get out and identify himself
͟d Mac behind the closed Venetian blinds. He
͟re he wanted to take the woman, and he
one who could possibly stop him was
͟ was stationed in the phone booth
͟ce. There was a slight parting of two

of the blind slats. A pair of fingers showed in the opening, wiggled themselves at him, and then disappeared. He waved at the blinds, got in behind the wheel again, and set the car in motion.

'Who's in there?' Ginny asked.

'Couple of hungry truck drivers,' he said, and chuckled at his own humour.

'Are you holding up the diner?' she said. 'Is that it?'

'Now, do I look like a holdup man?' he said, and grinned at her.

'Yeah,' she answered, 'you do.'

There was something odd about this one. He had never met a woman like this one before. He could scarcely sit still beside her. He couldn't understand this because she wasn't all that pretty, except for her legs maybe, and besides she was old enough to be his mother. In fact, he wondered why he was bothering with her at all when there was good young stuff right down the beach in the Stern house, waiting for his pleasure. Harry had told him to get back down there, hadn't he? Hadn't Goody told him to get back down there? All he had to do was meander into the house and tell Flack to take a walk or something and then go right over to that bed and have his pleasure with her, that was all. Only thing was that this one, this Ginny McNeil here in the car with him, she looked at him kind of funny. Well, she looked at him like she admired the way he carried himself, you know? Or admired what he was saying or doing, you know? Like she tried hard to make believe she didn't want him saying the things he kept saying to her, or looking at her legs that way, but he could tell she really *did* want him to. This was going to be something, he just knew it. And this was part of what it was all about, wasn't it? Wasn't this part of what Jason had meant when he'd told them about the greater glory, all that stuff? Wasn't this what he'd meant, didn't some of it come down to picking up a woman with a fine set of legs and taking her someplace where you could have your pleasure with her?

He took his right hand off the wheel and dropped it onto her thigh. She didn't move. She just kept looking th the window on her side of the car as if he hadn't put his hand on her leg at all. But he could tell she knew it was there. He could feel a trembling in her leg and in her body, like a high-tension wire singing in the wind, a high thin hum of excitement running through her and touching his fingers and setting his hand to shaking so that he had to grip her harder. Right then she said, 'Where are you taking me?' and reached down and picked up his hand as if it was a dead fish or something bad-smelling, and dropped it on the seat between them so that he had to laugh out loud.

He didn't answer. He pulled into the driveway to the left of the bait and tackle shop, glancing up the road to see if the phone booth could be seen from here, but it couldn't. He nodded, pleased. That meant *he* couldn't be seen from the phone booth either. He yanked up the parking brake and cut the engine, and then put one knee up on the seat so that it accidentally on purpose was against her thigh, and he said, 'We're gonna get out of the car now, Ginny.'

'Where are we going?' she asked.

'We're gonna go round back of the shop here, and to the other side where there's a door. You know where I mean?'

'You mean where Bobby lives?'

'Where the old wino lives, that's right.'

'Do you know him?' she said.

'Why sure, we're old buddies,' he said, and chuckled. 'You know you got the damn'est legs I've ever seen?'

'Yeah,' she said, and moved slightly away from him, closer to the door on her side.

'Now, when we get around to the other side of the shack here, we've got to be real careful,' Willy said. 'There's a phone booth just outside the marina office – oh, maybe two hundred yards up the road, you know where I mean?'

'Y..........' she said.

..........somebody in that booth, and I don't want him to

..........'d just spoil the party if he did, that's all.'

..........e are gonna have.'

188

'Don't count on it,' Ginny said.

'Honey,' he answered. 'I could get *rich* counting on it.' He paused, and grinned, and then repeated, 'Rich.'

'Yeah,' she said.

'Come on.'

They got out of the car and walked over the packed gravel in the driveway to the rear of the shack, and then around it parallel to the ocean. He stopped at the corner of the shack and peeked around it towards the phone booth two hundred yards away. Goody Moore was sitting there, just like he was supposed to be, waiting for them five-minute-apart calls from every house on the beach; there was such a thing as carrying things too far, Willy thought. He kept watching the booth, wondering how he could get the woman around the side of the shack and into the room without Goody seeing her. He held her tightly by the wrist. He could feel a pulse beating there. He was sure the old wino had a bed in his room.

Goody was reaching into his shirt pocket for a cigarette.

'As soon as he starts to light that cigarette,' Willy whispered, 'you go, you hear me?'

'All right,' she said.

'Get right inside there just as fast as you can.'

'All right,' she said.

'I'm gonna do you fine, baby,' he said. He looked over towards the phone booth. Goody had put the cigarette between his lips. He took a book of matches from his pocket, struck one, and ducked his head to the flame.

'Go,' Willy whispered.

He supposed she could have run away from him right then, but he knew she wouldn't, or at least was hoping she wouldn't. She did just what he'd told her to do. She ran as fast as she could around the side of the shack, and then opened the door and ducked inside, and closed the door again, all before Goody had got his cigarette going and shaken out the match.

He had to wait five minutes more for his next opportunity, and that didn't come until somebody in khaki (it looked like Clay Prentiss; he couldn't be sure b

189

he'd come up to the booth from the marina side) stopped to pass the time of day with Goody. Willy just sauntered out from around behind the shack with the rifle in his right hand, and walked to the door and opened it, and went into the room, and closed the door behind him, and then turned.

She was on the bed waiting for him.

She had taken off the white work dress and the flat-soled white shoes and the torn stockings. She was on the bed wearing only a white slip. Her face was turned to the wall. Her back was to the door. She did not turn to look at him.

He put the rifle down inside the door and went to the bed and sat on the edge of it, and said in a very soft voice, 'Hey. Ain't you even gonna turn around to make sure it's me?'

'I know it's you,' she said. Her voice was muffled.

He put his hand on her backside, just resting it there, not moving it. 'How do you know it's me?' he said.

Without turning, her voice still muffled, she said, 'Are you going to kill me?'

'No, honey,' he said. 'I'm gonna love you.'

She rolled towards him suddenly, the slip riding back over her knees. She looked up into his face and then she said, 'I have the feeling . . .'

'What feeling do you have, baby?' he said. His hands were moving on her thighs now, sliding over the nylon, gathering the nylon, bunching the nylon up over her thighs, pushing the slip up and away from her long white legs, 'What feeling do you have, sugar?'

'That . . . kill me or love me . . . it's the same with you.'

He eased her onto the pillow gently. The room stank of booze and staleness. Later, they would drink. He wanted to drink with her. He could see Ava Gardner's picture tacked to the white wall. He wondered what it was like to lay a mo͟ ͟ ͟ ͟. She had taken off everything under the slip. He ͟ ͟ ͟ ͟ slip high up on her thighs and looked at her ͟ ͟ ͟ ͟hed her, and she moved towards him wet ͟ ͟ ͟ ͟ gave a small moan and said, 'Honey, ͟ ͟ ͟ ͟n the straps of the slip. He kissed her ͟ ͟ ͟ ͟ hands on him and opened his eyes and saw Ava Gardner's picture again. He remembered suddenly that he had killed a man early this morning.

It ended for him in the next moment.

All of it, all the promised excitement of it, all the anticipated pleasure of working together with men who knew what they were doing, who had a definite scheme in mind and who were not afraid of its proper execution, all of it ended for him the moment he entered her because it was then that he ceased caring about Jason Trench or his plan, then that he knew the plan had been executed long ago, this morning when he had shot Stern. This, this now with a long-legged woman in a bed stinking of sweat and booze, this now was the reward to which he was entitled. This was where he wanted to be for the rest of the day. The hell with phase two of the operation out there on the water someplace. The hell with phase three, the hell with all of it but this woman spreading her legs under him. This woman – 'Honey, honey, do it to me, give it to me, do it, *do* it' – was the honour and the glory and the pride and the spoils of a war without trumpets and banners. He romped upon her with a glee almost childish. He could remember running across a field of tall grass holding a little girl by the hand. He could remember clouds unfolding on the brow of a hill. He could remember his mother wearing a white dress and tucking a handkerchief into the cleft of her bosom. Secret after secret seemed perched upon the edge of definition as he moved inside this yielding woman, imploring, entreating, questioning, searching.

He came before he learned any of the answers.

'I'm gonna keep you here all day,' he whispered.

'All right,' she said.

'Even after they're gone,' he said.

'All right.'

'Gonna keep you here forever.'

There had been twelve outside calls to the marina office so far that morning and afternoon. When the phone rang for the thirteenth time, Benny lifted it from the cradle and said, 'Costigan's Marina, good afternoon.'

'Who's this?' the voice on the other end asked.

'Benny.'

'Benny who?'

'Benny Prager.'

'Where's Luke?'

'Taking care of the boats, sir. Who's this, please?'

'This is Joel Dodge, up Ramrod way.'

'Yes, Mr. Dodge?'

'I was wondering how it is down there,' Dodge said. 'They keep yelling about a hurricane, but it looks fine here.'

'It's fine here too, Mr. Dodge.'

'What's Luke doing about the boats?'

'Well, sir, he moved some of them into the cove this morning, when he wasn't sure. But we're just leaving the rest where they are for now. He asked me to come in, and a few other fellows from Marathon, just in case he needs help moving them later on. I mean, if the hurricane should *really* start heading this way.'

'Then the boats are okay, huh? My boat's okay?'

'Which one is that, sir?'

'The white Chris-Craft. Thirty-four-foot Constellation.'

'Oh, yes, sir.'

'You think I ought to drive down anyway? Just in case?'

'I wouldn't advise it, sir,' Benny said. 'Not unless you'd planned to use the boat today.'

'No, I hadn't,' Dodge said.

'Then we've got everything under control here. Appreciate your offering help, though.'

'Well, I was just . . .' Dodge began, and then paused. 'Long as everything's okay.'

'Everything's fine, sir.'

'Okay, thank you. Give my regards to Luke when he comes back in, will you? Tell him I called.'

'I certainly will, sir.'

'Thanks,' Dodge said, and hung up.

Benny put the phone back onto its cradle and turned to the other man in the office. 'All they're worried about is their boats,' he said, 'each and every one of them.' He shook his head. 'Come tomorrow morning, they'll have a little bit more to worry about, huh?' He grinned. 'Just a little bit more, I'd say.'

The seven drunks pulled up to the end of the marina's pier at thirteen minutes past two. Jason, who had been watching the cutter through binoculars, barely had time to unstrap his automatic and throw it under some canvas on the nearest boat. The seven drunks were aboard a fifty-foot cruiser with twin Cadillacs, and they pulled the yacht into the pier as though anxious to carry half the pier away with them.

'Ahoy there!' the drunk at the wheel yelled down from the command bridge.

'Ahoy!' Jason answered.

'Ahoy!' the drunk shouted, and then burst out laughing. 'We are in need of fuel.'

'I can let you have some petrol,' Jason said.

'Are you Mr. Costigan?'

'No,' Jason said. 'I work for him.'

'I do not wish to deal with menials,' the drunk said, and laughed. 'And besides I do not wish petrol.'

'You said you wanted fuel, sir.'

'Freddy, tie us up to this mangy dock while this fellow runs to fetch Mr. Costigan.'

'Mr. Costigan is busy right now,' Jason said.

'You tell him Horace Carmody needs fuel and he had better unbusy himself right away.'

'I can fill you up, Mr. Carmody, same as Mr. Costigan could.'

Freddy and another drunk had stumbled ashore and were fumbling with the lines, trying to tie up alongside the Diesel pump at the pier's end. The other drunks aboard kept calling encouragement to the staggering pair while Horace Carmody on the command bridge put his hands on his hips and looked up at the sign and said, 'Welcome to Costigan's Marina! This is some auspittish welcome after travelling all the way from Bimini! You go get Mr. Costigan, young man, and tell him to get right down here to this pier right away.

193

Something funny going on *here*, all right, when he doesn't even want to come down to say hello to Horace Carmody.'

Jason had no idea who Horace Carmody was, except that he was a noisy drunk who said he wanted fuel but who also said he did not want fuel. Jason was expecting a signal from the cutter at any moment. Once that signal came, the next phase of the plan would be put into motion. He did not want Horace Carmody and his six drunken cronies cluttering up the waterfront with a yacht, not when an operation of this size was about to get under way. The two drunks on the dock had finally managed to get lines secured fore and aft, and one of the other drunks threw over some press lines while Carmody looked down from the bridge at Jason.

'What kind of fuel did you have in mind?' Jason asked pleasantly.

'Scotch,' Carmody said, and laughed. 'Gin,' he said, and laughed again.

'Bourbon,' one of the other drunks shouted.

'Canadian!' another drunk yelled.

'You fellows must be having quite a little party,' Jason said pleasantly.

'Yes, sir, quite a little party, and none of your business to boot. You go get Mr. Costigan and tell him we would like a case of Scotch and a case of bourbon and a case of gin and a case of martinis.'

One of the drunks on the dock began laughing and almost fell into the water.

'We don't carry liquor, sir,' Jason said politely. He was considering an alternate plan of action if he could not peaceably get rid of Carmody and his party. He would jump down into the boat where he'd thrown his .45, pick it up, and then escort Carmody and his drunken pals back to the repair shop at gunpoint.

'You are supposed to carry liquor,' Carmody said.

'Sir –'

'You are *supposed* to carry liquor.'

'I'm sorry, but –'

'There is a Coast Guard cutter out on the water there,' Carmody said, pointing vaguely out to sea with an over-the-shoulder gesture. 'I shall report you to them if you refuse to serve us.'

'Mr. Carmody, I'm not refusing to serve you. We don't *carry* liquor, sir, that's all.'

'You *do* carry liquor. Every marina in the United States of *America* carries liquor. That is the American way. It is the American *way* to carry liquor in *all* marinas!'

The drunks on the boat began applauding, and Carmody bowed from the waist and then turned again to Jason. He was a rotund little man wearing a short-sleeved sports shirt patterned with flags and pennants of the international code. A dead cigar stub was clamped between his lips. He smelled of whisky, or perhaps the stench of alcohol was simply something that permeated the entire yacht, rising on the air like a giant cloud of poison gas.

'Well?' he said.

'Sir –'

'There was *whisky* in the marina at Barbados.'

'Yes, sir, but –'

'There was *whisky* in the marina at Jamaica. B.W.I. *British* West Indies. There was whisky on *abundance* there. *In.*'

'Mr. Carmody –'

'And there was *whisky* in the marina at Bimini, our last port of call. So don't try to hoodwink me into believing there is *no* whisky here at Mr. Costigan's fine marina, with his big *welcome* sign overhead! How can you *possibly* welcome anyone to your shores without a glass of cheer, eh? Would you mind telling me *that?*'

'We can give you petrol and food, if you like,' Jason said patiently. 'We've got a Coke machine outside the office, a telephone booth if you want to make any calls, and a john if you want to use it. We don't carry whisky. I suggest, sir, that you try some of the bigger marinas on the way down to Key West.'

'I am not on the *way* down to Key West,' Carmody said.

'I am on the way to *Miami* from Bimini.'

'Well, I think you took a wrong turn back there someplace, sir,' Jason said.

'Horace Carmody does not take wrong turns.'

'No, sir.'

'Damn right.'

'When you pull out,' Jason said, 'I suggest you come around to the east and follow the coastline up to the bridge at Long Key. You can catch the Intercoastal Waterway up there.'

'I'm not interested in catching the Intercoastal Waterway,' Carmody said.

'I just thought you might like the quickest way to Miami,' Jason said.

'You're beginning to get on my nerves, young man,' Carmody said. 'Please get Mr. Costigan at once. At *once*.'

Jason looked at him a moment longer, and then sighed. He glanced out towards the horizon where the cutter was clearly visible, the Chris-Craft alongside it. He didn't want Carmody around when the boats began moving. He again debated reaching for the .45. But what kind of insane havoc could seven drunks cause in the repair shop? And even if he put them in the storage locker instead, what would he do for space when the others began arriving? He didn't want to end up shooting Carmody and his buddies. Not unless he absolutely had to. But he could not afford to have them hanging around, either.

'I'll get Mr. Costigan,' he said softly.

'Damn right, you will,' Carmody said.

Jason clenched his fists, turned on his heel, and began walking quickly towards the repair shop.

Early tomorrow morning the fat Horace Carmodys of the world would stand on the flying bridges of their fifty-foot yachts with twin Cadillac engines, and wonder what had happened to change the world so drastically. None of them would realize that Jason Trench had happened. None of them would know how long Jason Trench had been waiting for this day; none of them would know the resistance he had met from the others at first, including his own wife; none of them would know how difficult it had been later on to find men they could trust completely, men who would be willing to sacrifice their lives for their country if the situation demanded it.

How do you recruit a secret army?

You are not Horace Carmody, you do not have millions of dollars at your disposal, you cannot engage men to conduct your research, no. You have only the money from Japan, perhaps thirty thousand dollars left after the years of living in New York, that and the five men who were your closest friends.

By the spring of 1962, they had honed and polished every facet of the operation, and knew that they needed a total of fifty men to take the town and hold it, to hijack the cutter, to carry out the plan. But where could they find forty-four additional men who felt as they did, and who would be willing to back their feelings with action?

They turned initially to the many protest organizations Jason and Randy had belonged to over the years. At first the faces blurred together into a grey mass of professional agitators, confused malcontents, neurotic misfits, excitement seekers, misguided patriots, bigots, bloody anarchists, fanatics. But they began to sort out the names and the faces, surprised by the overlap in separate groups, more surprised to discover they could come up with a list of seventy-five remembered names between them, the names of people they had known, people who felt as they did and who were willing to attend meetings, distribute literature, contribute funds, join in protest marches and rallies. They plotted chance encounters, they asked discreet questions, they probed, they searched; they could not tell these people too much and yet they had to tell enough to elicit at least a tentative response. By the end of the year they had recruited only fourteen men they knew they could trust; what had earlier been six was now twenty. They were making progress, but they still had less than half the number of men they felt they needed.

They went over the plan again. If they could not find fifty men, they would have to carry out their plan with fewer.

They trimmed and cut and then, as with many economy measures, they discovered they had gone too far; they had reduced their needs too drastically. If they did not allow themselves a margin of safety, their plan had no hope of success. So they began revising once more, upward this time, moving away from their very low and impractical estimate and back towards their original figure. They finally decided they could do what had to be done with a total of forty-two men.

It took them almost seven months to find those men. It seemed at times as though this would be the hardest part of the entire operation, the enlisting of merely twenty-two additional men. They worked slowly and carefully, hand-picking their candidates and then exploring their backgrounds and their beliefs, avoiding personal contact until they were sure the aims and ideals of the group would meet with certain approval. Even then, after a man was accepted, the true and complete nature of the plan was not revealed to him until he had been with them for months and it was certain he would not defect. Perhaps they were too cautious in the beginning. They began to discover that men they had earlier enlisted were beginning to lose interest, were beginning to press for the action they had been promised. A man like Willy, who would have been considered poor material in the first several months of their search, was eagerly and somewhat recklessly courted towards the end. Harry Barnes was flatly denied acceptance by Jason when Alex Witten first offered him as a prospect. It was not until the plan seemed in total danger of collapse that Jason reluctantly allowed him to join the other men. By that time Alex was badgering him mercilessly. We've got to move on this, he kept saying. If we expect to keep these men together, we have to do more than talk of a vague operation that'll take place sometime in a misty future with faceless compatriots who haven't been found yet.

That misty future was today.

That vague operation was now in motion.

Those men now had faces, and guns, and they were willing to die for America.

By 1 A.M. tomorrow morning – or perhaps a trifle later, depending on weather conditions, but sometime early tomorrow morning – these men would change the course of history. What would all the fat pigs on their flying bridges say to that? Would they say, 'But I don't understand. I have been sitting up here puffing on my dead cigar with my drunken crony friends and ordering people to do my bidding. I don't understand what happened. I have been sitting here rich and fat and complacent and on the inside of everything, the inside of delicate blonde women who say shan't, the inside of expensive silent motorcars, the inside of stock market tips and plush restaurants, the inside of *everything*. What the hell happened?'

What happened is that you were *not* on the inside of Jason Trench's head; that is what happened. You did not appreciate Jason Trench, nor what he did on his floating piece of mayhem in the Pacific. No, you chose to remember instead the incident with the Japanese whore in the Tokyo alley, yes, that was important, wasn't it? Oh yes, that was very important. Well, you forgot that Jason Trench could change things. You forgot there was a man like Jason Trench who could and would die for his country if it meant restoring the country's respect and protecting freedom and equality.

Yes.

Tomorrow morning your flying bridges won't be worth a flying damn.

He threw open the door of the repair shop.

'Costigan!' he shouted. 'Get out here!'

They walked in silence to the end of the pier, side by side.

Jason carried no gun, and there was no gun trained on Luke's back as they approached the blue yacht. Luke's instructions were simple. He was to get rid of this party of drunks immediately, without giving them any reason to believe anything was wrong here in Ocho Puertos. Jason was fairly certain that Luke would carry out his instructions without causing any trouble. His confidence was based on the knowledge that Samantha Watts was being held at gunpoint in the shop, and Clyde had orders to shoot her at once if anything funny happened on the pier.

'Well!' the voice boomed down from the command bridge. 'Do I have the distinct honour of addressing Mr. Costigan at last?'

'How do you do, sir?' Luke said.

'I'm Horace Carmody.'

'Yes, sir.'

'Your man there refuses to sell us any whisky.'

'We don't have any to sell,' Luke said.

'You do not sell whisky?'

'No, sir.'

'It's uncivilized not to sell whisky,' Carmody said to his friends. 'The goddamn fellow is uncivilized.'

'I'm sorry, sir, but we don't have a liquor licence.'

'Yes, you *should* be sorry. If *I* did not have a liquor licence, I would be sorry as hell.'

There was a long silence on the pier. Carmody was apparently gathering his thoughts and catching his breath for a new onslaught. Luke had just noticed what Carmody was wearing.

He did not know whether the fat man's shirt carried *all* the flags and pennants in the international code, but it certainly seemed to be patterned with a great many of them. He could make out at least six different flags: Tango, Echo, Oscar, Uniform, Yankee, Foxtrot, wait, there were several more, Victor and November. He suddenly wondered if Carmody *knew* the code signals, and then wondered how he could possibly convey to a drunken sea captain the information that this town was being held by a band of armed men.

The silence lengthened ominously. He had been anxious to get rid of Carmody not three minutes ago, but now he was afraid that Carmody would leave before he could transmit a message to him. His eyes flicked again over the brightly coloured flags printed on Carmody's shirt. His mind raced through the code signals from H.O. 103, linking each flag with each remembered signal. Tango was DO NO PASS AHEAD OF ME, Echo was I AM DIRECTING MY

200

COURSE TO STARBOARD, Oscar was MAN OVER-
BOARD, Uniform was –

Uniform might do.

Uniform just might do it.

YOU ARE STANDING INTO DANGER.

But would the flag mean anything to Carmody and his
inebriated crew? And even if Carmody *did* understand it,
might he not, in his drunken state, simply shout, 'What do
you mean, I'm standing into danger?'

'Well, how about it?' Carmody said.

Wait a minute. Was Jason Trench familiar with flags and
pennants?

'He's talking to you, Mr. Costigan,' Jason said beside
him.

'How about what, sir?' Luke said.

'Do I get my whisky, or not?'

'We don't have any.'

'So I guess there's nothing to do but shove off, Mr.
Carmody,' Jason said.

'You see,' Luke said slowly, 'there are uniform
requirements for obtaining a liquor licence in this state, and
–'

'I'm not interested in the requirements for a liquor
licence,' Carmody said.

'Well, they're uniform,' Luke said.

'What?'

'Uniform,' Luke said again. 'Uniform, Mr. Carmody.'

'The goddamn man's a broken record, ' Carmody said.
'Stand by to cast off, lads.'

It happened too fast. The two drunks who were
Carmody's line handlers had the lines off and were back on
the yacht an instant before it began moving away from the
pier. 'Welcome to Costigan's Marina,' Carmody said
sourly, and one of the drunks added something obscene that
caused all the others to burst into laughter. The long blue
boat nosed out gently, and came around, and then put on a
burst of speed to leave the dock front area in a roar of
powerful engines and a spuming wash of spray, while Luke
watched helplessly.

'Nice try,' Jason said, and hit him.

The blow was unexpected. It came with the full force of Jason's arm and shoulder behind it, and it caught Luke on the bridge of the nose and sent him staggering back against one of the pilings. He put up his hands instantly, but Jason was upon him again, seizing the front of his shirt and pulling him away from the piling and then punching him furiously in the mouth once, twice, again, and saying all the time, 'You think you're playing with kids, you lousy cripple? You think you're playing with kids here?' Luke's nose was bleeding. Over and over again, his fury a monumental thing from which there was no escape, Jason's fists struck, in harsh and angry, terrible succession. Luke tried to block each subsequent battering blow, the fists striking his open palms and his wrists – heavy hammer-blows – his throat, his face again. He managed to double his left fist and threw it at Jason's chest, but Jason shrugged off the blow and bore in again savagely, his rage unfettered, his fists covered with Luke's blood now. He stopped suddenly.

He stopped with his right fist drawn back, his arm trembling, his breath hissing raggedly from between his parted lips. He stopped and looked out over the water. Luke turned and followed his gaze.

A light was blinking on the cutter.

Luke licked his lips and tasted the salt of his own blood, and began reading the message that came in short steady winks from the Coast Guard ship. He felt a sudden despair. He felt as though Jason Trench had tilted the world and everyone was sliding towards the edge of reality where they would fall off into nightmare oblivion. Out on the water the light blinked its short and frightening message.

The ship is –

Dah-dah-dah, dit-dit-dah, dit-dah-dit, dit-dit-dit.

Ours.

THE SHIP IS OURS.

12

There was a great deal of traffic at the pier.

Was some sort of naval manoeuvre in operation, was that it? Wasn't that a Navy ship out on the horizon, less than a mile off-shore?

Roger Cummings lay flat on the beach with his head raised above the dune, and tried to make out what was happening in the distance. He wished he had binoculars.

Something odd was going on, of that he was certain; and he was becoming more and more convinced that all of it was somehow linked to the man and woman who had come to the front door of the Westerfield house and tried the knob. He and Sondra had watched from the upstairs bedroom window as the man went around to the driver's side of the car and the woman got in on the side closest to the house, and then the car started, and made its way around the turnabout and went up the driveway and out of sight.

'What do you suppose *that* was all about?' he asked.

'I don't know,' Sondra said.

'You don't suppose that fellow was a hunter, do you?'

'Which fellow? Oh, you mean the one with the gun?'

'Yes.'

'He could have been.'

'Did it seem to you that he was threatening that woman in any way?'

'No. The gun wasn't even pointed at her or anything.'

'That's right,' Cummings said. 'Did you notice that?'

'They seemed very friendly, in fact,' Sondra said.

'That's what I thought. Perhaps they know Westerfield.'

'Who's Westerfield?'

'He owns this house. Myron Westerfield. Maybe they know him and dropped by to say hello.'

'Maybe. Where did you leave our car, Rog?'

'In the garage.'

'Then how would they know anybody was here?'

'They wouldn't,' Cummings said. He was frowning again. 'The odd thing about it, of course, is that *their* car was parked in the driveway at . . . what time was it, Sondra? When did I go out to take a look?'

'Oh . . . nine-thirty, ten o'clock. Around then.'

'Yes. So what took them an hour to get to the front door? *More* than an hour.'

'I don't know, Rog.' She kissed him on the cheek and said, 'Maybe they found something to do on the way.'

She looked at him then and giggled at the serious expression on his face.

'It's the rifle that bothers me,' he said.

He had left the house at two-forty, unable to sit still a moment longer, curiosity clamouring inside him. He had walked up to the main highway and then looked across to where the barricade was set across the top of the side road. The barricade was innocuous and commonplace; he associated it at once with the armed man who had come to the front door, and immediately looked upon it with dark suspicion.

Get back to the house, he warned himself.

You are Roger Cummings. Get back to the house before you find yourself in more trouble than you ever imagined.

Instead he had gone off to the right of the side road, swinging around past the barricade and into the thicket, passing behind the first house on the road and then cutting over to the beach.

Lying at the far end of the beach, he could see the maroon-and-black cabin cruiser coming from the ship directly to the pier. He could not tell how many men were aboard the cruiser, or how many men in blue – all carrying weapons – were waiting on the dock. There seemed to be at least a half-dozen. They climbed aboard the cruiser as soon as it reached the dock. The moment they were loaded, the boat pulled out again. Cummings watched it moving out to the ship. It stayed alongside for perhaps ten minutes, and then started back towards shore again.

The town seemed silent and deserted except for the activity at the pier, the boat coming in from the ship out there, more men in blue massing on the waterfront.

Weren't there any people in this town?'

Where are all the people? he wondered.

Cautiously he crawled up the beach and closer to the pier. Crouching behind an empty oil barrel, he watched the activity there unobserved. It was entirely possible, he supposed, that the Navy was conducting some sort of manoeuvres in the area. He glanced out over the water to where the ship sat in pale silhouette and saw the marking W 017 on her bow and wondered what kind of Navy vessel she was, and why she was in these waters. The nature of the manoeuvres puzzled him, too, because he could not imagine any naval games that would include a young man escorting a woman to the front door of a civilian's home, unless the woman was a Navy nurse, was that possible? She had, after all, been wearing white. But no hat. Didn't nurses always wear hats? Didn't Navy nurses have a little white hat with the gold stripe or stripes of their rank showing on it?

He crouched behind his oil barrel, confused, and tried to figure out the pattern of the manoeuvres. He could see the pier clearly now, could see the cabin cruiser tied there, could even read the name lettered across her transom, *The Golden Fleece*. There was a very fat man in khaki standing on the pier together with four other men in dungarees and chambray shirts, all of whom were armed. There were six men standing in the cockpit of the cruiser. One of them was holding a gun in his hand and the other five were standing with their hands clasped on the tops of their heads. All of them were dressed in the work clothes of Navy enlisted men, which made very little sense to Cummings unless the men in the boat were wearing little tags or buttons that distinguished the blue team from the red team, something like that. Otherwise, why would one enlisted man be pointing a gun at five other enlisted men who had their hands on their heads, while still more men waited on the dock?

The men in the boat were coming ashore now.

The one with the gun pointed it in Cummings' direction. Cummings immediately ducked his head down below the rim of the oil barrel and then realized the man was only indicating a long building forward of the pier. The building was made of corrugated metal. It seemed to have only one door and no windows, some sort of storage locker, he imagined. The men with their hands on their heads began marching towards the building, and a man with a rifle came out of the adjacent building to lead them away.

'You want to bring your men aboard, Fatboy?' a voice on the boat said. Cummings could not see who had spoken; the voice had come from inside the wheelhouse. The one called Fatboy nodded quickly and led his men into the idling boat. As the boat pulled away, another group of men moved on to the pier, this time led by a man who had pale white skin and jet-black hair. Cummings looked toward the storage locker in time to see the single door being slammed shut, a padlock being bolted into place. The man with the rifle stationed himself outside the door.

Out on the water *The Golden Fleece* sped towards the ship on the horizon. Cummings, frowning, watched it.

They had gone through one of the bottles of bourbon and opened the next, and now they lay on the bed drinking from two white coffee mugs they had found on Bobby's shelf next to the picture of Ava Gardner. There was no ice in the mugs, and no water, just straight bourbon, and the cups were filled almost to the brim. They were in a silly giggly mood, both naked, Ginny toying with the crisp blond hair on Willy's chest, and Willy lying with the back of his head between her breasts, her arms around him, giggling and trying to sip at the bourbon without spilling it all over himself. He managed to get a dribble of whisky down his throat and then choked on it, and sat up and began giggling again and Ginny said, 'You're the slobbiest man I know.'

206

'You're the sexiest woman I know,' he said, and rolled over and kissed her nipples and then made a ravenous slurping sound and bent swiftly to lick her navel. He burst out laughing.

'This's a massive navel operation,' he said.

'What?' she said, laughing. 'What do you mean?'

'This,' he said, and he put his tongue in her navel again and then reached for his coffee mug and held it high, spilling some of the bourbon on to his wrist. 'Here is to Jason Trench's massive naval operation,' he shouted. 'Did you ever have a massive navel operation?'

'Never,' she said, and giggled and picked up her own mug. 'Listen, do we have to have her staring at us?'

'Who?'

'Ave Gabor there, whatever her name is.'

'Gardner,' Willy said.

'Yeah.'

'We don't need her.' He moved toward the picture and placed his forefinger on the movie star's left breast with delicate precision and said to the photograph, 'Miss Gardener, have you ever had a massive navel operation? No,' he answered himself. 'I didn't think you did,' and tore the picture from the wall. 'There. No more Peepy Toms,' he said, and burst out laughing again. 'What it is, it's like a massive hernia operation,' he said and slapped his naked thigh and drank some more bourbon and said, 'Ginny, honey, let's do it again.'

'Let's do what again?' she said.

'Let's go shoot that guy.'

'What guy?'

'Sonabitch who wouldn't listen to me.'

'Let's shoot all the sonabitches who won't listen to you,' Ginny said.

'Well, that's a whole hell of a lot of people,' Willy said, giggling. 'There's fifty-five of them alone on that ship out there, *none* of them listening to me. We can't go shooting everybody don't want to listen to me, now can we?'

'Sure, we can, why not? What ship out where?'

'The masshole navel operation,' Willy said, and began

laughing again. 'Jason's asshole operation,' he said, and nearly choked. 'Oh my God, he's got fifty-five men out there who're taking orders from a preggen woman, how about that?'

'What? Who?' Ginny said, and laughed and threw one leg over his thigh and began moving against him rhythmically and without passion, almost as a reflex action.

'Out there,' he said, pointing to where Ava Gardner's picture had been. 'That's where the ship is. And what Jason's doing is taking 'em off, you see? Except engineers and such. You see?'

'Sure,' Ginny said.

'What, then?'

'What do you mean?'

'What is it?'

'What is what?'

'What he's doing?'

'He's taking them off.'

'Off what?' Willy asked.

'His bellybutton,' Ginny said, and they both burst out laughing.

'The cutter!' Willy said.

'What cutter?'

'The Coast Guard cutter. The *Mercury*.'

'Oh.'

'That's right,' Willy said.

'I say three cheers,' Ginny said.

'For what?'

'For Jonas.'

'Jason.'

'That's right.'

'Why?'

'He brought you here to love me,' Ginny said.

'That's what he did, that li'l sweetheart,' Willy said, and began giggling into Ginny's collarbone. 'Now, listen.'

'I'm listening.'

'Fifty-five men on that cutter, you hear?'

'I hear.'

'He's bringing almost all of them here, putting them in the storage locker.'

His eyes had narrowed, his voice had lowered. Ginny squinted her eyes in imitation and moved closer to him.

'But you know what?'

'What?' Ginny said.

'He's sending twenty-five of *us* out there!'

'Out where?'

'To the cutter. *On* the cutter.'

'What for?'

'To *run* it. To *drive* it. To, you know, make it *go*.'

'Can't the Coast Guard make it go?'

'Sure, honey,' Willy said. 'But not where Jason *wants* it to go.'

'Well, where does Jason want it to go?'

'Ah-ha,' Willy said. 'That's a secret.'

'Oh, you got secrets from me, huh?' she said, and teasingly tweaked his nose and then rolled into his lap and pulled her face back some three inches from his and pursed her lips and kissed him. 'Where's Jason gonna go, huh?' she said. 'Where's he gonna go? Tell me or I'll kiss you to death.' He giggled and she kissed his eyes and his mouth and his nose again. 'Huh? Where?'

Laughing, Willy said, 'It's a secret.'

'Where?' she said. 'Huh? Where? Huh? Huh?'

It was possible, of course, that the men moving out towards that ship were not bona fide United States sailors. Yes, that was possible, Cummings thought. If this were a real naval manoeuvre, then only Naval boats would be in use. That maroon-and-black cabin-cruiser was definitely not a Navy boat, and neither was the white Chris-Craft that had come in from the ship and was now unloading more men at the pier.

Prisoners.

Yes.

That was the accurate word.

Those men coming onto the dock with their hands on

their heads were prisoners, and they would be taken to the storage locker to join the others there under lock and key.

Cummings could hear muffled voices, 'Move along, let's keep it moving,' could see brass shining on khaki collars—some of the prisoners were officers, then – could hear a man shouting, 'Goody, let's move half those men out of the houses now,' and then heard the answering 'Right, Jase!' and the sound of feet clattering on the wooden dock. The men from the ship were moving towards the storage locker. 'How many more are on the cutter?' someone asked, and Cummings could not hear the reply, but he understood now that the ship out there was a Coast Guard vessel, and then he heard a phone ringing in one of the houses on the waterfront. He glanced over his shoulder, trying to locate the house. He thought the ringing sound was coming from the first house on the beach, more voices, the sound of an engine idling, the clattering noise that could come only from weapons, a door opening; he turned his head. A man with a rifle was coming out of the back door of the first house. Before the door closed, Cummings could see that another armed man was still in the house. The first man ran towards the pier, his rifle at port arms, and suddenly another phone was ringing in another house, another door was opening, another lone man with a rifle stepped out and moved swiftly and silently towards the waiting white Chris-Craft at the pier's end. The door to the storage locker slammed shut, the loud click of the padlock snapped on to the air, another telephone was ringing.

'Enjoying yourself, mister?' a voice said.

Marvin watched as they brought the stranger into the repair shop and threw him headlong across the floor, near where Costigan was sitting beside Samantha. They were behaving differently now, these men. It had begun, he supposed, when they brought Costigan back not more than a half-hour ago, his nose bleeding, his left eye squinted shut, his clothes stained with grease. A tenseness had come into the shop with his return. Harry had begun pacing the room with long impatient strides. Clyde, silent and lackadaisical before, had suddenly become alert and edgy. The same knife-edged tautness was apparent in the manner of the men who opened the door now, throwing the stranger in onto the floor. Marvin, watching them, sensing their tenseness, had the feeling that something outside was reaching a climax and that once the climax had passed, his life would be in real danger. He looked at the man on the floor. The right side of his face was bruised and swollen as though he had been hit once, sharply, with something blunt. On the other side of the room Harry held a hurried, whispered conversation with the two men who had brought the man in, and then nodded and said good-bye to them as they walked out. He went over to the man and stood beside him spread-legged, almost straddling him.

'What's your name?' he said.

The man did not answer.

Marvin, watching the pair, suddenly realized that Harry had his back to him. He almost reached for the bottle of thinner on the shelves, and then realized that Clyde was sitting on the workbench and that any move would be seen by him immediately.

'I said what's your name, mister?' Harry said.

'What have you done?' the man asked suddenly. 'Hijacked a Coast Guard cutter?'

Harry turned toward Clyde quickly, his eyes opening in surprise. Clyde got off the bench and moved towards where the man was sitting on the floor, standing opposite Harry so that one of them was on either side of the man. Marvin kept watching them carefully. Harry's back was still to him. Clyde was only half turned away from him.

'You must've seen quite a little bit out there on the beach, huh, mister?' Harry said.

'I saw enough.'

'What's your name?' Harry said.

Again the man would not answer.

'Get his wallet,' Harry said to Clyde.

'Cummings,' the man said. And then, very quickly, so quickly that Marvin knew at once he was lying, the man said, 'David Cummings.'

211

'Sometimes, Mr. Cummings, it ain't healthy to see too much.'

'Sure, listen to the gangsters,' Tannenbaum said. 'Talk from gangster pictures with James Cagney.'

'Shut up, Doc,' Harry said. 'Just what'd you see out there, Mr. Cummings?'

'What do you want with that cutter?' Cummings asked, ignoring the question.

'Clyde,' Harry said.

Clyde took two steps toward Cummings, his hand going up high over his head at the same time, and then descending in a long swinging arc that seemed almost a part of his forward momentum. Marvin, watching Clyde, frightened and fascinated, almost missed his opportunity to grab the half-gallon of thinner. He saw Cummings' head snap back, and he heard Cummings grunt in pain, and then suddenly realized that Clyde's back was to him. Quickly he slid to the end of the bench, rose, turned, grabbed a bottle from the shelf, put it down behind the bench, sat, and then turned towards the three men again, his heart pounding. They had not seen him.

He realized all at once how idoitic his sudden move had been. They could have turned at any instant. They would have beaten him up the way they had Costigan, who sat now with a bloody handkerchief to his nose, the way they were doing with this new man Cummings.

'Well?' Harry said.

Cummings got to his feet. 'Let's get something straight here,' he said.

'Only thing we want to get straight is –'

'No, you just –'

'– what you saw outside.'

'– listen to me a minute.'

The men stood facing each other.

'Mister,' Harry said, 'we're gonna have to hurt you.'

'Will that change what I saw outside?'

Harry grinned. 'Clyde, I think you'd better –'

Cummings took a step backwards and clenched his fist. 'This time I'm ready for him,' he said.

'You've got to be kidding,' Clyde said.

'This time, you'd better kill me.'

'How brave you gonna be when he hits you with that gun butt?' Harry said.

'Ask him to try it.'

'Mr. Cummings,' Harry said, 'we've got nothing to lose.'

'Then you *know* how serious this is.'

'How serious *what* is?' Clyde said.

'The hijacking of a government vessel.'

'Is that what we did, Mr. Cummings?'

'They're comedians, mister,' Tannenbaum said. 'They crack jokes from vaudeville.'

'Pop, keep quiet,' Marvin said, and Harry turned towards him, and fear crackled into his skull. Could he see the bottle of thinner behind the bench? Was the bottle showing?

'What's the penalty?' Clyde asked, grinning.

'What do you mean?' Cummings said. 'Penalty?'

'For hijacking.'

'I'm not sure.'

'Are you a lawyer?'

'Yes.'

'Then what's the penalty? Ten years? Twenty? Life? The electric chair? What?'

'I don't know. Hijacking a cutter isn't exactly an everyday occurrence.'

'Is that right? You hear that, Harry? I thought cutters *did* get hijacked every day. You mean they don't? Tch, tch.'

'If you want my opinion,' Cummings said, 'I think you ought to go to whoever's in charge of this little adventure, and ask him to forget it. That's my opinion. Get off that ship and out of this town before you're all in more trouble than you ever imagined.'

'Us?' Clyde said, and burst out laughing. 'In trouble? Man, we've been in trouble since six o'clock this morning.'

'What are you doing here anyway?' Bobby Colmore said suddenly. 'Why'd you come here?'

'To hijack a cutter,' Clyde answered immediately.

213

'The cutter's out on the water,' Costigan said. 'Why do you need the town?'

'How's your nose, Mr. Costigan?' Clyde said.

'My nose is fine. Why do you need the town?'

'Tell him, Harry.'

'I'm telling him nothing, Clyde. You want my advice, you better shut up right now.'

'Why? What's the matter?'

'Just cool it, that's all.'

'Why won't you let him talk?' Amos said.

'Sure, Harry, why won't you let me –'

'Clyde, shut up!' Harry shouted. He jerked his rifle up. 'Now, shut up. I mean it, man. I mean it. One more word –'

'Hey, come on,' Clyde said, and grinned.

'Man, you say one more word, and you're dead, man. I mean it.'

Clyde flushed crimson, and then caught his breath, nodded, and said, 'Sure. Take it easy.'

'How come he ain't laughing now?' Amos said.

Harry still had not lowered the rifle. It was pointed at Clyde's middle. Clyde, his face red, kept staring at the muzzle of the gun.

'I thought he laughed at just about everything you said. I thought you got along just like two brothers,' Amos said.

'We get along fine,' Harry answered, not taking his eyes from Clyde. Quickly he lowered the rifle. Clyde nodded again, and then walked directly past Harry without looking at him. He boosted himself on to the workbench, sat, and put the rifle across his lap. He closed his eyes at once, as though he were enormously weary after a long, gruelling ordeal.

'Just what did you see out there?' Costigan asked Cummings.

'Luke, don't –' Samantha began.

'I want to know,' he said.

'Go ahead, tell him,' Clyde said, his eyes shut.

Cummings hesitated a moment. Sighing, he said. 'I saw them moving armed men out to that cutter. And bringing men here, locking them up in the other building.'

214

'The storage locker?'

'If that's what it is. The one without any windows.'

'Then that's why they needed the town,' Costigan said. 'So they'd have a place to bring that cutter in and transfer their men to it.'

'But *why?*' Tannenbaum said, and turned to Clyde. 'Why are you stealing a boat? For scrap iron? For what?'

'For war,' Clyde said, his eyes still shut.

There was, for the space of a heartbeat, silence in the shop. Clyde's words hung without malice, almost without meaning, in the empty stillness. The silence seemed longer than it actually was. Clyde did not move from the bench. He kept leaning back against the wall with his eyes closed and a faint smile on his face as the silence turned in upon itself, second lengthening into second after second after second, all compressed and compacted into a split instant.

'What do you mean?' Cummings asked.

'Clyde –'

'Keep quiet, Harry. They know most of it already!'

'They don't know –'

'What is it?' Costigan said. 'Another –'

'Shut up, all of you!'

'Talk, Costigan.'

'No, never mind.'

Silence again. Marvin, his mind working frantically, could not for the life of him imagine what Costigan had been about to say. And what had Clyde meant? What the hell was a Coast Guard cutter? It was just a little boat, wasn't it? Like a pleasure boat?

'Well?' Clyde said. His eyes were still shut. He was not looking at anyone in the room, but Marvin knew unmistakably that he was talking to Costigan.

'Well?' he said again.

'You'll never make it,' Costigan said.

'No?'

'Never. She's too small a ship.'

'She's big enough.'

Costigan was shaking his head. 'What has she got aboard her? Seventy-five men? A hundred men?'

'*Fifty*-five,' Clyde said. 'Less when we get through with her.'

'And what's your armament? A three-inch gun on the bow?'

'That's all.'

'What do you hope to do with that?'

'Just what we have to do.'

'It'll be another disaster,' Costigan said. 'Just like the Bay of Pigs. Go tell Trench to forget it.'

Clyde shook his head. 'Too much at stake.'

'Like what?'

'The future.'

'Of what? Cuba?'

'Of the hemisphere.'

'Sure,' Costigan said. 'You're going to change the situation with a two-bit gunboat and a handful of men. Forget it.'

'We're going to change the situation by steaming straight into Havana Harbour, and –'

'Sure, past the Cuban radar –'

'– shelling the city.'

'– and past the Cuban torpedo boats and jets. You've got one hell of a chance to succeed.'

'Are you serious about this?' Cummings asked suddenly.

'The man wants to know if we're serious. Tell him, Harry.'

'I ain't in this,' Harry said. 'When Jason asks about this, I had no part of it.'

'Yes, we're serious, goddamn you,' Clyde said.

'You're going to invade Cuba?'

'Did I say that?'

'It sounded to me –'

'Nobody said anything about invading Cuba.'

'You said you were going to shell the city.'

'We're sure going to try.'

'The island is ringed with radar,' Costigan said. 'You won't get within fifty miles of it.'

'That's more'n halfway there, ain't it?' Clyde said, and grinned.

'You can't shell Havana from fifty miles out in the Caribbean.'

'I think we might get just a bit closer than that,' Clyde said.

'They'll still know you're on the way. Your little raid –'

'This isn't a raid.'

'It's not an invasion, and it's not a raid,' Tannenbaum said. 'So what is it?'

'Herbert, keep out,' Rachel said.

'Never mind,' he answered.

'Maybe it's both a raid *and* an invasion,' Clyde said. His smile widened. 'Or maybe it's neither.'

'Riddles,' Tannenbaum said.

'No riddles, Grandpa.'

'I'm getting Jason,' Harry said, and started for the door.

'Hold it!'

'Listen, Clyde –'

'You listen to *me!*'

'Jason said –'

'What am I doing to Jason?'

'You got no call to –'

'How am I hurting Jason, huh? What am I doing that's so terrible, huh?'

'You know what –'

'Well, I'm tired of sitting here on my behind! Why should Jason have all the fun!'

'The fun?' Harry said, astonished.

'Yes, the fun, the *fun!* We sit here like a pair of nursemaids while he –'

'Fun?' Harry said again.

'Why doesn't he take *all* of us with him?'

'Somebody has to stay here, you know that.'

'What for?'

'To keep these people here.'

'*Kill* the goddamn people,' Clyde said. 'Do it now! Why wait?'

'Gangsters,' Tannenbaum said. 'They grab a boat, they talk about kill –'

'A *cutter*, Grandpa,' Clyde said. 'A cutter is what we grabbed. Not a boat.'

'You'll never make it,' Costigan said again. 'There are dozens of Navy ships between here and Cuba. The United States doesn't *want* an invasion. Those ships'll –'

'We know all about the dozens of Navy ships between here and Cuba. You think any Navy ship is going to challenge a Coast Guard cutter answering a distress call?'

'Who'll buy that?'

'Who won't? A few hours after the *Mercury* steams out of here, she'll radio Miami and say she's answering an SOS about fifty miles north-west of Havana.'

'Miami won't believe it,' Costigan said.

'Why not?'

'They've got planes in the air. They'll send one down to check.'

'You're assuming Miami *knows* the cutter is in our hands, which Miami doesn't. Miami simply thinks the captain of one of her ships is radioing to say he's answering an SOS from –'

'That Miami never heard?'

'It happens all the time,' Clyde said. 'Radio signals are unpredictable.'

'They'd *still* send the plane down.'

'No. All the planes are back at Dinner Key by sundown.'

The room was silent for a moment. Costigan frowned, and Samantha suddenly covered his hand with her own.

'Those Navy destroyers would challenge her,' Cummings said.

'Why should they? They know there are Coast Guard ships on patrol between here and Cuba. They wouldn't give her a second thought. But even if they did, she'd say she was answering a distress call. Search and rescue is the Coast Guard's job – *not* the Navy's.'

'The cutter simply lies to everybody, is that it?'

'That's it.'

'There are some people she can't lie to,' Costigan said.

'Who?'

'The men on the Cuban patrol boats.'

'She won't lie to them.'

'She'll just tell them she's heading for Havana, huh? She'll –'

'No. She'll just open fire on them.'

'That'd bring out the jets,' Costigan said. 'That'd be the end of your little party.'

'No. That'd be the *beginning* of our little party.'

'They'd blow you right out of the water,' Cummings said.

'Yes.'

'What . . .?'

'They'll blow us right out of the water,' Clyde said. 'They'll blow a United States Coast Guard cutter out of the water.' He smiled. 'That's an act of war, isn't it?' he asked softly.

13

They'll have to kill everyone here, Luke thought.

If they don't, their suicidal plan is in danger of collapsing.

Their only hope is that the United States and the world will believe a Coast Guard cutter has been attacked and sunk by Cuban forces while answering a distress call. If the masquerade is less than complete, if the tiniest doubt exists about the genuineness of the cutter or the real identity of the men aboard her, the plan will immediately collapse.

Luke could see no possibility of anything going wrong out there on the water; the thing had been planned too carefully for that. They had captured Ocho Puertos and brought the cutter here, they were moving the sailors into the storage locker and putting their own men aboard, they knew there would be no patrol planes flying after dark. They also knew that the danger of the Navy's stopping them was practically nonexistent. And even if they were challenged, they had a cover story ready: they were answering a distress call. So they would head for Cuba, and they would fire on the first thing they saw, torpedo boat or jet aeroplane, or Havana itself. When the counter-attack came, they would radio Miami to say they were being fired upon by Cubans without provocation, and then they would radio to say they were being *sunk* by Cubans. The Cubans, of course, would protest that the cutter had opened fire first – but neither the United States nor the world would believe them.

The only hitch was Ocho Puertos.

In Ocho Puertos there were people who had been held captive since dawn, and who now knew about the plan. In Ocho Puertos there were sailors who had been moved from the cutter, and who knew the ship had been taken by force.

In Ocho Puertos there were men and women who could immediately squelch the elaborate lie off the shores of Cuba.

They would have to kill everyone in town before they left.

They would undoubtedly be listening for word on the radio, oh yes, the news would go out at once, the world would know in an instant what had happened out there in the Caribbean. And presuming everything had gone as planned, presuming the cutter and the men who had gone down with her were accepted as genuine, presuming the Cuban attack clearly seemed an overt act of aggression, then the men left behind here in town would have to wipe out all traces of themselves. They would strip their Coast Guard prisoners of clothes and identification, they would kill everyone in town, and then they would leave. Wasn't that what Clyde had said? 'Kill the goddamn people. Kill them now. Why wait?' Yes, and while the police tried to solve a puzzling and senseless mass murder on a tiny key called Ocho Puertos, the government of the United States would either immediately retaliate against Cuba with rockets and bombs, or else go through the more formal process of declaring war first. Either way, Jason Trench would have accomplished his goal.

It'll never work, Cummings thought.

We've had American aircraft shot down before, we've had pilots captured, we've had truckfuls of men detained at checkpoints, we've even had private citizens held prisoner behind the Curtain. None of these had ever led to even a limited war. This was a little different, of course; this was a little closer to American shores. And it did not involve an individual person or a small group of persons; it involved fifty-five men, which was almost a quarter of an Army company, mmmm. But even so, there wasn't the slightest possibility that America would respond to such an attack by declaring war. We were too sensible for that, we knew the awesome consequences, we would prefer sacrificing the ship and the men if it meant preserving the peace.

We would undoubtedly take it to the United Nations.

We would set a pattern for the rest of the world. We would maintain that even in the face of a ruthless, unprovoked act of aggression, we were nonetheless refusing to retaliate with our terrible, swift power. Instead, we were taking the matter to the world organization, where we had every reason to believe it would be settled. We would ask reparation from Cuba, of course, and then we would –

Oh yes, the newspapers would have a field day with that. What kind of reparation do you ask for fifty-five men dead or crippled, all or any part of them? How do you explain reparation to wives and mothers and children? Oh yes, that would be a sweet one for the yellow journalists. And there were men on Capitol Hill who would argue, perhaps rightfully, that no amount of reparation could restore our image in the eyes of the world if we let this unprovoked and unwarranted attack go unanswered. These men would leap upon the sinking of the cutter as an excuse for the action they had been demanding all along. They would seize upon the attack as an opportunity to restage the Bay of Pigs blunder, invade Cuba in force this time, eliminate her threat in the Western Hemisphere once and for all.

But of course the cooler heads would insist that the world organization be the arbiter. Let the United Nations try the case; if necessary, let the United Nations send a force in to disarm Cuba and remove any further possibility of wanton –

There were still Russians on the island.

He could not remember a single instance where the U.N. had forcibly disarmed a member nation.

If they tried it with Cuba, there would be a global war.

There were men in Washington who would argue that if the possibility of war existed either way, why waste lives? Push the buttons, send the rockets, get rid of the goddamn threat, do it now! They've sunk one of our ships! What do we have to do – wait until they wade ashore in Miami?

It could work, Cummings thought. Jason Trench could get the war he wanted.

No, Cummings thought. This is absurd. This entire

thing is absurd. There were fanatics in the world, yes, that was true. But authority had an uncanny knack of stopping fanatics before they ever carried out their plans. In a world of extremes, the extremists rarely were permitted to act. There was talk, yes, always talk. Talk on street corners and in assembly halls, heated oratory pouring from the lips of rabble-rousers, hatred shaped to fit the mould of democracy. In a free nation you can speak your mind, that is an inalienable right, stand on your soapbox and advocate the overthrow of a nation – but do not move into action. If you do, if you are foolish enough to translate your hatred, right or left, into movement, you are doomed. The Marines will always arrive just in the nick of time to foil your plot, whatever it may be.

It was difficult to think beyond this room. Beyond this room there was a cutter loading men dressed in the uniforms of Coast Guard sailors, men who would take that ship into Cuban waters and open fire on Cuban property in the hope they would be sunk. Beyond this room there were fanatics who had moved beyond their own rhetoric into sudden and decisive action.

I can stop them, Cummings thought.

I could make one phone call, just one; they would believe me, they would move immediately to –

He suddenly remembered that among the other dangers lurking beyond this room was a twenty-year-old girl in a house across the road, and she was his mistress. Even if he *could* get to a telephone, which was doubtful, he would have to say where he was; he would have to tell them the jumping-off spot for Jason Trench's plan was a town called Ocho Puertos in the Florida Keys.

For perhaps the first time in his life, Roger Cummings wondered if the Marines would indeed arrive.

The two highway patrolmen watched the car as it came out of the water, choked with grass, dripping, the winch tugging it reluctantly out of the mud. They were both big men, and the day was warm, and they were sweating across the fronts and under the arms of their tan uniform shirts.

The first patrolman was named Oscar, and his partner's name was Frank, and they kept making hand signals to the winch operator in the cab of the truck, until finally the patrol car was on dry ground.

'It's empty,' Oscar said.

'Yeah,' Frank answered.

Oscar opened the door on the driver's side, and looked in. A trooper's hat was resting on the front seat. He picked it up and studied the sweatband. The name R. HOGAN was stamped into the leather.

'It's Ronnie's car, all right,' Oscar said.

'What's that on the crown of the hat there?' Frank said.

'Huh? Where do you . . . oh.'

Both men stared at the hat.

'It's blood,' Oscar said.

'Yeah,' Frank answered.

'There's the keys, right there in the dash,' Oscar said.

'Mmm.'

Frank took the keys out of the ignition slot. He held them on the palm of his hand for a moment, looking down at them silently. Then he said, 'I reckon we'd better take a look in the trunk.'

They're not figuring on annihilation, Marvin thought. That's not in their plan at all. They may have to sacrifice the handful of men who are taking the ship down to Cuba, yes, but not because they expect America to be wiped out. On the contrary. They're hoping there will be swift and sudden reprisal from us, a counter-attack that will destroy Cuba's potential in this hemisphere. They are gambling that Russia will not step into this thing at all – why should she? Cuba will be labelled the aggressor, the nation that sank a ship answering an SOS. Why should Russia risk adverse world opinion by keeping her promise to a small country that has already been successfully invaded?

Your plan sounds good, Marvin thought. I like it, Jason, I'm almost tempted. You are going to sacrifice a small Coast Guard ship that doesn't even belong to you, plus two or three dozen men, but you're going to get Cuba in return.

That sounds like a good deal, a bargain for fanatics. The trouble with fanatics, of course, is that they never realize there are *other* fanatics in the world. What you're perfectly willing to assume, Jason, is that we will not risk nuclear warfare, but will instead fight a limited war with conventional arms. You are ready to assume – because it fits your plans – that Russia will stay out of it. But suppose she doesn't? Suppose she decides to push the retaliation button, what then, Jason?

You almost had me.

I can be had, you know.

If you'd only held out a realistic war to me, if you'd only extended a uniform glittering with brass, and a rifle I could shoot with impunity; if you'd offered me French girls with their eager pouting mouths or subjugated Russian peasant women obediently opening strong meaty thighs, or slender starving Chinese girls in slit skirts begging mercy from the American conqueror; if you'd offered me the spoils of war and the glamour of war, and the thrill of legal murder, rape and pillage; if you'd offered me all these things, Jason Trench, I would have walked across this room and shaken hands with your henchmen there, and joined your cause. I would have, I swear it. I would have kicked Selma in the ass and gone off to pick up glory like foreign coins at my feet. I would have done that.

But you offer possible ashes in my mouth; you offer possible blinding demolition and extinction, not escape. War is old-fashioned now, I guess. The killers have no place to go any more, except into the streets. Or, perhaps, on suicidal missions to Cuba to trigger what could become a holocaust.

If it's fire you wish, Jason Trench, I can accommodate you.

The radioman's name was Evan Peters, and he had relieved the Miami watch at 1545, and was now filing messages from the watch before. Big Chief Osama, who had stayed on to have a cup of coffee with the relieving watch section, was sitting at the desk alongside Peters, who was sorting and collating the sheaf of messages preparatory to putting them in their proper cabinets.

'I'm supposed to see this girl tonight,' Osama said, sipping his coffee. 'She says she's a Russian countess. You believe it?'

'I don't know.'

'She's got red hair. You think there's such a thing as a red-headed Russian?'

'Sure, there must be plenty of them,' Peters said.

'Why would a Russian countess want to go out with an Indian?'

'Why don't you ask her?'

'I did.'

'What'd she say?'

'She said we were both in the same fix. She lost everything when her parents got killed in the revolution, and I lost everything when the United States stuck my tribe on a reservation. What do you think of that?'

'I don't know,' Peters said. 'What do you think?'

'I think she's full of crap.'

'Maybe she's a spy,' Peters said.

'What do you mean?'

'A secret agent. She knows you work here in Search and Rescue, and she's trying to get information out of you.'

'Yeah, I'll give her some information, all right,' Osama said, and burst out laughing. He lifted his coffee cup, drained it, put it down on the desktop again, and rose. He stretched his arms towards the ceiling, laughed again, and said, 'I'll give her some fine information, all right.' Laughing, he took his hat from where it was resting on one of the cabinets, winked at Peters, said, 'Take it easy, kid,' and walked out of the message centre. Outside, Peters could hear him telling Mr. Bordigian that he had a date with a Russian spy, would Mr. Bordigian recommend him for a commission if he promised not to give her any secrets? Mr. Bordigian laughed, and the Chief laughed with him and even Peters, sorting his messages, was forced to smile a little.

226

The smile dropped from his mouth when he saw the word ZUG on messages from the *Mercury*.

He separated the message from the others in the pile, and read it over carefully:

```
P 061845Z
FM CGC MERCURY
TO CCGSEVEN
INFO CGAS MIAMI
GR 33
BT

ZUG
1. C/C GOLDEN FLEECE IN TOW.
2. PASSENGERS ABOARD MERCURY. WOMAN
PREGNANT AND IN NEED OF MEDICAL ASSIST-
ANCE. HELICOPTER UNNECESSARY.
3. PROCEEDING BEST POSSIBLE SPEED NEAREST
PORT.
4. CG 7272 RESUMING PATROL.

BT
```

Peters had no prior knowledge of anything that had happened during the noon watch, but the message in his hands told him a great deal. It had been sent from the *Mercury* at 1945 ZULU, which was 1845 Greenwich Mean Time or 1345 Eastern Standard Time. It had been sent to the commander of Coast Guard District Seven, with a copy of the message going to the Miami Air Station for information. The *Merc* had either intercepted or gone to the assistance of a cabin cruiser called *The Golden Fleece* and the boat was now in tow, with her passengers aboard the cutter. One of the passengers was a pregnant woman who was in need of –

But why the ZUG?

Peters read the message again. He knew that ZUG meant No or Negative, and he couldn't understand how anyone could have made a mistake like that, preceding the entire text of a message with the word No. Unless, of course, it wasn't a mistake, in which case the ZUG was a part of the message itself.

ZUG, Peters thought.

No.

Negative.

No what?

Negative what?

Negative everything following the ZUG?

Peters lighted a cigarette and debated bringing the message to the attention of Mr. Bordigian outside.

If the fire comes, Amos thought, we'll all be black. We'll all get roasted in that two, three seconds it takes for the big bomb to do it, that's it, man, zero. Black zero. We'll all be laying there on the ground and anybody comes along to take a look at us, he won't know if we coloured or white because we'll all be roasted the same. Governor Wallace up there, he's gonna be laying right next to some big black-ass nigger, and ain't nobody gonna be able to tell them apart. Jason Trench, he gonna bring true democracy to America at last. After a hundred years of arguing, Jason Trench is finally gonna end all the discussion. He's gonna take his boat down to Cuba and get it sunk, and then we'll send up our rockets and they'll send back their rockets, and black men and white men'll lay on the ground to-gether roasted like pigs. They'll be American whitemen-blackmen, and Russian whitemen-blackmen, and even Chinese yellowmen-blackmen, the whole damn world's gonna be black, all because of Jason Trench, he is cer-tainly the saviour of the poor coloured folk, amen. Only thing is, Jason, I ain't got a hankering to wake up dead in the morning, even if it means at long last I can wake up alongside some white American woman. Won't do me any good if she's laying there roasted, now, will it, since then she'd be just as black as I am? Everybody *knows* a nigger ain't got nothing on his mind but banging some white woman, so what good is a white woman who's black? And besides, what good is a coloured man who's dead?

Now, that's the thing, Jason. That's the little clause there. That's the fine print, man. You ain't giving me nothing, don't you see? You saying to me, man, come on, in the morning you going to be equal with everybody in the entire world, everybody gonna be black like you. Only trouble is everybody also gonna be *dead* like you. But never mind that, you want liberty and equality, don't you, man?

Jason, I want liberty and equality.

My mother used to say, Amos, you got to go to college. I used to say, Yes, Mom. She used to say, Amos, you got to better yourself. I used to say, Yes, Mom. She used to tell me, Amos, this a white world and you got to prepare yourself for it, you got to work hard, you got to study, you got to be *somebody*.

I used to say, Yes, Mom.

Someday, Jason, I'm gonna stop hating white men, and I'm gonna stop hating white niggers like Harry, maybe someday. But being dead ain't the way to do it. When I'm dead, it'll be too late to stop hating, and too late to begin loving, it'll be too goddamn late.

I wish I could stop you, Amos thought.

I wish I was somebody.

AND POSSIBLE IDENTIFICATION MIAMI MORTU-ARY XXX REQUEST INFO IN RELATION BURG-LARY SEPTEMBER 27 XXXX   XXXXX

                                        XXXXX
INFO
XXXX ALL CARS ALL CARS FLORIDA KEYS AND MIAMI AREA XXX MIAMI AREA XXX BE ON LOOKOUT MAN OR MEN BELIEVED ARMED AND DANGEROUS WANTED IN DUAL GUNSHOT SLAYING FLORIDA STATE HIGHWAY PATROLMEN HOGAN AND DI PIETRO TODAY OCTOBER 6 XXXXXX BODIES FOUND TRUNK
PATROL CAR LONG BEACH ROAD BIG PINE KEY FOUR PM EST XXXXXXXX BALLISTICS REPORT

FORTHCOMING POSSIBLE MURDER WEAPON
THIRTY EIGHT CALIBRE REVOLVER XX TYRE
TRACKS SCENE OF CRIME INDICATE SUSPECTS
DRIVING XXXXXXXX BE ADVISED NO ROAD-
BLOCKS KEY WEST TO MIAMI SUGGEST KEY BY
KEY SEARCH AND INTERROGATION XXXXXX
REPORT ALL INFO HQ COMMAND XXXXXX
XXXXXX
OCTOBER 6 GENERAL ALARM JUVENILE FEMALE
AGE FIFTEEN FIVE FEET SEVEN AND ONE HALF
INCHES ONE HUNDRED TWENTY FIVE POUNDS
LAST SEEN WEARING A

Traitors, Tannenbaum thought; they are traitors.

They have come here to murder reason; we cannot let them do it. They have come here to make a war, God forbid; we cannot let them do it. Here in this room, we must stop them before it is too late. Here in this room, these people, we must rise up and stop them.

In Nazi Germany they did not rise up until it was too late. Now, in the town where my father was born, there are only seventeen Jews. Half of them are very old men who are dying. The Jews of the world are all either dead or dying because no one stood up, no one got up on his own two feet to say, Stop! Enough! You cannot do this to us!

Someone in this room will stop them, Tannenbaum thought.

Slowly and with an almost painful scrutiny, Tannenbaum studied the faces of his allies. These are the people who will have to do it somehow, he thought. We are the sentries. We are standing here without guns, but it is us who will either stop Jason Trench or allow him to turn loose a terrible thing.

I am very happy here, Tannenbaum thought. I like this town, I like the sunshine here, I enjoy my life here. Why did Jason Trench have to come to us?

Someone in this room will stop him, Tannenbaum thought.

Someone will rise and . . .

No, he thought.

His brow lowered.

No one will stop him because everyone will be waiting for someone *else* to stop him. It will be the Jews all over again. Only this time the entire world could be an oven.

Unless.

Unless I, Herbert Tannenbaum, stand up.

But I have a bad heart, he thought.

'What we shoulda done,' Red Canaday said, 'was stop back there in Marathon. That's what we shoulda done.'

'We'll see something,' Felix Potter said. 'Don't worry.'

'You didn't wanna stop in Tavernier, you didn't wanna stop in Islamorada, you didn't wanna stop in Marathon. Now I'll bet there ain't gonna be nothing till we get down to Key West. How much you want to bet?'

'There'll be something,' Felix said.

'What time is it?' Red asked.

Felix took his left hand from the wheel and looked at his wrist. 'Four-twenty.'

'I'm starving,' Red said.

'You had lunch in Miami.'

'That was in Miami. And that was a long time ago.'

'It wasn't so long ago. You just got a tapeworm, that's all.'

'Sitting in a truck all day makes me hungry.'

'We'll see something, don't worry,' Felix said.

The truck rumbled westward, a huge 25,000-pound Diesel with silvered sides and a green cab. It seemed to occupy almost all of the road as it crossed the Seven Mile Bridge and then came on to Little Duck Key, continuing west to Missouri Key and then crossing the short bridge that led to Ohio Key.

'There you go,' Felix said.

'What?'

'Didn't you see the sign there?'

'Yeah, it said Ohio Key.'

'The one next to it, the one next to it.'

'What'd it say?' Red asked.

231

'It said you're gonna be eating soon.'

'What do you mean?'

'It said there's a diner just ahead.'

I need a drink, Bobby Colmore thought.

He tried to understand why Marvin had taken the bottle of thinner from the shelf and put it behind the bench. He realized that he was the only person in the room who had seen Marvin grab the bottle – everyone else had been watching Cummings – and he wondered now if his observation hadn't been something more than chance, something like divine providence. Surely there was no one else in the shop to whom the thinner meant anything. Surely he was the only person to whom the thinner represented something more than a fluid to mix with paint. But if that was the case, what was Marvin's interest in it?'

He studied Marvin owlishly.

He did not look like a drinker, but sometimes you couldn't tell about a man. Sometimes a man looked like a banker or a real estate agent, and it turned out he was really nothing but a sodden bum like all the others. There had been a guy in Boston whom everybody called the Preacher because he was always violently exhorting the guys to drop the booze and live a life of clean underwear and white sheets. But they had found the Preacher dead in Scollay Square one morning and everybody decided he'd been drinking wood alcohol. So you couldn't tell about a man. And if the doctor's son wasn't a drinker, then why had he snatched that half-gallon bottle of thinner? What could he possibly hope to do with it, if not drink it?

So you're a boozer, huh? Bobby thought. Shake hands, pal, only don't try to grab it all for yourself, huh? There's a second bottle right there on the shelf, and that's for me, okay? You keep what you've got, but leave one for me, okay? Leave some for little old Bobby. Or are you trying to keep it from me, is that it? Are you afraid I'll get obnoxiously drunk and dangerous? Are you afraid I'll curse in front of the ladies and vomit in front of the men and cause God knows what kind of trouble with those two hoodlums

232

and their rifles, trouble that would put your precious little hide in danger? Don't worry, buddy.

Those men are going to start a war tomorrow morning. Don't worry about what little trouble *I* can cause.

All I want is a lousy drink. That's all I've wanted since as long as I can remember. And not you or anybody else.

Marvin suddenly moved into action.

14

The cap was off the bottle; he had unscrewed the cap cautiously and slowly. The cigarette was between his lips, the lighter was in his right hand, his thumb was on the wheel. His left hand was dangling behind the bench, hovering over the top of the bottle. Harry had his back to him. Clyde was just turning away. This was the time, *now!*

His left hand hit the half-gallon bottle, knocking it over. His right hand thumbed the lighter into flame. The colourless fluid ran from the neck of the bottle and on to the wooden floor – God, don't let it be water, Marvin thought. Harry turned sharply and abruptly. The liquid was spreading; it ran from the neck of the bottle in a thin rapid stream, facing across the centre of the shop. 'What the hell?' Harry said, and Marvin dropped the flaming lighter into it. He reared back at once because the fluid at his feet went up in flames and backed into the bottle, which exploded under the bench sending flying glass fragments scattering like pieces of a hand grenade. The trail of flame shot across the length of the room, almost touching the oil cans where Amos and Selma were sitting. Harry was standing in the middle of the room, his mouth hanging open in surprise as the flames shot past him. Clyde whipped around with his rifle waist-high, ready to shoot somebody. Marvin was off the bench. He whirled towards the shelves. The second bottle was in his hands.

'Don't!' Bobby shouted, and he came off the packing crate to run towards Marvin who was lifting the second bottle over his head, ready to throw it. He caught Marvin's wrist in both his hands, struggling to loosen the second bottle of thinner from his grip. Marvin, like a quarterback trying to get off a pass against strong opposition, backed away from Bobby and collided with the wall and then rolled away from him and realized he could not get past him; this damn alcoholic fool was going to spoil everything! Costigan was on his feet and shouting, Marvin couldn't understand what. He saw his father rising, saw his father standing up, saw his father coming across the room to pull at Bobby's arm, to try to yank Bobby away from him so he could throw the bottle. The three men struggled grotesquely and silently for perhaps thirty seconds, with Costigan shouting and Marvin not understanding him, knowing only that he wanted to throw the bottle across the shop, but being unable to do so because Bobby was clinging to his wrist even though his father was trying to break the grip. He realized all at once what it was that Costigan was shouting to him, and he let the bottle drop into Costigan's hands where they were outstretched and waiting, entreating patiently for the bottle while Bobby and his father struggled. A shot rang out. He saw his father stumbling backward clutching his chest, and wondered if he had been hit with a bullet, and then realized the bullet had hit not his father but himself, and it was only then that he felt pain. Costigan threw the bottle. The bottle crashed into flames on the other side of the room near the open packing crate brimming with excelsior. Liquid fire went up and on to the crate and into the excelsior, ignited the petrol in the cans near the wall. There was an explosion, and suddenly the entire shop was ablaze.

Marvin dropped on his knees, clutching his bleeding chest.

There was another shot.

And another.

Sondra saw the flames from the bedroom window of the Westerfield house. For a moment she did not know what to do. She felt only panic because she knew that Rog had said he was going to take a look around, and now there was a fire someplace in the town.

She stood at the window motionless for several seconds, her breath coming fast, and then she bit her lip and moved swiftly to the telephone. She was about to pick up the receiver and dial the operator when she saw the list of numbers Myron Westerfield had left beside the phone. The second number on the list was for the fire department on Big Pine Key.

Quickly, she began dialling.

The moment Luke threw open the overhead doors, the ocean wind fanned the flames across the shop floor, sent them rushing up the tool-hung pegboard wall to lick at the ceiling timbers. Harry was running to the fire extinguisher on the wall near the bathroom door. Clyde was backing away from the flames, firing his rifle in panic, as though he could stop the blaze that way. Luke grabbed Samantha's hand and pulled her through the opening, fairly yanking her off her feet. Behind him he heard two more shots as Clyde fired again. His feet dug into the sand.

'Luke . . .'

'Run!' he shouted.

He had made his bid for escape, and now he lay on the floor of the shop with a bullet in his chest and a searing pain flaring across his shoulders and down his arms. Harry was shouting something to Clyde. There was the sound of running feet now, men arriving. 'Give me a hand here!' Harry was yelling. 'We need some water, some more extinguishers!'

'Marvin,' she said. She was leaning over him. He could not see her face clearly because his glasses had dropped from his nose when he fell. He looked up at her and winced again at the pain in his chest, and he thought, I almost made it, I almost escaped.

'Marvin,' she said, 'are you all right?'

'Leave me alone,' he said.

'Marvin . . .'

'For God's sake, leave me alone!' he shouted. 'Can't you even let me die in peace?'

'I love you,' she said. 'Marvin, I love you.'

That's fine, he thought. She loves me. That makes

everything just fine and dandy. Love will conquer all. Love will take away this burning pain in my chest, love will foil the plot of Jason Trench, love will save the world and the human race.

I've got news for you, he thought, and then his head fell back and his eyes rolled up into his forehead sightlessly.

'He's dead,' Selma said to no one.

She felt almost relieved.

Jason's men were running up from the dock, and Luke's first instinct was to drag Samantha in the opposite direction, towards the Tannenbaum house at the western end of S-811. He remembered then that these men were armed and that anyone running *away* from the shop would be immediately suspect and would probably draw fire. For a reckless moment he considered running directly into the midst of the advancing men, shouting orders at them, telling them what was needed at the burning shop, giving force and direction to a mindless moving body of men who were responding only to the immediate threat and presence of fire. Samantha, he thought. They might accept *me* as one of their band, but if they see a woman, no. The beach. 'This way,' he whispered, and his hand tightened on hers as he turned and ran on to the coral leading to the oceanfront. He had no clear idea of what he would do next. The important thing for the moment was to escape being seen by the men who were running up from the dock towards the paint shop. It seemed to him that the best way to do this was to get over the coral to where it dropped down to the beach, and then double back towards the dock. He had no plan beyond that, no scheme, not even a very clear idea of what might happen to them if they were caught. He had a vague notion that they would be killed, yes, but death seemed unreal in the same way Jason's invasion of the town seemed unreal, in the same way Jason's proposed suicide mission seemed unreal, in the same way everything that had happened since sunrise this morning seemed unreal. He could not muster fear, he could not allow himself the luxury of an emotional involvement,

237

because the basic thread of Jason's plan seemed intellectual in concept, reducing even the fear of death to an abstract idea rather than a reality that might overcome them within the next few minutes. His hand holding Samantha's was not sweating. His heart pounded only with the exertion of their wild scramble over the coral and on to the sand: he felt no fear. He knew they had to get away, had to get out of town to warn the authorities, but he didn't know which authorities he should warn – the police, the Coast Guard, the Army, who? He felt almost dismally certain that they would never get out of town alive, but he felt no fear. Jason's men were in the diner at the eastern end of the road, and the diner commanded a view of the entrance to U.S. 1 as well as the thicket across S-811, so that was out. But if he and Sam ran up the beach towards the Tannenbaum house, they might possibly be spotted by the men fighting the fire at the paint shop, where the coral shelf was lower and the beach clearly visible. And even if they got past the shop, there was Jason's men in houses all along the beach; any one of them was a potential danger. No, the dock was the place to go, and he headed for it only as a refuge at first, seeing the long empty wooden length of it, and the white Chris-Craft sitting at the pier's end, Joel Dodge's boat, and then realizing that the boat was a means of escape, and suddenly conceiving a plan.

Samantha responded to the slight pressure of his hand as though he were whispering instructions through his fingers.

They came up off the beach and on to the dock, using the steps at the western end, and then moving on to the planking, Samantha's sneakers making a slight squeaking sound as they ran towards the Chris-Craft – it was funny how he heard the sound of her sneakers, expecting a bullet in the back at any moment – and then miraculously climbing aboard the boat unharmed and ducking into the cabin. 'Get below,' he said to her, and automatically reached for the key in the boat's ignition. His hand almost closed on air; his hand almost did a classic take, grasping for the key, finding nothing in the ignition slot. And then he tried to remember whether the key was hanging on the keyboard in the repair shop or whether – wait, hadn't Jason been using this boat? Of course he had; it had been out on the water alongside the cutter not more than –

Then the key was up on the command bridge.

Samantha had gone down the two steps leading to the galley, and she turned now and looked up at him and whispered, 'What is it?'

'The key,' he said, 'I've got to go topside.'

'I'll go with you.'

'No. Stay below. If the key's up there, I'm going to start the boat and head out.'

'You'll need me to cast off.'

'There's only a single line on her.'

'Still.'

They stared at each other for a moment.

'All right,' Luke said. 'Come.'

They were moving out of the cabin when they heard the footsteps at the far end of the dock.

'What –'

'Shhh.'

They stood breathlessly in the boat's cockpit, waiting, listening to the sound of heavy boots on the wooden planking. The man would be armed; there was no question about that. If they tried for the bridge now – no, their only hope was that he would pass the boat by.

Luke said nothing. Again his fingers touched hers lightly, and he guided her below, past the galley and the dinette and into the forward stateroom where the sleeping berths angled into a V shape, one wing of the V on either side of the bow. Luke closed the door and then opened it again a crack, listening. The footsteps on the pier were closer. He listened.

The footsteps stopped.

Beside him, Samantha caught her breath. He pressed her hand reassuringly. He waited.

The boat moved only slightly, there was only the faintest creaking of timber, but Luke knew the man had stepped aboard. He quickly closed the door, and turned and looked directly into Samantha's face. Her expression was one of trapped horror, the eyes wide, the nostrils flaring, the lips slightly parted over clenched teeth. He suddenly wondered if the same expression was on his face. He heard heavy footsteps on the vinyl cockpit deck aft and above. The stateroom was perhaps eight feet across at the widest point of the V, with a narrow two feet of deck space between the berths. There was little more than six feet of headroom, and the apex of the V was no more than two feet wide with a curtained narrow locker pointing into the bow and with two larger lockers running beneath the berths, one on either side of the boat, the length of the berths.

There was nowhere else to hide.

He pushed open the sliding door on the locker below the berth on the starboard side. Samantha did not say a word. She dropped to her knees and crawled into the narrow space, utilizing a curiously awkward half-sliding motion, getting in head-first and then pulling her knees up, and unfolding her legs only when she was completely inside the locker.

'Okay?' Luke whispered.

'Yes,' she whispered back.

'I'm going to slide the door shut,' Luke whispered. 'Don't move from where you are, and don't say another word until I open it again. Have you got that?'

'Yes,' she whispered.

'Good. I'll be here. Don't be frightened.'

He slid the door shut and then turned rapidly to the port side of the stateroom. He heard footsteps on the ladder leading below. He slid open the locker door quickly, and then tried the same crawling, sliding technique Samantha had used, but discovered his legs were too long; he could not pull his knees up. The footsteps were in the galley now. He came out of the locker and tried the opposite approach, putting his legs in first, bending them at the knee as he lay on one side and then hoisting his behind up over the sill and rolling over on to his shoulder as the footsteps hesitated just outside the closed stateroom door. Ducking his head, he was entirely inside the narrow locker now. He put his palm flat against the inside of the sliding door and prayed it would not squeak when he closed it.

He pushed it closed in one swift movement not an instant before the door to the stateroom opened.

In the darkness, lying with his arms folded across his chest and his legs cramped against either side of the locker, he closed his eyes and waited.

In a little while he heard the stateroom door open and close again. Someone greeted the man just outside the stateroom. They laughed and began talking. He could not hear their words clearly. He kept listening.

The men were not leaving the boat.

The volunteer firemen from Big Pine Key, twenty-five men in two modern fire engines, arrived on Ocho Puertos within five minutes after Sondra Lasky had telephoned. They made a screeching right turn on to S-811, almost knocking over the barricade at the mouth of the road. Danny Latham, the fire chief, swung down from the cab of the first engine, swore under his breath and yelled for a man to help him clear the road. They hopped back into the trucks as soon as they had moved the obstruction, and then rolled into the town, directly to Costigan's Marina, where smoke was still billowing up from the paint shop.

'How'd this get started?' Latham asked a coloured fellow who was trying to fight the blaze, along with six or seven other men in dungaree trousers and chambray shirts.

'We're Coast Guards,' the coloured fellow answered. 'Checking the boats here at the marina because of that hurricane.'

'Oh yeah, I see,' Latham said. 'How'd the fire start?'

'Somebody smoking there in the paint shop,' the coloured fellow said.

'Well, we'll have it out for you in no time,' Latham said. He glanced around and then asked, 'Where's Luke?'

'He was with the skipper last I seen him. Taking care of the boats.'

'You really think this hurricane's gonna hit?' Latham said.

241

'We'll know better when we get the next advisory,' the coloured fellow said.

'When'll that be?'

'Five o'clock.'

'Yeah,' Latham said. 'Get that hose in there!' he shouted to one of his men. 'My name's Latham,' he told the coloured fellow, 'Danny Latham.' He extended his hand.

'Harry Barnes,' the coloured fellow answered, and shook his hand.

In five minutes' time, the fire was out.

Latham's men hosed down the shop once again, and then packed their gear. A Coast Guard officer named Jason Tench came over to thank Latham for his assistance, and promised to deliver Latham's good wishes personally to Luke Costigan as soon as he returned from the cove where he was mooring some boats.

The fire engines left at four thirty-four.

'Well, this is Ocho Puertos,' Red said.

Felix slowed the truck at the side of the road. 'This is it, all right. Where do you suppose the diner is?'

'Search me. Must be in there someplace.' He gestured with his head.

'The sign there says the road's closed for repairs.'

'We can always *walk* in,' Red said.

'Yeah, I guess so.'

'What do you say?'

'I don't know.'

'You want to or not?'

'Leave the truck up here, you mean? On the highway?'

'Sure, what's wrong with that?'

'Nothing. You want to?'

'What do *you* say?'

'If you want to, I'm game.'

'Okay, so let's.'

They got out of the cab and were starting across the highway when they saw the police car approaching from the west.

'Cops,' Red said.

'Yeah,' Felix answered.

The two men crossed the road and stopped near the barricade, watching the patrol car as it approached. The car slowed, and then came to a stop beside them. The door closest to the edge of the road opened. A state trooper got out of the car.

'Afternoon,' he said.

'Afternoon,' Red answered.

'Afternoon,' Felix said.

'That your truck?' the trooper asked.

'Yes, sir.'

'What are you doing walking out here on the highway?'

'Going to the diner,' Red said. 'The road's closed for repairs, so we figured we'd walk in.'

'That right?' the trooper said, and he glanced at the FLORIDA STATE ROAD DEPARTMENT barricade and the ROAD CLOSED FOR REPAIRS sign. 'Where you bound?'

'Key West.'

'Where in Key West?'

'A & L Furniture,' Red said. 'We've got a truckload of outdoor stuff for them. Wrought-iron. You know.'

'You been to Big Pine today?'

'Where's that?'

'Down the road a ways.'

'No, we just came from Miami. Never made this run before.'

'Who's driving?' the trooper asked.

'I am,' Felix said.

'Let's see your licence.'

Felix handed it to him, and the trooper studied it carefully. 'Looks okay,' he said, and handed it back. 'You plan on leaving the truck right where it is?'

'I tried to get it as far off the road as I could. That's a soft shoulder on the side there, isn't it?'

'I just don't want you blocking traffic,' the trooper said.

'You want me to move it over a bit?'

'Well, I guess it's okay where it is,' the trooper said. 'You smell smoke?' he asked, and sniffed the air.

'Yeah, there must've been a fire,' Red said.

243

'Maybe the road gang's burning something,' the trooper said. He walked to the barricade and moved it aside. 'Okay, Jim,' he called to the car, and the trooper behind the wheel turned in on to S-811. 'You fellows want a lift to the diner,' the first trooper said, 'we'll be happy to drop you.'

'Thanks,' Red said, and all three men got into the car, the trooper up front with his buddy, and the truck drivers in back.

'What's this back here?' Red asked conversationally.

'Oh, a riot gun,' one of the troopers said.

'Bet you don't get many of those down this way.'

'Many of what?'

'Riots.'

'No, not too many.' The trooper paused. 'There's the diner, Jim. Why don't you just pull up and I'll step inside.'

'Okay,' the driver said.

'Looks like it's closed,' Red said.

'Shouldn't be,' the trooper behind the wheel answered.

'Yep, it's closed all right,' Felix said. 'Sign hanging right there on the door.'

'Truck parked in back, though,' the first trooper said. 'Must be *some*body in there to take delivery.' He paused and said, 'Jim, why don't you drive up to the marina? Maybe Costigan knows why it's closed.'

The patrol car moved slowly up the road towards the marina office. In the distance they could hear a telephone ringing, and then the sound stopped abruptly.

'Must be somebody at the marina, anyway,' the first trooper said.

'How come?'

'Just answered the phone, didn't they?' The first trooper paused. 'I don't see any work gang on the road, do you?'

'Nope. Just 'cause they closed the road don't mean they're working. Not on a Sunday, leastways.'

'Lester usually opens that diner of his every day of the week, don't he?'

'Yep.'

'Today a holiday or something?'

244

'Not that I know of. Maybe he kept closed 'cause of the hurricane.'

'Yeah, that's a point.'

'You know any place we can get some coffee and pie before Key West?' Oscar asked.

'Lots of places on Big Pine.'

'How far's that?'

'Oh, no more'n three, four miles.'

'That's not so bad, Red.'

'No, that's fine,' Red said.

'Lots of cars in town today,' the first trooper said. 'Seems like almost every house on the beach has company.'

'Yeah.'

'You want to pull up here, Jim?'

The patrol car came to a stop before the marina office. The trooper opened the door on his side. 'I won't be long,' he said to his partner behind the wheel, and then went up the walk to the front door. He opened the door and stepped inside.

Bobby Colmore was sitting behind the desk. A stranger was sitting beside him. There was a jacket thrown over his lap.

'Hi, Bobby,' the trooper said. 'Where's Luke?'

'Out moving some boats.'

'Everything okay here?'

'Fine,' Bobby said.

The trooper kept looking at the stranger.

'Howdy,' the stranger said.

'Hi,' the trooper answered.

'This here's a friend of Luke's,' Bobby said.

'How do you do?' the stranger said, smiling. 'My name's Benny Prager.' He extended his hand, but he did not rise from his position next to Bobby.

'How are you?' the trooper said, and shook hands.

'Luke said I ever needed a boat, I should stop by,' Prager said. He grinned. 'I finally took him up on it.'

'You picked a fine time,' the trooper said. 'Hurricane's supposed to be coming this way.'

'Well, maybe it won't,' Prager said.

'Maybe not. Bobby, when's Luke gonna be back, do you know?'

'Well, that's hard to say. He's moving boats.'

'Up the cove?'

'Yep.'

'Maybe I can catch him there,' the trooper said.

'Maybe,' Bobby answered.

'Couple of state policemen got killed on Big Pine,' the trooper said.

'What?' Bobby said.

'Yeah,' the trooper answered.

'Gee, that's too bad,' Prager said.

'Yeah. You didn't see anybody suspicious hanging around town, did you?'

'No,' Bobby said.

'Well, keep your eyes open, huh? You see or hear anything funny, just give us a ring. You've got the number?'

'Yeah, it's stuck to the phone there.'

'Good,' the trooper said. 'Nice meeting you, Mr. Jaeger.'

'Prager.'

'Right, Prager. Which way you gonna be heading?'

'Beg your pardon?'

'With the boat.'

'Oh. Key West. I'm supposed to pick up some friends there.'

'Watch out for Flora,' the trooper said, and laughed.

'I'm hoping she'll blow out in the other direction.'

'Next advisory should tell you,' the trooper said. 'You just come down?'

'Yep, from Miami.'

'How's it up that way?'

'Well, pretty windy this morning.'

'That's all them Jews yakking it up there on the beach,' the trooper said, and laughed. 'That's what causes the wind.'

'I wouldn't be surprised,' Prager said, and laughed with him.

'Well, I'll see you, Bobby,' the trooper said, and went to the door. At the door he paused and turned, 'Diner's closed, you know,' he said.

'Is it?'

'Yeah. Lester sick or something?'

'Not that I know of,' Bobby said.

'Must be taking the day off, then.'

'Maybe.'

'Mmm,' the trooper said. 'Do you smell smoke, or is it just me?'

'We had a little fire over in the paint shop,' Bobby said.

'Oh, no wonder.'

'Firemen just left a little while ago.'

'Oh. Anybody hurt?'

'No, they put it out all right.'

'Oh. Well, good. Good.' The trooper put his hand on the door-knob. 'Tell Luke I was by,' he said.

'See you,' Benny Prager said.

'Right,' the trooper answered. He opened the door and stepped outside. The door closed behind him. Bobby Colmore and Benny Prager sat behind the desk motionless. Outside, they heard the patrol car starting. They heard tyres pulling at the road. The sound of the car's engine moved into the distance. They listened until it was out of earshot.

'That was very good, Mr. Colmore,' Benny said, and he pulled the gun from beneath the jacket on his lap. He rose swiftly and walked to the door at the rear of the office. He knocked on the door three times. The door opened.

'Are they gone?' Jason asked.

'They're gone,' Benny said. 'Good thing Johnny called from the diner.'

'Bring the wino back here with Tannenbaum and the others,' Jason said.

At four forty-five, Harry Barnes went to the marina office and discovered that neither Luke Costigan nor Samantha Watts was among the prisoners in the back room. He told Jason that they had both run out of the paint shop during

247

the fire, and that he had automatically assumed they had been recaptured. Jason said he was a fool for automatically assuming anything, and Harry apologized and said he'd had his hands full with the fire, you know, and the volunteer firemen from Big Pine, and Jason said, All right, all right, let's search the town.

In the room behind Bobby Colmore's shop they found Willy in bed with a woman. Both Willy and the woman were naked and unconscious, and the room stank of alcohol. Jason posted a guard outside the door with instructions to shoot them if they tried to get out. They searched the town from end to end, house to house, from mangrove jungle to beachfront. They went aboard every boat at the pier, including the white Chris-Craft. Alex Witten and Clay Prentiss were sitting below in the dinette booth, quietly talking.

'Anyone come aboard here?' Jason asked.

'Nope,' Clay answered.

'Okay,' Jason said, and he and Benny went ashore again.

'What do you think?' Benny asked.

'I don't know.'

'Were they in town when that patrol car was here?'

'I don't think so.'

'Then they got away,' Benny said. 'They're outside, they're –'

'Probably,' Jason said. 'Most likely.'

'Jase, they'll call the police.'

'They haven't yet.'

'How do you know?'

'Do you see the police here?'

'No, but . . .'

'If Costigan called them, they'd have been back by now.'

'Maybe he hasn't gotten to a phone yet.'

'Big Pine's only a few miles away.'

'Still . . .'

'I'm not worried. I can't worry about it.'

'Jason, if he gets to the police –'

'I can't worry about it.'

'Jason, you *have* to.'

'This country is going to declare war against Cuba,' Jason said. His voice was very low, his eyes serious. 'We are going to declare war as soon as the full impact of what happens out there in the Caribbean' – he pointed out over the water – 'has had a chance to register.'

'Jason, what's that got to do –'

'I can't worry about Costigan. I can't worry about a cripple roaming the highway. What do you think'll happen if the police *do* get here, Benny? Tell me that.'

'Well, Jase, they'll –'

'Benny, the men who stay behind here have orders to kill everyone in this town before they leave. They'll do it. They'll do it unless they know for certain we've failed out there, unless they know the plan has gone wrong. In that case, they'll clear out fast. It's as simple as that. Do you understand me, Benny?'

'Yes, but –'

'But, Benny, they are *ready* to kill everyone in this town. They are *expecting* to kill everyone in this town.'

'I know.' He looked at Jason curiously. 'I know, Jase.'

'If anything happens here after we're under way, they'll do it sooner, that's all. They won't risk the plan, Benny.'

Benny shook his head. He still seemed troubled.

'Don't worry,' Jason said. 'The only thing that can possibly stop us is Flora.' He looked at his watch. 'We'll know what she's going to do in ten minutes' time.'

'Well,' Benny said dubiously, and then nodded and began nibbling at the inside of his mouth.

At five minutes to five, the radioman Peters went out to talk to Mr. Bordigian, the lieutenant j.g. who was the watch officer. He handed him the afternoon message from the *Mercury* and said, 'What do you make of this, sir?'

Bordigian read the message, and then looked up at Peters, 'What do I make of what?' he asked.

'The ZUG, sir.'

'The ZUG?' Bordigian looked at the message again. 'Oh,' he said. 'Yeah.'

'Kind of funny, isn't it, sir?'

'Mm,' Bordigian said. 'Yeah.'

'What do you think we ought to do, sir?'

'Do?' Bordigian said. He scratched his head, looked at the message again, and then said, 'File it, Peters. Somebody goofed, that's all.'

MIAMI WEATHER BUREAU ADVISORY NUMBER 33 HURRICANE FLORA 5 PM EST SUNDAY OCTOBER 6.

RESIDENTS IN THE SOUTHEASTERN BAHAMAS SHOULD TAKE ALL POSSIBLE EMERGENCY PRECAUTIONS IMMEDIATELY AGAINST HURRICANE WINDS HIGH TIDES AND ROUGH SEAS.

AT 5 PM EST ... 2200 ZULU ... THE CENTRE OF HURRICANE FLORA WAS ESTIMATED TO BE NEAR LATITUDE 21.1 NORTH LONGITUDE 75.7 WEST AND PASSING INTO THE ATLANTIC NEAR CAPE LUCRECIA. THIS POSITION IS ABOUT 80 STATUTE MILES NORTH NORTHWEST OF GUANTANAMO BAY AND 440 MILES SOUTHEAST OF MIAMI.

FLORA IS FORECAST TO MOVE IN A GENERAL NORTHEASTERLY DIRECTION AT AROUND 10 MPH DURING THE NEXT TWELVE HOURS. SHE WOULD APPEAR TO OFFER NO FURTHER THREAT TO EXTREME WESTERN CUBA CENTRAL AMERICA AND FLORIDA AND NO FURTHER THREAT TO THE REMAINDER OF THE EAST COAST OF THE UNITED STATES AS WELL.

15

Dusk was a long time coming.

The sky sketched from horizon to horizon and there was nothing to hide the sun in its slow descent towards the rim of water. There was a stillness to the earth as the spreading stain of sunset covered the sky, touched the sea, tipped the scattered clouds in glowing colours. Close to shore the ocean was calm, unrippled, reflecting the dying sun like a mirror of molten gold.

Jason stood on the shore, a black shadow against the burning sky, and watched the end of day.

A warm breeze touched his face like a maiden's kiss.

Out on the horizon he could see the cutter in sharp silhouette. A light winked a brief signal, and he turned away from it, not bothering to read it, and watched the sun drop slowly into the water, savouring the stillness, feeling oddly and curiously at peace.

'Jason?'

It was Annabelle's voice, whispering into the stillness of near dusk, carrying from the pier across the coral to the beach. He turned, and nodded, and walked slowly towards the pier with the sun behind him. He could see Annabelle standing in vague sun-washed gloom near the white boat, the boat tinted gold and orange by the drowning sun, her face a blur, her silhouette softened by the fading light. He stopped beside her and took her hand, and together they turned to watch the disappearing sun, the ocean consuming it, the sky turning violently red and then purple, the red tones extinguished by the water, blue dominating the horizon, spreading, the suddenness of a single star.

'The cutter just signalled,' she whispered. 'They want us.'

'Right,' he said.

Lying in the darkness beneath the port sleeping berth, Luke heard the boat starting and then felt it moving away from the pier. There were footsteps above, and then the sound of muffled voices just outside the stateroom, someone greeting the newcomer, another voice, someone laughing. He heard the footsteps moving closer to the stateroom door, an indistinct voice, and suddenly the door opened, '. . . right in here, honey, like I told you,' Jason's voice said.

'But I'm not tired,' a woman's voice said.

'I know, honey,' Jason said. 'But you can lie down, anyway, can't you? We'll leave the door open so we can talk, okay?'

'All right,' the woman said.

Luke held his breath. The woman had undoubtedly moved into the stateroom; he could hear the shuffle of her feet not six inches from where his head rested behind the sliding door of the locker. He drew his chin back into his chest instinctively, as if certain her unseen feet would touch him momentarily, even though the sliding locker door was between them.

'You need some help there?' Jason asked.

'No, I can manage.'

Luke heard a small grunt as the woman lifted herself on the berth. Above his head the wooden base of the berth creaked as it took her weight.

'How's that?' Jason asked. 'Comfy?'

'Yes, it's fine. This is silly,' the woman said. 'We'll be out to the cutter in no time.'

'You need all the rest you can get,' Jason said.

'Why?' the woman answered, her voice suddenly sharp. 'So I can be ready for annihilation tomorrow morning?'

There was a long silence. When Jason spoke again, it was not in answer to the woman's question. He seemed to have turned away from her to address the third person in the cabin outside.

'How's the skipper taking all this?' he asked.

'Not much he can do about it, Jase,' a man's voice answered.

'Where've we got him?'

'Locked in his cabin. Alex had one of the boys weld some two-inch chain to the bulkhead and the door.'

'Is he having any trouble with the ship?'

'He's got the engines warming up now. Just waiting for us to come aboard, that's all.'

'Good,' Jason said.

'I'd better get topside, see how Clay and Benny are doing.'

'Right.'

There was another silence. Luke heard retreating footsteps. The footsteps died, but the cabin remained silent. Luke made a mental count of people aboard. There was Jason and the woman, the two named Clay and Benny who were topside, and the one who had just left to join them. Five.

'Annabelle?' Jason said.

'Mmm?'

'You want your baby to grow up in a world where he's got to be afraid all the time?'

'Jason . . .'

'Is that what you want for your baby?'

'I'm doing this with you,' Annabelle said.

'I know you are.'

'Then all right.'

'What you said before isn't all right,' Jason said.

'I meant it.'

'No, you didn't mean it.'

'Don't tell me what I mean or don't mean, Jase. Tomorrow morning you're going to blow up my unborn baby, aren't you? Well, if that's what you're going to do, then I've got a right to –'

'If that's as far as you can see –'

'Jason, I wish to hell you'd –'

'– just about past the tip of your nose.'

'Jason, let it alone,' Annabelle said. 'Let's not even talk about it any more.'

'If all you're concerned about is your own personal self and your baby, well, that's something else again. I happen to be worrying about all the other unborn babies, Annabelle, all the babies that won't even get a chance to be born if we let the Commies –'

'Oh, for God's sake, the hell with the Commies!'

'You're tired,' he said gently.

'I'm *not* tired.'

'What you did today –'

'Jason, please leave me alone. I don't want to know about what I did today, and I don't want to know about what we're going to do tomorrow. I just want to forget all about it, all right? You're going on about this the same way you went on about . . .'

Annabelle stopped talking.

'About what?' Jason said.

'Nothing?'

'About the Jap whore,' Jason said.

Annabelle said nothing.

'Right? About the Jap whore, right?'

'I don't know what she was.'

'She was a whore.'

'I wasn't there.'

'Take my word for it.'

'I know you too well,' Annabelle said.

'She was a lying old bitch!' Jason shouted. 'And anyway, what the hell has she got to do with this, would you mind telling me?'

'I don't know.'

'You *bet* you don't know.'

'I only know what you wrote me.' Annabelle paused. 'And I know what the others said.'

'What others?'

'The others.' Her voice was very low.

'The newspapers, you mean? *Stars and Stripes?*'

Annabelle remained silent.

'That's an *Army* paper. What did you *expect* them to say? That I was innocent?'

'Were you, Jason?'

'Yes!'

'Then why did they throw you out of the Navy?'

'Because . . .'

'Because the woman told the truth, Jason.'

The cabin fell silent. Luke, cramped into the space beneath the berth, heard the wood above him creak again, and knew that Annabelle had shifted her position.

'Why are you in this with me?' Jason asked suddenly.

'You're my husband.'

'That's no reason.'

'It's enough reason.'

'You want to know what I think?'

'I don't care what you think,' Annabelle said sharply. 'I'm scared!'

'You're not scared!'

'I don't want to die. My baby . . .'

'The hell with your baby!'

'Jason . . .'

'I said the hell with your baby, you hear me? I say the hell with all babies that come from chickenshit bellies like yours! How can you talk about *dying* when we've got the whole future of the world right here in the palms of our hands, right here in these hands? You talk about *dying*, you little bitch? Hold up your goddamn head!'

'Jason . . .'

'Look at me. Hold up your head.' His voice dropped to a whisper. 'Hold up your head.'

From above somewhere a voice called down to Jason. He did not answer. 'Jason,' the voice shouted again, 'we're coming alongside the cutter.'

'Be right with you,' Jason said.

There was a silence.

'Jason?'

Her voice was curiously soft.

'It's because I love you,' she said. '*That's* why I'm here. Because I love you.'

He wished there were no choice. He wished there were only a single possibility for action, clear and undebatable. But unfortunately, there were several courses open to him, and the decision had to be made now, immediately, before the cutter got under way.

He could wait until that happened, of course. That was one possibility. He could lie here in the close darkness of the locker below the berth and wait until he heard the cutter moving out, and then wait until he was sure it was gone, and then simply go topside and take the boat back to –

Provided they had left the keys.

But even if they hadn't –

No, the boat didn't have a radio; he had talked to Joel Dodge about putting one in, but Joel had –

The other way was to go aboard the cutter and try to stop them right there; no, that was stupid.

He slid open the locker door.

He knew that the five of them had left the boat already, and he knew that it might be only a matter of minutes before the cutter got under way. But he also knew he could not risk detection, not now, and so he moved with an exaggerated caution, sliding quietly out of the locker and then stretching to his full height and trying to work the cramp out of his shoulder, and then stooping to whisper, 'Samantha,' and sliding open the door of the other locker.

She was asleep.

He almost burst out laughing, and then smiled instead and put his hand gently on her shoulder and whispered again, 'Samantha?'

Her eyes opened instantly. She looked into his face, startled but immediately awake. He helped her out of the locker, and she peered past him into the empty cabin and asked, 'Are they gone?'

'Yes.' He hesitated. 'Sam, I don't know what to do. Should I try to board the cutter and –'

'No,' she said.

256

'I want to stop them.'

'Then stay here. We can get the boat back to shore and notify the police.'

He hesitated again. 'What if they've taken the ignition keys with them?' He looked at her searchingly, wanting her to convince him that it was really much safer and much wiser to stay aboard the Chris-Craft, get back to shore somehow, put the entire matter in the hands of the police.

'You can swim,' she said.

He shook his head. 'We're too far out. I'd never make it.'

'All right, someone'll spot us right here. You wouldn't have to –'

'In the dark?'

'The boat's white. We can put on our lights, and –'

'Who'll be out on the water after dark?'

'Someone, you can't tell, there might be . . .'

'There *might* be,' he said. 'Or there might *not* be.'

'Luke, it'll be hours before they get to Cuba. We can certainly –'

'Seven hours,' he said. 'Eight hours at most. Honey, we could spend the *night* out here without being seen.'

'But in the morning . . .'

'The morning is too late.'

'Look . . .'

'What?'

'Look, we're . . . look, if the keys are up there, we've got nothing to worry about.'

'And what if they're not?' Luke asked.

Benny Prager stood on the main deck of the cutter with his back to the rail and looked up at the wheelhouse where Jason and Alex were preparing to get under way. Below him and behind him the white Chris-Craft bobbed gently on the water. Above him and beyond him and around him the Florida night was dusted with stars, the air was balmy.

He sucked in a deep draught of sweet night air and suddenly felt the arm circling his throat and putting him into the shadows near the forward stack. He tried to shout, but the arm was tight around his throat, unrelenting. He tried to free himself, he clutched at the arm with his fingers, tried to claw it loose; he opened his mouth and gasped for breath, he could feel himself getting dizzy, his lungs would burst, he was being dragged towards the rail, he was being lifted, his eyes were bulging, frantically he tore at the tight iron band . . . black . . . reeling . . . Jason please help . . . don't . . . night-star . . .

Harry Barnes stood on the end of the pier and watched the shop move out.

Something was bothering him.

At first he thought it was simply the fact that Jason Trench – to whom he had given his trust and his loyalty and his devotion – had left without even saying good-bye. Well, that's a white man for you, he thought, and stopped the thought before it went any further. That was not what he'd meant; he did not want to think that way. The only reason he was in this expedition at all was because he didn't believe in all that blackman-whiteman garbage. He believed in a free and united world without the danger of communism hanging over it, without the threat of nuclear extinction over-shadowing everything the human race tried to do. So he certainly didn't mean that about Jason. Jason's being white had nothing to do with his not stopping off to say good-bye. Jason had more important things on his mind than saying good-bye to just another one of the troops.

Still, he'd have liked to say, Good luck, Jase. Do it, Jase, he'd have liked to say. Go down there, and clear them out, get rid of them, Jase, take away the danger. Do it, man.

He'd have liked to shake Jase's hand and tell him that.

Well, maybe Jase was sore because he'd let Costigan and the girl get away. And yet he hadn't *seemed* particularly sore, even when they couldn't find them. He'd just sort of shrugged it off and –

All at once, Harry knew what was bothering him.

He suddenly remembered that Costigan and the girl had been present when Clyde shot off his mouth. They knew *exactly* what Jason was planning, and now they were somewhere free and clear of the town while Jason was out there on the cutter, maybe heading into Navy guns.

Oh God Almighty, Harry thought.

I should have told him, I should have warned him.

It was too late now. The cutter was on its way.

And then Harry wondered why he *hadn't* told him.

The initial memory, the initial wash of feeling that came over Jason as he stood outside the wheelhouse on the bridge of the cutter and tasted the first tingling kiss of salt on his lips, the first sensation was one of unadulterated joy, of wild soaring freedom, the memory of those golden days aboard the 832 when the entire Pacific Ocean was his, the world was his.

Nine men in the crew, including himself, and a feeling he had never known before in his life, a feeling of belonging, a feeling of being liked and respected. At the university he had waited on tables in the student cafeteria and the upperclassmen had called him 'boy', as though he were a nigger. His older brother used to send him clothes he no longer had any use for, and then he went into the Army in January of 1942, immediately after Pearl Harbour, and stopped sending anything. His name was Caleb, his name used to be Caleb, he was killed in Italy some years later. By that time Jason was in the Pacific with his own command, and he didn't learn of his older brother's death until two months after it happened because that was when Annabelle's letter finally caught up with him. Alex Witten, who was exec on the 832, an ensign from New Haven, Connecticut, looked at Jason as he read the letter and then said, 'What is it?'

'Nothing,' Jason said, and crumpled the letter into a ball and threw it over the side. That night he got roaring drunk on grapefruit juice and torpedo fluid. Clay Prentiss couldn't wake him the next morning, and thought he was dead because his eyes were partially opened and he was lying on his back like a corpse.

Nine men aboard the boat, one who shot himself with a stolen Army .45 that night in Pearl when they were in drydock after that foolhardy attack on the Jap minesweeper

– what the hell was his name? He'd been a very thin man, a machinist's mate second, Schroeder, Schneider, something like that. He'd gone ashore and into the heads of a USO canteen and then put the barrel of the gun into his mouth and pulled the trigger. They'd found him with the back of his skull splattered all over the bathroom walls. One of the USO hostesses said to Jason when he went to identify the body – the face was still intact, it was only the back of the man's head that was gone – she said to Jason, 'I wish he'd picked someplace else to do it. That bathroom was freshly painted only last week.' Nine men to begin with, and then Schroeder or Schneider (*which* the hell was it?) killed himself in Pearl and the seaman, Phillips, asked for transfer to the U.S.S. *Little*, a destroyer that was later sunk by kamikazes off Okinawa. Jason often wondered if Phillips had been among the men killed that day in May of 1942. Two other men left the 832, a gunner's mate third named Kuzinsky – who was wounded in the summer of 1944 during an air attack on the base, and who was sent home with a Purple Heart – and the replacement for Schneider or Schroeder, a man named Palucci who had two brothers killed in the battle for Cassino (where his mother was born) and who was shipped back to the States gratuitously. Five of the original crew members stayed with the 832 until the war ended, forming the fighting nucleus, providing the generating force and spirit that took all the others through the war alive. They were Jason Trench, Alex Witten, Arthur Hazlitt, Clay Prentiss and Goody Moore.

There was nothing you couldn't sell in Japan during the winter of 1945, and only several things you could buy. Jason Trench was an officer in the United States Navy – he had been promoted to full lieutenant by this time – and his occupation assignment was the inspection of Japanese warships for armament, radar, or other forbidden military contraband. He would go aboard each Japanese ship with a .45 strapped to his side, accompanied by Clay carrying the walkie-talkie and Goody carrying the camera. Alex would remain aboard the 832 with the rest of the crew, moving out and away from any ship they were inspecting, as a precaution against the defeated Japanese trying to capture the boat. Alex's orders were to fire across the bow of any ship from which Clay did not radio at five-minute intervals. In all the while they were in Japan, and up to the time of the Tokyo incident, Alex never had to fire a single shot.

The 832's home base was theoretically Sasebo, but her assignments carried her north and south throughout the Japanese islands. She ranged from Kagoshima to Tokyo, from Yokohama to Hakodate, from Fukouka to Kushiro. Jason detested each and every port because he still considered the Japanese enemies of the United States and, consequently, personal enemies of Jason Trench. The only saving grace Japan possessed was that it didn't cost anything to be there. Jason's expenses ashore were usually taken care of by the cigarettes he smuggled off the boat and sold to the Japs for yen. There was something enormously satisfying about dickering with the Japanese over the price of a package of cigarettes. They were bringing the equivalent of a dollar and eighty-five cents a pack when the 832 first arrived on Sasebo, and Jason would not accept less, and often insisted on more. He enjoyed the bargaining, refusing to sell unless his price was met, knowing all the time that such transactions were illegal, but somehow feeling he was exacting a sort of tithe from the Japs by selling them cigarettes at exorbitant prices – almost as if he were continuing the war against them in this way.

He went ashore in the tiny northern town at about 2 P.M. that January day, planning only to pick up the mail at the local Army base, and not dressed for liberty, wearing grey trousers and a new foul-weather jacket upon which he had not yet stencilled his name. Technically he was out of uniform, but he found himself wandering into the town nonetheless and then found himself on a narrow side street and realized all at once that he was being followed. The man behind him was Japanese, and he stopped whenever Jason stopped and then began walking again whenever Jason did. At first Jason was alarmed. Then, as the game of pursuit continued, Jason found himself wondering if the Jap would attack him. He began looking forward to the attack. He knew unquestionably that he could kill the man without effort, and with the certain immunity of self-defence. Confidently, eagerly, he anticipated the man's approach. When it came, Jason was so startled he burst into laughter.

'You sell coat?' the man said.

Jason's laughter eventually subsided.

He sold the foul-weather jacket for the equivalent of a hundred and twelve dollars in American money.

By the time the thing in Tokyo happened –

'Jase?'

He turned. Alex was at the wheel, his face illuminated by the binnacle light.

'Did you want to come left at Looe Key?' he asked. 'We're almost there now, Jase.'

'Left to two-zero-zero at the key,' Jason said.

'Left to two-zero-zero,' Alex repeated.

The men had come down out of the low foothills of the Sierra de los Órganos range in the province of Pinar del Rio. They plodded through the same teeming rain that had inundated the island for the past four days, lashed now by a strong wind that moved the storm northward and eastward towards the Bahamas. The heavier boxes were strapped to the mules, but the men carried all the others on their backs and the rain was merciless, the wind whistled through the vegetation on either side of the muddy rutted road that led towards Cabo San Antonio and the extreme western end of the island.

There were fourteen men in all.

They were dressed protectively, most of them wearing rubberized ponchos, all of them wearing rubber boots, some of them wearing hats. They were all armed. One man carried an American burp gun, a leftover from the Bay of Pigs invasion. Occasionally one of them would slip in the treacherous mud and curse loudly in Spanish as he extricated himself from the slime. When an animal bogged down or simply refused to move, the men would patiently pull at his reins or shove at his backside, the rain beating around them, their hands working swiftly, their mouths moving with an ever-present Spanish curse.

It would be a twelve-mile hike to La Fé, where the boat was waiting.

The leader of the men was called El Feliz, which meant 'The Lucky One' in Spanish. He was called El Feliz because once, back in 1958 when Batista was in power, he had won a lottery for a hundred and twenty-five pesos on a ticket that had cost him twenty-five centavos. That was in the days when Batista was in power. El Feliz had spent part of his winnings to see a circus with a fellow named Superman who had the largest weapon on the island and who performed with two putas, mostly for the benefit of American tourists. That was in the days when Batista was in power.

El Feliz was a chunky man with powerful muscles on his back and arms and shoulders from cutting sugar cane, and with dark and wary eyes that seemed suspicious of every fluttering palm frond on either side of the road. He made no attempt to quiet his men, and yet he studied the road with darting eyes, the burp gun slung over one shoulder, the left arm stretched behind him as he tugged at the reins of one of the animals. Struggling in the mud behind him, his head ducked against the rain, was El Feliz's friend and lieutenant, a man named Angel, who tugged at the same reins and then stopped abruptly as the mule sat in the mud. Angel turned to the mule, muttered, 'Hijo de la chingada,' and then immediately walked behind it and delivered a sharp-pointed kick to the mule's haunches. The mule changed its mind about sitting in the mud, and immediately struggled to its legs under the load of the heavy wooden box on its back. The box was covered with a tarpaulin, and the wind tore wildly at the covering. The mule almost lost its balance, and then found its footing and pushed through the mud as Angel whipped it from behind.

In Spanish, El Feliz said, 'Do not force the animals. They cannot go more rapidly than the men.'

'The men go too slowly,' Angel replied.
'Too slowly for what? It will still be there on Tuesday.'
'Then I long for Tuesday,' Angel said fiercely.

16

The ship was too small.

Luke was unfamiliar with its layout, and he was certain that whichever passageway or ladder he took he would lead into a nest of Jason's men squatting on their haunches with rifles across their knees. He had circled to the fantail with Samantha, and then had come forward again until they were now back to where he had attacked Benny and dropped him over the side. A set of ladders went up on either side of the ship and he supposed they led to the bridge, which was where he definitely did not want to go. Even moving here on the main deck was extremely dangerous; there were too many open spaces, Samantha's blonde hair caught too much starlight.

He wished he knew where the captain's cabin was; he did not think it would be on the main deck. As he moved aft of what seemed to be some sort of deck structure behind the forward stack, he saw a companionway and a ladder leading below. He listened at the top of the steps for perhaps ten or fifteen seconds, heard no voices, and then tugged gently at Samantha's hand and began leading her down. He stopped in the middle of the ladder because he realized he was entering the engine room and further realized there had to be men down there, undoubtedly Jason's men, and probably some of the ship's engineers as well. He could hear the engines pounding. From where he stood midway on the ladder, he could see clear to the other end of the compartment where a work-bench and a lube-oil tank were against the bulkhead. A man with a rifle leaned against the tank. Luke put his hand flat against Samantha to stop her forward movement, and then they eased themselves up the ladder and on to the main deck again, slipping to the port

-side of the engine-room trunk as they heard voices approaching from aft and starboard. The voices passed into the night.

He said nothing to Samantha, but only increased the pressure on her hand tight in his, and moved aft again, circling around the stack and finding there a pair of ladders that led below. He reasoned correctly that it was impossible for the entire deck below the main deck to contain only an engine room and nothing else. There had to be sleeping compartments, there had to be mess halls and offices and storage lockers. There had to be a magazine. There had to be a place where they kept guns. He listened at the top of the ladder on the port side, again heard no voices, and again decided to chance it. He started down the ladder with Samantha behind him.

The ladder led into what obviously was a mess hall of some kind, with a long table against the port bulkhead, and a bench in front of it. There was a clock on the aft bulkhead of the compartment – the time was six thirty-five – and a door to the left of that. Luke stopped just outside the door and listened. There were no sounds coming from behind it. He grasped the knob and slowly turned it, opening the door a crack and peering into the room. There were two chairs in front of a long desk on the port bulkhead, and a pair of typewriters rested on the desktop. A small cabinet was against the aft bulkhead and alongside that a larger filing cabinet. Diagonally across the room from the entrance door, on the starboard bulkhead, there was a hanging curtain, partially opened.

Luke tiptoed into the room and looked around the curtain and into the next compartment. He knew immediately that this was the wardroom. There was a transom seat angled into the corner formed by the aft and starboard bulkheads, padded, covered with either leather or a plastic facsimile. A table with several chairs around it rested inside the angle formed by the corner seat. There was a serving board and a coffee maker and a toaster and a cabinet with dishes and cups and saucers in it and a radio and a bookcase.

And a telephone.

He moved to the phone where it hung on the bulkhead. A small black rectangular box was bolted below it. There were three buttons set into the face of the box. Transparent plates beneath each button covered three small typewritten labels. The label under the first button read BRDG, which Luke assumed was the bridge. The label under the second button read ENGR, which he supposed referred to the engine room or the engineering officer. The third and last button was labelled CABN. He figured this was either an abbreviation for the 'cabin' or else a misspelling of an abbreviation for the word 'captain'. In either case, he didn't see how he could lose. He didn't know how many cabins there were aboard the cutter, but he was willing to bet the only CABN that had a direct line to the wardroom was the captain's. He lifted the phone from its bracket.

There was a button on the handgrip. It was marked PRESS TO TALK. He looked at the labelled buttons on the bulkhead once more, pushed in the one marked CABN, caught his breath, and waited.

When the sound-powered telephone buzzed in Cates's cabin, he looked at it in surprise and debated whether or not he should answer it. He had decided long ago that the only reason they had kept him aboard was that they had a future possible use for him, and he had further decided that he would let them kill him before he would help them with their plan, whatever the plan was.

The phone buzzed again.

No, he thought. If you want something, come in here and ask for it. Then I'll spit in your eye and tell you to go to hell.

The phone buzzed again, insistently.

Cates looked at it.

He was being childish. The ship was in their hands. He would not help them, but neither would he behave in a manner unbefitting an officer. He lifted the phone from its bracket.

'Yes?' he said.

'Is this the captain?' the voice on the other end asked.

The voice sounded cautious. He could have sworn the man was whispering.

'Who's this?' he asked.

'Is this the captain?' the voice asked again.

'Yes. Who –'

'My name is Costigan. We've never met, and it doesn't matter,' the man said. He spoke quietly with restraint, but the words came rapidly and tensely with an urgency that immediately demanded Cates's full attention.

'Go on, Mr Costigan,' he said.

'I'm in the wardroom right now, trying to keep away from the people who've taken this ship. They're heading for Cuba, Captain, where they hope to involve the United States in a shooting war.'

'What?' Cates said.

'Yes, sir.'

'How –?'

'Sir, I'll explain later, if there's time. Right now, I need a gun.'

'The armoury locker,' Cates said.

'Where?'

'Aft of the exec's quarters. On the first deck.'

'Where's that?'

'Where did you say you were?'

'The wardroom, I think.'

'Through the ship's office?'

'Yes, it seemed to be that.'

'Was there a curtain over the hatch?'

'Yes.'

'All right, that's the wardroom. Go out the way you came in, through the ship's office, and then through the CPO's mess, back up the ladder to the main deck. If you come forward on the main deck to . . . well, just aft of the gun there are two deck hatches, and then my cabin, and a hatch leading into a passageway. About midships in the passageway, you'll see a ladder leading below . . . wait a minute.'

'What's the matter?'

'The armoury's always locked. There's a padlock on the door.'

'Who's got the key?'

'It's in the safe,' Cates said.

'What safe?'

'The one here. Right here in my cabin.'

It was five minutes to seven and he wasn't back yet, and she didn't know what to do. She stood near the window in the big old house on the beach, the house silent and grey around her, looking out over the road and to the town beyond, where she had first seen the fire and later the fire engines coming to put it out. She hadn't supposed anything had happened to him. They had put the fire *out*, hadn't they?

She wondered suddenly if he'd taken off.

Well, no, he wouldn't do that.

No, she didn't suppose he'd do anything like that.

Still, he'd been acting very jumpy ever since those two came to the door. What had that fellow been doing with a rifle, anyway? Even Rog said it was the rifle that bothered him – it bothers *me* too. I'll tell you the truth.

Maybe I ought to take a walk across the road.

He wouldn't just walk out on me, would he?

I don't know. Who knows with married men? I should never have started up with him in the first place, in the snow that day, he wasn't wearing a hat. She had thought at first his hair was white, but that was only the snow in it. He had parked the Cadillac around the corner from the Bureau of Printing and Engraving, and walked in the snow to where she was standing by the bus stop, and then had just asked her right out if he could drop her someplace. She'd looked at the white hair and then realized it was only snow, and thought he was very good-looking and said, 'I live in Maryland.'

'Did I ask?'

'No.'

'Let's go,' he said.

'What's this?' she said. 'A pickup?'

'Yes.'

'Well, so it's a pickup,' she answered, and shrugged, and went with him to where the car was parked, noticing the VIP licence plate immediately.

He wouldn't just walk out on her, would he?

And leave her here in the middle of the swamp all alone with alligators or whatever was outside, fellows coming to the door with rifles no less?

Well, she thought.

Well, gee, what am I going to do? And suddenly she laughed.

Her laughter came back to her hollowly in the empty house.

Fatboy and Rodiz were sitting in chairs near the chart table, smoking and talking in quiet voices. Rodiz said something in Spanish, and Fatboy, apparently understanding, broke into quiet laughter. Their earlier dispute about leaving the dead policemen in the automobile seemed to have been forgotten. Jason watched them from the wheelhouse, and smiled in pleasure. Everything would be all right. There was a feel to the entire operation that told him nothing could go wrong any more. He closed his eyes and felt the gentle rocking of the ship, listened to the pleasant hum of Rodiz talking in Spanish.

It started with the sale of the foul-weather jacket, for which he got what amounted to a hundred and twelve dollars in yen. He began stealing regularly after that, he didn't know why. The 832 would pull into a Japanese port and her skipper would go ashore and visit here and there, and then the 832 would vanish for a little while and a little sugar would vanish with her, or a few machine parts, or some grapefruit juice, or some rice, all of which he would later trade in Tokyo or Yokohama for more paper money than he knew existed in the world, money that could buy saki or broads or crumby souvenirs, but not much of anything else – or so he thought, at first. He enjoyed taking money from the Japanese. He enjoyed hearing them plead, watching their eyes grow round with greed and longing, holding to his price each time, ten dollars in yen for a sack of sugar, fifty-three dollars in yen for an Army blanket he stole in Fukuoka, two hundred dollars in yen for a Jeep tyre he stole in souvenirs he wanted to ship back home. That was the first and only time anyone ever asked him what he was taking ashore with him. The person who asked was a new Shore Patrolman at the gate. He apologized and giggled and kept calling him 'sir' afterwards. 'Yes, sir, sorry, sir, but I'm *supposed* to ask, sir. All *kinds* of stuff has been finding its way ashore, sir,' two hundred bucks in yen for the tyre.

He counted up his money in February and discovered he had close to fifteen thousand dollars in occupation yen, which was *real* money to the Japs, the only money in circulation in the country, the only money that could buy fish or rice or vegetables. It seemed grossly unfair to Jason that these dirty little cock-eyed brown bastards could spend the money on things they actually needed, and here he had a fortune in the stuff and all he could do was wipe his ass with it. He couldn't cash it in for dollars because of the strict monetary regulations, and he couldn't send it home to Annabelle to cash because it was clearly marked 'Occupation', and was about as valuable in the States as the fake money in a game of monopoly.

Along about that time, well, maybe it was a little later, yes, it must have been early in March, he heard about a machinist's mate who had taken apart a motor launch and was shipping it home piece by piece, the rudder, the screw, the carburettor, the whole damn thing, part by part, listing each separate part as a souvenir he was sending to his mother. Jason knew intuitively that the story was exaggerated, but the machinist's ingenuity gave him an idea. If he couldn't cash in his yen or send it home, why not spend it on something he *could* send home?

Why not spend it on something like pearls?

Kemo was a smart little whore he was shacking up with in Tokyo. It was Kemo he sounded out about maybe buying some Japanese pearls. He had already hinted to her that he was picking up a few things here and there, making a few bucks on the side by selling a few choice items to her countrymen, all of which Kemo understood perfectly because first of all she was forty-three years old, a good deal older than he at the time, and also she was a whore with a whore's honest enjoyment of larceny. He didn't trust her enough to tell her exactly how *much* he was pulling in – no sense getting her all excited, right? – but he did give her some idea of his operation, and the kind of stuff he was picking up. Like one night he told her about the fan he'd stolen in Kagoshima, right from under the eyes of the yeoman first class in the office. That was back in January. He still had to laugh when he thought about that fan. Kemo laughed too. She always covered her mouth when she laughed. He thought that was cute as hell. Kemo knew he thought it was cute, and she did it because she knew he thought it was cute. She referred to her genitals as her 'monkey'. 'Monkey catch Jasonn,' she would say. 'Monkey take Jasonn from Annaburr.' Jason would laugh and tell her nobody in the world was going to take him from Annaburr, especially not an old Jap whore who lived in a bombed-out Tokyo alley. 'You better be careful,' he said, 'or I'll report you to the M.P.s and MacArthur himself will come down in person and put a scarlet letter right here on your left one.'

Maybe she believed him.

Anyway, it was natural for him to sound her out about the pearls, and it was natural for her to know somebody who knew somebody – everybody in Japan always knew somebody who knew somebody, especially the whores. Especially the smart whores like Kemo.

'It coss much,' she said.

Jason said it was up to her to find some that didn't cost much, you dig? and Kemo said she would investigate the matter. She then asked him to get out because an Army sergeant friend of hers was coming in ten minutes, and he was a very jealous man. Jason wanted to know if she had warned the sergeant that he might easily catch the clap from her, and then he left and didn't see her again until the boat came back to Sasebo in the middle of March. He borrowed a jeep from the base and drove up to Tokyo, parking the jeep

272

outside the makeshift tin-and-wood shack where Kemo lived, and rapping on the door and then going in to find her asleep near the small burning hibachi.

'Hey, wake up, you old whore,' he said, and nudged her with the toe of his shoe.

Kemo looked up at him with all the unveiled malevolence of a conquered people, and then came immediately awake, and smiled and told him she had made contact with someone who wanted to sell some very good pearls. She asked Jason if he understood that the pearls would be stolen pearls, which was why he was getting such a bargain on them. He hadn't thought of it until just that minute, but it didn't matter a damn to him whether they were stolen or what they were. So he said sure, he understood, and they made arrangements to buy a whole potful of them for the fifteen thousand dollars, more than he could have bought in the States for twice that price, good pearls, too, the real, thing. He told Kemo to get more for him. He told her he'd have at least another five grand by the beginning of April, and that he wanted more pearls of the same quality. Kemo, always willing to oblige, said she would get them, and then archly asked if he was going to have them strung for Annaburr. 'String *this* for Annaburr,' he said, and laughed and pinched her naked breast until a huge purple bruise showed near the nipple. Again the same look crossed Kemo's face, the look she had awakened with the day he had returned to Tokyo.

Jason did not notice it.

He was beginning to realize that he would be a very rich man before he left Japan. It never occurred to him that he was selling property belonging to the United States government. Oh yes, it occurred to him; it simply never bothered him. The way he looked at it, these Jap bastards had it coming to them. Each time he sold them something, he felt as if he were gouging them, as if he were somehow taking food out of their mouths. He sold them all this worthless crap that was lying around all these bases just gathering dust, and he got yen for it, which he then used to buy the only good things the Japs had ever come up with, their pearls. The United States government had nothing whatever to do with it. This was something personal between Jason and the Japs. He was giving it to the enemies of his country. He was doing it in his own way and in his own time, but he was giving it to them as surely as he was giving it to little Kemo in that crawling Tokyo shack, the old bitch.

On the third of April Jason returned to Sasebo from a tour of Hokkaido, where he had inspected four Japanese destroyers and seven Japanese cargo vessels, and where he had stolen and sold enough material to bring him not the five thousand dollars he had expected but the equivalent of two thousand five hundred and twenty-one dollars in yen, not bad for a short voyage. He tried to check out a jeep, but there weren't any available, so he took a train up to Tokyo and then walked up Kemo's street through the rows of rubble on either side of the street itself, Toyko flattened, the shacks springing up everywhere like weeds in a vacant lot. At the far end of the street a man was building a house, working silently and rapidly in the flat afternoon light. The house was a real house and not a shack like Kemo's. It was only half built, partially roofed over, but the sliding doors and windows were already in place, and a finished deck jutted out from the entrance door. He suddenly wondered where the man had got enough money to buy the lumber that was stacked alongside the house. He put the man out of his mind and knocked on Kemo's door. He knew there was someone with her immediately. There was a short tell-tale hesitation, and then her voice came to him huskily, in Japanese, asking who was there.

'It's me,' he said.

'Mo-men,' Kemo answered, and he heard her shuffling around inside the shack. He waited angrily. He heard her footsteps approaching the door. At last the door opened. Her face showed in the crack. Her hand was clutched into the closed front of her kimono. 'Yess?' she said.

'Who's in there with you?'

'Friend,' she answered.

'Get rid of him.'

'He good friend.'

'I'll give you five minutes.'

'Jasonn, you verry minn,' Kemo said.

'I'll break you and him in half, both,' Jason said. 'Get him the hell out of there.'

'Oh you so strong,' Kemo said, and grinned wickedly and closed the door. Angrily he walked away from the shack. He felt suddenly chilled. It was cold for April, with a wan pale light glowing flatly on the rubble, the stench of smoke and fish and humanity hanging on the air, the sound of the carpenter's hammer ringing sharp and clear with each stroke. Jason lifted the collar of his jacket. He found a few scraps of wood in the gutter, and carried them into the lot, lighted them with his Zippo, and made a small fire over which he squatted, warming his hands. She seemed to be taking a very long time in there, the old bitch; that was because she knew he was waiting. The flames were dying. He searched around for some more bits and pieces and then looked off to where the carpenter was working and strolled down to the end of the lot, watching for a moment. The man glanced at him apprehensively, smiling, bowing, and then turned back to his work.

'Hey,' Jason said.

The man turned, smiling again, waiting.

'You need these scraps here?' Jason asked.

The man did not understand English.

'You need this wood here?' Jason said. 'These chips, do you need them? Oh, go to hell,' he said, and picked up the scraps and walked back to the fire with them.

They burned very rapidly.

It was three o'clock in the afternoon, but it seemed later because of the curious light that day, the clouds hanging in dark folds, refusing to allow the sunlight through. The hammer rings seemed to add to the feeling of coldness, each sharp biting clang reverberating on the air, carrying to where Jason squatted over the rapidly dying fire. He would need more wood. Unless she came out soon, he would need more wood. He got up and walked back to where the Japanese carpenter was working. He looked for some more

275

scraps, but there didn't seem to be any.

'You got any more wood you don't need?' he asked.

The carpenter bowed and smiled.

'For the fire,' Jason said, pointing.

'Ahhh,' the Jap said. 'Ahhh.'

'Have you got any?'

'Kemo,' the Jap said. 'Kemo.' And he grinned.

The dumb bastard thinks I want to get laid, Jason thought. He's giving me the phone number of the local whore. 'Yeah, I know all about Kemo,' he said. 'I want wood. You got some wood for me. To burn. Some junk you're not going to use. Oh hell, what's the sense?' He turned away from the Jap and was starting back for the dying fire when the door to Kemo's shack opened.

He had expected her 'friend' to be an American, perhaps even the sergeant he had kidded her about one time. But the man who came out of the shack was a Japanese, still wearing his uniform, his face browned and bearded, as if he had just come back from some Pacific island where he'd been holed up in a cave eating his buddies and shooting at Americans. Jason turned and walked to the neatly stacked pile of fresh lumber near the house. He picked up a long slat.

'I'm taking this,' he said, and began walking away. He very carefully avoided looking at the touching scene in the doorway of Kemo's shack, the man bowing his little brown ass off, Kemo hanging in the doorway like a teen-ager coming home after the big Saturday night prom. He went to the fire, and he broke the wood in pieces over his knees and threw the pieces on to the waning flames. An idea, an impulse, came to him. He walked back to the house again and climbed up on to the partially finished deck where the carpenter was working.

'You building yourself a nice little house, gook?' he asked. 'Get the hell out of my way.' He shoved the carpenter aside and grabbed a partially fastened slat with both hands and pulled it free from the wall. The carpenter's eyes opened wide. Jason threw the plank off the deck and then kicked his foot through the sliding door of the house and ripped the thin dividing pieces of wood from the door frame while the carpenter stood by in helpless indecision.

'Well, what you say, you dumb bastard?' Jason shouted. 'I'm tearing apart your crumby little house, how about that?' He ripped another slat free, he kicked his foot through another paper panel, the whole damn house was falling apart, cheap crap, Made in Japan, the only good thing they had was pearls. He picked up an axe from the deck and swung it fiercely, chopping at one wall and then another, splitting paper and wood, wrecking the house with a wild angry glee, and finally throwing the axe down at the feet of the shocked, trembling carpenter. He leaped off the deck and began to walk back to where Kemo was watching him from the open door of her shack. Her 'friend' was gone now. He was going to give it to her, all right. If she thought what he'd just done to this house was something, then she had a little surprise coming because he was really going to give it to her.

The carpenter said something.

It might have been only a sob, because when he turned, the man was standing on the deck of the demolished house with his hands clenched tightly around the head of the hammer, both hands squeezing the head of the hammer, both hands trying to fit on to the small head of the hammer, trembling, the tears running down his face with the effort to contain his anger.

'*What'd* you say, pal?' Jason asked.

The man shook his head. Sobbing, trembling, he avoided Jason's eyes.

'Did I hear you *say* something, pal?' Jason asked.

The man did not reply. He was shaking violently now. Behind him, Jason could hear Kemo's approaching footsteps. He leaped on to the deck and yanked the man to him with one angry grabbing pulling motion and smashed his fist into the man's face. The man fell to the deck and Jason kicked him in the head. Behind him he heard Kemo screaming. He whirled, jumped off the deck, and ran after her, catching her near the fire, grabbing her kimono and swinging her around, the kimono flaring wide over her

277

naked belly and legs. He slapped her and called her a cheap little whore and then slapped her again. The fire leaped high with the flames of the dried wood he had fed to it. He kept slapping her in the light of the blaze until she dropped to her knees with blood streaming from her nose and her mouth, the kimono open. He barely realized that two Marine M.P.s had grabbed his arms and were holding him. He looked down at Kemo and said, 'You don't mess with *me*, honey. You don't *never* mess with me.'

Kemo looked up. Through her broken teeth and her bloody lips she said in English. 'You son a bitch basturr brack marker thief nogood basturr crook.' For good measure , and to ingratitate herself with the military police, she added, 'Tojo nogood crap.'

The Marine colonel who searched Jason found that he was carrying two thousand five hundred and twenty-one dollars in yen.

'That's a lot of money,' the colonel said.

'Mmm?' Jason answered.

'Where'd you get all this money?'

'I got lucky in a crap game.'

'Why'd you beat up that woman?'

'They tried to roll me.'

'Who?'

'Her and the guy working on that house. I was just strolling up the street and they jumped me.'

The colonel squeezed the bridge of his nose with his thumb and forefinger, and sighed. The two M.P.s who had picked Jason up stood just inside the door of the hut, their hands clasped over their white clubs. 'The woman says you're involved in black market activities,' the colonel said. He had a flat dry voice. He sounded as if he were from the Middle West someplace.

'She's crazy,' Jason said. 'I never saw her in my life before tonight.'

'She says she knows you.'

'She's lying.'

'She says your name is Jason Trench.' The colonel

suddenly released the bridge of his nose and looked up. '*Is that your name?*'

Jason did not answer.

'She says you bought more than fifteen thousand dollars in stolen pearls last month, and that you were there to buy more today.'

'Where would I get that kind of money?' Jason asked.

'I don't know.' The colonel shrugged. 'Where would you get two thousand five hundred and twenty-one dollars in yen?'

'I told you. In a crap game.'

'Where?'

'Aboard the boat.'

'What boat?'

'The PT 832.'

'You the skipper?'

'Yes.'

'We're going to ask your men about that alleged crap game while we keep you here. Is that all right with you?'

'Sir . . .'

'Yes?'

'Sir, are you going to listen to an old Jap whore, or are you –'

'No,' the colonel said.

'Good. I was afraid –'

'What we *are* going to do is keep you here while we question your crew about that crap game you say took place aboard your boat. Then we're –'

'Well, I don't remember if it was aboard the boat. It could have been with some Army guys up in –'

'Then we're going to ask to see your ID card and your dog tags. Maybe your name isn't Jason Trench. Maybe that woman's talking about somebody else.'

'My name's Trench,' he said.

'Oh?'

'They tried to roll me. She stopped me in the street and he came up behind me, and together they tried to roll me.'

'Is that your story?'

'That's my story.'

'We found the man on the deck of that house, Trench. He —'

'Yeah, he tried to drag me inside there.'

'I thought he jumped you in the street.'

'Well, he . . .'

'We had to take him to the hospital,' the colonel said. 'Somebody kicked him in the head.'

'I did. He tried to roll me.'

'Yes, I know, you said so.'

'It's the truth.'

The colonel shrugged. 'Truth or not,' he said, 'you're stuck with it.'

The thing he shouldn't have done – well, actually there were a couple of things he shouldn't have done, but the first thing he shouldn't have done was turn back when the Jap muttered whatever it was he'd muttered; that was plain stupid. He should have just kept walking to where Kemo was standing in the door of the shack, and grabbed her and quietly taken her back inside, that was it, no sweat, instead of losing his head like that. He shouldn't have lied about there having been a crap game aboard the boat either, because naturally when they questioned the other men, all of them – with the exception of Arthur – had tried to protect him by saying exactly the wrong thing. A crap game? Heavens, no, we never shot dice aboard our clean little boat, they had said, golly Moses, no, all except Arthur. Arthur had possessed the good sense to know something was in the wind, and he had picked up the lie almost as if he were carrying radar. Yes sir, he had said, there *was* a very big crap game aboard the boat, there are *always* a lot of very big money crap games. Even so, the lie hadn't work. Nor had he been very smart in pretending not to know Kemo either; that was really dumb. Not only was she able to tell them *his* name, and his *wife*'s name – 'Annaburr,' she said, 'he send the perrs to Annaburr' – but she was also able to tell them the number of his boat and the names of several of the men aboard her; it was amazing the things a man said to a woman when he was in bed with her. He had also

280

apparently told her about a particular escapade in Kagoshima, where he had audaciously stolen an electric fan from the desk of the yeoman first, in the office ashore, a fan he later sold for seventy-five dollars. The funny thing about this particular fan was that the yeoman had painted it pink.

Kemo didn't understand English too well, and she spoke it pretty badly, especially when it came to naming colours. Had she described the colour of that fan wrong when the court asked about it, things might have worked out differently. But Kemo was remembering all the indignities she had suffered at the hands of Jason Trench, Kemo was remembering the bruises he had left on her breast and thighs, remembering that he had never treated her like anything but dirt, never like a woman even when he was inside her, remembering his wife Annaburr to whom he had sent the pearls. All these things combined to make it absolutely essential that there be no mistake about the colour of the fan that had been stolen in Kagoshima. Kemo lifted the hem of her kimono clear up over her thighs, showing the court a splendid pair of whore's legs, and also showing them a nylon slip that had been given to her by her Army sergeant friend.

'This,' she said, and glared at Jason.

The slip was pink.

He always felt later that they were being particularly hard on him because he had pulled down that Jap house and beaten up Kemo. He could not understand it. Kemo and the carpenters were both enemies of the United States; what difference did it make what happened to them? But he knew that this was why they were being so hard on him. After all, he was an officer in the United States Navy, a *combat* officer; they didn't have to throw the book at him that way. Oh yes, the yeoman from Kagoshima came down to testify that a pink fan had been discovered missing from the office shortly after the visit of the 832 in the second week of January, a visit confirmed by the record of harbour traffic that month. He also testified to having seen Jason in the office on at least two occasions, but all this was circumstantial since the missing pink fan was

281

at no time offered in evidence. (How could it be? Jason had sold it to a shopkeeper in Kyoto.) It seemed to Jason, in fact, that the only few things they really had him on were the ones the Japs had testitied to, and he couldn't understand why the court was willing to accept *their* word over his.

The charges included violation of Paragraph 187, Article 108 of the Punitive Articles, *Selling or otherwise disposing of military property of the United States;* that was the pink fan, all circumstantial. Then they charged him with the *Wasting, despoiling or damaging of any property other than military property of the United States*. That was the Jap house. The court valued the fan at between twenty dollars and fifty dollars, and the house at more than fifty dollars. In either case, the punishment – if he had been an enlisted man – could have included dishonourable discharge and forfeiture of all pay and allowances, as well as six months' hard labour for each offence. That wasn't all, though. They charged him with two counts of assault. The asssault of the Jap carpenter was called *aggravated* assault, because it turned out the bastard had suffered a concussion when Jason kicked him in the head. They called the assault on Kemo an assault with intent to commit rape, which couldn't have been further from the truth but which carried a possible twenty-year sentence as opposed to six months for simple assault and battery, and five years for aggravated assault. They also added looting and pillaging to the list of offences, because he had taken a slat of wood and tossed it on the fire, and – as an ironic fillip to the whole episode – they charged him with misbehaviour before the enemy in that his intentional misconduct in the presence of Kemo and the carpenter had endangered the safety of the place (Japan) which it was his duty to defend.

According to the code, an officer could not be sentenced to a bad-conduct discharge, but he *could* be dismissed from the service for an offence in violation of an article of the code, and Jason was convicted of several such offences. His dismissal included a forfeiture of all pay and allowances and immediate transfer back to the United States. Back in

282

Louisiana, Annabelle was waiting with the pearls he had sent to her, and which he estimated to be worth about thirty-five thousand dollars.

Many years later he would use the money he received from the sale of those pearls to buy a cabin cruiser named *The Golden Fleece*, to rent a warehouse and a truck in Miami, to acquire automobiles and rooms in Key West, to pay for plane fares, to buy pistols and rifles to support an invasion. He thought it supremely ironic that he had taken this money from a past enemy of the United States and was now using it against a present enemy.

The sound-powered phone at his elbow buzzed. He opened his eyes and blinked at it curiously for a moment, as though his mind were still elsewhere, and then lifted it from the bulkhead bracket.

'Bridge,' he said.

'This is the captain,' the voice on the other end answered.

17

'Well, how are you, Captain?' Jason said pleasantly. 'Everything all right down there?'

'I . . . I don't like to ask for favours,' Cates said.

'What is it?'

'I've got a bad tooth,' Cates said. 'It's been . . .'

'Yes, what about it?' Jason said.

'We have a hospital corpsman aboard. I thought –'

'Oh, do we?'

'Yes,' Cates said, and waited.

'Did we leave the corpsman aboard?' Jason asked Alex.

Alex turned from the wheel and said, 'I think so.'

'You sure he's not ashore?'

'No, I think he's down in the engine room with the others.'

'Tell him I'm about to have my baby,' Annabelle said, and giggled. 'I want to see him go pale again.'

Jason laughed and pressed the button on the phone grip, 'Captain,' he said, 'we *do* have a corpsman aboard. What is it you want?'

'I thought he could pull this tooth,' Cates said. 'I'm in pain.'

'Well, I don't like to see anybody in pain,' Jason said, and hesitated. 'I'll send somebody for the corpsman. He'll be down there soon. Why don't you take a swig of brandy meanwhile? You've got some in your safe, haven't you?'

'I've already had some.'

'Don't get loaded, Captain. We may need you later on, just in case anybody gets too curious.' Jason laughed again. 'I'll have the corpsman brought down. You just relax.'

'Thank you,' Cates said.

'Sure,' Jason answered, and hung up the phone. He

turned to where Rodiz and Fatboy were seated at the chart table. 'Anybody feel like taking a walk?'

'What is it?' Rodiz asked.

'Captain needs a tooth pulled. I'd like somebody to go get the corpsman and take him to the captain's cabin.'

'I'll go,' Fatboy said. 'Where is he?'

'In the engine room.'

Fatboy stood up and stretched.

'You'll need a key,' Alex said from the wheel. 'The cabin's locked.' He reached into his pocket and then extended his hand back to Jason, who took the key from it and passed it on to Fatboy.

'What's the corpsman's name?' Fatboy asked.

'I don't know. Just go down there and ask for him. Who's down there, anyway?'

'I think Johnny and Sy.'

'Yeah, well, tell them you want the corpsman, that's all.'

'Okay. I'll see you,' Fatboy said, and went out through the wheelhouse door and on to the bridge deck, walking aft to the ladder that led to the main deck, climbing down, and then going past the forward stack and into the companionway and down the ladder to the engine room. There were perhaps a dozen men in the compartment, including Johnny and Sy. Sy was standing near the workbench, the butt of a rifle at his feet, his hand around the muzzle near the sight. Johnny was sitting on the bench. Both men looked up as Fatboy came down the ladder.

'Hey, how's it going?' Fatboy asked.

'Nice and quiet,' Sy answered.

'You got a hospital corpsman here?'

'Search me,' Sy said. He turned to the men who were standing near the bulkhead just forward of the starboard main engine. 'Any of you guys a corpsman?' he asked.

None of the men answered. But some of them turned automatically to look at a thin young man who glanced up nervously and then tried to hide behind the man next to him.

'You the corpsman?' Fatboy asked.

The young man nodded.

'What's your name?'

'Bunder.'

'Let's go, Bunder.'

'Wh – wh – where? Where?' Bunder said.

'Come on,' Fatboy said, and drew his .45. Bunder glanced at the gun and nodded, and swallowed, and looked at his shipmates pleadingly. 'Up the ladder,' Fatboy said. Bunder went up the ladder ahead of him. Over his shoulder Fatboy called, 'Take it easy, now.'

They came out on to the main deck. The sky was sprinkled with stars, the ship moved steadily southward and westward, there was the constant hiss of rushing waters against its sides. 'You'll need your kit,' Fatboy said. 'Where's sick bay?'

'In officer's country.'

'Where's that?'

'On the berth deck, amidships.'

'Where we just came from?'

'Well, forward of the engine room.'

'How do we get there?'

'We can take a passageway going by the captain's cabin.'

'Good. That's right on our way.'

'What do you mean?'

'The captain's cabin.'

'Well, sick bay's on the deck below.'

'That's okay.'

They came down the starboard side of the ship. Bunder opened the hatch leading into the passageway. As they passed the captain's cabin, he saw that two pieces of chain had been welded to the door and bulkhead, and that a padlock had been passed through them. A ladder about two feet beyond the door and across the passageway led below to the armoury locker, the officers' staterooms, and sick bay. A hatch was at the other end of the passageway. The hatch was closed.

'Down here,' Bunder said. 'Listen, you could tell me where we're going and what I'm supposed to do? So I'll know what –'

'You gonna pull a tooth.'

'What?'

'Yeah, the captain's tooth.'

'Oh, brother,' Bunder said.

'You'd better bring pliers or something,' Fatboy said.

Bunder nodded dismally. From the surgical tools in the medicine cabinet he took heavy forceps and bandage scissors, and hoped they would suffice to yank the captain's tooth. This had been the worst day of his entire life. First a pregnant woman – well, they *thought* she was pregnant – and then all the shooting, and now he had to pull the *captain*'s tooth, the tooth of a lieutenant commander in the United States Coast Guard. Wouldn't this day ever end?

'Listen,' he said, 'maybe *you* ought to do it.'

'What are you talking about?'

'Pull the tooth.'

'He asked for you specifically.'

'The captain did?'

'Uh-huh.'

'Oh, brother,' Bunder said, and picked up his kit. He looked up at Fatboy, and then said conversationally, 'What are you guys doing, anyway?'

'None of your business,' Fatboy said.

'Oh,' Bunder said.

They went up the steps again. Bunder walked directly to the captain's door, looked at the padlocked chain again, and then said, 'This is locked.'

'I've got the key,' Fatboy said. 'Stand aside.' He waved the gun at Bunder and reached into his pocket. Bunder backed off against the bulkhead. Fatboy fitted the key into the padlock and opened it. He was putting the key back into his pocket when he saw the look of surprise in Bunder's face, and immediately turned. Luke Costigan was bounding through the hatch at the other end of the passageway some four feet from where they were standing, both hands clenched together and going up over his head like a sledge hammer. The element of total surprise had been totally wasted on Bunder, who still stood flat against the bulkhead alongside the door, his eyes wide, his mouth gaping as Fatboy moved forward like a boxer to meet Luke's rush.

287

The surprise element might have equalized the .45 in Fatboy's hand, but Bunder had very carelessly blown Luke's advantage, and now Luke rushed forward with both hands clasped together over his head, and then stopped dead and swung them down and sideways at Fatboy's head just as Fatboy brought the .45 into firing position. For the first time that day Bunder acted like a hero. He stuck out his foot just enough to catch the tip of Fatboy's shoe, throwing him off balance. Fatboy hurtled forward clumsily as Luke's clenched hands came around like a solid iron mace at the end of a swinging chain, colliding with Fatboy's jaw and sending the .45 flying out of his hand and spinning down the length of the passageway. Fatboy crashed into the bulkhead and then turned, dazed, to find Luke coming at him again. Luke's hands were bunched into separate solid fists now, and he threw one with all his strength into Fatboy's midsection and then tried a fierce right uppercut that missed Fatboy's jaw by inches. Fatboy was still doubled over, his arms clutching at his midsection, a sustained grunt coming from his lips in a steady *urgh-urgh-urgh* struggle for breath. Luke clenched his left fist and brought it down on the back of Fatboy's neck in an angry rabbit punch that sent him sprawling to the deck. He bent over him, straddling him, caught his collar in both hands, and banged his head against the deck once, without anger. Fatboy lay still. Bunder stood against the bulkhead, his face pale, his eyes wide, his palms pressed flat to the metal, and looked at Luke as though he wondered which of the men was the lesser of the two evils.

Luke threw open the captain's door. 'Help me get him inside,' he said. 'Quick!'

There were some men who claimed Virgil Cooper could see in the dark. Well, maybe he could when he was on dry land with dirt under his boots and with nothing more to worry about than just looking. He sure couldn't see anything out there on the water, though it was a wonder ships didn't just go banging into each other all the time. Well, he supposed they had radar. He looked out over the rail to

288

starboard and couldn't see a thing but the stars in the distance and even they seemed to be hanging in total darkness, with ocean and sky blending into one, and without a man being able to tell where one started and the other began.

It was a dark night, all right, with no moon and with the ship plunging ahead without running lights into a blackness as deep as hell. It made Coop uncomfortable. It reminded him of that Korean night when the Mongolians came charging out of the darkness blowing their bugles and beating their drums. You'd think the stars would throw just a little more light than they did.

He was walking back aft near the fantail where the canvas canopy was spread like a tent. He paused for a moment to watch the small white tongues of water licking the sides of the ship, to listen to the whispering hiss of steel pushing against ocean, and then began walking forward again.

He was passing the after stack when something on the deck caught his eye. It rested just alongside the companionway and ladder leading below. He thought at first it was a cartridge someone had dropped, its brass case catching starlight and glowing feebly in the shadow of the bulkhead. He stooped to pick it up.

He held it in the palm of his hand and stared at it, puzzled.

It took him several moments to realize he was looking down at a woman's lipstick.

They opened the door to the armoury locker quickly and silently, each of the men taking a .45 and an M1, strapping on the handguns, putting clips into the rifles and then moving swiftly into the forward stateroom on the starboard side, the exec's cabin, and closing the door behind them. Bunder was still frightened; he had the feeling he was going to be killed; he had the feeling they were all going to be killed. He didn't like the way the captain and this man Costigan looked at each other with hard eyes; he didn't like the way they talked in whispers. He was a hospital corpsman; he wasn't expected to carry a rifle and a strap on

289

a handgun. He was afraid he would get killed. They were planning their next move. He tried to listen to them, but his heart was pounding and all he could think of was that he would be killed tonight. His girl's name was Effie. He wondered what she would say when they told her he'd been killed on a routine patrol originating out of Key West.

'Where's the radio room?' Costigan was saying.

'Just aft of where we are now,' the captain said, 'But up on the main deck.'

'Is there a lock on the door?'

'Yes.'

'Can it be locked from the inside?'

'Yes. But there should be a duplicate key right here in this cabin,' the captain said. 'The executive officer has a dupe of every key aboard, except for the magazine and the armoury.'

'We might need it,' Costigan said. 'They may have locked themselves in there. They plan to radio back and say they're answering an SOS about fifty miles north-west of Havana. Is that possible?'

'Yes, it's possible,' the captain said.

'I mean, that you'd go in that close to the island?'

'Yes, that's not too close.'

'Then Miami *would* believe it.'

'Yes. *I* would, if I were the officer on duty.' The captain paused. 'Mr. Costigan,' he said, 'I want to regain control of my ship.'

'I don't think that's possible,' Costigan said.

'Why not?'

'Trench has too many men aboard.'

'We're armed now. We can –'

'I don't want to try it.'

'This is not your ship, Mr. Costigan.'

'That's true, Captain. But it's not yours, either. It's Jason Trench's. And if we try to take it back and fail, the United States'll be at war tomorrow morning.'

'I don't think we'll fail, Mr. Costigan.'

'If there's even a chance of failure –'

'I want the ship back.'

'Captain,' Luke said, 'it's too late for this kind of crap.'

'What?'

'You shouldn't have lost the ship in the first place. We shouldn't have let them take the town, either. But we did, and you did, and there's nothing to be done about it now. Except stop them.'

'That's why I want to –'

'Captain, the only way to stop these men for sure is to go into that radio room and call Miami and tell them exactly what's going on. That's the only way. Miami'll contact the Navy, and the destroyers'll take care of the rest.'

'They won't believe us. They'll think somebody is playing a practical joke.'

'They'll believe us,' Costigan said. 'But if they don't, you can give them a frequency to call back on. They can check it that way.'

The captain hesitated for a long time. It seemed to Bunder that however they worked this, they were going to get killed. If they stormed the bridge or whatever it was the captain wanted to do to get control of the ship, they'd be shot down in their tracks. If they tried to get into the radio shack, wouldn't the men in there be armed?

'Captain,' Costigan said, 'I'm going ahead with this whether you're with me or not. It'll make it easier if you send the message. I'm not familiar with your gear, and the Miami Coast Guard doesn't know me from a hole in the wall. But if I have to do it alone, I will. Now, where does your exec keep those duplicate keys?'

'There,' the captain said, and indicated the key locker on the bulkhead. He hesitated a moment. He sighed. 'What's your plan?' he asked. 'What do we do when we get to the radio shack?'

'We'll have to –'

Quite unexpectedly, even to himself, Bunder said aloud, 'We're all going to get killed tonight.'

It was very quiet up on the bridge. Coop didn't know exactly what he'd expected up here, but it seemed altogether too quiet. Maybe the darkness had something to do with it. The only real light burning was the one near the wheel, and it shone up on Alex's face and made him look kind of eerie. The other light came from the Sperry Mark 3 radar gear against the port bulkhead. Jason and Annabelle were standing near the gear, looking down at the scope in its slanted top, their faces bathed in its bluish-white electronic glow. Neither of the two was talking. As Coop approached them, he saw that they were holding hands. He grinned.

'Hey, I hope I'm not interrupting anything,' he said.

'We're watching television,' Jason said, and laughed.

'Anything good on?' Coop asked.

'Nothing. I thought maybe we'd catch Ed Sullivan. This *is* Sunday night, isn't it?'

'Yeah. Couldn't you get him?'

'Nothing but a lot of junk on it,' Jason said, and turned away from the gear.

'Hey, I found something belongs to you, Annabelle.'

'Oh?' Annabelle said, and looked up.

Coop reached into his pocket and pulled out the lipstick. He handed it to Annabelle.

'Oh, thanks,' she said.

'What is it?' Jason said.

'My lipstick,' Annabelle said.

'I found it near that ladder back aft.'

'Thanks,' Annabelle said. She paused a moment and then said, 'Back aft?'

'Yeah. Behind the stack there. You know, there's that –'

Annabelle had risen and was walking towards the binnacle. She held the lipstick on the palm of her hand, the hand extended towards the binnacle light. She was shaking her head when she turned back towards the two men.

'It's not mine,' she said.

I love him, Samantha thought. He'll be back any minute. He said he would come back as soon as they'd got the message off. He said to stay here and wait. I love him.

Fear crackled into her skull with every strange sound that clanged or clicked in the wardroom where she huddled in a corner of the transom seat. The curtain over the bulkhead opening was closed; he had told her to leave it closed. The wardroom was black. She had never liked the darkness. It was always a comfort to have the cats around the house, first Fang and Fong and then the others; she had not fed them this morning. The ocean rushed past on the other side of the transom seat, beyond the thick skin of the ship. She could hear its angry haste, and the sound frightened her because she knew that if Luke did not get that message off as he had promised to do, the ship would be blown apart before dawn, the rushing water outside would flood into compartments and passageways, they would drown.

I'm afraid, she thought.

Now don't, she thought. Don't.

The cats must be starving.

It was always so damn dark in that house on the beach, I like it with his arms around me at night.

He had held her in his arms here in the wardroom, how long ago had it been? They had stood very close to each other, the curtain drawn, the wardroom dark and silent.

'I want to come with you,' she said.

'No. You stay here. If this goes wrong –'

'If it goes wrong –'

'– I don't want you to be . . .'

'– there's nothing left.'

She could not see his face in the darkness. She could only feel his arms around her and his body tight against her, the way she had felt his arms around her and his body against her in bed with the darkness around them in the house on the beach. This could have been the house on the beach, her darkened bedroom with the jalousied windows overlooking the slate patio outside; this could have been a night like all those others that began in the back of the marina office when she'd been half drunk and he'd told her he loved her. This could have been a night just like all the others, but it was not.

There was something strange in his voice.

'I don't know if we're going to come out of this tonight,' he said.

293

The room was silent and black. His mouth was close to her ear, he was speaking in a whisper.

'The whole idea of going out there scares me. I don't even know if it'll work. The whole thing . . .'

He shook his head. She said nothing.

'I wish someone else could do this, I want to stay here in the dark and hold you in my arms and never move, never. I don't want to go out there to ambush somebody and maybe kill him.'

She still said nothing. He was trembling now – she could feel his body shaking against her – but she said nothing and did nothing.

'I don't want to go out there,' he said.

'I know.'

The room was silent.

'Sam?'

'Yes?'

He sighed. 'I wish it didn't have to be me.' He sighed again. 'I'll come back for you,' he said. 'As soon as we get the message off, I'll come back.'

There was another silence.

'Sam, I don't know what there is for us.'

'I don't either.'

'But maybe something. I love you.'

'I love you, Luke.'

'Wait for me,' he said, and was gone.

She could not see her watch in the dark. She worried about the cats and she worried about Luke and then thought perhaps she was only worrying about herself. She told herself she loved him and that he was doing a very courageous thing, going out there against a shipful of fanatics; he was a brave and responsible man. Then she told herself she hated him for leaving her alone here in the dark while he went out on a hopeless mission. They would kill him and then find her and kill her, too. He was a fool.

She wondered what time it was.

She heard something clanging someplace.

Footsteps?

She caught her breath. Someone was coming down a ladder; it sounded as if it was on her left someplace. She counted the steps down, six, seven, eight; there were footfalls on the deck now. She waited. Silence. She heard a door opening. Someone was entering the ship's office. A light snapped on. 'Anything?' a man asked. 'No.' More silence. Footsteps. She knew she would faint. She struggled for breath and knew that she would faint if they pulled open the curtain. 'Got to be down here someplace,' the first man said. They were right outside the curtain now. She pulled herself into a corner of the seat, small and huddled and frightened and gasping for breath, and remembered what Luke had said about wishing it could be someone else, about not wanting to ambush and maybe kill a man, about not wanting to go out there.

But he had gone.

With her breath rattling in her throat, she moved off the seat, and as she was groping in the dark along the top of the cabinet for a knife, a utensil, a glass she could break, anything she could use for a weapon, the curtain rasped back on its rod.

Light from the ship's office flooded the wardroom.

A tall pale man with black hair looked in, smiled, and said, '*Vamanos senorita*. We have something of yours on the bridge.'

They had unburdened the mules, and now the large wooden crates stood at the water's edge, waiting to be loaded. It was still raining, and so the tarpaulins had not yet been removed from the boxes. El Feliz and his men squatted inside their ponchos around the open fire on the beach, drinking coffee and chewing cold pork. The boat was tied alongside a ramshackle dock that jutted out lopsidedly into the water. Angel looked at the boat every few seconds.

'Está tranquilo,' El Feliz advised.

'When will we load it?'

'Soon. When our meal is finished.'

'I want to *get* there.'

'We have two days,' El Feliz said. He grinned and spat

295

into the sand. 'If we go too rapidly, amigo, we will overtake the lady. Is that what you wish?'

'What lady?' Angel asked.

'Flora. La dama ventosa.' El Feliz laughed. 'We have had enough of her, no? Let her march.' He made a shooting motion with his hands, and then wiped the rain from his face, picked up his coffee mug and held it out to one of the men. The man filled it. El Feliz drank from the mug and then glanced again at Angel, who was still looking out towards the boat. 'Calm,' he said again. 'Slow. Moderate yourself.'

Angel grunted sourly, and El Feliz burst out laughing. 'Amigo,' he said gently and reasonably, 'we cannot follow a hurricane too closely.'

'We do not have to follow it at all,' Angel said testily. 'We can come south around the cape and then through the basin.'

'Past Guantánamo?'

'Not if we land on the peninsula.'

'But we will *not* land on the peninsula,' El Feliz said. 'We will land on the northern coast.'

'The first plan was for the peninsula.'

'That was before Flora.'

'We still do not know the extent of the damage there.'

'And we do not wish to test fortune. The centre of Flora crossed the peninsula. It is reasonable to assume there was at least some damage to the docks and beaches. Besides' – El Feliz shrugged – 'they have already been told the landing will be in the north. The plan cannot change itself again.'

'Why did Flora have to come?' Angel asked angrily, and slapped his fist into the open palm of his other hand.

'Because she came,' El Feliz said philosophically, and again laughed. 'My friend, you have all the energy, all the devotion to a cause, all the resolve of a true fanatic, but –'

'A fanatic?' Angel said, annoyed.

'Cómo, no! A fanatic, yes, what did you think? But you also have the impatience of a fanatic and the stubbornness of one. More coffee,' he said, and extended his mug again. 'You refuse to believe that Flora forced us to change our

plans. You refuse to believe that she is still angry up there' –
he pointed with his finger – 'and that it could be extremely
dangerous if we followed her too closely. You refuse to
accept the fact that chance, and coincidence, and
unforeseen accidents can force a man to alter his plans – and
can sometimes change the course of history. Gracias,' El
Feliz said to the man who filled his cup. He drank again. 'Be
patient. The boat will be loaded by nine o'clock. We are not
expected until sundown Tuesday.'

'We should have loaded it at the other end of the island.
We should have –'

'Again, there is Guantánamo at the other end of the
island. That is a fact. Flora is a fact, Guantánamo is a fact.
Accept them,' he said, and drained the remainder of the
coffee from the mug. 'We will leave La Fé at nine tonight.
We will proceed to the northern side of the island and follow
the coastline some thirty or forty miles offshore, past
Havana and Matanzas, Caribarién and Cayo Romano,
Puerto Manati and Moa, all the way down past Baracoa. At
our top speed, we will have need of two days to travel where
we are going. But we will be moving well behind Flora and
well away from the eyes of Guantánamo. Those are the
facts, Angel. That is our plan.'

On the beach, the wind lashed at a tarpaulin, pulling it
free from the crate it was protecting. Angel leaped to his feet
and ran for the tarpaulin as it flapped into the air like a giant
bat. He clasped the tarpaulin in his arms and brought it
fluttering to the sand. Annoyed, he dragged it back to the
crate. The wind drove the rain against the crate's exposed
raw wood as he struggled to cover it again. On the sides of
the crate two stencilled Spanish words screamed a warning
in bold black letters:

!PELIGRO!
– DINAMITA –

The trouble with hanky-panky, Sondra Lasky thought, is that you can't complain to the hotel management if the tap leaks.

Roger Cummings was just a human being, just a person like any other person walking the streets of Washington or anyplace else. And being only a person, he could be expected to notice a good pair of legs outside the Bureau of Printing and Engraving every day of the week except Saturdays, Sundays, and holidays. Being only a person, he could be expected eventually to try a pickup. Who wouldn't? Being a person, and also a man besides, he could naturally be expected finally to leave a girl in the lurch in the middle of a swamp infested with cottonmouths and crocodiles and probably wild naked Florida Indians with their hair in bangs.

Or maybe not.

That was where the hanky-panky came in.

Maybe Roger Cummings the *person* was leaving her in the lurch and maybe he wasn't. Maybe Roger Cummings the *person* was really in trouble someplace, maybe he'd got hit by a truck on the highway, or bitten by a snake in the swamp, or scalped by one of those wild Indians – who could tell? Maybe Roger Cummings the *person* wasn't really being a rat at all; maybe he was gasping for breath and calling her name, with one hand stuck out of the water, all covered with mud like Stewart Granger – who could tell?

But Sondra couldn't call the management to tell them the tap was leaking, because then she would have to say she was here with Roger Cummings, who was a United States senator. And if anybody found out that Roger Cummings the *senator* was maybe in trouble, wow, he would *really* be in trouble!

So what the hell, he was a big boy now.

If he wanted to go wandering off across the swamp into some one-horse town that was having its yearly fire, that was his business. As for her, there were plenty of things she could do with her time, instead of hanging around a Godforsaken dump on the edge of the ocean when maybe a hurricane was coming. Wasn't that what they were saying, or was it the other way round? Was the hurricane *going?*

The rented car had been left in the garage by Roger. She had driven it to Key West. The NO SMOKING-FASTEN SEAT BELTS sign went on at the front of the Twin Beech. Sondra fastened her belt and then glanced in turn at the other three passengers in the small aeroplane, making sure they had also obeyed the sign. The pilot's voice came over the loudspeaker system. He told them at what altitude they would be flying, and he told them the temperature in Miami, and he said they would be there in fifty minutes.

At 8 P.M. the Key West tower cleared the plane for takeoff, and it taxied down the field into the wind.

They heard the plane on Ocho Puertos.

The sailors in the storage locker, the men and women in the houses along the beach and in the room behind the marina office heard the sound of the aeroplane and listened to it cautiously at first. The sound came from a long way off, a steady rumble that moved closer and closer. As the plane approached, they allowed themselves to hope. They had been waiting for salvation for a long time now, had been waiting since dawn for someone to deliver them, and now they heard the sound of the approaching aeroplane and hoped silently that it would land here on Ocho Puertos, wished desperately that it would be an amphibious Coast Guard plane that would put down on the water and rescue them.

The plane was overhead now.

Some of the people in the town dared to raise their eyes.

There was a brief moment where hope hung suspended. The sound of the plane seemed to indicate it was preparing to land, and yet at the same time seemed unchanged. The steady rumble remained unbroken. The plane droned noisily in the sky.

They listened until there was nothing more to hear.

Fang was the one who finally ripped the hole in the screen door. He had been clawing at a small tear for the better part of three hours, and now he had enlarged

299

the hole enough to squeeze through, first his head and then his body. An odd feline shudder of triumph seemed to work down the length of his back to the tip of his tail as he crawled through the hole and on to the slate patio outside. Fong was right behind him.

They were starving.

Their mistress had not fed them, and they prowled the beach like wild scavengers now, sniffing the air, waiting to pounce on anything that seemed even barely edible, willing to eat carrion or drink blood, ready to accept sustenance from whoever or whatever offered it.

It did not take long for the other cats to discover the hole in the screen door. In five minutes' time the beach was alive with prowling, crying, desperately hungry animals.

Their eyes glowed greedily in the darkness.

Luke could hear voices inside.

With the .45 in one hand, he stood with Cates and the corpsman on the main deck, just outside the hatch to the radio room, and tried to the ease the door open. The door was locked.

On his right, some three feet from where they stood before the door, a ladder led to the bridge deck and the wheelhouse. The plan as they had outlined it below in the executive officer's quarters was simple and direct, and necessitated silence and speed. The silence was imperative because the bridge was only three feet to the right, eight feet above, and sixteen feet forward of where they stood. They could not risk any shots or shouts that would bring help from the wheelhouse before they could radio Miami. The speed was essential because Jason Trench had sent one of his men down with Bunder more than a half-hour ago, and he might begin wondering about him at any moment now. If he became concerned, he might possibly call the captain's cabin and get no answer; his man was alone down there, bound hand and foot, and stuffed into the captain's berth.

The plan was to unlock the door with the key they had taken from the exec's cabin, rush the men in the radio room

– from the outside, it sounded as if there were two of them, but there might be three, or even four – and silence them. Cates would then warm up the transmitter if it was not already in operation, and send his voice message directly to Radio Miami in Perrine. That was the plan. The only tricky part was overcoming the men inside before they could shout a warning or fire a shot.

'The key,' Luke whispered.

Cates handed it to him. They looked at each other for a moment. Cates nodded. Behind them Bunder wiped his lip. Luke slipped the key into the lock slowly, soundlessly. Inside, the men were laughing. He turned the key. The tumblers made a small clicking sound, but it was drowned by the laughter of the men inside. The door was unlocked.

Luke took hold of the handle.

'Ready?' he whispered.

'Ready,' Cates said.

'Ready,' Bunder said, and wiped his lip again.

Luke pushed on the handle and threw open the door to the radio room just as the ship's loudspeaker erupted with sound. Bunder and Cates were rushing past him into the room, but Luke stopped short because the loudspeaker was calling him by name. The loudspeaker was shouting in its scratchy mechanical voice, '*Luke Costigan, we know you are aboard, we have the girl on the bridge. We will kill her if you do not surrender.*' The loudspeaker was bellowing like the echoing voice of God. '*We will kill the girl, we will kill the girl, we will kill the girl!*'

The men in the radio room whirled at the sudden sound of the loudspeaker. There were three men in all, and two of them had left their rifles in the far corner of the room. The third man sat near the transmitter with his rifle across his lap, and he brought it into firing position the moment he saw Bunder and Cates rushing into the room. The captain of the ship was carrying out the plan just the way they had outlined it below – he was rushing these men and trying to put them out of commission without firing a shot. Bunder, following his captain, was attempting to do the same thing. The loudspeaker was shouting a warning. The two unarmed men were moving towards their rifles in the corner. The man sitting in front of the transmitter slipped his finger inside the trigger guard of his rifle, curled it around the trigger, and began shooting. The first volley caught Bunder in the chest, and he shouted 'No!' and that was all, and then began staggering forward. The second volley came from the far corner of the room where both of the other men had picked up their rifles. Luke saw Cates drop his .45 and stumble back against Bunder who was bleeding profusely, and then both men dropped to the deck and Luke turned away and ran for the ladder leading up to the bridge.

It occurred to him as he took the steps up – he took them two at a time despite his bad leg – it occurred to him that the men in the radio shack were now behind him with the same guns that had felled Bunder and Cates, and that Jason Trench was above him and ahead of him on the bridge with more men and more guns. It occurred to him that the entire world had disintegrated into groups of men holding guns, some behind you and some ahead of you, and that the only thing you could do was remain unafraid in the face of whatever was happening, cling to the hope that mankind had not completely lost its reason, resist long enough and loud enough until they all put down their weapons.

A shot rang out behind him.

He was on the bridge now and running for the wheelhouse. There was another shot behind him, and he thought at first he'd been hit but he realized he'd only slipped momentarily on the wet bridge deck, and suddenly felt invincible. Nothing could possibly harm him now, he thought. He knew that what he was doing was right, he knew that his own unselfish motives, his own brave and courageous attempt to stop these maniacs before they destroyed themselves and the world would somehow succeed. He would storm that goddamn wheelhouse and pull Samantha out of their clutches and save the world, because what he was doing was good and right, and what they were doing was evil.

He threw open the wheelhouse hatch.

Jason was still at the microphone. The loudspeaker was still bleating; he hadn't even heard it after those first arresting ominous words. He heard it again now, '*We have the girl, we will kill her, we will kill –*' and then the words stopped as Jason turned from the microphone and Luke said, like the hero he felt he was, like the man who was about to save the world, 'This is it, Trench.'

Jason fired four times.

Each of his bullets caught Luke in a different part of his body. Samantha, who was being held by Rodiz across the wheelhouse, screamed when the first bullet struck Luke and tore away half his face, and then screamed again as the second bullet exploded into his throat. Luke's finger tightened around the trigger of his own gun in that moment, more as a reflex spasm than as any consciously directed action – all thought, all feeling, had been blown from his head with Jason's first shot. His finger jerked fitfully against the trigger as he began falling towards the deck, the single bullet exploding from the muzzle of his gun and slamming into the metal deck and then richocheting wildly across the wheelhouse, screaming from bulkhead to bulkhead like a wild buzzing hornet, finally smashing into the sloped top of the radar gear and shattering the scope. He was dead before he struck the deck, but Jason fired two more bullets into his back and shoulders.

Samantha broke away from Rodiz and ran screaming to where Luke lay in his own blood. She was lifting his head into her lap when Annabelle fired at her with the .22, killing her instantly.

The world was poised for anarchy.

18

One of the men in the bunker was a corporal in the Cuban Army, and the other was a Russian civilian who had been in Cuba for eight months and who wanted to go home. He was writing a letter to his wife when the corporal called to him from the other room. Reluctantly he put down the clipboard to which his single sheet of stationery was attached, rose, and went to where the corporal sat in semi-darkness before the Russian-built radar.

The corporal did not know any Russian, and the Russian knew only a little Spanish, so they would have had difficulty communicating even if they liked each other, which they did not. Moreover, it was almost two-thirty in the morning, and both men were tired, and both were annoyed by the radar which had been flashing electronic echoes from high ocean waves all night long, and which seemed to be performing erratically and irrationally because of the hurricane. The Cuban corporal secretly felt that the Russians did not know how to build radar anyway, even if they *were* capable of shooting people off into space, and the Russian civilian secretly felt that these indolent Spaniards were incapable of operating anything more complicated than a straight razor. So the feeling in the bunker was hardly one of understanding, even before the Cuban picked up what now appeared to be a target some forty-five miles north-west of Havana.

The corporal pointed to the illuminated dot of light on the scope as the sweep line went past. The Russian nodded and watched it fade. The electronic line made its 360-degree sweep, and the orange dot appeared once again. The men continued to watch the scope in silence. The target appeared each time the sweep line went past, a bright clear echo that seemed to indicate there was a vessel out there on the water, a vessel moving steadily and inexorably towards the Cuban coastline.

The corporal did not know exactly what his role was in relation to all these Russians who were instructing them and buying their cigars and laying their women, and besides he was a cautious man by nature. His job was to watch the radar, and that was all. He did not want to make any decisions about the target which was now about forty-two miles offshore, *if* this Russian radar could be trusted, and *if* this wasn't simply another wave echo, although none of the other wave echoes had kept moving steadily towards Havana. The Russian, on the other hand, was nothing more than a civilian adviser who was standing this foolish middle-of-the-night watch with the corporal only to make certain he mastered control of the machinery, a feat he was sure the Cubans would never accomplish. He wasn't quite sure to whom they should report this target, if indeed it was a target at all.

Silently, they kept watching the scope, each secretly hating the other, and each secretly hoping this was nothing more serious than a wave echo.

The second target appeared on the screen suddenly.

If there had been a lack of understanding in the room before that moment, there was a total understanding now. If there had been a lack of sympathy before, there was now agreement bordering on wild hysteria. The corporal and the civilian looked at the screen and then turned to face each other. For the first time that night, they were ready to admit that somewhere out on that water – somewhere about forty-one miles away, to be exact – there was not only *one* vessel heading for Havana, but possibly *two* – in fact *def*initely two, because the second target was now sending back an echo as bright and as strong as the first.

They watched the scope in fascinated terror, expecting to see yet another electronic dot appear, and another, and still another, until a huge invasion armada filled the scope. They stared motionless as the two dots approached each other in what seemed to be a calculated manoeuvre, watched and waited breathlessly, wondering what their next move should be – should they sound an alarm, should they call the patrol boat command, should they alert the airfield?

All at once, a third dot appeared, a huge electronic burst that startled them both, overwhelming the two dots that had been on the screen earlier. They knew immediately that an enormous vessel had joined the formation, either a battleship or an aircraft carrier, hiding the other two from view. The sweep line came around again, a bright thin orange line coming nearer and nearer to where the invasion armada was massing. They watched silently, their terror rising, waiting for confirmation of what they had witnessed only seconds before. The sweep line moved towards the exact spot, closer and closer.

Nothing appeared on the screen.

The Russian and the Cuban turned to stare at each other and then blinked and then turned their attention back to the radar again. The sweep line was advancing towards the same spot once more, a position forty miles north-west of them, moving swiftly, and then passing the point again – and again there was nothing on the screen. There had been an enormous burst of electronic light not more than a minute ago, surely marking the appearance of a third huge vessel, and now there was no sign of anything. The third vessel, if such it had been, seemed to have disappeared, and with it the two other vessels as well. Puzzled, they continued to watch the empty screen.

None of the targets appeared again.

Radio Miami knew the cutter *Mercury* had been answering a distress call some fifty miles off the coast of Cuba, because she had radioed them at midnight to report her position and her destination. About a half-hour after that, they monitored a conversation between the *Merc* and a Navy destroyer on patrol duty. The destroyer had raised the *Merc* to ask whether there was anything wrong with her running lights. The *Merc* replied that there had been an electrical failure.

'Are you in need of emergency equipment?' the destroyer asked.

'Negative, negative,' the *Merc* said. 'We have just about located the difficulty.'

'Ah, roger,' the destroyer said. 'We will stand by until you are functioning properly again.'

The *Merc* apparently located the difficulty and repaired the malfunction, because Radio Miami later monitored a conversation between the destroyer and another ship in its squadron, stating that the *Mercury* was on its way again with its lights functioning, and the destroyer was resuming patrol. It was possible, of course, that there was a later electrical failure, which once again put out the cutter's running lights. Considering the storm conditions off the coast of Cuba, however, it was difficult to fathom why the cutter would not have made use of battery-powered lights if there had been such a failure. In the beginning, no one even imagined that the cutter was deliberately running without lights. In the beginning, everyone was too involved with trying to figure out exactly what had happened.

It was supposed at first that the other vessel involved was the very vessel that had sent the SOS to which the *Merc* was responding. There was some confusion there, too, however, because if this had been the ship in distress, she would have been expecting the *Merc* and certainly looking for her, even if she was travelling without lights. Moreover, since the vessel came out of the storm just about where the *Merc* knew she would be, at latitude 23°37' north, longitude 81° 54' west, the *Merc* should have been actively searching for her with radar. The possibility of a second electrical failure that had knocked out the *Merc*'s single radar scope as well was, of course, discarded once all the facts were in. Nor was there speculation on any other possible malfunction of the radar, a broken cable, a shattered scope face. The only logical assumption was that the storm had raised waves high enough to prevent anything but intermittent radar reception. The second vessel, it was assumed, had simply materialized out of the night, undetected by radar, if indeed anyone aboard the *Merc* was even monitoring the scope.

307

The cutter, travelling without lights, had not been seen either. The collision was almost inevitable.

The accident was reported to Radio Miami by a second patrolling Navy destroyer. Miami received the message at 0238 from the U.S.S. *Bunt*. The *Bunt* reported an enormous explosion south-south-west of her position, and advised that she was proceeding at best possible speed to investigate. At 0316, the *Bunt* reported that she was at the scene and gave the latitude and longitude for the first time. She advised that there was no sign of any vessel, but that debris floating on the water indicated there had been a collision between two ships or a ship and a boat, it was difficult to tell. At 0324, the *Bunt* called in again to state that she had recovered debris marked with the name of the *Mercury*.

At four-thirty in the morning, the first public news broadcast went out over a Miami radio station. It said simply that a 165-foot Coast Guard cutter had accidentally collided with what was assumed to be a small fishing boat, and that both vessels were reported sunk some forty miles north-west of Havana. There were, the announcer said, no survivors.

Harry and the others in Ocho Puertos must have known at once that Jason Trench's plan had failed.

At ten minutes past five, a little more than an hour before dawn of the morning of October seventh, the Florida State Highway Patrol received a call from a man who identified himself as Amos Carter. He told them that the people of the town of Ocho Puertos had been held as prisoners from early yesterday morning until just a few minutes ago, and that a man named Marvin Tannenbaum had been shot and killed. Within the next ten minutes the police received telephone calls from four other people in the town, all of whom reported having been kept there as prisoners. One of the callers said her name was Lucy Nelson and that someone (they could not understand the name she gave because she was crying into the phone) had been killed early yesterday morning and was out on the porch covered with a blanket.

The police arrived a half-hour before dawn.

The people of the town were standing in the road.

They were all very excited, all talking at the same time, to themselves and to the troopers. It was all over now, and now they could afford to rehash it with the same sort of excitement that followed any adventure. It was all over now, and those who had survived could relate the tale with a curious sort of tragic glee. Amos Carter took them to the storage locker, and the troopers shot the lock off the door and released the men there. One of the men said his name was Michael Pierce and that he was executive officer of the Coast Guard cutter *Mercury*, and then he went on to relate what had happened aboard the ship yesterday. The cops, who had not yet heard any news of the disaster off Cuba, listened very calmly. One of them looked somewhat confused. Pierce excused himself and said he wanted to call the Coast Guard in Miami. The trooper said, Sure, go right ahead. Amos Carter was telling them about a scheme to involve the United States in a war. A woman named Rachel Tannenbaum was asking them to call an ambulance for her husband, who had suffered a heart attack. The man, who was lying on a blanket in the back of the marina office, kept telling them as they made their call that his son had been a hero. 'My son was a hero,' he said. 'My son was a hero.' A tall good-looking gentleman with greying hair said he had only wandered into all this by accident and asked whether or not they would need him any longer. The others verified his story, and the police said they guessed he could go. One of them asked his name and address. He gave his name as David Cummings and his address as Scranton, Pennsylvania.

About fifteen minutes after they had arrived, the troopers found the drunken man and woman in the back of the bait and tackle shop.

'My name is Willy,' the man said. 'This here is my girl Ginny.'

'I never saw him before in my life,' the woman said.

'We got some questions to ask you, Willy,' one of the troopers said.

'Yeah? Like what?'

'Like where all your friends ran off to.'

'I don't have to tell you nothing,' Willy said.

The trooper smiled. 'Sure,' he said. 'But we think you will.'

About ten minutes past dawn on Monday morning, October seventh, the USS *Bunt* radioed Miami to say it had recovered some additional material from the water.

'Only thing we can figure,' the *Bunt* reported, 'is that the boat was heading for Haiti.'

'Which boat?'

'The one the *Merc* hit.'

'Oh, really? How do you get that?'

'Well, this crate we fished out of the water was loaded with pamphlets.'

'What kind of pamphlets?'

'Communist stuff.'

'What do you mean?'

'Communist propaganda. It's in French – that's what they speak in Haiti, you know – but one of our men translated it for us. It's all about Duvalier, the dictator down there, and how the people should rise up against him the way the Cubans rose up against Batista, and how they would be helped with arms and explosives and food and whatever else they needed. You should read this stuff. It's wild, believe me.'

'Just the *Merc*'s luck, huh?'

'What do you mean?'

'To run into a bunch of Communist fanatics,' Radio Miami said.

'Macabre, moony and plain strip-joint sleazy'
SUNDAY TIMES

McBAIN
A MATTHEW HOPE MYSTERY

SNOW WHITE
AND ROSE RED
by ED McBAIN

Sarah Whittaker, said her attorney, was nuttier than a
fruitcake. When Matthew Hope visited her in the institution he
was half-expecting some shaven-headed basket case in a
uniform that looked like mattress ticking.

Instead Sarah Whittaker was wearing a wheat-coloured linen
suit and a saffron silk blouse open at the throat. She had a
generous mouth and eyes as green as the Amazon jungle and
Matthew Hope fell in love with her on the spot.

'So why are you here?' he asked. 'Ah,' she said, and started
to tell him a story. And it certainly wasn't the kind of tale a
mother would read to her children at bedtime . . .

'A swift and adroitly plotted mystery . . . events leave the
reader devastated'.
PUBLISHERS WEEKLY

'Laces its horrors with some good running gags and
some gamey writing . . . everything one looks for in
vintage McBain'.
THE FICTION MAGAZINE

0 7221 5726 6   CRIME

All Sphere Books are available at your bookshop or newsagent, or can be ordered from the following address: Sphere Books, Cash Sales Department, P.O. Box 11, Falmouth, Cornwall TR10 9EN.

Please send cheque or postal order (no currency), and allow 60p for postage and packing for the first book plus 25p for the second book and 15p for each additional book ordered up to a maximum charge of £1.90 in U.K.

B.F.P.O. customers please allow 60p for the first book, 25p for the second book plus 15p per copy for the next 7 books, thereafter 9p per book.

Overseas customers, including Eire, please allow £1.25 for postage and packing for the first book, 75p for the second book and 28p for each subsequent title ordered.